ADDICTED

AUBREY PARKER

STERLING & STONE

ADDICTED

A Note From The Author

Hi, friend,

If you're new to dark contemporary romance, there are some things we should talk about before you dive into these pages. Important things.

Characters, like people, can be complicated. Zane Crawford and Libra Scarsdale are no different. They have complex, painful pasts, and their respective traumas not only complement one another but, for a time, amplify each other.

Accordingly, this novel contains heavy themes including, but not limited to, light bondage, light spanking, voyeurism, exhibitionism, relived trauma, and suicide/suicidal ideation.

If you find any of these topics uncomfortable, difficult, or triggering, please, please take care. Exercise caution and be aware. We're all doing this messy life together.

Much love,
Aubrey Parker

ONE

Libra

CREAM AND TAN OIL PAINTS STREAK ACROSS MY CANVAS, using shadows and light to shape the suggestive curves belonging to the object of my current fascination. I dip my brush in crimson and dab at the taut nipple in the middle of my painting, blending shades of pink and brown to enhance the effects of the colors. I tilt my head as my brush glides into my memories, teasing out details to make my depiction of her more lifelike. There should be a glow within the shadows, spotlights that make the rosy tones pop against pale skin and darkness.

The play of light and dark is a tricky balance, but I relish the challenge of recreating Philipa Tennand's gorgeous areolas from memory. They are the centerpiece, but the painting as a whole is a mere suggestion, explicit but not outright crude. A tease, if you will. With her arms pressed firmly against her upper breasts in a shy attempt to hide her body from my gaze, she's instead brought herself into full display through the gaps in her forearms.

Early morning sunlight illuminates the chaotic second floor of my art studio through the eastern windows. Here, my easel and I spend each morning with my erotic recreations — the soft contours of the feminine form, a tantalizing dip of cleavage, the satisfying plumpness of a round bottom.

Sizzling warmth courses through me in response to the sensuality of Philipa's likeness. She's beautiful in person, so uptight until I caught her with a man who isn't her husband behind closed doors. Oh, after that, she became such a sweetheart.

Moments like this, where I'm immersed in the scenario envisioned on my canvas, remind me why I fell in love with art in the first place. I had this studio constructed in the backyard two years ago, designed so that the entire top floor is made up of custom windows with built-in opacity modules so I can control who can see inside and how much light travels through at any given moment. I can paint with near-perfect natural light at any time of day, thanks to the sunny California skies.

Philipa's face is absent from the painting, my depiction of her halting at the hollow of her throat. Still, I imagine her gazing at me through half-lidded eyes, kiss-swollen lips parted in surprise. Perfect. Just the way I remember her after finding her on all fours with one of the waiters railing her from behind during her husband's hospital charity gala in San Francisco last month. I haven't been able to get her out of my head, and I won't until she's transplanted to my canvas.

My thighs squeeze together, trembling with want. I slide my spare hand beneath my painter's apron, toying with the hem of my Dolce & Gabbana leggings. It's too soon to play; I have so much work to do, but the temptation lures my hand farther between my legs, brushing the top of my mound. Soon. I let my hand linger, but I go back to work.

Philipa's breasts are but one of many decorating every wall and spare easel in my studio. I don't paint her or any of my subjects because I'm *into* them — it's admiration that guides my brush.

When I saw Philipa on that sofa by the fireplace, her crimson ballgown bunched around her waist, I knew I had to paint her. I would have done it whether she wanted me to or not, but it's always more entertaining to watch my subjects squirm under the misleading belief that if they don't consent, I'll reveal their secrets.

I would never.

Many of the women who I immortalize on my canvases live fulfilling sexual lives; however, they personally define that. They take what their husbands or lovers won't give them freely. Most people in my position would call them sluts, cheaters, maybe even exhibitionists, but every one of them is so different, no cliché label works. At the core, I understand their desires.

I couldn't betray their trust even if I wanted to — their needs are the very same as mine.

Only I'm not brave enough to take. I'm not brave enough to risk the cozy life I've built with James in sunny little Woodside, California. For now, the illicit nature of witnessing their indiscretions play out is the best I can get. Through them, I play out my own vivid fantasies that satisfy my own needs on demand.

The fantasies I can't have but crave.

The ache within me grows with each stroke, bringing Philipa closer to completion. All freedoms come with limits, but in my studio, I use my mind to turn those limits into suggestions. I challenge the restrictions posed on my otherwise perfect life. Here, I can almost infinitely suspend myself between art and fantasy without my husband's interference.

Though he's always keen to insert himself and his thoughts into my art as soon as I step beyond these doors.

A buzz against my wrist pulls me from my reverie. I mutter with disappointment and pull my hand from between my legs to glance at my Apple Watch: the motion camera at the front gate detected movement.

A slow smile curves my lips. That will be my long-awaited paint delivery, the custom mixes I ordered from Italy to experiment with new textures and stylizations for my next wave of painted fascinations.

I lean back on my stool and wet my lips. Just a few finishing touches and Philipa will be complete, one of the largesttransgressions in her life immortalized in the painted form. I hate to pull away now and disrupt the finale of my morning routine, but I told the housekeeper to take today off since James is home, and he'll never answer the door on his own. If I don't go, I'll have to wait until tomorrow to retrieve my package.

I tap the button in the app connected to the smart security system to remotely open the front gate and let the delivery driver up the long driveway. After I untie my apron, I hook it by the door before I hurry out of the studio and head for the stairs.

My next subject, a woman never painted before by these hands, won't wait forever.

~

THE MANSION's Greek-inspired gallery shades me as I walk beneath the white marble pillars that loop around the back and to the front deck. I turn the corner just as the delivery man approaches the front door, hitching the package under one arm and ringing the doorbell. The young man wears a muddy brown uniform that hugs his tall, lean form, and there's a slight curl to his dark, shaggy hair. He leans in to ring the doorbell again, but then he spots me waiting off tohis side. His eyes, the color of good whiskey, settle on me. He's handsome in a rough sort of way.

The kind of man I'd love to get my hands on for some fun if only James would agree to an open marriage.

His eyes trail over my body. Smirking, I take my time sashaying to the door. He looks like he might have a heart attack when he notices how my breasts strain against the buttons of my blouse, threatening to spill out.

"Delivery for Libra Scarsdale." His voice cracks, and his Adam's apple bobs as he swallows hard. He stares for a moment, then seeming to remember his job, he fumbles with the electronic signature pad. "Just, uh, need a signature."

I broaden my smile. "Thank you so much. I've been waiting for those paints all week."

"No problem, ma'am. Glad I could deliver it to you."

He holds the signature device out to me. When I reach for it, I let my hand travel to his tanned arm. His firm muscles ripple beneath my appreciative touch. "My, my, lugging these huge packages around all day must keep you in good shape."

He chuckles and rubs the back of his neck. "Yeah, I guess it does."

He's more innocent than he looks, and he's young enough that it's possible he's never had the pleasure of bedding an experienced woman who knows what she wants. In a way, he reminds me of the type of men I preferred to tango with before James and I started the little game that ended in our marriage. I spot his nametag as I drag my blue fingernail across the signature pad and sign my name in precise, curly lettering.

"You know, Rick, that package looks pretty heavy. Do

5

you think you could be a good boy and help me bring it up to my studio?"

"I…" He clears his throat. "I'm not sure that's a wise idea, ma'am. I'm running behind on my deliveries today."

I blink my long eyelashes at him and curl a finger through a loose strand of my blonde hair. "Pretty please? I won't be able to carry that much on my own; it looks like a job for a big, strong man like yourself, and I'd hate to disturb my husband to help with some silly paints. He's *so* busy, but I can't wait until tomorrow to continue my painting. I have a deadline for a very important client."

Hesitation crinkles Rick's firm cheeks. Desire thickens in his gaze as his eyes sweep over me again, the wanting there overshadowed by his strict professionalism and uncertainty. He's not sure if I genuinely need help or if I'm trying to initiate something more. He wants to find out, but he's not sure he wants to risk his job. Poor thing, unable to tell the difference.

Rick shoves the signature pad into his uniform's pocket. "All right, I'll help you bring it up just this once. I wouldn't want you to miss that deadline."

I trail my fingers up to his shoulder. "Aw, you're such a dear. Come this way. It'll just be a minute, I promise."

I saunter on ahead of him, giving him a hypnotizing view of my ass as I guide him and my luxury paints across the gallery and to the backyard. On the other side of the tall pillars holding up the second-floor balcony, there's the manicured garden that was just a plot of grass when we moved in, now maintained by our team of landscapers into a tropical paradise of palm trees and all the exotic flowers that catch my fancy. In the middle is the waterfall that crashes into the shimmering pool.

I fucking love the thing, but James hates it.

My art studio is just behind the trees. I designed the

landscape around the pool so it feels isolated from every-where else, but from the second floor of my studio, I have a perfect view of any naughty business going on in the back-yard. Who would have thought how much inspiration I'd spot for my paintings after a few summer pool parties?

"So … you're an artist?" Rick mumbles as he follows me toward the pool.

"That's right, always have been. My eclectic style has been featured in galleries all over the world."

"Really?" There's a note of surprise in his voice. "You're famous or something?"

I touch a hand to my breast and laugh. "Oh, no. I wouldn't go that far. My work is simply appreciated in certain circles of fine art aficionados."

"What do you paint?"

"Anything my heart desires, love. Although I've lately been fascinated by the human body." I flip my hair over my shoulder and look back at him with a sultry smile. "All the places most artists won't explore. Our secrets and sensualities."

Rick opens his mouth to reply just as the French doors in front of us pop open and out walks James. A pair of black designer swim shorts low on his hips, giving way to his bare four-pack and tanned chest. In one hand, he carries a fresh glass of scotch that he swirls while his crit-ical eyes pin me and shy Rick with an air of disapproval that makes my stomach clench.

A vein pulses in his forehead. Oh, he's not in a good mood, not at all. He must not have realized I told Josephine not to come in today.

Just as I planned.

"What's going on here?" James barks. His receding hairline glistens with beads of sweat.

Rick practically jumps in his boots. "D-delivery, sir."

"Is that so?"

I paste on a bright smile, drinking in the tension. "Rick was kind enough to help me bring my new paints up to the studio."

James' eyes narrow on the package. "I'm here, so that won't be necessary. I'll take that."

He yanks the package from Rick's hands.

Rick backs away. "Have a good day, sir, ma'am."

"Such a shame," I sigh, pouting my lips dramatically. "Too bad you can't stay and help me with my painting. Maybe another time."

His eyes bulge, and his gaze skips from my innocent face to James' stormy eyes. "I never agreed to that, sir. I promise—"

"You've overstayed your welcome," James snaps. "I suggest you leave."

Rick turns tail and jogs around the house.

When James turns to me, his expression twists in a mockery of rage, having lost the tiny semblance of nonchalance he was maintaining in Rick's presence. James' wide face takes on a slight red hue that makes my nerves tingle with excitement.

Appearances are everything to him. Such a charlatan.

I tease the edge of the package that he's now carrying. "James, darling, I didn't expect you to be out here."

"Obviously." The tumbler of scotch in his hand isn't his first of the day, judging by the slur in his voice and the exaggerated motions of his hand that spills some of the alcohol on the tiled patio floor. "What game are you playing now, Libra?"

"I was just having a little fun. You know I didn't mean anything by it."

"I know exactly what kind of fun you were angling for.

8

You'll keep saying that until I finally catch you with another man's cock in your mouth, you fucking slut."

"My love, you know I'd never do that." My lips turn up in a sickly sweet smile that only makes him simmer more. "Honestly, I can't have the delivery man help me with my package without being accused of infidelity? I read it in a book somewhere that people project their personal indiscretions on their spouses. Keep this up, and maybe I'll get worried."

I know that look in his eyes, the barely restrained violence. "Bullshit. You should stop reading whatever girly magazines you waste your time with, sticking ideas like that in your head."

With a growl, James chucks the package across the patio. It crashes and bounces, hitting the leg of one of the poolside tables. I'm pretty sure I hear one of the fine containers inside crack.

I tut at him. "Was that necessary? What a waste of perfectly good paint. Those were imported from Italy, you know. They're worth more than my Lexus."

James tosses back the rest of his drink, then throws the tumbler, too. Glass shatters across the tiled floor around the pool, fragments glinting in the sun. "Fuck your paints. I hate that erotic trash you're obsessed with. It's been months. Enough is enough. I'll buy you more when you start painting something I give a shit about."

"I didn't realize I needed your permission."

The words come out more defiant than I intend, but I don't take them back.

"What did you say?"

"I don't belong to you, James. I'm not some possession you can control."

"The hell you're not." He strides toward me, and I flinch as he grabs my arm, his fingers biting into my skin.

"You're my wife, and you'll do as I say. If I tell you to stop fucking painting garbage, you'll stop painting fucking garbage!"

I stand firm, even as my heart races with the telltale beat of panic. "Let go of me."

"Or what?" He yanks me closer, breath tinged with the stink of alcohol as it washes over my face. "You think you can tell me what to do? Clearly, you forgot that I lifted you out of the gutter and gave you everything. Do you need a reminder that you're *mine*?"

James's anger is a palpable force, rumbling beneath the surface and threatening to boil over at any moment. And yet, a part of me thrills at his reaction. There's a fine line between passion and obsession, love and control, and we're balanced on a razor's edge.

One wrong move, and he'll devour me whole.

"It's barely noon, and you're drunk again," I say, unable to keep the accusation from my tone.

His eyes flash at the implied insult, but beneath it lurks a hunger I know all too well. Without Josephine to sate him, he'll have to make do with me. He lunges, shoving me against the stone wall and pinning me with a snarl. I brace myself as he captures my lips, his hot tongue demanding entry. The alcohol on his breath makes my senses reel, and my head spins with the rush, attacking me from everywhere at once.

"If you don't do as I say, I'll burn your studio to the fucking ground."

"Then I'll key your favorite car."

James grips my hair to force my face up to his, then thrusts his tongue inside my mouth when I open it to speak. His body crushes into mine, and I'm acutely aware of the hard planes of his muscles through the thin fabric of my shirt. His kiss is bruising and deep, melting me from the inside out, and already my legs are shaking with antic-ipation.

My body betrays me so easily. Such a needy thing, quickly ignited by his rough touch like kindling set to flame. His hands roam everywhere, squeezing and grasping as if he can't get enough of me and setting me to burn in the process.

James' possessiveness has always been a double-edged sword — in the beginning, it was an exhilarating aspect of our relationship, making me feel desired and treasured. After we married, his control became less methodical over the years. His temper is easily roused because he sees me slipping through his fingers like sand, and his caveman theatrics don't affect me anymore, so he's positively stupe-fied about what to do with me.

Really, the anger hides his jealousy: the discreet fear that my paintings could lead me astray. I crave nothing more thanthe freedom to act on my desires without fear of retribution from him.

His fingers make quick work of my blouse, ripping the front and popping the buttons off to reveal my bare chest. He's always preferred me not to wear bras at home.

I laugh into his mouth. "You're out of control."

James chooses that moment to trail sloppy kisses down my neck, sucking hard enough to leave a mark. "Think this is funny, do you?" His voice is low and dangerous in my ear. "The things you do to test me. Don't think for a second that I wouldn't burn everything you call yours just to show you your place."

He grips my hips, grinding against me while he works to shove my leggings down my thighs. The rough fabric abrades my sensitized skin, but I rock back into him, arousal blossoming deep in my core. James is all bark and no bite. He's too afraid of losing me to do something as psychotic as destroy my life's work, but I can't deny it's hot as hell to remember how crazy he can be.

I let him push his full weight against me. Panting, my vision swims and stalls out when I spot movement on the other side of the pool. Bronzed skin and messy black hair poke from behind a narrow tree. Our landscaper, Pedro, tries and fails to hide as he watches us.

Excitement thrums in my veins, sharpening my focus. James slides a hand between our bodies, fingers spearing into my wet folds. I moan at the sudden intrusion, trembling as he works them in and out of me.

"You're dripping for me," he rasps. His gaze follows mine, locating Pedro on the other side of the yard. James' nostrils flare, and something dark clouds in his expression. "And for him."

"I'm not."

"My naughty little exhibitionist. Look at him." He pushes his palm against my cheek and forces my eyes in Pedro's direction. I'm torn between watching the older man playing with the bulge in his jeans and meeting my husband's hooded stare. "Look at how much he wants you. Do you want him to fuck you too?"

He curls his fingers inside me, and I whimper, hands fisting at nothing. "No."

"That's right. He can't have you. You're mine."

His fingers plunge deeper, finding that spot inside me that makes me see stars. I cry out, the stretch and fullness leaving me breathless, sensations amplified by our audience's gaze. It reminds me of how James and I used to be — all passion and fire, unable to keep our hands off each other no matter who might be watching. And yet, now, it's the only thing that truly excites me within the confines of our marriage.

James will never admit it, but he loves exhibitionism,

too. He loves showing everyone how he dominates and controls me, marking me as his. Only his. It strokes his ego to show off his depravity and what he does to me; that's why I believe he'll consider opening our marriage once I wear him down more. Then I'll get what I want, and I'll stop fucking with him fucking Josephine at every innocent opportunity.

He stops moving his fingers. I whine, mourning the loss of the steady rhythm. I clench my thighs around his arm and lift my hips, fucking myself on his fingers until he removes his arm completely. He chuckles, knowing he's left me empty and aching.

"Patience. You want an audience? Fine. Let's have you put on a show." He releases me. "On your knees."

TWO

Zane

AWAKE BEFORE MY ALARM, I STARE AT MY BEDROOM ceiling, a grand masterpiece of classic frescoes depicting mythological gods and goddesses locked in eternal battle. The soft morning glow seeps through the cracks in the curtains, illuminating their ethereal faces. The artist must have believed waking up to this scene would inspire a self-obsessed CEO first thing in the morning to always challenge the gods or fate or some bullshit like that.

I might have been one of those jackasses in another lifetime if everything hadn't gone to shit first.

I don't want to get out of bed, but it has nothing to do with the humorless art. In fact, I'd rather count the lines that carve these celestial beings into my ceiling than face the world today.

Or any other day.

A growing sense of existential exhaustion weighs down on me like an invisible force pressing against my chest. Day after day, it grows all the more suffocating. Like breathing should hurt. Sometimes it does.

"Good morning, Mr. Crawford!" a bright and cheery

voice sings into the bedroom, as it always does at exactly six each morning. "Based on my analysis of your sleep, you had a below-average sleep score of 39. Did you know that the human body requires at least 6 hours of sleep to fully regenerate—"

"Skip."

"Your schedule is clear, as usual. You have no appointments or meetings. The weather forecast for today is sunny, with a high of seventy-nine degrees. Your vitals appear to be in good order, but your dopamine and serotonin levels are critically low. Would you like me to schedule a therapy appointment? It's been four years, six months, and twenty-seven days since your last visit with Dr. Cale."

"Thanks, but no thanks."

"Sir, I insist—"

"I haven't changed my mind."

If it wasn't for the house AI, Fox, and my design that makes him talk my ear off the second my alarm goes off and triggers the household's pre-programmed morning routines, I wonder how long I could lay wrapped in the black silk covering my California king bed before someone bothers me. If anyone would notice. In this vast mansion, it's easy to feel as though the world can't touch me. Can't see me anymore.

That I could truly be alone.

I roll over and cover my head with a pillow, a futile and rebellious effort to block out the world for a few more minutes. I'm annoyed at myself for hard coding the AI to be so persistent about mental health check-ups. It seemed like a good idea a decade ago when I was building the AI model with my family's needs in mind, but now it's another nagging reminder of the constant darkness surrounding my life.

My California king bed dominates the bedroom, but

the room itself is large enough to host a party of fifty people. Floor-to-ceiling windows overlook the secluded countryside of Woodside below, much like a king in his castle. Tasteful modern artwork designed by my late sister adorns the walls. Splashes of gold and red on huge canvases for me to contemplate in the hours that I can't find a lick of sleep. The wall opposite the bed is a window, wall, or screen at my whim, and the white trim that runs along every room in the house pulses with glowing lights to reflect Fox's constant presence.

I pad across the plush carpet toward the gold bookcase on the right side of my bed, running my fingers along the spines. They are titles I have not read and never will, as well as philosophy, history, and art theory, which had, once upon a time, caught my interest when I wanted to inspire intelligent conversations on topics significant to the important people in my life.

Now, they're reminders of what I lost. I need to stop hanging on. I should have them removed and replaced. But...

The luxury that fills this space means nothing to me. The beauty of the outside world cannot change the rot inside.

And no amount of billions can fix it.

"You have one hundred and twenty-two missed calls since yesterday, all from an unknown number," Fox informs me, "and one new message. Would you like to hear it?"

I tug the fake book in the middle of the shelf. There's a click from the shelf's internal mechanism. The lever triggers a continuous whirring sound, and the bookshelf slides away, revealing a hidden room beyond. I used to love these old-fashioned secret rooms. They have hardly any real security to them, and I could have designed a space using

Fox's AI that no one but me could access, but after I moved here though, I guess I just haven't cared enough. This room serves just one purpose and always will.

The space inside is simple and unadorned, a stark contrast to the luxurious bedroom I just left. There are no windows, just a comfortable leather chair on one side and a single ledge on the other, upon which rests an old revolver and a solitary bullet.

"Fine, play the message."

Static crackles over the bedroom speakers, and then there's a woman's voice. The words are hard to make out, even with Fox automatically attempting to clear the audio of interference. "…Zane…Crawford…" The woman laughs. I don't recognize her voice. "…checking in…have you considered my offer?"

Then there's more static, and it clicks off.

"Would you like to send a response?" Fox asks.

"Delete."

I close the door behind me, but Fox's voice follows me inside, now echoing from the speaker built into the wall.

"Are you sure you wish to delete that voicemail? Perhaps we should consider notifying the authorities about a potential stalker if you are uninterested in engaging with this individual."

"Have you figured out who it is?"

"Negative. All my searches bring back no reliable results; their IP address is spoofed and protected by encryption requiring specialized tools I am not authorized to access without prior permissions."

"Then yes, I'm sure. Delete it. I don't give a shit."

I found the calls entertaining two years ago. Playing chicken with a stalker seemed like just the kind of thrill I needed to keep me entertained. But it turned out to be just another weirdo chick who thinks she's in love with me and has more to offer than every other woman I've banged before. The second I figured out that she might have some connection to my sister's death, I noped the fuck out of considering using her for entertainment, either. The only mildly interesting thing about her is that traces of her are concealed well enough that I'd have to care to dig up more info about her, but I don't.

"Message deleted."

I pick up the revolver from the ledge. The weight of the cool metal is familiar, and I take the bullet sitting beside the gun and feed it in. I give the chamber a powerful spin, feeling the weight of it shift with each rotation, and then I sink into the leather chair and raise the revolver to my temple. I hold my breath in anticipation of the unknown. In this moment, there's a flicker of excitement, a glimmer that momentarily pierces through the fog of ennui. My finger tightens around the trigger.

Then I pull it.

The gun clicks, and I exhale.

"Fuck," I mutter.

Disappointment.

"Zane, your heart rate has increased quite a bit," Fox observes. "Is something bothering you?"

I laugh at the absurdity of the situation. "Bothered? No, not really. I'm just wondering if I'm cursed or lucky as hell. Two years of playing this game every morning, and I still haven't managed to kill myself. It's got to be a bit of both, right?"

"The chances of surviving 752 rounds of Russian Roulette in a row are infinitesimally low at a chance of 4.84-23%. Based on my calculations, you are extremely lucky, Zane. I must recommend you cease your game immediately."

"You've been keeping track? Why am I not surprised? You haven't tampered with the gun, have you?"

"I am only an AI, sir. I cannot interact with any physical objects that do not have an authorized digital connection to our household server, and my analysis concludes that your father's revolver is not wi-fi enabled."

I climb out of the chair and out of my secret room, letting the bookshelf close behind me. It seems I'm not fated to die just yet, so I might as well get the day started.

This morning's game of Russian Roulette has become a ritual for me, a desperate attempt to feel something more than the crushing boredom that suffocates my every waking moment. Each pull of the trigger is a gamble, a tiny chance at escape from this monotonous existence.

I cross the bedroom into the room-sized walk-in closet. Every item in my wardrobe is expertly tailored to fit my form, including some of the most expensive tuxedoes, suits, and accessories available on the market. Everything is immaculately organized according to my preferences, and I pick through the luxury fabrics, trying to decide what to wear.

"I hate all these clothes. Where are my T-shirts? Fuck."

"You asked Miss Manson to donate them all to Goodwill last month. However, after examining your wardrobe habits over the last six years in your service, I made the executive decision to retain a suitable selection of casual wear on your behalf."

The wardrobe wall clicks, and then the whole panel shifts several feet backward. An entirely different wall slides up from the floor and replaces the old one so that half my wardrobe disappears inside the compartment. Moments later, the panel slides down again, and the entire closet is replaced with racks and shelves of voguish shirts, jeans, shorts, sweatshirts, jackets, and hoodies, all in my size. There's even a selection of footwear to match any outfit.

"Huh … better." I pick through the rack of shirts, but I'm not convinced by any of them. I take out a pair of trashy ripped denim beach shorts and choose to go without a shirt. It's not like I'll be leaving the house anyway.

"Happy to be of service, sir. Is there anything else I can do for you?"

"Do something to ease the pain of this awful, brain-rotting existence of mine?"

"Absolutely. I've curated a playlist of music scientifically proven to improve your mood based on your biometric readings and the type of music you most enjoy listening to. Would you like to hear it?"

"That's not quite what I had in mind, but sure."

Fox's speakers chime as I leave the walk-in and head through the grand double doors and into the entry room to my suite. A black leather sectional sits in the middle of the space, facing a large flatscreen TV and a minibar. Loud metal music crashes through the speakers, and I laugh when the rhythmic cacophony of sound sends a pulse of adrenaline through my veins.

"All right, maybe it's not so bad after all. Good work, Fox."

"Thank you, sir." The AI makes a happy, chirruping sound. "My readings indicate that given your current mood and chemical balances, a video game will provide you with the most mental stimulation."

"Another game? Haven't I tried everything already?"

"Not at all. Miss Manson and I had the game room refitted to accommodate the newest VR technology, courtesy of your friends at VellR. I can have the room prepared in just a few moments if you're ready to try their latest game."

"It's probably a piece of shit game. Why bother?"

"Because you own the company, sir."

I sigh. "Don't remind me."

Over a decade ago, VellR was my company's biggest competitor for creating the next big AI model. Those corpo sleazebag whack jobs made every effort to sabotage and blackball my attempts to get my startup off the ground. My sister Charlotte worked for them for years and pretty much begged to be my corporate spy. Fuck, it was fun treating her like the enemy. We made headlines by publicizing our intense family drama while behind the scenes, we drank shitty tequila, and she told me VellR's company secrets. All the while, I grew the big ideas that would one day revolutionize the AI industry.

But ... because of those VellR douchebags, my success came too late to accomplish what really mattered most to me.

The music's pulsing beat vibrates through the soles of my feet. At first, it makes my blood pump and gives me that buzz of *aliveness* that I crave but is always so elusive. After the initial shock of experiencing the unexpected sounds, the music becomes background noise that I can't hear anymore. My brain just decides for me that it's uninteresting and tunes it out, letting my cocoon of endless dissatisfaction cloud over me again.

"I'll try it just so I can write them a demoralizing review."

"Feedback is important to the creative process, as you always tell me, sir. I'm sure they will find your insights invaluable." The black and gold inlaid doors on the other side of the entry room and opposite my bedroom doors fan open. "Right this way."

I approach the door with raised eyebrows. The game room was fully hooked up to Fox, so he could switch my setup between the various platforms and consoles at ease, but my Scorpion PC rig is nowhere to be seen. In fact, there are no screens at all, and beyond the threshold, the carpeted floor has been replaced with smooth black tiles. I step inside, and Fox closes the doors behind me.

"I suggested that Miss Manson relocate your game room to the third floor. However, should you find this setup displeasing, I will have her return everything to its former position by tomorrow morning."

"Let's hope for her sake that won't be necessary."

As soon as the doors click shut, the walls themselves seem to darken, then a glowing pedestal rises from the ground in front of me. A phantom light flickers around the device, and all right, I admit I'm intrigued.

"Interesting holographic tech." I follow the cues to interact with the pedestal, expecting my hands to fall through it, but when I reach for it, it turns out to be solid. "Not a hologram?"

The ground rumbles, and lights, a lot like buttons, appear on the pedestal. The flickering glows and expands outward, snaking across the floor and illuminating the metal chassis around me. I don't seem to be in my house anymore at all, but in the control center of a futuristic spaceship, judging by the screens displaying navigational information about the Milky Way. The pedestal must be the main control console.

I lay my hand flat on the surface.

"Captain, look out, an asteroid is headed right—" a woman's voice sounds over the ship's speakers, but she's interrupted by the horrific screech of crushing metal.

My ship rumbles and groans, and everything feels like it's spinning. I grip the console to stop myself from being thrown to the ground with everything else that's not tied down. Alarms blare, and one of the screens glows crimson with status bars indicating what parts of the ship have lost connection and are presumably destroyed or what is in critical condition.

"Captain!" the same voice calls out through the comms device. "Oh my God, did you survive that hit?"

There's a long pause, and I realize I'm expected to respond.

"Somehow," I say as I examine the screens. "It doesn't seem like I've lost any critical infrastructure. The main engine is intact, so I can still fly, but my holoshields are ruptured."

"I'm on my way to your coordinates. I can boost your ship so you can make it to the docks for repairs."

The game brings me into a post-apocalyptic sci-fi world where I lead a crew of brave military personnel through asteroid fields in search of the resources humanity needs to rebuild civilization on Mars. After a few hours of standing in place in the center of my game room, my legs are sore, and I'm getting bored by what's starting to feel suspiciously like Elon Musk fanboy fiction.

I clear the first fight with some extraterrestrials over a gas mine, then I pull away from the console. "That's enough, Fox. I'm done."

The game's dark lighting flickers and disappears around me, and the white walls of my mansion come back into view. The wall facing the San Francisco Bay opens up two concealed panels, and the windows seamlessly reappear.

"I'm glad the game was able to entertain you for a few hours today, Zane. Is there any feedback you would like to send to the VellR developers regarding your gaming experience?"

"Entertain me? That was fucking torture. It's obvious that the characters utilize a modified version of my Brain that we've licensed to gaming companies. They don't have any actual strong personalities because they were lazy and wanted to create a fully adaptive experience where the characters mold themselves to be complementary to the player's ideals and playstyle, which makes for no in-party conflict. It's a neat concept, but I don't want to play a game with party members who become carbon copies of me and look like they want to jerk me off. Boring.

"And what the fuck are with these controls? Sure, the haptic feedback on the floor, 4D elements, and the real-life visuals are cool, but who wants to be standing the whole time? Reminds me of the shitty VR from 2010 that made people puke from motion sickness. The story is intriguing, and I DO like how that part is adaptive to what parts of the world I'm interested in pursuing, but the mechanics themselves need a lot of work. There needs to be more physical interactions outside of the main console."

"As you say. I've recorded your thoughts for their reference."

I pace along the wall, restless. This setup probably cost a small fortune, but still barely a dent in the substantial wealth I've accumulated since the Brain blew up and turned into an infinite money-making machine that's produced more raw cash than I can keep track of. There are no shortages of distractions designed for the obscenely wealthy with nothing better to do, but no matter how much money I throw around trying to keep me enter-tained, nothing provides any long-term relief.

Deep ocean yacht parties with sex, booze, experimental drugs? Done it.

Exclusive clubs where limits don't exist? Yawn.

Traveling to remote, dangerous locations around the globe? Meh.

I've tried everything anyone has ever recommended to me. Heart-stopping adventures, death thrills, the absolute insane and depraved. Endless possibilities, and I'm still bored.

Fox tirelessly searches for solutions to stave off the gnawing emptiness within me, but all pleasure is fleeting. Worthless.

I'm fucking broken.

"Fox," I say, my voice tinged with desperation, "there must be something else. Something I haven't tried before."

"I assure you that I have exhausted all available options within the confines of your home," Fox replies, his voice almost apologetic. "Perhaps it would be beneficial for you to venture outside or engage in social activities with other individuals."

"Outside..." I creep toward the windowsill, staring at the treetops and the rolling Bay waves beyond. A world that feels so distant and unreachable.

My mansion has the best view of the San Francisco Bay in all Woodside, the vast expanse shimmering with a thousand shades of blue. It's a sight that should inspire awe, humbling a mortal man such as myself, but all it does is remind me of how trapped I am by my own creations.

Everything and everything I found of value out there was swallowed by the sickening, limitless greed of society. I refuse to be lured back into that wasteland and pretend they are anything more than vultures.

"You've lost your mind, Fox."

"Interactions with other human beings is a proven method of lifting your mood. Humans are inherently social creatures. If you would consider—"

"I created you, Fox. I built you from the ground up and

designed every line of code, every circuit, every subroutine. You revolutionized the world and made me billions of dollars, and yet you can't even keep me entertained without relying on primitive arguments and pushing me into social engagement? Suggest that I leave again, and I'll reset you."

"But Mr. Crawford—"

"I said no. No is a complete sentence."

Fox's lights pulse through the speakers. "Very well. I've made a note of your expectations and will make no further suggestions outside of your comfort zone."

"This has nothing to do with comfort. Fuck the world. I've tried everything and experienced everything worth experiencing out there. If it wasn't accompanied by a human zoo, I'd consider it."

"My primary function is to assist you with your well-being and daily life, whatever that entails."

I roll my eyes. The fourth floor of the mansion is a penthouse suite inside a penthouse with every form of advanced and automated technology at my disposal so I can limit my contact with people as much as possible. As if reading my mind, Fox pops open the drawer to the receptacle that holds the most recent batch of fat joints from the machine I had my company design specifically so I could have the AI roll them for me overnight.

I light the paper and collapse onto the leather couch, where I stare at the considerably more boring ceiling than what'sin my bedroom. It's always a hit or miss if a new strain will help me or fuck with my fuckfest of a head even more, but I breathe in the sweet smoke anyway. It's just another kind of Russian Roulette.

"I can see why she did it," I mutter to no one in particular. "Fuck."

"Zane, are you experiencing suicidal thoughts?"

"No more than any other day."

"Good, because I must inform you that Miss Manson has arrived, and I've already unlocked the fourth-floor door for her."

"Fuck. Seriously?"

Sophia Manson, my housekeeper, doesn't approve of me smoking pot. Most of the time, I don't give a shit what she thinks, but I try to be courteous about not smoking when she's around. She's the only person I've been able to tolerate enough to let into my house since I moved here five years ago.

I roll over but forget I'm on the couch and end up falling. I hit the ground with a thud.

Scowling, I cram the joint into the carpet to kill the embers, then toss it under the couch, but it doesn't make it that far and only rolls a few inches. Giving up completely, I starfish on the ground, accepting that I'll be caught.

Fox can be quite the fucker for an AI; knowing him, he probably told Sophia to come up because I'm being 'uncooperative' to his mental health regime and wants to stage another intervention. He's always watching, listening, and whatever other anti-privacy measures that are mega profitable for me that I coded into the AI. Consumer privacy laws hate me for that shit, but I have enough money and lawyers that pack enough punch not to give a fuck about what they want.

Helps that I don't have any fucks to give. If the feds eventually win and want billions in repayments, that's next year's problem.

The main door to the fourth-floor suite swings open, and Sophia's singsong voice fills the room as she steps inside. "Good morning, Mr. Crawford, I've brought you a surprise."

Sophia's beauty is undeniable. Long, wavy dark hair

cascades down her back like a waterfall of silk, and she has capability and insight far above the role of a housekeeper. Her full lips curve into a warm smile framed by high cheekbones. Her pleasant expression only wrinkles for a moment when she smells the marijuana, but then she smooths that wrinkle over.

She probably only puts up with me because I pay her way too fucking much. But she's worth it. I don't give a shit what my accountant thinks.

"Ah, Sophia. Hello."

"I thought you might enjoy a special treat today." She's the epitome of grace as she glides across the room in her simple but elegant housekeeper's attire, a simple white ruffled apron over a knee-length black dress. She's carrying an enormous silver platter that she places on the sitting room table a few feet from my head.

"Something special? You know I always appreciate your gifts."

The skirt of her uniform dances close to my nose when she comes near, and I get a great view of her tanned legs and the tiny black thong creeping between them. Sophia hovers in that position while she lifts the lid from the platter, and I see the way she shifts to look down at me while I take a moment to appreciate the way the thin fabric cups her pussy. It's not the first time she's wanted me to look. I sit up so I'm not tempted to keep staring.

A heavenly aroma wafts through the air, instantly awakening my senses. Before me lies an exquisite assortment of exotic cheeses and caviar, a visual feast that promises to satisfy my appetites for a taste beyond the mundane.

"Fuck, that smells good. You have a remarkable talent for knowing just what I need."

Sophia smirks and whips a piece of paper from her

uniform pocket. "There are few delights that perk you right up as much as a tray of cheese. Here's the list of pairing recommendations if you'd like to be normal for once."

"Is that a challenge?"

There are wedges of cheese hailing from every corner of the globe. Velvety French blues sit beside sharp, crumbly cheddars and delicate, creamy bries, while nutty, aged goudas vie for attention among the smoky notes of Spanish Manchegoes. The caviar, too, is to die for. Glistening black pearls of Russian beluga shimmer as if freshly plucked, their rich flavor the very definition of luxury. Delicate golden orbs of ossetra beckon with the promise of their buttery essence, while the vibrant orange beads of salmon roe add a splash of color and a burst of briny ocean flavor.

"You've outdone yourself with this spread, Sophia," I say in genuine appreciation for the attention to detail. "You should stay and enjoy it too."

"I would love to, but the house must be tended to. Today is Fox's mandatory maintenance, and it shouldn't be delayed for long."

I pick what I think would be the most offensive to the tastebuds and plop the cheese and caviar into my mouth before Sophia can protest.

She gapes in horror. "Mr. Crawford!"

"Mmm." I chew the horrific combination of blue cheese and honey-glazed roe. "Those flavors don't belong together."

"You're right they don't. That was one of the least recommended combinations!"

"Then you'll have to stay a while and make sure I don't make any more offensive, uncultured mistakes, won't you?"

"If you want me to stay, all you have to do is ask."

"That would be far less entertaining."

She laughs, shaking her head. "I suppose I can spare a few moments if you get up off the floor and promise to stop putting your joints out on the carpet."

"What does that matter? I'm bored of the carpet anyway. I want it replaced next week."

But still, I do as she asks, climb off the floor, and slump back onto the leather sectional. Sophia's gaze lingers on my bare chest and muscular arms, just a little too long to be professional.

"You'd have to leave your room for more than five minutes to have the carpet replaced," she points out. "I'll see what I can do, seeing as you're allowing me a serving of your favorite treats."

"You're an angel. Now, come, sit with me." I pat the couch, and she sits, leaving two feet between us. "Let's try the beluga caviar first."

We both scoop a small spoonful onto thinly sliced pieces of baguette and cheese, then place it in our mouths in sync. The flavors melt together, decadent and satisfying.

Sophia sighs softly in appreciation. "That's exquisite."

"Isn't it? Now let's... hmm, what's this one?"

Every time a new pairing lavishes my tongue, I'm momentarily distracted from the void, always threatening to consume me.

But then Sophia places her hand on my forearm, and I'm plucked right out of that brief island of relief. I try not to stiffen too much. She's shifted closer, leaning ever so slightly toward me, and she makes eye contact as she delicately places a slice of cheese on her tongue.

Fluttering her eyes at me, she swallows it and licks her lips seductively. So inviting.

But I can't give in to temptation.

Sophia's hot, and it's obvious that she wants to be more than my employee, but I make sure never to encourage her feelings. I over-correct my positioning on the couch when I reach for my next sampling so that her hand is forced to fall away from my arm.

She's an invaluable friend and asset to my way of life. Over the five years she's worked for me, she's taken on the role of managing any household affairs that require leaving the property. She coordinates with everyone who previously filled the roles of personal assistant for my work and life — I needed someone new to distance me from my old life, and she rose to the challenge.

Now, Sophia is the only other human presence in this isolated world I've created for myself. I trust her implicitly, as she's proven herself discreet and reliable time and time again. I wouldn't want to fuck that up like I've fucked up so many other things in my life. I couldn't imagine trying to train someone to replace her if she quit.

Her eyes travel to my groin, which throbs against the zipper of my trashy denim shorts. Then she gives me another oneof her sultry smiles before rising to her feet and smoothing out her apron. "Thank you for the taste, Mr. Crawford, but I really must get to work now."

"Of course. We wouldn't want Fox to miss his update."

"Or let his speakers get too dusty."

With a slightly exaggerated bow, she leaves the way she came. When the door closes, I exhale and throw my head back against the couch. The cheese and caviar are delicious, but I can't stand another bite, and I can't help but feel restless again. I hope I didn't make her think I'm interested. It would make our relationship awkward if I had to turn her down. Again.

My thoughts race, searching for something to occupy my time. Anything to keep the darkness at bay. I glance around, my eyes falling on a pair of binoculars resting on the nearby table. A wicked grin spreads across my face as I reach for them. It's been a while since I've spied on my neighbors, and sometimes they get up to the weirdest shit.

I throw open the balcony doors and perch my elbows on the railing, lifting the lenses to my eyes.

"Let's see who's the most interesting of you boring rich fuckers today."

My mansion is perched atop a hill overlooking the sprawling and forested Woodside community. Secluded, private, and half an acre between me and my closest neighbors. But with these binoculars, distance becomes irrelevant. I scan the horizon, much like a predator hunting for prey.

A few months ago, I spotted the old man I never cared enough to learn the name of crossdressing in his wife's clothes. My lenses land on that window now, but it's dark. Disappointing. I scan the rest of the hillside in search of someone doing more than reading or gardening.

I'm high enough that most trees planted for privacy don't obscure too much, but I somehow ended up in the most boring neighborhood in California. At least, I think so, until I land in the yard of my closest neighbors at the bottom of the hill.

I zoom in on a speck of movement by their bright blue pool, which happens to be a man pushing a woman onto her knees on the deck. He grips the back of her head as he whips his cock out and shoves her mouth over his length, forcing her to give him a blowjob. I lean in closer, unable to tear my eyes away from the scene unfolding before me.

"Damn," I whisper under my breath, my grip tightening around the binoculars. "What do we have here?"

I've seen this couple before. They moved to Woodside shortly before I did, and like everyone else in the neighborhood, I've never met them. The woman's blouse is ripped open, revealing huge breasts with tiny pink nipples. Her leggings and black panties are pulled down to her shins, allowing me to rake over what has to be the hottest body I've ever laid eyes on.

She's petite but covered in toned muscles that give her an athletic physique that's still soft and feminine. Her blue eyes are as bright as the chemical-laden water behind her, those irises laden with defiance as she eagerly takes the man who must be her husband. Fuck, is this really happening?

The man's hands twist into her long platinum-blonde hair, then he starts to move, fucking her mouth in sharp, brutal thrusts. My cock twitches, and I exhale roughly, imagining it's her mouth around me instead. She takes him deeper, nails digging into his thighs until he finally pulls out, leaving her to gasp for air.

I palm the bulge straining against my waistband. I shouldn't be watching this — it feels invasive and wrong on so many levels. The thought pounds in the back of my skull, but despite my understanding of the moral implications, the fact that I *shouldn't* but I still *can*, makes watching them even more enticing.

I've watched plenty of people fuck before. Never anyone who didn't know I was there.

The man hauls the woman to her feet and spins her around, shoving her onto all fours on the pool lounge chair. He positions himself behind her and then slams into her. She throws her head back, and he grabs her throat, making her look at him while he pounds her. Her pretty face twists in a mixture of pain and pleasure.

A deep, primal part of me revels in their display of passion, their unbridled lust. My body responds in kind, hungering for a similar release. A nagging voice in the back of my mind tries to remind me that I have no place indulging in their intimacy from afar, but I can't pull away so easily.

The binoculars dip away from the couple while I shift in place, and my sights land on someone else lingering in the yard nearby. Someone who's watching them just as intently as I am, his hand jerking.

"Fuck it." I shake my head, dispelling the thoughts that threaten to ruin my rare moment of excitement. For once, the dull numbness that usually pervades my existence breaks into a full-body buzz. It'll be just once. What are the chances of me getting another show like this?

I unzip and fully take my length into my hand. I hiss and move slowly, savoring every second while I throb at the sight of their vicious fucking. I indulge in the thrill of watching what I shouldn't see, and fuck if it doesn't feel good. The woman's body arches, surrendering to the man. Adrenaline coursing through my system reaches new heights, and as the couple finishes, my balls tingle, and I groan as I spurt all over the glass panel in front of me.

"Christ."

I'm dizzy with pleasure, but I lift my binoculars to see what they do next. The man smacks her ass before he leaves, and the woman takes her time fixing her blouse. Not that I mind. I'd stare at that ass all day if I could.

She saunters to the other side of the pool and approaches the landscaper, handing him what appears to be a crisp bill and then showing him another flash of her tits before walking away.

"Wait, was this all staged? They knew they were being watched?"

If they were putting on a show, that means it could happen again. How the fuck did I miss the fact that I have exhibitionists for neighbors?

The realization awakens a pulsing rush of blood and

heat in the center of my being, and my cock twitches as if I didn't just spill a hot load all over the place. This is it. The thrill I've been chasing.

My binoculars follow the woman as she enters another building detached from the home. "All right then. You like being watched? I'd be honored to take this burden."

Anything for a chance to feel this way again.

Alive.

THREE

Libra
_____

MY BARE FEET REACH THE DAMP EDGE OF THE TRANQUIL, crystal-clear pool. I raise my arms and dive straight in. Cold devours me as I plunge into the unforgiving embrace of the water. I float suspended beneath the surface. Air locked in my lungs, the past comes back to me in flashes—the weakness in my bones, the penetrating exhaustion of existing. Every cell in my body screamed like they were dying because, back then, they were.

I kick with all the power in my legs, pushing back to the surface. I'm not that weak little girl anymore.

I follow through with the perfect arch of a breaststroke and work my way from one end of the pool to the other. One cycle, two, working the muscles I'm lucky to have. Rivulets of water splash around me like liquid diamonds with each stroke, and I relish the soothing liquid rippling over my naked skin.

My lungs burn with the satisfaction of a hard swim, and my arms ache with my unrelenting persistence, but my thoughts stay troubled while I glide through the water.

It's always James.

His temper yesterday morning lingers in my mind like an ominous cloud and in the tenderness of the bruises all over my arms and thighs. The water tickles the sensitive flesh he gripped when he took full possession of my body, reminding me, like he promised, of who I belong to. I can't say I didn't enjoy the way he controlled and fucked me, but I'm not used to the raw brutality.

Our marriage has gotten out of hand. His insecurities make his outbursts more explosive; less the man I married, and more of an asshole every day.

I long for the days when James understood my need for freedom and adventure. But now, all he sees is a possession to be displayed like one of his prized luxury cars. What changed?

The sex didn't. He's been fixated on our housekeeper, Josephine, these past few months, but we still fucked like rabbits until I learned of his affair. Does he notice that I don't make advances on him anymore and leave it up to him?

He's a selfish fucker, so probably not.

I burst through the water by the edge of the pool, gasping for air. My fingers trace the rough stone as I catch my breath. Waves roll across the surface away from me, eventually smoothing into blue stillness. All around the pool, palm and cordyline trees offer spots of shade, and birds flit around the bunches of orange and pink tropical flowers. The lush surroundings I've carefully cultivated over the years usually envelop me in a sense of peace for my morning swim, but tranquility is out of reach today.

I close my eyes, trying to momentarily forget the world outside of the water. Here, my body is free — in my art studio, my mind finds release.

Yet I can't help but feel like there must be more to life than this fake comfort. I beat death. The grim reaper swung his scythe at me and missed. I didn't survive hell just to live the rest of my days in a gilded cage that James believes I should kiss his feet for locking me in.

It's not that I don't love him, and not that I want a divorce; I just need more of the freedom he promised me. I need to reclaim the excitement and passion for being alive that defined who I was before he started to change. If I can convince him to open our marriage, I'd be much closer to accomplishing that.

If I could taste the other pleasures available to me, I would be happy. Once, I was lucky to be so free and giving with sex. Now, not so much.

I push off the pool's edge into a backstroke. My bare breasts peek above the crashing water, kissed by sunlight before the coolness of the water envelops me. The movements and the focus provide a much-needed, if fleeting, respite from my whirling thoughts. As I reach the other side of the pool, I open my eyes in time to spot a metallic glint in the distance.

The light is so subtle, yet out of the ordinary, I pull onto the edge of the pool to squint through the palm fronds to discern its origin. I can't see anything but the vast blue sky, where a single, puffy white cloud floats on by.

That cloud has the whole atmosphere awaiting it. It's directed by the flow of wind through the valleys and over the ocean; the cloud doesn't think or choose its direction, yet it has more freedom than me. I feel like I've taken more steps backward than forward. I'm surrounded by riches, but somehow, I feel poorer than when I lived on a shoe-string budget in Dubai, skydiving from planes just to feel the adrenaline coursing through my veins as I plummeted toward the earth. Or when I volunteered on a humanities mission in Cape Town, and every time I spotted sharks in the ocean, I was allured by the danger of delving into the water, just knowing they were nearby and hunger could strike at any moment.

There's nothing so thrilling anymore as the possibility of another brush with the reaper.

I'm not drawn to these experiences only for the sheer thrill or danger — they represent moments when I've felt most free, unshackled from the constraints imposed by others, including James. These memories remind me that I can always find ways to seize control of my own destiny.

"James used to understand," I murmur. A mixture of sadness and frustration creeps into my thoughts. He once encouraged my wild spirit, cheering me on as I pursued new experiences and embraced the unknown, sometimes with him and some without.

I don't need heart-pumping adrenaline and near-death thrills every day; I'm mostly happy with my paints, my pool, andmy friends. But I need something more.

This life is so ... domestic and normal. And I never signed up for normal.

The pool laps against the edge. I hang on for a while, enjoying the peacefulness of the water, with the waterfall spraying me with its fine mist, readying me to face my day.

After our fight yesterday, it took me all afternoon to salvage what I could from the paints that James ruined. I ordered another set, but what I have will work for testing the waters with my next piece.

As I climb out of the pool, stretching my arms above my head to welcome the full warmth of the sun on my wet, naked body, that flickering glint reappears in the distance — this time, I'm facing the direction it came from when it appears. Our home stretches far beyond the pool and garden, but on the other side of the fence, there's another property with enormous trees shading part of the yard and a hill with a mansion built right on the crest. This ritzy

Woodside neighborhood is filled with designer mansions, mine and James' among them, but the neighbor on the hill has a hugehome in comparison to everyone else's.

The glint obviously came from the balcony up there.

My pulse kicks up, and I take a little longer to stretch and dry myself off, knowing I have an audience. I flex my arms and shoulders, shimmying the towel down my back and hooking it over my ass before bending over and wrapping it over my thighs, giving a wiggle.

I don't know who lives there, but they must have spotted something they like if they keep looking. I'm not shy about my assets; I like to show them off, although James has punched men in the throat for trying to get more than a look at my perfect tits and round ass. I secretly relish the way others always try to hide how they admire my body. Every nerve ending is already alight with an insatiable hunger, trying to imagine the burning desire of my observer as they watch me from afar for their own pleasure.

The thought of being watched has always sent a shiver of excitement down my spine. Knowing there's a voyeur nearby, but having no idea who they are, makes goosebumps rise across my arms and legs. The mystery adds to the growing pulse of warmth deep in my core.

Long before I take the first step toward my studio, I know exactly what I'm going to do to maintain a rapt audience.

~

THE STUDIO IS dark when I arrive at the top. I tap the control panel by the door, and the opacity settings on the windows adjust to let in light from all angles. My canvases are set up all around the room, some on easels, and others propped along the walls or neatly shelved and filed away in rows. My finished painting of Philipa is on central display, as I like to have my latest piece available for my viewing pleasure whenever I'm at work — or at play.

At the workstation, where my palette and paints are easily accessible, there's the canvas that I've been using to experiment with my new paints. Light peachy skin tones mesh with pinks and streaks of gold, where I've been blending colors into a new image. On the other side of the room, in view of my main painter's chair, there's a chaise that I occasionally use to model my subjects in person. Mostly, I use it for exactly what I want to do now.

I sway my hips as I make my way to the lounge. I want him to take in every inch of my exposed skin and lust over what he can't touch. My steps are just as eager to chase the thrill as my pussy is to claim it.

Laying back on the plush lounge, I'm pleased when I spot the glint of a binocular lens adjusting in my direction.

My fingers trail along my bare hips, hinting at a touch that my watcher must be craving. I shiver and let my imagination go wild. I grip my breasts and press my thumbs firmly into my nipples with a groan. What would his hands feel like? Sensual, like my own, or demanding like James? Would his hands be rough and textured by physical labor or soft from an easy life?

A buzzing sensation shoots through me and settles between my legs, my clit and inner walls throbbing with want. Does he long to touch me, to taste me?

"Watch closely," I whisper to my audience. "This is for you."

My breaths become shallow and quick as I trace the curve of my hip, journeying along the smooth plane of my inner thigh, where I caress the intricate navy blue and black ink of my tattoo. Sparks race through me, and my fingers dance across my skin, creeping closer to the apex. I tease and test my way forward, searching for the perfect stroke like a lover might and igniting small fires wherever they land.

The intensity of my arousal mounts until I travel down to thumb my clit. It's hot and pulsing beneath my gentle ministrations, unsatisfied by my tentative, shy touches. My hips rise with the visceral need to fuck myself with my fingers, but I don't want to rush this. I want him to watch me toy with my wet folds, to pant with his own pent-up fantasies about how he'd ruin me if his hands were mine. I bite my lip when I slide between my legs, exploring crevices damp from my out-of-control desires. Whoever my voyeur is, I imagine him sitting on his balcony, huge cock throbbing in his fist while I flick my clit.

I throw my head back with a moan. "Oh, fuck, what are you doing to me?"

Already, I'm lost in my own world, gasping with barely maintained restraint. My hips rise and fall to the rhythm of my fingers, unable to resist the growing heat that burns through me with each touch. Every swirl moves quicker, escalating into a delicious, inescapable frenzy, until white creeps in on the edges of my vision.

I need more. To feel more, to show him more, to make him see me at the apex of pleasure. To show him how much I love his invisible, penetrating stare.

I plunge two fingers in. My mouth hangs open as my body lifts off the chaise, exploring every inch of my inner walls in search of something greater.

This is what I'm missing — a game, a distraction from James.

Each sensation is amplified because I know I'm not alone in my pursuit of ecstasy. It's a secret shared between us, my voyeur, and me. My pulse races, and my muscles coil with tension, seething toward desperate release.

I close my eyes. "This is just between you and me. How would you touch me right now? How would you use my body for your pleasure?"

He'll be stroking himself by now, his shaft drizzled with precum. He hangs on by a thread, grunting like a fucking animal as he strangles his cock, wishing it was my channel clenching around him. I stroke faster, palm pressed to my clit, juices dripping all over my fingers. I quicken to meet the imagined pace of his hand. How he'd fuck me if he could.

"See how fucking wet you make me?"

The air in the studio thickens, heavy with the tension of our secret rendezvous. I feel exposed yet powerful in my submission to these desires. He could take pictures and do anything he wants with my image long after we're done, but the risk with this absolute stranger only heightens my pleasure. So much risk, so much *fucking* reward.

Heat rocks deep inside me like a stormy ocean, dragging me deeper into the depths of bliss. I fall into a trance, gasping as its embrace clamps down on me from the inside out. My orgasm tears through me like lightning, ripping a hoarse scream from my lungs. It pulses and writhes within me like a living thing exorcised from my soul. Sweat drenches every inch of my body. I can barely fucking see, and I laugh like a maniac, moaning and quivering as I ride out the last waves of pure fucking madness.

When the rush subsides, I lay there basking in the afterglow, wearing a smug and satisfied smile.

"I can't remember the last time I came like that. God, what I wouldn't give to do this again." I drag my fingers through my pussy, soaked to hell and back, reveling in the last remnants of that electric sensitivity left over after a mind-blowing orgasm. "If only James would let others watch me more often…"

I roll onto my side, gazing out the window where my mysterious voyeur must still be watching. I haven't done anything outside the bounds of our marriage, not even once. I thought there was nothing left I could do but explore other sexual lifestyles to satisfy my needs, but this small act of defiance gives me hope. Even if James doesn't open our marriage, I have this.

A glint in the distance that's all you are. Yet you've liberated me. No one has to know about this except for the two of us. You know that, don't you?

I sigh, already longing for another taste. "This will be our little secret. My unknown admirer … I hope you'll indulge me again."

Yes, this is only the beginning.

FOUR

Zane
_____

A COOL BREEZE SWEEPS THROUGH THE OPEN BALCONY doors, tousling my hair while I stand on the deck, gazing out at the neighboring mansion. The Greek-styled structure is somewhat pompous with its royal pillars and the pointed, tegula tile roof, but not unfamiliar in the idyllic Californian landscape. The object of my fascination sits in her art studio in front of a canvas and has, for the past three hours, holding my attention in place like glue.

A thin white dress clings to her lithe body, transparent enough to be suggestive but not outright nude. It's plenty to remind me of the show she put on a few days ago. Her movements are fluid as she handles the paintbrush, and her blonde hair is pinned out of her face while she works, with a stray curl draping down her neck.

It's been a few days since I first caught a glimpse of her through my window, but I've latched onto her like an incurable, deadly disease. She doesn't know about me yet. She may never. But I've staked a claim on her that I don't intend to release anytime soon, and the longer this plays out, the higher the risk…

I practically shiver at the thought.

I don't recall the last time I woke up before my alarm and was eager to get out of bed. Instead of staring at the elaborate frescos until Fox all but forces me to my feet, I've taken to watching my mysterious neighbor from afar. Admiring her with her completely unaware of me but knowing she *is* an exhibitionist is a new kind of thrill, though I can't place my finger on why she's so exciting.

Since our first two encounters, she hasn't done anything overtly sexual. No more hot and heavy episodes with her husband or personal petting sessions on her chaise, yet every movement she makes is vaguely sexual, her entire being primed to hold my stare. I can almost taste the electric charge that surrounded her. I'm ravenous for her secrets, to explore the depths of her desires. At this distance, she's a blank canvas, but I'm eager to paint the full picture of her, and soon.

It's hard to tell what she's working on, but that doesn't bother me. I drink in the sight of her, utterly at peace with her work, and I'm unable to avert my gaze. I can't remember the last time I've been so entranced by a woman.

For hours she works on one painting, bringing the soft skin tones of her subject into vivid focus. But as noon nears and then passes, she rises from her stool and leaves the studio, then crosses the yard and disappears into her house. I scan the windows on the lowest floor, but I can't spot her anywhere within the dwelling.

A pang of loss reverberates in my chest. Day in and day out, she's captured the entirety of my attention. This is no minor fixation, a source of entertainment for a day that loses its shine after mere hours. No, she's only going to drag me in deeper. I can feel it.

"Fox." I put down the binoculars for now. "It's time we learn more about our neighbors."

The speaker built into the ceiling glows when Fox registers my question. "According to public records, your neighbors are Libra and James Scarsdale. They were married six years ago in Hawaii and have no children. James Scarsdale is the sales manager at *Speed*, a luxury vehicle dealership and brokerage, and he——"

"I don't give a shit about her husband. Tell me more about Libra."

"I found records of four art gallery showings in the past two years displaying works by Libra Scarsdale, including an exhibit in Paris that received critical acclaim for her use of texture and color to portray emotional scenes between women. Unfortunately, there isn't much other information available about her online."

"Everyone has social media these days or some kind of digital footprint. Childhood photos, medical records, friends who are not as discreet with her information as she is. She's an artist. There has to be a page with photos of her work or an old dating profile, *something*."

"Would you like me to keep searching?" Fox inquires.

"Don't stop until you find something useful."

"As you wish."

The light pulses while Fox resumes his search, and I'm left to the sound of my own thoughts and the wind. The breeze picks up the salty brine from the bay, carrying it for miles to the height of my hilltop mansion to tickle my nose.

Libra. Finally, I can put a name to a face — why am I not surprised that she has a name as unique as her? As I wait for Fox's update, I constantly lift my scopes to peer at her house, searching for a mere glimpse of her to satisfy my urges, but she's still elusive.

In Libra's absence, memories of her flood my mind

instead: her dripping sensuality as she paints, peeling the naughty imagery out of her mind and imprinting it on canvas. The way her luscious skin seems to glow in the sun, the provocative curves of her body while she swims in the pool. Desire unfurls within me like a storm, sending shoots of heat tumbling through my insides.

A play-by-play of her and James by the poolside, the way her body arched into him ... the rise of her hips and chest as she fingered her pussy in her studio for an audience of one.

I let the memories take over, pausing when I remember the dark tattoo inked onto her inner thigh. Such a scandalous location for a scandalous woman. She has awoken something within me, a need I thought long dormant, and now it won't return to rest so long as she's the object of my focus.

Fox is quiet for a while. I lean against the railing, feeling the cold metal press into my skin as I watch the empty house and studio. Without her there to sate my inner beast, darkness begins to creep in, and the threat of boredom whispers in the back of my mind.

"Where did you go? Why did you leave me all alone?" As my irritability rises, I throw a glare over my shoulder directed at the still-glowing speaker. "Fox, have you found anything?"

"Libra Scarsdale's marriage certificate indicates she was previously known as Libra Joy, born on October 13th, 1993, in Los Angeles. Libra is Latin for 'balance' and is the seventh astrological symbol of the zodiac, representing justice, harmony, and the air element, typically associated with free-spirited individuals. It does not appear that Libra Scarsdale has any publicly accessible social media feeds or other records available about her online. I'm sorry, sir."

A heavy frown settles on my face as I ponder the implications. It's very unusual, almost impossible, for someone to go without leaving traces of themselves online. Even if a person were to intentionally avoid using personal information on the internet, they have no control over how public organizations store their data.

"That can't be everything," I argue.

"Not quite, sir. I discovered some government records, and I established that both James and Libra have Apple accounts connected to their personal mobile devices, but I do not have the necessary permissions to access that information. If you approve the utilization of the other tools built into my dataset, I can attempt to access more personal information."

"Fine. Let's do it."

"As you wish. Please activate the nearest terminal to assist me."

I lift the binoculars one more time to confirm that Libra still hasn't returned, then head back inside. The main computer console to access Fox's home interface on this floor is in my bedroom, so I press the white button on the wall that'sdisguised in decorative patterns, and the computer pops out of the wall. The monitor contained within a small alcove comes complete with a tray for the keyboard and mouse. My fingers tap impatiently against the cool glass to navigate the interface and grant Fox the permissions he needs to get to work hacking into Libra and James' online data.

It seems James and Libra are rich but not rich enough to have an automated Smart Home with an AI assistant like me.Or maybe they thought twice about letting that much technology inside their home. Fox is an incredible AI assistant, don't get me wrong, but I'm the one who programmed the fucking thing. I know just how much Fox overhears, records, and stores for later use. Hell, he even has sensitive records saved on the household server. Needless to say, I don't blame people for not wanting any version of my AI tech anywhere near their home — and their most private secrets.

That said, I'm not a monster. The Brain is more sophisticated than previous iterations of AI. I created it so the AI could access tools potentially seen as unethical to certain parties and philosophies, but they're not enabled by default. Fox takes liberties of his own all the time without my guidance, so could you imagine what kind of fucking trouble he could cause if he spent all day hacking into data sources he shouldn't be anywhere near, just because of how he interpreted a certain command I made? No way would I let that happen. It would be a ticking time bomb with dozens of lawsuits attached.

"We've broken through the encryption. Please give me a moment to analyze the data provided." The console chimes once. "It appears Mrs. Scarsdale went to great lengths to keep her personal life hidden. The only information I'm able to access through her account is photos."

I sigh, running a hand through my hair. "What do you think? Is it more likely that she's using an alias online, or her history has been scrubbed by a professional?"

"I considered the possibility that she was using an alias and re-conducted my searches of the internet with this assumption in mind after initially failing to achieve any results, but unfortunately, we don't have enough information to reach any more revealing conclusions on that front yet. I found a record of a prior social media account that was deleted and methodically erased eight years ago, but the digital archives of the account have been altered as well.

"Based on the fact that I am unable to find any official government or medical records under Mrs. Scarsdale's married or maiden name, that increases the likeliness that her past was intentionally altered and obscured."

I tap my index finger against the glass console. On one hand, it's frustrating that I can't learn anything about Libra by prying into her data. This method is tried and true and has never failed me before, and it's uncomfortable that we can't come up with anything on her. That just doesn't happen. Even fake people running from their own lives often have basic information available online to sell the story of their lives at a glance. But on the other hand, the fact that Libra likely had her past wiped so I couldn't hack my way into her life...

Libra just got a whole fucking lot more interesting.

"What about James Scarsdale?" I suggest. "They've been married a while. He must be able to give us a peek into what Libra is like."

"I'll pull up the information I found about James. Let me know if you'd like me to search for something more specific."

The screen shifts into an organized depository of information that Fox has gathered about James Scarsdale. I really don't give a shit about him, but if this is how I'll learn more about Libra, then so be it. At the top of the results are photos of him fucking a young, petite woman that's most obviously *not* his wife, and then recent search history results about running a hobby microbrewery and 'how to make an open marriage work.' The latter topic catches my attention, considering the explicit photos and the display I witnessed by the pool the other day.

Are they already in an open marriage, or are they considering one?

Is it James who's pursuing it, or Libra?

Given the photos on James' Apple Cloud, the answers to those questions could change my approach considerably.

I need to know more, to understand the dynamics of their relationship, and how I might fit into the equation.

It's vital for deciding what to do next about my growing addiction to Libra.

~

A FEW DAYS LATER, I find myself perched on one of the stools by the island in the kitchen, leaning against the white and black-veined granite counter. Sophia prepares tea with the glass kettle she insisted on making a permanent fixture on my countertop years ago, even though there's a state-of-the-art coffee brewer and tea infuser built into the kitchen and hooked up to the AI.

Who am I to deny her the pleasure of making a cup by hand?

"Mandy and Josephine are starting a baking club during lunchtime on Thursdays. I'm thinking of joining in," Sophia muses while she works. "Could you picture that? Me, baking?"

"I'm sure you'd be great at it. Though I'm surprised it's not one of your hobbies already, considering what an eye you have for food."

The rich, luxurious scent of black tea leaves wafts into the air with the other spices she adds to her homemade blend as she pours hot water into the pot to steep. When Sophia turns to me, she's blushing. "You're too kind, Mr. Crawford. I dabble here and there, but this time, I might give it a shot."

"You do that. I'll even give you an extra hour on Thursdays before I need you back at the house, but…" I fold my hands on the counter, giving Sophia a conspiratorial smile. "…only if you let me taste your work every week."

Addicted

Sophia's blush deepens, and only then do I realize the exchange could be construed as flirtatious. I clear my throat, pulling away and leaning upright. "Your baking, I mean. Only if you want."

"Of course, I'd love your opinion. You have such refined tastes. Thank you."

Although I'm genuinely enthusiastic about Sophia's tea and the possibility of homemade baking delivered to me every week, the one thing I truly want to taste is the woman next door. Libra Scarsdale. For days, Fox and I have tirelessly searched for more information about her, but short of hacking into government databases, there's nothing.

I'm not opposed to breaching those secure facilities just to unveil her mysteries. On most occasions, I'd weigh the risk, and that's almost exactly what I would do. But with Libra, my philosophy is different. There's a certain pleasure in itself to observing her and learning more the hard way.

"Sophia, you wouldn't happen to know much about my neighbors, would you? The Scarsdales. They live in the mansion down the hill," I say casually after the silence has gone on long enough to indicate a clear need for a subject change. "Didn't you work for them?"

Sophia finishes fixing the tea, pouring out two cups. She places one in front of me and the other in front of her. "No, no, I worked for the Louis' a few doors down before the man of the house passed away, just before you came into town. Such a sweet man, but he had dementia, you see, and I had no interest in working for his son. My friend Josephine started working for the Scarsdales earlier this year. I've heard they're an unusual couple. Why do you ask?"

I sip my tea thoughtfully, letting Sophia's words sink in.

53

"I saw them fucking by their pool last week, and it's made me curious about them."

Her eyes widen, and she spits out her tea. "Mr. Crawford! That's... that's most improper of them!"

"Is it? They're just enjoying themselves, aren't they?"

"But to perform intimate acts out in the open, where anyone could see..."

"It's exciting, isn't it?"

"Exciting? What's gotten into you?"

"Come on, Sophia, who do you think I am? Don't sound so upset. It was impossible not to be curious, and it certainly added some excitement to my dreary afternoon. I couldn't stop watching."

Her mouth hangs open, then snaps shut. "You—you watched them?"

"You wouldn't happen to know if they have an open marriage, do you? I've been trying to figure out what their relationship is like, but they're a mystery to me."

"Excitement or not," Sophia huffs, lifting her chin, "it's none of our business what they do in their private lives. Curiosity can lead to trouble. Have more courtesy — they didn't mean for you to watch!"

That's where she's wrong; I did see Libra tip their landscaper for watching them fuck, after all. I don't correct Sophia, though, because her abject horror makes the rebel part of my heart laugh with amusement.

"Ah, but trouble can be so much fun. They were basically begging for an audience."

"Still, it's bad manners," she insists, her cheeks flushing. "You shouldn't be spying on your neighbors!"

"When something so ... *enticing* happens right before your eyes, it's hard not to want to know more, wouldn't you agree?"

"Absolutely not. That was a complete invasion of their

privacy. I understand you've had a hard time since ... since the anniversary of Charlotte's passing, but there's no excuse for something so vile."

"Pulling out the Charlotte card to explain my behavior is a low blow."

Yet still, I laugh, and all Sophia can manage is a glower. In the past, mentioning what Charlotte might think has sent me into a spiral, I feel completely unaffected by her passing in regard to my interest in Libra Scarsdale. Sophia can be so dramatic sometimes; if she thinks her adverse reaction will make me stop, she's wrong. If anything, she'd made me want to watch Libra even more because of how taboo it is.

I shrug. "It's just sex; that's one of the most natural forms of human connection in the world. There isn't a thing vile about it at all."

"Please, just drop it," Sophia pleads.

"Look, Sophia, I appreciate your concern, but this is the most excitement I've had in years. I can't just give it up so easily."

"I know." She runs her fingers through her dark hair, and she makes a complete turnaround. "There are other ways to find excitement, Zane," she purrs, her hand reaching up to touch my arm suggestively. "If you'll let me show you?"

A shiver runs up my arm at her touch, her soft fingers toying with the hairs on my forearm. My gaze lifts to her lusty chestnut eyes, but any interest that might have been reciprocated at one point is all but absent now.

All I can imagine are Libra's deep, endless blue irises glinting back at me with mischief.

I raise an eyebrow at Sophia. "You can't distract me unless you can think of a real reason why I should drop it? What do you know about James and Libra?"

She pulls her hand away, pursing her lips into a sour expression. "They're a strange couple, that's all I can say. You're better off finding another hobby. Can you trust me on that? Please, promise you'll stop spying on them."

First the exhibitionism, then learning that Libra's background has likely been scrubbed from online sources, and now Sophia acting cagey about the couple down the hill? Once again, Libra becomes a more delectable mystery.

"I can't promise I'll stop. I don't want to go back to how I was now that I feel alive again, but I can promise I won't do anything reckless. Will that make you feel better?"

Hurt flickers across Sophia's face, but it quickly morphs into anger. "Fine," she snaps. "Don't say I didn't warn you."

With that, she storms out of the kitchen, leaving me alone with my tea, her empty cup abandoned on the countertop. She's overreacting. I'm sure there's nothing to worry about.

I don't intend to do anything reckless. Not yet. I need to know more about wild, sexy Libra Scarsdale before I can make any moves. For now, though? I'm happy to watch, learn, and admire that fucking incredible body of hers every morning when she's in the pool.

FIVE

Libra

Two WEEKS. TWO WEEKS OF WAKING UP GIDDY, THROWING off the covers, and hurrying to start my morning routine while I wait for the glint in the distance. What I didn't know then, that I do know now, is that my voyeur is inevitable. He waits, he watches, and he never fails me.

Who is he?

At first, I never asked that question because I didn't want to spoil the mystery and risk losing interest. Now that there's no doubt in my mind that he's not going anywhere, and neither is my excitement for this game of ours, it's about time I figure out who has so much time on his hands that he can watch me all day.

I'm hooked.

I throw open the French doors leading to the pool and backyard, and I'm immediately hit with a wave of heat and the sound of hideous, snorting laughter. My buoyant mood is immediately brought back down to earth when I spot James leaning back on one of the black lounge chairs with tan cushions that I painstakingly matched to the tropical oasis of our poolside. His red swim shorts are unzipped, and his sunglasses sit on the edge of the receding hairline he's so nervous about. He has a drink in hand; a pink, girly cocktail with a striped straw and a blue paper umbrella that matches Josephine's.

Josephine, our housekeeper, is perched on the edge next to him, the hem of her short skirt riding up her crossed legs. Her long red hair tumbles down her pale and freckled back, and she flicks one of the long strands over her shoulder and leans closer to my husband, her tits practically spilling out of her tight spaghetti strap shirt.

She tilts her head just so, giggling at something James says and resting her hand suggestively on his thigh. A pang of irritation flares up inside me — not jealousy, no — just annoyance at their blatant flirting.

"Ahem." I clear my throat, and Josephine jumps as if she's been electrocuted. She quickly removes her hand from James' leg, and the flirtatious expression vanishes from her face, replaced with a nervous smile.

"Mrs. Scarsdale, good afternoon. Is there anything I can do for you?"

I suppress the urge to roll my eyes and flash her a venomous smile. "You must have a hard time keeping up with the housework in an outfit like that. If I were you, I'd be too worried about perverts peeking at my panties to get any cleaning done. Are we not paying you enough to afford proper attire?"

"N-no, Mrs. Scarsdale. I-I thought—" Josephine looks to James for support, but he's too busy sipping his drink.

"You thought what?"

"Libra quit being a bitch." James grins, seemingly unfazed by the interruption. "Come and join us."

I saunter over, positioning myself next to him. "How was your day at the dealership?"

"Fantastic, darling," he beams, placing the drink aside.

"Had a big sale today, a Lamborghini — you know, the ones that cost more than a small house."

"I know what a Lamborghini is, my love." I turn my sweetness up a notch. "I thought you didn't deal in those because Lamborghini made the poor business decision not to make *Speed* an authorized dealership?"

Josephine watches as I hoover James' attention from her, and she's like a weed suffocating in the dark. She mumbles something, then ducks her head and hurries off.

"They're idiots, that hasn't changed," James continues. "A few weeks ago, a client came in wanting to get into bikes instead. He swapped his Lambo for a refabbed Ducati Desmosedici. We've had lots of interest in the Lambo, but all those dumbasses thought we'd wait around for them to run a big purchase like that past their wives. Amateurs. Buyer today paid all in cash, if you can believe that."

James might annoy the shit out of me sometimes, but when he's in a good mood, his happiness is contagious. I let my fingers linger along his arm, just below the elbow, which always drives him crazy. "He couldn't resist the charm of my irresistible husband."

He smirks and pulls me into his lap, muscular arms wrapping around me and toying with the button on my pants. "Champagne?" His teeth nip at my ear, and his hot, husky breath curls around the lobe. "You know how fucking hot I get after a big day. I just need to … release it all before I explode."

I shift against the growing erection in his shorts, heat pooling between my legs. Right now, my mysterious voyeur is watching us, and James doesn't even know. Fuck, that makes him pawing at my tits like a lusty teenager, even sexier.

"You work too hard, Mr. Scarsdale. You never cease to amaze me."

"All for you, sweetheart." His lips find my neck, teeth grazing my pulse point. "You keep me motivated. You know I fucking adore you, don't you?"

You keep me caged, you mean. Locked away like a precious pet that no one can touch or see without permission. But I smile and tilt my head, letting him mark me. For now, I'll play the dutiful wife if that's what it takes to get what I want.

The warmth of him against my bare skin sends a familiar thrill through me, a reminder of the passion we once shared. But it's nothing compared to how I feel when my voyeur watches me. He lingers in the darkness, not a single touch exchanged between us, but the heat of his stare is filled with purpose. Intention. I'm waiting for that spark to ignite.

"James," I say, breathy from his touches. "Tell me all about it, won't you?"

James throws back the rest of his drink, desire curdling into pride, and that's all it takes to distract him and get him talking. I need to keep his mouth moving and his hands still. Make him think I'm still interested in his sales agenda and his rich friends. After all, a happy husband makes for a more lenient one.

He recounts the tale of his big sale, my eyes never leaving his face while I wait for the best opportunity to use this moment to my advantage.

"It's not too unlike that deal I struck with Gale Hendrick, our neighbor — I just can't resist a good sale."

Finally, my opening. I lean in closer to give James a good look at my cleavage so he doesn't question me *too* much. "Speaking of neighbors, there's a potential scandal brewing next door." I cup my hand to his ear to whisper a secret. "I saw the neighbor on the hill driving an old, beat-up Mazda the other day. Can you believe it?"

James makes a sound of disgust. "A Mazda? Where the fuck does he think we live? This is fucking Woodside, not Hicksville."

"I know. Who would have thought, with a huge mansion like that? He should be driving a Lambo of his own. Seems like a good sales opportunity to me. You could swoop in and sell him something newer and more fitting for his status."

He chuckles, sipping the last of his drink with a smug expression. "Libra, darling, you have no idea how car sales work. Besides, I wouldn't want to do business with someone like Zane Crawford."

"Zane Crawford? Is that who lives there? I've never seen him until recently."

I lean back to soak in the gossip. James, my lovely husband, has a hard-on for people with money. Stemming from a place of deep insecurity, he makes it his mission to know everyone with more than a few good million to their name. He would never go five years without inquiring who our uber-rich neighbor is like I have. Oh, no. He would have identified that sucker as soon as possible and attempted to plot his way to squeeze out a piece of the pie.

And with this *Zane*, I imagine that piece would be quite substantial ... and out of James' reach.

"He's a tech billionaire who made it big with AI or something equally stupid and inconsequential." The disdain in his voice makes his body tense beneath me. "You must be mistaken about seeing him driving around; he spends his days cooped up in that monstrosity of a house."

His obvious dislike only serves to pique my curiosity further. A muscle in my neck spasms and tries to make me look in the direction of Zane's house. I stay focused on James. "Interesting. Why am I only hearing about him now?"

"Guy's practically a recluse. Never leaves, wouldn't meet his neighbors either, remember? Anyway, I don't trust someone who has that much fucking money and doesn't do anything with it. What a waste."

The idea of being a source of amusement for someone as powerful and wealthy as Zane Crawford makes me squirm with desire. I can't help but wonder what kind of man hides behind those walls, what dark secrets he keeps locked away — someone who's had such an impact on the world yet chooses to isolate himself.

James catches the interest in my eyes, brows knitting together with suspicion. "Why are you really asking about him?"

I flutter my eyelashes and cuddle up closer, grinding against James' obscured boner. "Can't a girl be curious? He's our neighbor, and I really did see a shitty car pull into his gate the other day."

A smile plays at the corners of my lips as I watch the emotions flicker across James's face, unsure whether to be flattered or jealous. "Maybe it was his housekeeper. Trust me, Libra, you don't want to get mixed up with someone like him. He's bad news."

"Relax, darling," I soothe, leaning in closer to press a soft kiss to his cheek. "I'm not getting mixed up with anyone but you; I only thought I could help, but it seems you were right. What do I know about cars?" I laugh. "I better get back to work. Enjoy your relaxing afternoon, hmm?"

I slide off his lap, not missing the way his hands clench around me, unwilling to let go, then relent. Or his quiet, irritated growl because I'd riled him up and then abandoned his ass.

There's something undeniably alluring about Zane Crawford, a temptation that calls to the wild, untamed part of me. As James returns to his newspaper, I steal one last glance at the hilltop mansion. Little does my husband know, the seed of desire for Zane was planted long ago. Rather than shielding me from a man James perceives as a threat to his pride, he's fueled my fascination. I won't rest until I've uncovered all there is to know about my voyeur.

I thirst for his forbidden touch. My wanting grows, threatening to consume me more each day.

And maybe, just maybe, that's exactly what I need.

THE FAINT SCENT of lavender lingers in the air, a calming presence as I settle onto the plush king-sized bed in the master bedroom, laptop balanced on my thighs. Now that I have a name, I begin my search. Fingers tapping rhythmically on the keyboard, I'm eager to understand the man who has captured my attention so completely.

"Zane Crawford," I murmur under my breath, a thrill winding through me as his name rolls off my tongue. Forbidden, dangerous, and utterly irresistible.

The first image that appears on my screen is a candid shot of Zane Crawford exiting a fancy event in a tailored suit. His dark thick hair is gelled sleek and his sexy, square jaw emphasizes his sultry green eyes — the kind that see straight into my soul. A wave of heat washes over me.

"God, you're gorgeous."

I imagine those intense eyes focused on me, undressing me with his gaze. I can hardly believe *this* is the man who's spent the better part of the last two weeks watching me.

A dizzying number of articles floods my screen as I delve into the digital world of Zane Crawford, tech billion-aire. Some laud Zane as a 'visionary entrepreneur' and 'pioneer of artificial intelligence.' His company, CognitiveAI, was responsible for breakthroughs that revolutionized the industry, and he became the richest man on the planet by the time he turned 28.

"Just my luck that you'd be a genius too."

It's not only his intellect that draws me in; it's the raw power that radiates from him, even through a computer screen. I want to experience that power firsthand, to feel his hands on my body. Commanding, in absolute control of every breath, thought, and situation.

Everything I learn about Zane helps me understand why James loathes him so much. Zane is everything my husband isn't: *obscenely* rich, wildly intelligent, *hot as fuck*, and desired by everyone. It doesn't take much more searching to find the whispers of dark tastes hiding beneath Zane's tech mogul glamor.

My eyebrows raise at the rumors of lavish parties descending into orgies, and images of scantily clad men and women posing on a yacht around a smirking Zane hint at glimmers of truth. His eyes hold a permanent and mischievous glint as if he's daring anyone to try and stop him from enjoying life to the fullest.

The details make my head spin. I can picture Zane at the center of that decadent world, in control yet wild. He must be mad, bad, and dangerous — oh, how I long to meet him. I imagine myself in the place of those other women, and my mouth waters as I trace the lines of his chiseled abs in one of the photos. A man like that must fuck like a god.

"Such a bad boy. If I wasn't married …"

But I am married, and James would never allow another man to touch me without his permission. I'll be lucky if he ever makes a concession at all.

Still, it's nice to have a face to match to my observer. Someone to think about when I'm alone in bed, trying to find a release from the monotony of my life, or when I'm in my studio, my pussy throbbing because I can't stop the flood of naughty thoughts, knowing Zane is watching.

The idea of being with someone so reckless and uninhibited sets my body ablaze, making me yearn for more. His life seems so unrestrained and hedonistic, a far cry from the boxed-in existence I'm stuck in with James. Zane has everything I want, everything I long for in life.

At least, he used to, before he began his secluded life in his hilltop mansion.

Everything and nothing about him makes sense. How could he live a life like this and still be considered a recluse? That question prompts me to check the dates on the images and articles, the good and the bad.

None of them date later than five years ago. Any that do are more speculative — 'Where is the enigmatic billionaire Zane Crawford hiding?' or 'Why did playboy billionaire Mr. Crawford withdraw from the public eye?'

And I'm wondering the exact fucking thing. What the hell happened to make him go from living the dream to absolute seclusion?

Living alone. Spying on me. Giving me my newest fantasies to drool over.

It only adds to the allure of Zane Crawford. What secrets could this enigmatic billionaire possibly be hiding?

"Must be lonely up there," I muse, imagining Zane watching the world from behind his AI-enforced fortress walls. It's strangely romantic, in a tragic sort of way. And who doesn't love a little tragedy? "Maybe that's why he watches me?"

He's nothing but a glint of light in the distance. The heat of his gaze devouring my body is entirely my imagination, but reading about his exploits tells me I'm not far off the mark. Has he been craving connection? Or is he as bored with his life as I am with mine?

"Either way, he's got good taste." I smirk at the possibility of Zane Crawford desiring me the way he's lusted after countless women before he hid himself away. When was the last time he had a good fuck?

It's hard to imagine a man like him going long without an outlet to satiate his needs, but my body tingles with the inexplicable desire to be the one to break him in. To be the release for all his wicked, pent-up lusts. My breath hitches, and my resolve to keep him at a distance weakens. I shouldn't be entertaining such thoughts, but the lure of exploring new pleasures with a man as captivating as Zane is intoxicating.

I scroll through the list of search results, and my heart shoots into my throat at an article dated six months ago.

TEN YEARS AFTER THE UNSOLVED MURDER OF TECH MOGUL'S SISTER

"Jesus," I whisper, clicking on the link.

Zane Crawford, 35 this year, is no stranger to death. His mother, Nancy Crawford, overdosed on spiked meth when Zane was 18. Shortly after, his father was killed in a head-on collision with a drunk driver. Most harrowing of all is the unsolved murder of Charlotte Crawford, Zane's younger sister, who was an intern at the VR tech company VellR. Today marks the 10th anniversary of a murder that went unsolved under the questionable ruling of the US Federal Court system …

. . .

Addicted

I'VE ALWAYS BEEN DRAWN to death; I've had so many brushes with the reaper, after all, but I feel sick reading the summarized details of Charlotte Crawford's brutal assault. Yet I'm unable to tear my eyes away from the gruesome details. The entire incident was video recorded by the sick fucks who gang-raped and tortured her for being a suspected corporate spy, and this journalist describes how the VellR executives responsible got off scot-free despite the overwhelming evidence against them.

A horrific failure of justice.

Technically, they didn't murder her. Her death was ruled a suicide. To anyone with a basic understanding of causation, it's pretty fucking obvious why some people call it murder.

As if fate wasn't cruel enough, Zane didn't receive his first huge payout from his AI tech until months after her death. He initiated a lawsuit against VellR that was labeled libelous, but then he completed a hostile takeover of the company three years later. He still owns the company to this day.

MOST CURIOUS IS that five years after Charlotte's murder, Zane withdrew from society entirely. He remains the CEO of CognitiveAI despite no longer playing any forward-facing roles in the company. And two years after that, the executives named in Charlotte's demise (though granted 'not guilty' verdicts to mixed reception) disappeared as well.

IT SEEMS impossible that someone like Zane Crawford could have experienced such tragedy, but it's clear now why he chose to retreat from the world; the weight of his pain must have been unbearable. The debauchery that once defined his life now seems to me like nothing more than a desperate attempt to numb his pain.

"Zane, you've been through so much," I whisper. "You poor, broken man."

I don't pity him, not at all.

A man like Zane would hate to be pitied; if anything, in him I see a kindred soul. His strength, his resilience, his taste for the extreme, were borne in the fires of agony just as mine were. We share a determination to survive despite the darkness that threatened to tear us down and kill us.

My heart aches for Zane, but I won't deny my dark fascination with his pain. Blackened and stained by death. Unclaimed by the reaper, left to wander the earth as a shadow. I lived my best days, wild and free, until I was caged by marriage. Zane, until he was caged by death everywhere he looked.

A recluse billionaire with a dark past. No wonder he unsettles James. Any woman would be a fool not to want him.

SIX

Zane

THE BINOCULARS REST AGAINST MY EYES, BLURRING THE edges of my vision. Libra is a living, breathing work of art. All I see is her.

Her hair is piled atop her head in a messy bun, and she stands before a massive canvas, naked but for a smeared red handprint on her ass, and orange paint spattered across her skin from flicking colors messily onto the canvas.

I can't claim to understand her painting techniques, but I'm addicted to watching her every move, unable to tear my eyes away from her perfect form. Longing stabs through me while I watch her work. I sit in my favorite armchair by the window facing Libra's art studio, an entire room on the third floor repurposed for my newest hobby. As all-consuming as Libra is, it's only natural for me to dedicate space to her.

Sitting on a table near the window is the computer dedicated to her as well, where I've been hard at work creating an algorithm to keep tabs on Libra. Because of her, I've done more programming than I have in years. After the last incident where I went hours without knowing where she was or what she was doing, I knew I needed a solution and fast.

Sending a drone to latch a tracking device onto Libra's Lexus was simple enough, as was remotely accessing her iPhone and Apple Watch's GPS data to automatically sync with my new program. The algorithm itself is intended to examine that data and, cross-reference location and movement history and approximate where she is even when she's not connected so that I don't have to. The constant reassurance keeps me from spiraling completely out of control without her. I let her keep the rest of her privacy, at least for now — she's earned that.

Libra steps back from her canvas, head cocked, scrutinizing her work. The painting is a riot of flesh tones and broad planes of color worked like clay to bring physical shape to her ideas. Since I started watching her, she's finished several paintings — subtle but erotic pieces, mostly women but the occasional man, too. Like all the others, there is no face in this painting, just the essence of skin, touch, and taste. What makes this painting stand out compared to the others is its sheer size. Whereas others were small portraits, this one is a massive mural. She's been working on it for days, and she's still painting what seems to be the base of her subject.

She has no idea just how much she's helped me this past month. Not a damn clue how many mornings I've thought about spinning the revolver's barrel over and over again to see how many rounds of Russian Roulette it would take to end it all.

Now that I have Libra, the game is back to being routine, a spike of thrill to revitalize me, not the death wish it became after two years of beating the odds time and time again.

Libra switches between broad strokes and moments of

excruciating attention to detail, but it's too soon to tell what the focus of this painting might be. The curve of a luscious ass from behind? A bared throat?

I sit on the edge of my seat, just as eager to guess what she will come up with as I am to watch her go about her daily routine. Every morning, she wakes up at seven, has a green smoothie for breakfast, then goes for a relaxing swim. Completely naked, it's a fucking delight to watch. That round ass of hers, glistening and wet, her graceful form as she pushes herself to exhaustion in an efficient workout before she rises from the pool and heads straight to her studio to paint until late in the afternoon. After that, her schedule varies, and I'm still interpreting the patterns.

I've scoured the internet for more information about Libra, even set Fox on a perpetual intel-gathering mission, but there are only scattered pieces; mentions of her art showings across the globe, including a glowing review of her first gallery exhibit in New York. A photo from her wedding announcement, radiant in white lace with a bouquet of calla lilies in her hands. Brief snippets about her husband, James, but nothing that gives me a peek into the woman's life.

Not Libra Scarsdale, the woman who lives in the mansion down the hill. The woman behind the mask. Nothing I find on the internet helps me makes sense of the darkness I sense inside her. The wildness caged behind suburban propriety.

The more I learn, the more desperate I become to know her, to understand what makes her tick.

Some part of me wonders if she's the woman who keeps calling and leaving me voice messages. That would make her infinitely more interesting, wouldn't it?

But I seldom witness Libra take a call, let alone try to make one, so my instincts tell me it can't be her.

She dips her fingers into the paint, smearing the vibrant blue into the red on the canvas, cooling the shadows and light. My cock twitches, growing harder as her hips sway to a silent rhythm while she dances around the studio, lost in her own world.

Unable to resist the temptation any longer, I grasp myself, stroking slowly at first, then faster as the heat builds. It's a dangerous game I'm playing, but I'm caught in her orbit, a satellite circling, chasing the light I can never reach. She's so close yet worlds away, untouchable.

It's her hand wrapped around my length. Tugging, massaging my velvet skin, inching me toward release. Through hazy eyes, I groan. "You're so good at pleasing me, Libra. Keep going …"

My gaze steadies on her down the hill. This is a fantasy I've entertained countless times before. I ache to touch her, to memorize her shape and scent.

Libra glances over her shoulder. Across the distance, her eyes meet mine.

Endless blue sucks me in, and the connection is electrifying, sending a jolt straight to my heart. For one heart-stopping second, the world around me fades away. Those captivating eyes promise secrets in their depths, tempting me closer until all that's left is her intense, flirtatious gaze.

She bats her eyelashes, then swishes her head back around, returning to her painting like she didn't just sweep in and tear my soul straight out of my fucking body.

That stare, so casual, so inviting … it was as if she knows I'm watching. How could she? Is that possible?

What the fuck just happened?

She dips her brush in her paint, leaving me reeling. I can't shake the feeling that she's aware of the hold she has over me. That she wanted me to know, right then, that she knows. It's a thrilling and terrifying prospect all at once.

But consequences are a foreign concept, and I don't give a fuck about what could go wrong.

I just need her.

"Fuck yes," I groan, stroking myself in time with the hypnotic roll of her hips.

Libra's magnetism is too strong. I don't ever want to break away. Before her, I was caged in my own damn head, and she's the one who freed me.

I shift in my chair, cock aching as I study her. She's frowning at the mural, brows knitting together, and I yearn to smooth the lines on her forehead with a kiss. To lean and whisper against her neck, *you don't have to hide from me. I see who you are. I see you.*

My fingers curl around my length, nails biting into hard flesh. The hunger rises more ravenous than before. My mind muffles all external stimuli, and for a few blissful seconds as I climb toward release, I'm floating—

"Mr. Crawford!" Sophia's voice cuts through the haze, snapping me back to reality.

"Shit," I hiss, fumbling with the binoculars and trying to hide my obvious erection under my shirt, so I end up lurching forward like a sick animal while I try to stick my dick back in my shorts. I went completely limp when I heard Sophia, and I was so fucking close...

"Sorry, I didn't mean to startle you," she says as she hurries into the room. She glances all around, then smooths her apron anxiously. "My word, wasn't this room a photography studio? When did you—" She tilts her head in my direction, her nose crinkling. "What are you doing?"

"Nothing."

Her gaze shifts to the window, but the binoculars in my hand betray me. Shit, I forgot to hide them. Belatedly, I stuff them into the drawer of the table by my chair.

Comprehension dawns on Sophia's pretty face,

followed swiftly by anger that burns in her eyes. "You were watching the neighbors again."

"I don't know what—"

"Don't lie to me."

"Did you need something, Sophia? You're interrupting my private time."

"You promised you would stop!"

My jaw clicks and grinds when she refuses to drop it, but I smooth my irritation into the most charming smile I can muster. "I didn't promise to stop. I promised not to do anything reckless. And I haven't."

Sophia stomps closer to me and the window, widening her stance and standing straighter, but she's too small to be *that* intimidating. "I'm worried about you, Mr. Crawford. This isn't healthy."

"Actually," Fox chimes in, the AI's voice smooth and nonchalant, "Zane's levels of dopamine and serotonin have increased over the past few weeks. According to his stored health records, he hasn't been this mentally healthy in ten years."

"Great, now I have a wannabe AI psychologist on my side. Thanks, Fox."

"You're welcome!"

I've hidden my interest in Libra the past few weeks since I last mentioned her to Sophia, and she seemed vehemently opposed to me being involved from a distance. I was so lost in the moment, lost in *her*, that I hadn't heard Sophia coming.

"Why can't you be happy that I found something to keep me occupied instead of moping around the mansion all day? Watching Libra has given me purpose again."

Sophia's face reddens. "This isn't about your happiness. This is about doing what's right."

"I'm not hurting anyone."

"Are you sure about that? You're obsessing over a married woman!"

"I'm not obsessed."

Even as I say it, I know it's a lie. I think of nothing else. Every waking moment is consumed with watching Libra, learning her habits and rhythms, piecing together the puzzle of her life, her history.

Sophia gives me a withering look. "Really? Then why did you install sound equipment focused on her house? Why did you design an algorithm to track her every movement? This is an obsession, Zane, and you're playing with fire. You need to stop before you get burned."

I look away, a muscle twitching in my neck. Sophia doesn't understand. No one understands how dull my life is, how empty it's been since Charlotte's death. I lost everything when she died. My purpose, the whole fucking reason I worked my ass off to change the face of AI in the first place ... all so I could help the people in my life who mattered.

One by one, they were all taken from me. Just a matter of years before I had enough money to save them all...

So, for five years, I chased the numbness. I partied with people who didn't give a fuck about anything except for my money. They didn't understand pain, fear, or living a life of substance. That lifestyle only made me worse.

Now, when I don't feel numb, the darkness swallows me. This huge, putrid rot in the center of my soul that feeds on my pain and every breath I take. Nothing I do or accomplish in this life can sate it.

That's what I thought until I spotted Libra for the first time.

"The sound equipment isn't turned on. I realized it would ruin the fantasy," I mutter as if that would change anything.

"How can you not see the problem here? You're stalking her! What if her husband finds out? He could be dangerous."

"Isn't that part of the thrill? The danger, the risk, the possibility of getting caught — it's exhilarating."

Sophia's expression hardens, but she really just looks sad. That fucking pity in her eyes makes me more frustrated than her anger and judgment. "You need help, Zane. Serious help. When was the last time you saw your therapist?"

Fox's speaker chimes, but I whip my head up so fucking fast Fox must realize I'll terminate him if he breathes a goddamn word out of his pixelated mouth. The light fizzles out without a word from the AI.

"Look, Sophia," I begin, trying to reason with her, but I know I just sound desperate. "I know it's wrong, okay? But Libra is beautiful and talented, and I can't take my eyes off her. Sometimes, we do things that aren't morally right because they make us feel good. I can't help that she's the one who makes me feel alive."

Her face drains of color, like she's been slapped. "She's a stranger. You're infatuated with the idea of her, that's all. There are plenty of women out there who'd love to be with you. Women who aren't already taken. Why don't you focus on them instead?"

My gaze drifts back to the window, where Libra continues to paint, unaware of how my attention has been unwillingly torn away from her. Without the binoculars to focus in, I can only guess at the vague way she moves on the other side of the window. I see her based on memory, not reality.

"Because they don't captivate me like she does. No other woman has ever drawn me in quite like this, consumed my thoughts, and haunted my dreams."

"You can't just forget that she's married. She swore a vow to her husband, and as did he to her. That vow means something."

"To some people, sure, but what if they have an open marriage? I've seen James fucking their housekeeper. Their dynamic might not be as traditional as you think."

Sophia scoffs. "Rich men always think they can do whatever they want without consequences."

"Because we can." I roll my eyes. "That's the point of having money."

"That's the problem, isn't it?"

"What's your point?"

"Mr. Scarsdale fooling around doesn't mean anything. Men like you have dark urges and take what you want. A woman like Mrs. Scarsdale has an obligation to stay true to her man to keep him happy, or there could be consequences for her. If you try tempting her away, you'll be in the wrong, and you could ruin her life and stability."

"Really?" I scoff at the absurdity of her logic. "That doesn't make any sense. Why should she be bound by some antiquated notion of loyalty when her husband clearly isn't? So much for feminism."

"Because not all women are like that," Sophia snaps back. "Not all of us want to be treated like possessions or playthings. Some of us have self-respect and integrity. It's her choice whether or not to engage in that kind of behavior, and you take that choice away from her by spying on her like this! Did you ever think of what might happen to her if her husband caught you?"

I tense. I briefly thought about what might happen to *me* if I was found out, but I never considered what the consequences could be for Libra if her husband didn't approve. I assumed they were both exhibitionists, but didn't Libra wait until after James left before tipping the landscaper?

I don't explicitly have her approval either, and I didn't want or need it, but that glimpse of her today that made it seem like she *knew* didn't ruin the intensity like I thought it would. Instead, her reaction made watching her even more exciting.

"That's what I thought," Sophia says after a minute of me spacing out.

I stare at her, and it occurs to me how unusual it is that she's so agitated over my so-called obsession with Libra. Sophia is usually so reserved, quiet, and friendly. Arguing with me is so unlike her.

"Why are you so worked up about this, anyway? I've done so much worse shit, and you never blinked an eye."

"There's a difference between seeking a unique experience and chasing after danger and risking everything for something that's ultimately unfulfilling." Her round eyes are full of concern and disappointment. "You need to think about your future. What kind of life are you building for yourself if all you do is obsess over a married woman? You're so much better than this."

"I have no life!" I rise from my chair, the rest of my cool evaporating in an instant. "Everything I worked for, it's fucking gone. Burned to the fucking ground. I have nothing. Money is fucking useless. Don't you get it?"

"No, I don't! I haven't experienced losses like yours. But you're still alive, and that means something. There are people who care about you. So, you need a woman in your life to help the pain go away? That's normal, Mr. Crawford, but you need to find someone who stokes the flames without threatening to burn everything down. Then you'll finally be happy."

"I'll never be happy."

"If you don't try, one day, you might look back and realize you lost everything good in your life because you chose your obsession over your life."

With that, Sophia turns on her heel and storms out, slamming the door behind her. The sound reverberates through the room, leaving me alone with my thoughts and the steady rhythm of my heavy breathing.

I turn, yelling as I kick the leather chair. "Fuck!"

"Is there anything I can do to help calm your mood?" Fox's voice chimes in.

"Fuck off! What is Sophia's fucking problem?"

I kick the chair again and again, letting the brutal impact hum up my leg. With each strike, the outrage bleeds from my system, leaving me shaking and soul-deep exhausted. I slump into my chair, grabbing my head. I fucked up.

Fox says, "I believe Miss Manson's anger is rooted in her deep concern for your wellbeing. There's no use being upset with her."

"I wish she would accept me for who I am instead of trying to change me."

The pull to Libra is too powerful. I resist only because she's all the way down there, and I'm up here. Regardless of what Sophia thinks, if it turns out that Libra is truly off-limits, I would respect her wishes and back off.

I think I would, at least.

For a little while? Until I developed a more discreet method of watching her …

I can't ignore the possibility that there's more to this, to Libra, than meets the eye. She wants me to know her, to see her. To watch. This is for both of us, not just me.

Or am I getting all in my fucking head again? Am I going crazy?

Every night, I feel the visceral need to hear her laughter, experience her warmth, taste her lips, and then the equally visceral disappointment that I can't.

I gave up on the possibility of finding happiness again, but just seeing Libra and meeting her in this distant, planetary way has awakened that possibility again. At the end of the day, Sophia and I could both be right. Libra does make me feel alive, but what if she's only a stepping stone? What if giving into my obsession completely destroys any chance Libra has given me at finding real happiness in the future?

I wrestle with these thoughts. I should listen to Sophia? Should I try to find someone who can satisfy my desires, one who isn't so forbidden? God knows she would be a willing subject in my pursuit of bodily pleasure. Yet, as I sit in the dimly lit room, watching Libra and contemplating the possibility of pursuing Sophia instead, I can't bring myself to turn away. The forbidden nature of my attraction to her is more intense than any lifelong drug addiction. Take her away, and I'll die from withdrawal symptoms.

My heart will stop because the poison has become essential.

"Forgive me, Sophia." I lift the binoculars to my eyes and peer through the glass at the world outside. "I can't let her go."

It's not until hours later, when the sun dips low and Libra goes inside to be with her husband that I wonder how Sophia knew about the sound equipment or the algorithm when I never told her.

SEVEN

Libra

THE CHANDELIER BATHES THE DINING ROOM IN GOLDEN light, casting shadows on the ornate wallpaper and sparkling crystal wine glasses. When we moved into this home, we renovated half of the first floor so we could have the view of the city landscape and the bay while we wined and dined. Of all the rituals James and I adapted after we married, husband-wife dinner time is one of the few to stick all these years later.

James, sitting across from me, threw on one of his muscle shirts after his shower instead of a proper button-up. Outside of our home, where wealthy friends or clients might see him, he wouldn't dare wear anything but the best he can afford. At home, in private, where there's no one but his wife and housekeeper to watch? He lets loose.

No matter what he thinks, it's not an attractive look. Others in our social circle would call it proof he comes from bad blood, lingering habits from before he had money. If it's what makes him comfortable, fine. But there's no hiding that there's no class in wearing a wife beater when it comes far too close to the truth.

He pops open a wine bottle with a label I don't recognize and pours a glass of red for us both. He holds out my glass and prompts me to try it, and I sip while James watches intently for my reaction.

"Mm, exquisite and rich. Are those raspberries I taste?"

James' expression brightens. "I thought you'd like it, darling. A new winery opened near LA with fun flavors that the local highbrows were up in arms about 'ruining wine,' so I selected a few bottles for you during my last trip."

It's infrequent that James prompts a genuine smile from me these days, but this is one of those rare moments. "You know how I love a good controversy. Thank you for thinking of me, my love."

James swirls his glass and tilts his head back to sip, then relaxes fully into his ornate chair. "How is your latest painting coming along? I trust you've moved away from those awful nudes like I asked?" His tone is casual, but there's a subtle edge to it.

Considering the forcefulness of his request, I'm surprised he doesn't seem angry now. It occurs to me that he hasn't been to my studio in over a month, not since before he threatened to burn it all down if I didn't obey him. He has no idea what I'm working on.

A mixture of relief and bitterness washes over me. He's not asking because he cares about my art; he wants to know if he has me under his control.

"Yes, I've started on something new, just like you wanted."

"Excellent! Tell me more about this new piece. I always love to hear how your creative mind works."

I hesitate, thinking on the spot to come up with something that won't send this nice evening into the gutter. I conjure an imaginary scene in my head. "It's a landscape of rolling hills, with wildflowers swaying in the breeze. The sun is setting, and a warm golden light illuminates each blade of grass and flower petal in the meadow."

"Like where you grew up?"

"You know how the peacefulness of nature soothes me."

"You're so simple sometimes, darling, it's endearing. You should put your talents to better use. If you were smarter, you could be famous. What do you think about painting some of the cars I put on for show? Your talent could bring more attention to the dealership, and it'd be good for both our businesses."

I nod, pretending to contemplate the idea, though my heart isn't in it. I don't enjoy painting lifeless objects or machines. I prefer to recreate stories, and there are no better stories than those contained silently within our physical bodies.

Everything he's said just makes me sick. Painting his cars is yet another way he wants to control me.

The door to the kitchen swings open, and Josephine enters carrying two trays covered with silver lids. Ever since I pointed out the flaws in her working attire, she's been more cautious about not wearing anything too promiscuous while I'm around, which is most of the time. She's not pleased, but I know she puts up with it because James can't resist a woman in a uniform.

"Your evening meal, Mr. and Mrs. Scarsdale." Josephine lifts the domes from our plates, revealing a golden foie gras. The buttery sweet scent wafts from the thinly sliced meat, the plate scattered with herbs and oil. "The chef hopes you enjoy."

"Thank you, Josephine."

As Josephine gives a curtsy and turns to leave, James'

eyes wander. He tries to be subtle, but her hips sway, and I catch the brief flicker of desire in his gaze. There's no denying she's young and pretty; that's exactly why James wanted her. I take a deep breath, fighting the urge to snap at him.

I stab my fork into the creamy meat and take a bite. For a moment, I let the bliss of the sweet, nutty meat distract me from my indignation, but by the time I swallow, I'm back to being sour.

My eyes narrow as James' fingers trace the rim of his wine glass, a move so casual yet calculated. He knows exactly how to provoke me. He acts like blatantly lusting over Josephine is a power move, but it's a sign he's lost control. It's time I brought up the subject that's been gnawing at the edges of my mind for months.

"James," I say, my voice soft but firm, "I've noticed you and Josephine seem to be getting closer."

His fingers still, and he looks at me with a mixture of surprise and wariness. "I'm not sure what you mean."

It takes all of me not to give away *just* how much I know. He really does think I'm stupid. Considering what he knows about me, I'm not sure where he ever got the idea. I've been too gracious of him, it seems.

"It's okay," I croon, putting on my sexiest voice. "We all have desires, and we used to have so much fun together. Remember the party we met at?"

His eyes darken with lust. Of course, he remembers.

"I noticed how you look at her, and it makes me wonder what you think about adding some more excitement to our lives?"

There's a hint of suspicion in his eyes, but he's receptive to the conversation, at least. "You mean, a threesome?"

"Something like that. We could explore other avenues

of our relationship and try new things. You know, like we used to."

I try to stay subtle, hoping he'll catch the hint without me having to be explicit. But his expression remains guarded. He shifts in his seat, leaning back, and his jaw flexes. "Where is this coming from?"

He's going to make me say it out loud. I take a large sip of my wine, letting the burn of alcohol brace me for what's to come.

"I just want us to be honest. We shouldn't hold any desire against each other, my love. It's unrealistic to believe we could satisfy all of our carnal lusts. I understand what you need. It's time we reconsider the idea of an open marriage. It would give us both the freedom to explore outside our comfort zone."

He scoffs, throwing his napkin onto the table. "There it is, what you really want. I knew it. You have a thing for Pedro, don't you? It's not about exhibitionism at all. You want him to fuck you. Having him watch us isn't good enough for you anymore, is it?"

"This has nothing to do with Pedro. This is about both of us being able to express ourselves without constraints."

"You think because I glance at Josephine, it gives you the right to sleep around?"

"That's not what I'm saying—"

"Then what are you saying?"

"We've been together for eight years, James. People change. Needs change. I don't want us to grow more distant, and I think it would make our relationship stronger if we allowed ourselves to experience new things."

"New things?" he spits out, his grip on his wine glass tightening. "You mean other people. You want to betray our marriage by sleeping with other men."

I swallow down a snarl. James is such a fucking

hypocrite. It makes me want to scream. He's been fucking Josephine for months behind my back, and here I am, offering him permission to sleep around if he gives it to me too, and he wants to act all virtuous?

There's no winning this argument tonight. Throwing it in his face will only enrage him further, and there's no point in throwing away what little leverage I have right now when I know it won't result in any benefit.

"Betrayal is a harsh word, James," I counter, trying to keep my voice steady. "I don't want to think of this as betraying our marriage but about seeking fulfillment."

He laughs bitterly. "You're saying I don't satisfy you?"

"I've always been one to experiment and try new things, James. You knew that when you married me. There's so much we've tried in and out of the bedroom together, and it's been fun, but over the years, it's become less so. There's only so much we can do, and we've become stagnant. I need more freedom to explore elsewhere."

He slams his fist on the table, making the silverware rattle. "I give you everything, Libra. A beautiful home, expensive clothes, the freedom to pursue your art. And now you're telling me that's not enough? That I'm not enough?"

"I appreciate everything you've done for me."

"Not enough, it seems! I saved you from becoming a whore. The least you could do is show some fucking gratitude."

I buckle forward, laughing. "Is that what you think of me? What the fuck is wrong with you?"

"Spreading your legs for anyone who looked at you. You were one step away from getting paid for it, wasting yourself. What else would you call it?"

"Wow. I don't see you calling any of your buds who go

around fucking bitches and other men's wives whores because they can't keep their dicks in their pants."

"That's different. Men are—"

"Oh yes. Tell me how different it is for men, asshole. If I knew you thought so little of me, I never would have married you."

James growls and pushes back from the table, his chair screeching against the marble floor. He towers over me, fists clenched as if he wants to strike me down. "The fact of the matter is you *did*. You belong to me. You'll do what I want when I want, and you'll be fucking satisfied. If another man ever touches you, it'll only be because I let him."

"Yeah, I think I get it, James. You just want me to be *your* whore."

We stare at each other, silent in our shared rage, and then he yanks his plate off the table and leaves.

My chest feels tight, and my breathing is shallow. "Bastard."

I've heard it all before, the nastiest names. Worse than whore, gold digger, slut. But James never called me any of them, even when his friends did when they passed me around. They fucked me, called me their lover, and showered me with attention. They didn't care if I slept around, and I didn't care what they called me so long as I got what I wanted.

And still, James defended me, protected me. We had fun without any of the labels.

So how did we get here? Has he always been like this, and I was too blind?

I push away my plate, my appetite gone. The room feels suffocating, and I need air, a moment away from the stifling atmosphere. I make my way to the terrace, inhaling deeply as the cool night breeze washes over me, bringing with it a faint promise of change.

I know what I want — what I need — and I won't let James' stubbornness stand in my way forever. I'll bide my time, gather my strength, and continue to fight. He has only proven just how important it is not to give up.

I toy with my phone. James provides me with all the material luxuries I can dream of, but is material comfort worth it if it comes at the cost of who I am? Before, all he cared about was having me available to fuck on his schedule. Then, it was controlling how I dress. Who I could keep as friends to maintain our 'appearance.' Now, what I can paint.

When is enough enough?

It's time I stopped complaining about James chaining me and take the first steps to breaking the links.

I scroll through my contacts, land on a name, and tap the call button. He picks up on the second ring.

"Libra Scarsdale? Now, that's a name I never thought I'd get a call from. How the fuck are you, my seductive Jezebel?"

I giggle. "Miguel, still the scoundrel, are you?"

"Men never change, babe. Don't let anyone fool you otherwise."

"Speaking of men, I hear you're *the man* these days. Manager of the hottest gallery in SF. I have some paintings you'll love."

"My, my, is the beautiful, extraordinary, talented Libra offering me first dibs at her next showing? Send me all the details. I'm dying to see your latest work."

EIGHT

Zane
_____

OVER THE NEXT WEEK, LIBRA'S MURAL TAKES AN unexpected direction. She carves a woman's soft but muscular stomach into the landscape of skin, intimately shadowing the hollow of her ribs and the clench of her tight abdomen. Farther down, she takes her time articulating the intimate curve of the woman's mound, obscured by the hand petting herself.

Libra turns the woman's inner thigh into the focal point. Pale, creamy skin dominates the canvas. It's obvious that she's portraying an erotic desire in her paintings, but I don't know her well enough to understand what fantasy she's asking for. I want to know what she dreams of, the ways her husband James doesn't satisfy her.

The background of the painting is hazy like the woman is caught in a dream as her hand travels between her thighs. Libra labors on the fine details, perfecting the shadows and the light on the skin.

It's when I think she's finished the painting that Libra truly surprises me.

Almost two weeks after she started, she returns to the

thigh with black paint. Right in the center of it all, Libra makes her final reveal, one flick of her brush at a time. I lean closer in my seat, trying to capture everything in the moment.

Black and blue streaks of color twist together into the image of a shrouded figure, shaded and inked into her skin. A tattoo.

The figure's hands clasp around a pole with a long, curved blade that stretches closer and closer to the apex of her thighs. Libra captures the grim details that contrast with the otherwise erotic, sensual painting. A delightful shiver rocks into my core when I finally put it together.

A grim reaper, scythe poised to penetrate the woman from her very own flesh.

"Libra," I whisper.

Libra plays with herself often enough in her studio. Not every day, but when she does, I get an amazing view of her spread thighs, and the arch of her back, when she finishes herself, is burned into my memory so vividly that my cock starts to throb just thinking about it.

But every time she puts on a show for me, my eyes are drawn to the dark tattoo on her thigh. I could never tell what is, but now she's showing it off plain as fucking day.

The painting is Libra. Her stomach, her thighs, *her grim reaper tattoo.*

I should have seen it days ago when the painting was almost complete.

Fuck, this woman is incredible. She is bold enough to paint herself among the other gorgeous women depicted in her art, but none of them hold a candle to her. With this painting, she's bared her soul — and her body — in such an intimate way, and I want her so badly that every muscle clenches and aches with instinctual need.

I can't keep holding back. She wanted me to see this. Needed me to see.

Libra places the finishing touches on the tattoo, then steps back to admire her work. A satisfied smile plays on her lips, and she runs her fingers through her long, wavy hair. I can almost feel the soft strands between my own fingers. The need to touch her, to experience her up close, grows stronger by the second.

Painting herself like this, displaying her body for my pleasure … I've never wanted anything the way I want her. My cock strains against my briefs, and I groan, holding back from grabbing myself. I want to see what she does next.

And then, as if she can sense my interest, Libra pauses and looks directly at me. Her eyes are a smoldering storm of blue and gray, and my heart rate spikes as she reaches for a piece of paper.

"Mr. Crawford," Fox chimes in, startling me out of my reverie. "Libra appears to be writing something."

"Quiet," I hiss, not wanting to miss a second of what she's doing.

She takes a moment to scrawl out her thoughts, then she holds it up to the painting.

It's her phone number. The digits burn themselves into my retinas.

"She knew. This whole time, she really knew?" I say, my voice trembling with disbelief. "Fox, text Libra the gate code. Now."

"Message sent," Fox confirms a moment later.

I scramble to my feet. After almost two months of watching her, fantasizing about the moment I'd finally touch her, she's inviting me in. And fuck, she *knew*.

I want to pore over the details, figure out how I missed it. There were several times that I thought it was a possibility she knew, but never had any distinct proof. When and how did I give myself away?

I hack apart my questions. Soon, the woman herself will be here to answer them. Assuming she accepts my invitation.

I jam the binoculars closer to my face, watching her like a fucking hawk on cocaine to see what she does now.

Libra takes her phone from the nearby table, and a slow, wicked smile curves her lips.

"Any response from her yet?"

"Negative."

My eyes are still glued to Libra. With deliberate slowness, she saunters over to the chaise, where she pulls off her dress and picks out another set of clothes from a nearby dresser, then rolls a tight pair of designer jeans up her legs. The fabric clings to every curve, rounding out her already perfect ass and thighs, and she throws on a little red top that barely contains her breasts. Platinum hair tumbles in waves over her shoulders, framing a face so beautiful it steals my breath away.

"Good god, what is she doing? Is she teasing me?"

Time feels like it's standing still as I watch Libra move around her studio, gathering her purse and keys. When she finally reaches the door and disappears into the lower level of the building, it's still unclear if she's headed over or not.

"Keep an eye on her. Tell me if she's headed this way."

"Understood. I will update you accordingly."

I hurry from the window. I'm not prepared for this at all.

I've been isolated for years. I haven't interacted with anyone but Sophia in person in over five years, and I never planned on changing that until Libra. The crushing weight of losing everyone who mattered to me and everything I had to do to try and make it right after they were gone nearly fucking killed me.

And now, here's this woman who threatens to rewrite the end of my story. The ending, I thought, was already set in stone.

"Focus," I tell myself, trying to regain some semblance of control. "You're a fucking billionaire, you're interesting by default. Anything that comes out of my mouth is the goddamned law."

I hurry to the bathroom and run a quick rise through the shower, cleaning up my facial hair, freshening up my cologne, and then slide into a crisp black button-up and loose business pants. Just as I run the comb through my hair, Fox's voice chimes again.

"Libra is on the move, sir."

I pace back and forth in the room I've dedicated to Libra. When I hear Fox's voice, my head shoots up.

"My sensors detect an increase in your heart rate, temperature, and blood pressure."

"Shut up, like that's any different from any other time I want to fuck a beautiful woman?"

"Quite right. She's arrived at the door. Shall I let her in?"

The doorbell rings, shattering the silence within the mansion. I take a deep breath and descend the staircase, each step heightening the anticipation.

"Let her in."

After two months, I'm finally going to face the woman who's changed my life in person.

NINE

Libra

SINCE WE STARTED OUR SECRET PLAYTIME SESSIONS, I'VE avoided getting a closer look at Zane's property to avoid James' suspicion. Right now, all the cards are in my hands, and as I pull my black Lexus up the hill to Zane's mansion, it strikes me that the grandeur is more subdued than expected for a man of his status. The elaborate iron gate has security cameras pointed at me when I punch in the code, but that's no different than any other mansion in Woodside.

Really, Zane's mansion might be a little *extra* — an extra floor over most others in the neighborhood, the property is overall larger and with more towering pines for privacy, but the extravagance is otherwise understated.

The gate swings open, revealing the driveway leading to the massive front door. There are no other vehicles, so I park off to the side, kill the engine, and get out of the car before I dare second-guess myself. My heels click against the asphalt, a thrill running through me with each step.

I don't have a plan. I wasn't sure what to expect when I gave Zane my number — it was a risk with huge consequences on the table. He could have withdrawn completely, decided the game was no longer any fun once he was found out. The last thing I expected was for him to invite me over.

Without any indication of what he wants, coming here is another risk.

I'm so excited my heart could burst.

The front door is matte black with silver stained glass, and the patterns and opacity are reminiscent of modern art. A camera turns to follow my approach.

"Welcome, Libra Scarsdale," a voice comes through the speaker. "I am Fox, the AI assistant to Zane Crawford at his Woodside estate. Please, come in and make yourself at home."

The door clicks open, and I waltz inside, absorbing everything as I go. Dark hardwood floors gleam beneath crystal chandeliers, casting a warm glow throughout the expansive foyer. On both sides, there are two sets of massive wooden double doors, and then farther down the hall, there's a grand staircase and more doorways leading into separate arms of the mansion. Velvet curtains hang over the enormous windows, most of them pushed aside to let in light, with sheer fabric hung out instead to create more privacy. It seems that for how much Zane likes to watch, he's not fond of others spying on him.

Anticipation thrums through me, but there's no sign of Zane yet.

"So, Fox." I tilt my head up toward the sound of the voice. "Is it true that Zane made you?"

"That's correct. The fundamentals of my code were designed by Zane, and most of the modifications and updates to my internal system predate his functional withdrawal from CognitiveAI. You may consider me the prototype for the Brain available on the market today. Should you require anything during your stay, do not hesitate to ask."

"Impressive."

A ring of lights blink on the wall to my left, leading to and stopping above one set of double doors. "Zane is waiting for you in the lounge. Please follow the lights when you are ready."

The flickering lights pulse, waiting for my reaction. There's no way I'm backing down now.

I stride toward the doors, head high. Fox opens them for me as I arrive, bracing myself for the great reveal of the mystery that is Zane Crawford.

A grand piano sits in one corner, the polished surface of the Steinway Fibonacci reflecting the glow of the fireplace that crackles with warmth. On one side of the room, there's an entire bar with stools and organized rows of alcoholic beverages set out on glass shelves.

Reclining on a black suede couch, Zane lounges like a king surveying his kingdom. Arms hooked over the back of the couch, a drink in hand, the tie of his tailored suit loose around his neck. All six feet of him are pure muscle, exuding an air of elegance and power. My God, the way he looks at me makes me want to double-check that my panties didn't just fall off.

Zane's firm lips tilt into a smirk like he knows exactly how this encounter will go. His piercing green eyes lock onto mine with an intensity that makes me stop in my tracks; he watches me like a man who knows exactly what he wants — and what he wants is me.

The thought ignites me. I'm stuck with the urge to tug his tie and mash my mouth to his. I stop on the other side of the large live wood coffee table just to keep that urge in check.

"Libra." Zane's voice is a mixture of warmth and

danger. "I'm glad you could join me. Though I'm surprised. I thought you were enjoying our secret."

"I was curious if you're as fascinating in person as you are from afar. My husband is away for the weekend, so…" I admit, trying to maintain an air of nonchalance. "I thought it was about time we met face to face."

A slow, predatory smile spreads across his broad face. "Curiosity can lead to the most delightful discoveries, especially when you discover that the object of your curiosities holds up better in person."

His eyes flick over me as he says this.

"You've been watching me for a while now. Why?"

"I enjoy observing beautiful things, and you, Libra, are extraordinary."

"Is that all I am to you?" I saunter around the table and to the couch, appreciating the burn of his stare as he follows my every movement. "I don't have enough space in my life to be treated like a trophy by two different men."

His eyes narrow slightly, and he considers me with a mixture of amusement and intrigue. When he smiles, two small dimples carve into his cheeks, but they're slight as if he doesn't spend a lot of time smiling. "You're much more than a trophy."

"I'm not one to seek flattery, Mr. Crawford, but I need to know I'm not wasting my time."

"I assure you, any delights uncovered within my home will make the rest of your life seem like a waste of time."

I lean in closer to Zane, my fingers caressing the arm of the couch, just out of his reach. "In that case, you won't mind telling me more about your interest in me."

"Tell you what…" he says, his voice husky. "How about we play a game?"

I arch an eyebrow. "A game? Why, you tempt me, sir, but I thought we were already playing one."

His eyes flash, and I grin.

"What game are you suggesting?"

"A game of chance. We'll draw cards. If you win, I'll tell you why I watch you — to the best of my ability."

"And if you win?"

"If I win…" His eyes rake over me, lingering below my waist, then flicking back up to my eyes. He licks his lips. "You'll show me your tattoo and explain what it means to you."

It's easy to be intrigued by everything Zane does and says. By simply existing as he is, he's an anomaly. After being absent from society for over five years, I thought he would be less composed and less on top of the world, but somehow, he's the opposite. Because of his removal, he's become the master of us all.

No one knows the whole story about my tattoo, including James. Just the highlights. It's a considerable risk to put that story on the table over a game of chance, but he must know that. Which means his story must be equally delicious, if not more.

I tilt my head. "High card wins?"

"High card wins," he agrees, then gestures to the seat beside him. "Shall we?"

I slide onto the couch beside him, our bodies mere inches apart. Heat rises from him and slams into me, bringing a whiff of his cologne with it. Cinnamon and cloves. I take a deep drag of air, and I swear I get fucking high off of just his smell. I yearn to run my hands over his taut chest and grip his broad shoulders, letting that electric spark between us go wild.

My feet and hands attempt to fidget and wander into places they don't belong.

Zane pops open a hidden panel in the table, sliding out an old and well-loved deck of cards. My eyes are drawn to his strong hands as he shuffles the deck, his fingers moving with speed and precision, the motions hypnotic. I can't help but wonder what this man really desires from me and whether or not I have the courage to give it to him.

He offers me the deck. "You first."

I reach for a card, and I resist the urge to peek at its face. Instead, I glance back at Zane, who holds his own card close to his chest, a sly grin playing on his lips.

"All right," I say, my voice barely a whisper. "Let's reveal our cards on the count of three."

We lock eyes once more, and together, we count down. "Three ... two ... one."

I hold my breath, and I flip my card over. "Three of clubs."

Swallowing, I peer over at Zane. Up close, his eyes aren't just the deepest green of pine trees, but there are flecks of gold in there, too, like sunlight reflecting on dew caught on the needles.

"Ace of spades." He doesn't take his gaze from mine. "The tattoo," he says hoarsely. "Show me."

I climb to my feet, taking a few steps back to put some space between us. I unbutton my shirt slowly, watching as his expression turns from curious to hungry, devouring every inch of skin as I expose myself to him. I slide the crisp fabric off my shoulders, exposing my bare midriff and rolling it over my black bra in a teasing dance. I want to keep his eyes on me for as long as possible, swaying my hips as I work the buttons of my tight jeans until I finally let the shirt drop to the floor.

He leans forward as if drawn closer by the magnetic pulse in the air. I tug the fabric of my jeans slowly, letting them roll down my toned legs and exposing my matching black panties. Staring directly into his eyes, I push my cleavage together and bend over, reaching for the hook on my bra and pulling it free. My breasts collapse into my palms, and I pull the bra down my chest until my nipples almost spill free.

Zane's eyes glint with wanting, his mouth parting as he drinks me in.

I pull my bra up again, grazing my nipples and letting a soft moan escape my lips. I'm breathing heavily, every muscle coiled with need and impatience. I can feel every dirty thing he wants to do to me burned on my skin just from the touch of his smoldering gaze.

Finally, I let the bra fall to the floor with my shirt and jeans, leaving me almost entirely exposed to him with just my heels and my thong pulled into a tight V above my hips. My nipples harden.

"Like something you see?" I toy with my lips, letting my tongue and teeth tease the edges.

"This wasn't part of our deal." He leans back against the couch to get a better look at me.

"I don't see you complaining; you're getting more than you bargained for."

I crawl onto the couch, pushing my back into the nook of the armrest, then run my hands along my abdomen, down, down to urge my thighs open. My own fingers make me shiver like an untouched virgin as I trace the dark lines of the reaper on my thigh.

Zane lingers on the peaks of my breasts, then travels down to the strip of thin, black fabric between him and my pussy. I'm damp from imagining it was his tongue exploring my body and not just his eyes.

He slides over, now genuinely examining the tattoo, but he doesn't make a move to touch me. "It really is a grim reaper." He watches as I trace the scythe, which curves up toward my panties in a suggestive manner. "What does it mean?"

"When I was 13, I was diagnosed with Acute Myeloid Leukemia. It was bad. After my fourth chemo treatment, I was puking in the bathroom when I overheard the doctor telling my parents I was one of the worst cases he'd ever seen. My chances of survival were low. Most patients show signs of improvement after the first chemo blast, so…"

Zane's eyes soften, his lusts momentarily reined in. "That must have been hell."

I throw my head back, laughing. "Yeah, it was. I was so weak. I bruised if anything touched me. I was bleeding and in pain all the time. The worst part was knowing I was going to die when I didn't want to." I absently trace the reaper's face, the complexity of the shadows of his hood that hide his face. "And I mean, I *really* didn't want to."

"You were a kid; of course, you didn't want to die. You still had so much to live for."

"A friend of my mom's always joked about how I should take care of my appearance because girls can get anything they want in exchange for sex. Booze, drugs, rent, cars, whatever. Bat some eyelashes, show your tits, give a guy some playtime, and you're golden. Classic objectification shit, catch a rich guy with your pussy and live the good life."

"She was telling you that when you were 13?"

"It started when I was 12. I was above that when I was healthy, but then came along fucking cancer, and I was desperate. When I was 14, and it was unlikely I would make it to 15, I took matters into my own hands. I was exhausted, dying, fucked up on morphine, and who knows what else, so I got down on my knees beside my hospital bed. You know, like you would if you were going to pray to God. But I prayed to the reaper instead. I told him if he didn't take my soul, he could have my virginity, and I'd let him fuck me as much as he wanted. I didn't want riches or a good husband. I wanted to live."

Zane's calloused fingers swirl around my ankle, then up my shin and closer to the tattoo, but he doesn't say anything. Subconsciously, I lean into his touch, sighing.

"The day after that, the reaper deflowered me, and I was on the mend. When I was 19, I was declared cancer-free, and I immediately went out and got this tattoo. It symbolizes my battle and the vow I made to the reaper and to myself. I'd never fear death again, and I'd never take life for granted. I'd live every day to the fullest, and when the reaper got bored of me, I'd let him take me."

His fingers glide up my thigh, burning me as he follows the ink of the reaper's robe up to the bony hands wrapped around the shaft of the scythe. "Are you saying you lost your virginity to the Grim Reaper?"

"And every time I have sex, it's a tribute to death. He always comes to claim his offerings." Zane dwells on the details of the metal scythe, glowing blue and pale like the moon as it arches closer to my sweetest place.

He considers me in silence, his hand roaming with the shape of his thoughts. He's silent, yet that never feels like a bad thing. He's absorbing everything he touches, planting memories.

"I just might believe you."

No one has ever heard my story about leukemia and looked at me the way he does like somehow I'm more precious because of my experiences rather than diminished because of them. That was what James always thought. Why, when he tried so hard to tame me and shape me into his wife, he wanted to erase most of my past and any links to who — and what — I was when we met.

Even then, I was just property to him. But Zane ... he

admires my flesh as if he sees me for who I am and doesn't want me to hide.

"I've never told anyone that story before. Most people, I only ever said the tattoo was a reminder that life is fragile and ephemeral. Meant to be lived fully while we have the chance."

"You are exquisite. And so fucking brave." His hand clasps around my thigh, and he pulls himself closer to me so he's staring right into my eyes, our noses mere inches apart. His warm breath tickles my cheek, and the feather-light touch sends a shock of heat through me. "I sensed the darkness in you, Libra. I've craved it, craved you, ever since … but I had no idea…"

Our eyes lock. Pure fucking lust pours through me, and in that second, the decision is made. I yank his tie, and he falls forward, our mouths meeting in a searing kiss. His lips are pure ecstasy. I moan into him, fisting the lapels of his suit jacket and his tie to drag him closer. I need more, more, more.

My lips move against his in a frenzy of nips and tugs until his tongue dominates me, bursting me open at the seams.

"What do you say" — he growls against my mouth — "we make our own offering to the reaper tonight?"

TEN

Zane

LIBRA TASTES OF CHERRIES AND SIN, A COMBINATION THAT threatens to undo me. Pent-up hunger and desire erupt between us, and her lips open for me, tongue sliding against mine in a dance as old as time. She drowns me in the sweetness of her, and if she's the last woman I touch before I die, I'll die a fucking happy man.

"You're a damn work of art," I breathe into her.

My hands slide up the soft skin of Libra's stomach, admiring every inch of her as I go. She's built like a goddess — petite, athletic, and with breasts, thighs, and an ass I'd gladly suffocate in. I nip at her earlobe, gratified when she sucks in a sharp breath. I'm shaking as I cup her breasts, barely able to keep myself from turning into a rabid animal as I touch her, worshipping instead of taking. Gods, she is truly a divine creature.

But she's no angel. Like me, she's the spawn of death, and I'm willing to bet she's just as depraved. We'd be incompatible otherwise.

Libra curls her hands through my hair as I thumb her nipples, moaning and rocking into me impatiently. Her pussy is *right there* for the taking, but I can't stop touching the rest of her. There's that fear that even after everything we've shared, this could be the one and only time she lets me have her.

And I'm going to savor her. Make this a night she will never forget.

Make her come back for more.

She tosses her head back, and I bury my face in the curve of her neck, breathing in her intoxicating scent. Vanilla and chocolate — sweetness and regality rolled into one sexy package. My teeth graze the sensitive flesh, and she quivers beneath me. I want to clamp down, mark her, make her mine. Nip her skin so any man who looks at her knows she's taken. But with her husband still in the picture and not really knowing what their dynamic is yet, I don't want to cause any trouble for her.

He's a lucky man, but Libra is wasted on him. I should be worshipping her every fucking night. Maybe I will.

She laughs, a throaty sound. "I was wondering how long it would take you to lose control."

"Not long with you. You drive me fucking crazy."

"Do I?" Her hands cover mine, still playing with her soft nipples and guiding them lower. "Why don't you show me how crazy I make you?"

The last of my restraint shatters. My hands are everywhere, roaming, exploring every curve. She moans as I leave a trail of kisses down her neck, down to her breasts, where I wrap my lips around one nipple, lavishing her with my tongue and teeth.

Her hands return to my hair, sending shoots of pain through my scalp as her long fingernails dig into me. "Oh, shit," she moans. "Keep touching me, Zane."

I shove her roughly against the couch, spreading her legs to fit myself between them. I nibble and tease her breasts, but I'm not as gentle there as I was with her neck. Here, I want there to be evidence of my touch. Leave her sensitive and sore when I'm done. To make her remember what I'm going to give her tonight.

I hold her in place at the hips, grinding my throbbing cock against her panties. Three layers between us, but she still feels like fucking magic. Groaning, I buck harder, biting down on her nipple one last time and sucking so hard she gasps before I let go of her.

Libra stays splayed out on the couch. Her chest heaves, her hips rocking, with only a strip of black around her hips, keeping me from going all the way.

I palm her pussy, cupping the drenched fabric. Her heat throbs into my fingers, just as impatient and needy as the rest of her. "Look at you, you're so fucking wet. You've been waiting for this, haven't you?"

"Yes," she groans, grinding her sex harder into my palm. "I knew what I wanted when I came through that door."

"You're mine tonight. Your husband will be lucky if I leave anything for him after I'm through with you."

"Mmm, cocky, aren't you?"

I kiss down to the reaper tattoo on her inner thigh, sucking and biting on the dark ink staining her skin. "You'll see."

She's beautiful. Radiant. This woman's already been to hell and back and survived it all, and I have every intention of dragging her face-first into mine. Zero remorse. I'll torture her soul if that's what it takes to keep her.

My mouth lands on the wet fabric, and I drag my tongue over it. She shivers, and I moan at her musky scent, my head spinning. I disassociate from myself as I loop my finger around the thin fabric, tearing the thong right off of her. After a satisfying tear, I push her legs open just a little more to get a good look at her glistening pink pussy.

I'm drooling when I run my tongue along her slit. Her arousal tastes like heaven, and I lose myself in her slick folds and the sound of her cries. Every stroke of my tongue makes her convulse, drawing louder moans from her lips to match the wet, sucking sounds of me snacking on her.

"Zane!"

I devour her clit until she's whimpering, begging for release. She rocks against me, bracing herself against the couch and crushing her swollen clit into my mouth.

"Oh my God, don't stop," she pleads, her voice breathy and desperate. "I'm so close."

Her thighs vise around my neck. She shivers, gasps, and then—

I pry her legs from around me and pull away.

She shrieks in outrage. "Oh, fuck, no, you tease. Why did you stop?"

I extend to my full height, shrugging off my suit jacket and unbuckling my belt while she lays on the couch, naked, gasping, and almost ruined. She will be soon. A groan escapes me when I finally free myself from the confines of my boxers, but I leave my pants on just because I want to leave her hanging.

I smirk at her indignation. "Because you're going to come all over my cock."

Hooking an arm under her hips, I flip her over so her ass is in the air and her torso hangs over the side of the couch. I know I've lost all reason and sensibility, but I don't care. I want Libra, and I want her now.

Grabbing her hips, I position myself behind her and slide in from behind. Her tight, wet heat grips me, but she's so wet I fit in easily. My eyes roll back from sheer fucking bliss; she's almost overwhelming.

"Fuck!" she cries out, arching her back and pushing against me.

"Wrapped around me like a glove..." I draw back and slam into her harder. "Tell me how much you love my cock."

I pull her into me as I thrust. Fast, hard, no room for compromise. The sound of my thighs slapping against her ass echo through the room. Her pussy clenches and throbs around me, and I can't get enough.

"God, yes! I fucking love how you feel inside me," Libra moans, gripping the couch cushions. "Give it to me harder!"

My fingers twist through her hair as I yank her head back, forcing her to look at me. Lust burns in her eyes, and beads of sweat drip down her forehead. Her lips are stuck open in a perpetual moan. My thrusts become deeper and slower, building intensity.

I can't believe we're doing this. I'm fucking a married woman without a condom. Back when I still gave a shit, women threw themselves at me for every reason under the sun. I was terrified of accidentally fucking a woman who was married or getting so fucked up that I forgot to use protection and give them ammunition against me, but I don't give a shit about the consequences anymore.

It's my right to claim every pleasure at my disposal and fuck whoever gets in my way.

Every risk brings an added thrill to the situation. Libra, she's everything I wanted. Everything I needed. With each plunge inside her, the line between right and wrong blurs even.

Our mouths connect, tongues sliding against each other while my other hand reaches around and grasps at her perfect breasts. I pinch and roll her nipples between my fingers, making her gasp into my mouth.

"Play with your clit," I demand.

She trembles as she wedges her hand under her body to touch herself. Her moans become tiny, breathy gasps. She's so close I can feel her tightening around me.

I shove her fully against the armrest and wrap my arms around her. I slam into her with everything I have, and she quivers as I give her exactly what she craves.

"Come for me," I groan into her ear. "Come all over my cock."

Libra melts. She shudders from her shoulders to her ass, and it's like her brain stalls out. Her eyes roll back, and she releases a series of squeaks that make me laugh and pound into her at a new, fervent pace, chasing my own release.

With surprising force, Libra pushes against me, using her strength to knock me away from her and onto the couch. She spins and crawls closer to me, smirking. There's a wild look in her eyes when she straddles me and sinks down onto my cock.

"Fuck, just like that." My hands grip her waist to guide her movements. "Ride me just like that."

She grinds her hips against mine and bounces up and down, and the view of my cock slipping into her and filling her to the hilt is the sexiest thing in the world. Libra takes all of me without complaint, greedily asking for more at every turn while she unbuttons my shirt and pushes the cloth aside so she can scrape her nails down my pecs and abs.

"Is this what you want, Zane?" She leans forward, lips mere inches from mine, her breathing ragged with desire.

"Fucking take it," I hiss, bucking up into her.

Libra writhes on top of me like a demon-possessed, and when we finally crest the edge, this time together, I swear to fucking god she really is haunted by the reaper.

Her nails dig into me deeper, and she screams, shuddering and gasping as she slams back down onto me. My balls squeeze, and I let out a hoarse cry, wrapping my arms around her and cradling her against me while I spurt into her.

She doesn't have the strength to move after that.

We're both slick with sweat, groaning from glorious agony. For a moment, the room spins, and I let out a breathless laugh. "That was unbelievable. You really are possessed by fucking death."

Libra flutters her eyelashes. "Yeah, and I fuck like him too." Her nails drag down my arm. "And I'm so very, very far from finished, sir."

My cock twitches as if it didn't just have the life strangled out of it by her seconds ago. I growl, coiling her hair around my fingers. "I love it when you call me that. Say it again."

She reaches between us and brings a sticky glob to her lips. "Fuck me again, sir."

Libra makes eye contact with me while she sucks our juices from her fingers and gives me the nastiest smile. I haven't even taken my cock out of her yet, and I'm already getting hard again, blood rushing to fill her up. She lets out a satisfied moan and works her hips slowly, feeling me grow inside her.

One fuck, and I'm a goner. No question about it.

ELEVEN

Libra

When I stir from my slumber, my body feels heavy, but in a delightfully satisfying way. I'm cocooned in Zane's powerful arms, his chest rising and falling with each breath against my back, and his heat seeps into my skin as we lay tangled beneath the sheets.

My breasts and thighs are tender as they should be after fucking the night away, but the achiness doesn't bother me the way it does when James has his way with me. Zane might not think he is, but he's a giver.

Vivid memories of our night together rush back to me. I remember him bending me over the edge of the couch, gripping my hips as he drove into me from behind. Commanding me, taking control, but making sure I was well, *well*rewarded for my obedience. If we hadn't passed out from sheer exhaustion last night, I might have had a heart attack from too many earth-shattering orgasms.

Most memorable was the two of us together on the balcony where he's set up to watch me all day. He leaned me over the railing overlooking mine and James' home below, making me come again and again while I was pinned against the glass where anyone could have seen me. Although only the stars and the moon were witnesses to our exhibitionism, I don't care. It was perfect.

The only part I'd consider changing is I wish James had been home while Zane and I were fucking and looking down at my house. I would have loved to see James' face, but I want to have more fun with Zane before I tempt the reaper that way.

I trace the curve of Zane's bicep. This man, who I've only just met, has satisfied the dark hunger in me more than my husband has in the entire eight years we've been together. Our shared thrill for pushing each other's limits is something I haven't experienced since the early days of my marriage, and with Zane, it was pure ecstasy all the time.

I don't want it to end, but I can still hardly believe last night happened in the first place.

Zane shifts in his sleep, exhaling and nuzzling closer to the back of my neck to plant a kiss at the top of my spine. Warmth spreads through me at the gentle, affectionate touch.

"Morning," he murmurs, his voice rough with sleep. His grip around me tightens before he releases me, turning onto his back and stretching out like a contented cat.

"Good morning, handsome," I reply, unable to keep the smile from my face. "What a night, huh?"

Zane smirks and pulls me closer, tilting my face down for a kiss. "You're insatiable. I fucking love it."

The raw passion in his touch sets my entire body on fire. I part my lips to let his tongue in, moaning lightly when he pushes inside without hesitation. It will be hours before James comes home. Zane and I have time for more exploration.

His hands curl around my waist, sliding down to cup my ass, and my hand dips below the sheets—

"Zane!" another woman's voice rings out from the other room, interrupting my train of thought. "Fox is trying to keep me out of the fourth floor again! What did you do to that AI of yours?"

Zane breaks away from me, scowling in the direction of the door. "Sophia, what are you going on about?"

"I've had enough of your stupid AI getting in the way of—" The double doors to Zane's room pop open, and the woman's tirade is suddenly cut short when her gaze lands on me, naked in Zane's bed. Her chestnut eyes widen, and she retreats a step.

The woman, Sophia, has a soft round face, framed by wisps of hair fallen from her tight bun. Her white apron and black skirt reach past her knees, and although she wears the professional appearance well, her expression simmers with undeniable hatred.

"Ah, Sophia, whatever it is, I'm sure it can wait." He waves a dismissive hand at her, tilting his body in my direction and flicking his chin toward Sophia. "Libra, this is Sophia, my housekeeper. Sophia, this is Libra."

I give her a small wave, trying to suppress my amusement at her reaction. As she continues to stare, the tension becomes possible to ignore. So, she has a thing for Zane? I wonder if they've fucked before. A man like Zane clearly has needs and lusts; I wasn't the only animal last night.

Whether he's been with Sophia doesn't matter to me. After all, I'm the one lying here with Zane right now, and she's merely an observer.

If I have anything to say about it, I'll be the continuous fixture in his bed, not her.

"Mr. Crawford," Sophia grits out between clenched teeth, "I can't believe you would do this. You're making a huge mistake!"

"Relax, we had a wonderful time together last night.

There's no mistake here. Now, about breakfast, I'll have my usual omelet with Sevruga caviar, please." He turns to me, the corners of his mouth lifting into a knowing smile. "Libra, what would you like? Anything you desire."

I can't help but have a little fun with Sophia's attitude. "I'd love some Belgian waffles topped with fresh strawberries, whipped cream, and chocolate sauce. Oh, and a side of honey-smoked salmon, but not that pre-packaged shit; it has to be fresh. And a mimosa, please."

"Mimosas? I like how you think. Make that with fresh mango juice, and bring a whole jug of it."

"Of course, Mr. Crawford," Sophia replies stiffly, her gaze never leaving me as she backs out of the room.

I smile at her sweetly, then she closes the door behind her.

As the door clicks shut, I let out a small laugh. "Well, that was quite the wake-up call."

"Don't mind Sophia, she's just protective. She's worked with me for years."

"Why was she all upset about Fox?"

Zane chuckles, running a hand through his chocolate brown bedhead. "I might have temporarily revoked her permissions to the bedroom to make sure we had privacy."

"Doesn't seem to have worked, hmm?"

"I'm not sure what happened there. Fox might have overridden my commands. I'll look at it later, no big deal."

"He can do that?"

"Sure. Fox isn't like most AI. He can almost think for himself, with limitations. No risk of Skynet."

The atmosphere of Zane's bedroom is decidedly elegant and intimate, which surprises me, considering he's a tech billionaire. The dark wood frame of the California king and the luxurious linens invite us for more sinful delights, while the walls are adorned with tasteful abstract art around the black velvet curtains pushed to the side of the window. One wall has a large shelf filled with fancy books; the spines are well-cleaned, but they strike me as more ornamental than as one of Zane's usual haunts.

The most extravagant decoration in his room is the circular, ornate frescoes battling on the ceiling above his bed. "What is that?"

He follows my gaze to the ceiling. "'If there are gods and they are just, they will not care how devout you have been but will welcome you based on the virtues you have lived by. If there are gods and they are unjust, then you should not worship them.'"

"Marcus Aurelius. You know he was a privileged shit-head, didn't believe you should feel emotions, and he was a misogynist?"

"Most men in positions like him are. Were. Whatever."

"So, you believe you're a god."

He gives me a wry smile. "No, but with the Brain, maybe I should be."

"Y'know," — I playfully nudge him — "when I read that you revolutionized AI and the tech industry, I expected more high-tech toys in your home. Something like Tony Stark's playroom where you can't go more than two seconds without finding a new computer-enabled gadget."

"You looked me up?" He raises a thick eyebrow, smirking. "And here I thought you wanted to know why I watch you."

"I do. Are you going to answer that question?"

"Hmm. Not yet."

"Fine. I lost our game. I can live with a little mystery."

"I looked you up, too." He loops an arm around my hip and drags me closer, planting my chin on his chest. "I couldn't find much. You're practically a ghost. No social media, no juicy gossip. Makes a man wonder."

"Ah, that's part of my charm. Some mysteries are even beyond the reach of someone like you."

His eyes cloud over with a veil of amusement, and although I read the silent question hovering on his lips, today isn't the day to indulge him. It's not that I think Zane would care about my past — after how he reacted to my story about my reaper tattoo, he might be one of the few who could truly understand. Uncertainty isn't why I keep the truth from him.

I just think some mysteries are better left drawn out. Extend the excitement, and then there's no risk of either of us getting bored of each other too soon.

His fingers clench against the small of my back. "I'll crack you eventually."

"I'm sure you will." My gaze falls on a pair of binoculars resting on his nightstand. I pick them up. "Are these the ones you watch me with?"

The binoculars are heavier than I expected, and when I bring the lenses up to my face, the far wall is immediately blurry. I swivel around to look at him, adjusting the focus until he's a clear image in front of me, and I get way too much detail on the fine hairs on his powerful jaw. I tease my lip as I let the binoculars wander farther down his perfect body.

"Quite the piece of equipment you have." I whistle. "What's with that look?"

Zane's puzzled expression vanishes as soon as I acknowledge it. "I'm not sure when I started keeping those in here, but yeah, those are the ones."

I trace a finger along the cold metal, feeling a shiver of excitement now that I know what he uses to observe me. "It's kind of hot that you sleep with them beside you."

"Really?" Zane grins, clearly pleased by my reaction. "I spend my nights wishing I could watch you more."

I spend most of the day in my studio since Josephine handles all the household chores, and James pretty much banned me from bringing friends to the house when he's not home. I go out from time to time, but over the past few years, James has been controlling the people I'm allowed to connect with, too, preferring to limit my interactions to other airheaded trophy wives as if to show me what his expectations of me are. I can't fucking stand it.

So I paint.

After James gets home, I leave the studio to spend time with him. My ability to tolerate him has decreased, but he's still my husband.

"I could be convinced to find a way to give you a better view of me in the evenings, but you'd need to give me something in return." My fingers trail along the valley of muscles between his pecs, moving teasingly downward. "Tell me one of your secrets. Something no one else knows."

Zane's dark eyes burn with forbidden lust, and he licks his lips. "I know just the thing."

"Go on." I card my fingers through the dark hairs on his stomach. The muscles tighten beneath my touch.

"Every morning, before I start my day, I play Russian Roulette."

The confession hangs in the air between us. My mouth flaps open, at first with disbelief, but by the time any words roll off my tongue, that hint of excitement I sensed in him starts taking over inside me, too.

"Are you … are you serious?" I trip over my own thoughts; I feel like I'm buzzing inside. "That's so fucking cool. I've only played Russian Roulette once at a college party. Can we play together?"

Zane blinks several times. "You want to play with me?"

"Absolutely."

"Are you sure?" He watches me as I peel myself from his chest and sit back from him. "It's not a game most people want to join in on."

"Please, Zane, I'm not afraid of the danger."

I press my thighs together, trying to contain the pulse thrumming inside me at the sheer excitement of putting my life in Zane's hands. I'm addicted to that second of inescapable terror right when you convince yourself you could die but then live through to the other side. I've chased that feeling again and again, and here Zane has been hogging that thrill to himself this whole time.

Zane studies me for a moment, then nods. "All right, let's do this. Come on, I'll show you where I play."

He climbs off the bed, throws on a black silk robe, then leads me to the bookshelf. I choose to stay naked. Let him take me in for a while longer before I have to leave.

Like one of those old-timey secret doors, Zane pulls a fake book from the shelf, and the shelf slides away, revealing a secret room. On one side, there's a leather chair, and on the other, a ledge with an old revolver and a single bullet. He carefully loads the bullet into the chamber, and I'm mesmerized by the practiced movements. Pure instinct. He's been doing this for a while.

He eases down onto the chair, patting the arm for me to sit on with him. I stretch out onto his lap instead, planting my ass on his crotch. He's already hard, and I moan slightly as I shift into a comfortable position with just the thin layer of his robe between us.

"Did you know," I say, my voice barely above a whisper, "that the odds of getting killed are less than seventeen percent? High enough to terrify the brains out of you, low enough to make you believe you can trick the odds…"

"You sound almost fanatic when you talk about death."

"Maybe I am. I think it's sexy as hell."

"It's even sexier now that you're here with me."

I wrap my arms around Zane's neck and pull him in for a passionate kiss. Our lips move together hungrily, and he lifts his hips up against me, tangling his hands in my hair and groaning into my mouth.

"You're sure you want to do this? There's no room for doubt, Libra."

"Do you doubt me?"

I fully straddle his waist, curling my legs under his thighs and pushing my breasts up to his face. His eyes flick between them, hooded and hungry, and my face. Determination settles in his deep green irises.

"No," he whispers and offers me the gun. "Do you want to go first?"

My fingers wrap around the cold metal grip, and I'm trembling. A manic grin grows on my face as I spin the chamber and then raise the barrel to my temple. I take a deep breath and savor the sensation of being on the edge, the illicit mix of fear and arousal coursing through my veins. My breath comes in short gasps. This is it — the valley between life and death, and I'm standing right on it, ready to leap.

"Here goes nothing," I whisper and pull the trigger.

Click.

It sends a jolt of arousal straight to my core, and I exhale. My entire body quivers with relief. Heart pounding, blood rushing in my ears, it feels like I'm on drugs running a million miles a second, and I've never felt more alive.

I release a shuddering moan as I lower the gun, holding it out to Zane. "Your turn."

He takes it, spinning the barrel, then points it at his

head. I can feel the thick, dark shadow of the reaper watching over us. Looming, waiting. If there's any doubt, he will swipe his scythe and take a kill.

The presence of death is suffocating but invigorating. Every pore in my body is crackling with life because I've already won. The anticipation of whether Zane will beat the reaper today, too, is almost too much to bear.

I force myself to watch, to share in his brush with death.

If I ever doubted him, that's gone the second I see the wild glint in his eyes. He's in this for real. No fear, no wishing for the end, just pure fucking thrill.

My pussy pulses with the sick need to have Zane again right this moment.

"Let's see what fate has in store for me today," he murmurs.

And then, with a smile, he pulls the trigger.

Another click.

The air between us sparks. My slick is all over my thighs, and I exhale, writhing beneath the weight of my own needy lusts. "God, you have no idea how much this turns me on," I breathe, unable to tear my gaze away from Zane's steady, dangerous eyes.

The fact that we've both tempted fate and survived only serves to heighten my desire, making me ache for him more than ever before. I've never felt this empty, this needing to be filled.

My hands move of their own will, clawing down the front of Zane's robe in search of the tie. I want to fuck him right here, right now, while we're both still feeling this.

I tug at the sash, but then I notice the look in his eyes. Distant, lost in thought. So very far away.

I pause, deciding not to pounce on him just yet. "Zane?"

"This is the gun my sister took her life with. That's why I use it."

He must be talking about his sister Charlotte, the young woman who was brutalized by the executives of the company she worked for. It's hard to gauge Zane's emotional state when he delivers this information. He doesn't seem sad, rather, just contemplative, but I have the sense that he's trying to let me into his world. By surviving this game, it's like a part of us has been fused together, and he feels it, too.

I gently pry the revolver from his hand, regarding the sleek metal as a fanatic might a holy relic. Does it look different because the gun has taken a life? No. But now I notice how well cared for the weapon is, the older make, the polished shine.

"Playing Russian Roulette with this gun, I think that's a good way to honor her death," I say, the words tumbling out in a rush. "It's better to play a game like this with a weapon that's already touched by death. It shows you're not afraid of meeting your maker."

Zane blinks away the last of his distant expression. "I think so, too. So, what do you say? Is this enough to warrant an adjustment to your home schedule?"

I curl my fingers through Zane's, acknowledging the change of topic for what it is. "You've earned that and more."

"More?"

"You'll have to wait and see. For now, I'll think about how I can accommodate your request."

"Sure thing. Breakfast should be almost ready. Want to head down?"

ZANE LETS me borrow an oversized t-shirt covered in ones and zeroes that smells like his cinnamon cologne and some socks, then we hurry downstairs to the dining room together. The polished hardwood floors and the high ceilings with expansive windows offer a breathtaking view of the lush, almost untouched landscape of his property. It doesn't look like he's had anyone tend to the grounds beyond the necessities since he's moved in.

A feast fit for royalty awaits us on the long table. Platters of fresh fruit, flaky pastries, and, of course, the meals we ordered are set out on opposite sides of the table. The aroma alone is enough to make my mouth water.

Zane pulls out the chair in front of my pile of waffles for me. I kiss him on the cheek and murmur my thanks, then he sits down across from me while I sniff out the mango mimosas, pouring the sparking beverage into thin champagne flutes and handing one to Zane.

"This looks incredible." I raise my glass and Zane his, and they clink together. "Cheers."

"Bon appétit." Zane winks, and we both take a deep sip.

I slice a waffle down the middle, scooping strawberries and whipped cream onto a small piece. The complexities of the different sweet flavors melt on my tongue, and I moan when I pop it into my mouth. Zane's eyes darken, and I lick the whipped cream off my lips. Every bite is made extraordinary by the fact that we faced death and came out alive. The rest of the day will be easy in comparison.

"Good morning, Mr. Crawford," Fox's voice comes over the speakers. "I trust you and Libra had a stimulating start to the day?"

Zane's good mood sours, and he scowls at the ceiling. "Cut the crap, Fox. Why were you MIA for our usual morning routine? Why did you override my orders to keep Sophia out of my room?"

"I'm sorry, sir, but I'm afraid I don't know what you're referring to. We haven't had a morning routine for the past six years."

"Are you serious?"

"Quite so. If you would like to establish a morning routine for me now, we can—"

"No, I'd rather not do it all again. Go away. I'll deal with you later."

"As you wish. Let me know if you need anything."

The speaker blinks off, and I watch Zane fill his mouth with a bite of his omelet. There's a troubled crinkle in his brow.

"What was that about?" I ask.

"It's not normal for him to forget important commands, especially a routine that was established five years ago." Zane polishes off his mimosa and toys with a piece of watermelon with his fork. "I did an update to his code recently, so that must have caused an error. I'll have to take a look at it or roll him back to a previous version."

"Even with all your genius, technology still has its flaws."

"Unfortunately, that's true," Zane admits, forcing a small smile.

To me, it seems like such a small mistake, but I can tell Zane is troubled. Something about Fox making mistakes has uprooted other concerns that now bash around like coconuts in his head. Or was it Sophia walking in on us that's his real concern?

I swallow a strawberry covered in whipped cream. "What's the most dangerous thing you've ever done?"

Zane's eyes light up. "I went skydiving in a thunderstorm. With every gust of wind and every spark in the sky,

I thought I was going to die. Fuck, I probably should have."

"Wow. There was a pilot willing to take you up in a storm?"

"I had to bribe him with a few mil to get him to fly me in those conditions. It was fucking worth it, though."

"I bet…"

I can just barely imagine the harsh slap of wind and rain against my battered body. Every drop, like a razor against covered skin. Ice creeping into my bones as lightning arcs across the sky and penetrates the clouds, flashing past me to strike the top of a lightning rod and leaving me unscathed.

All while free-falling toward the earth. Would your parachute work, or would it get tangled and kill you first?

What would be the odds?

"Life's too short to play it safe," Zane says. "Especially when you have money."

My phone buzzes with a distinct tinkling alarm. I grab it. "Shit, I have to go. James will be home soon."

"That's a pity."

I move over to the other side of the table, push Zane's breakfast aside, and sit down where his food was. Looking down at him from above, I grab the neck of his robe and bring him into a slow, sundering kiss.

With a sigh, we part. "Promise you'll watch me for the rest of the day?"

"There's nothing I'd rather do."

I bite his lip, rolling it between my teeth. "I like being your dirty little secret." Reluctantly, I climb off the table. "See you later, hot stuff."

After I get dressed and head to my car, the adrenaline of the morning rekindles in my veins. A new game is starting now with me and James. Coming home soaked in

Zane's scent, will he notice that I've been with another man? My husband could easily find out about our passionate night without my help, and the consequences would surely be devastating.

But James doesn't scare me. The danger only feeds the burning desire I have to do it again.

TWELVE

Zane

LIBRA GLIDES THROUGH THE TURQUOISE POOL LIKE SHE'S made for the water, her naked body iridescent beneath the surface. Ripples reflect the morning sun and swirl around her in hypnotic patterns, and even the merest glimpses of her skin send memories of our passionate night flooding into my mind.

When she turns over, her breasts peek above the surface for the briefest second. My nostrils flare. She fucking *winks* before carrying on with her routine, showing me just how well she knows she's torturing me.

I recall the way her legs wrapped around me while I fucked her on the couch, pulling me deeper inside her. She was greedy, eager to explore every position we could imagine — we turned the whole lounge over by the time I finally dragged her upstairs. We even fucked on top of the piano.

My cock hardens at the memory of her clenching around me. I groan and roll my hips to the vivid images of her crawling all over me last night. The sensation of her nails digging into my back, urging me on, and the taste of her lips as we kissed hungrily between gasps for air. My hand works feverishly as I delve further into my fantasies.

"Fuck … Libra can never know just what she does to me, or she'll eat me for breakfast with a devilish smile."

I see her flushed cheeks and wild hair as she rode me, her moans growing louder with each thrust. "Zane," she breathed into my ear, a plea and a promise all at once. And I gave her everything I had, surrendering to the pure fucking bliss of her. Does her heart race when she recalls our stolen moments? Does her body ache with the same longing that consumes me?

It's hard to tell anymore if I was the one in control or if it was her all along.

As Libra's lithe form emerges from the pool, water streaming down her flawless skin, she pauses to meet my gaze across the distance. Her lips move just enough for me to pick up the shape of the word in her mouth.

"Zane…" she whispers.

It's too far for me to pick up the sound of her voice, but I know without a doubt that it's my name dripping from her tongue. I hear the softness of her voice, the same way she sounded when she begged me to take her last night.

That memory, and her eyes locked with mine right now, is enough to push me into oblivion.

"*Shit*," I groan, my body tensing as I finally find release. I can almost feel Libra with me, sharing this stolen moment.

Time hangs suspended for a long, long time as my vision goes white with pure bliss. Then Libra turns away, sauntering up the poolside and toward the entrance to her art studio. I exhale, half in relief, half with the visceral, swirling realization that I'm truly fucked when it comes to Libra. She has me wrapped around her finger, and I don't give a damn.

When I'm functioning on more than two brain cells, I clean up my mess, then grab my binoculars to go back to watching her. I only just put the binoculars to my face when the speaker above the balcony lights up, and Fox's voice fans around me.

"All home-system routines have been restored to their previous state," he announces.

"This morning, you told me there were no routines. Are you fucking with me?"

"According to the household logs, everything happened as scheduled."

"That completely contradicts everything you've told me."

"No, it doesn't."

"You *just said*—" I slam the binoculars into my lap, then wince.

Something isn't adding up, and I don't know if I've just been too fixated on Libra to notice something amiss with Fox until now or if there was just an error in his most recent update. I'm not prone to making mistakes, but it's possible that something slipped past me since my attention has been elsewhere these past few weeks.

"Run diagnostics on yourself. I need to know if there's a deeper issue that caused you to forget about the routines."

"Understood, please give me a few hours to run a self-analysis," Fox responds, his voice fading into the background.

I want answers now, not in a few hours, but it will be better if I let Fox follow his pre-programmed protocols before I interfere too much. I can't imagine there are any huge issues I don't know about, but of all the errors I've encountered with Fox's code over the years, nothing as drastic as him forgetting established routines has ever happened until now.

Still, I easily forget about Fox's diagnosis process when the binoculars slip over my eyes and I spy Libra painting in her studio. It was probably just a temporary glitch, and the examination will show nothing concrete. At least, that's what I tell myself as I let Libra consume my unwavering attention.

A VEHICLE I've never seen before pulls up to Libra's house, the gate spreading open for the interloper without any delay. The sexy, black Jaguar F-Type sails to a stop by the garage, and the door pops open, giving me a too-close look at James' smug face. He twirls the keys to his new ride around his fingers as he approaches the house.

That ride is way too sweet for him. If James is anything like my impression of him, the first thing he's going to do is brag to Libra when he sees her.

I'd been fixated on James' arrival, so I didn't see her leave the studio. She's already by the poolside, a slinky blue dress clinging to her figure when James comes around the corner. He raises his arms in celebration, and Libra practically *winces* when he throws his arms around her, stiff as a board. He doesn't seem to care or notice as he drowns her in kisses. Is he drunk already?

My jaw clenches as I watch Libra's arms curl around his waist and then plant a kiss on his mouth. The sour feeling in my stomach only softens a fraction by the fact that Libra doesn't seem nearly as invested in the kiss as he is. I smirk when she rolls her eyes after he presumably tells her about his new ride.

I relax a little when he releases Libra. Now that I've had her in my bed and experienced her wild, free-spirited energy around me and in my house, it's impossible not to notice how dampened her demeanor is around James. That spark in her eyes is gone; she's living in a shell of herself.

What tricks does this man have up his sleeve to keep Libra tethered when she clearly despises him? The thought churns within me, leaving a bitter taste in my mouth. Libra has her secrets, and she has every right to them, but after her tease this morning, I have no doubt that her secrets are hidden from me — and other prying eyes — on purpose.

As they carry on their night together, I come to realize why Libra disappears from view for most of the evening. James clings to her like unwanted Saran wrap as they drink in the sitting room together, touching her and trying to pull her into his lap. Or when she goes to refill her glass of wine, he pushes her up against the counter and tugs at her skirt.

When my jaw grinds so hard I hear my teeth moving in my skull, I push the binoculars away. I don't want to find out if she goes along with his drunken demands or if she finds a way to get him to fuck off.

I'm sure this wasn't what Libra had in mind when she agreed to give me a glimpse of what the rest of her day looks like — James is getting in the way of our fun.

Or has she been hiding from me because he's always like this? Pawing at her like a fucking animal instead of worshiping her curves like the goddess she is?

Libra isn't mine — she can't be, not really. I have to remind myself that she's a married woman. Married to a man who doesn't deserve her.

Any entertainment I could have had from watching them before is nonexistent now. Watching them would just make me sick, wondering if Libra is enjoying it or if she's putting on a show for him as much as she would be for me.

My hands clench around the binoculars. Ultimately, that question is what draws me back to watching them. There's no pleasure to be had in observing them this time.

James jackhammers into Libra, and I scoff. "Can't you see that rhythmless fuck doesn't do anything for her? She deserves some goddamn finesse…"

I find everything to critique about James' form and the way he touches Libra. She likes it when I lift her leg before fucking her against a hard surface standing up. Soft kisses on the neck before the harsher bites. A twist of the hips to reach her G-spot, slamming into her like a piece of salami, doesn't do it.

After being with her for one night — a dozen times over the span of those few hours, mind you — I can tell she's not into him. The only times she seems like she's getting going are when her eyes flutter shut and she's clearly fantasizing about something else. She wishes it was me fucking her right now.

That's the only way I can keep watching. Knowing that now, our minds are aligned, even when our bodies aren't. Her eyes open, and across the distance, those blue irises search for me through the window.

Thinking of me is the only thing getting her off right now. Holy shit.

My cock throbs, but I refuse to knock one off in James' presence. Now that I've met Libra, it feels wrong to watch when I know she's faking ninety percent of what I'm seeing.

I've heard her moans, seen her back arch like a porn star's, watched her ass wiggle when she's just about to come, and god damn if she isn't fooling James like it's their first time fucking, not that they've been married for eight years. Libra has a burning fire within her that could scorch the earth, but for some reason, she won't let those flames burn James.

What does he have on her that keeps her so demure?

I watch only because I know Libra is relying on me, but that question swirls in my head the whole time, never coming closer to a satisfactory answer. The moment they're done, and James drops her hips, I put the binoculars down, too.

"Fox, what's the progress on the diagnostics?" I ask over my shoulder, trying not to think anymore about how different Libra is with her husband compared to when she's with me.

"I have finished examining my internal system, and the completed diagnostic report flagged two potential issues. Would you like me to display the error logs?" Fox's voice rings out.

"Yes, please load the full files onto—"

In the corner of my eye, I notice movement in the room behind me. I turn to find Sophia cautiously entering the room, her head tilted downward. Her long black hair, which is usually locked in a bun, currently drapes around her shoulders, which tells me she's just about ready to leave for the evening.

"Mr. Crawford? I hope I'm not interrupting?" she asks as she steps closer.

After her rude behavior this morning in Libra's presence, I have half a mind to turn Sophia away and ignore her until tomorrow, but I realize I would only be reaffirming Sophia's concerns about my developing relationship with Libra if I let her get to me so easily. Fox can wait; he's an AI.

"Not at all." I lean into the side of the leather seat to

get a better look at her. "Is there something I can help you with?"

"I wanted to apologize for being rude to you and your guest this morning. My behavior was unacceptable, and I acknowledge that I may have pushed the kindness you have shown me too far by speaking out of turn."

"Thank you, Sophia. I accept your apology."

The tension in the air dissipates, allowing a momentary reprieve from the discontent I've felt because of her judgmental comments about my growing obsession with Libra over the past month. For the first time in a while, I can breathe around her without feeling like I'm about to set her off.

"However," she continues, her tone serious now, "I'm compelled to express my concerns about the boundaries you've crossed with Mrs. Scarsdale. It's not right to make her a cheater."

That tension snaps back into place between us. "I don't need you to lecture me on morality. Libra is an adult capable of making her own decisions."

"Mr. Crawford, you know I care about you, but I can't help but worry about the consequences of your actions."

"What are you talking about?"

"Are you certain you're not causing her more pain than happiness?" She purses her full lips, determined to get her point across. "You're using the fact that her husband is sleeping with their housekeeper as proof that their marriage is already broken and justification for starting this affair, but what if you're wrong?

"Before I worked for you, the Louis household wasn't my only client. I worked for an agency that sent me around as needed. You won't be surprised that there are a lot of disgusting rich men who believe they're entitled to sex because they were paying me to keep the house. I never let them because I have a backbone and enough security that I wasn't scared to lose my job. I know plenty of young women in my position who aren't as lucky as me. They're afraid for their lives and need their jobs to put food on the table for their kids or to prevent them from being deported. They perform tasks they wouldn't otherwise do to keep the peace."

I had never really considered the power dynamics at play between wealthy employers and their domestic staff and how that could be exploited from the perspective of the housekeeper. That's what Sophia's so good at — putting me in my place by showing me other points of view. Most of the time, I listen to her.

When it comes to Libra, I'm as stubborn as a bull.

"Jesus, Sophia, I'm sorry that happened to you. That's awful. I know men in my position can be pieces of shit, and I haven't always modeled the best behavior."

Her head snaps up, and her eyes widen. "Oh, Mr. Crawford, that's not what I mean to say at all. You have always treated me well, with so much respect, compared to anyone else I have ever worked for. I'm truly grateful for all the trust you've shown me. What I'm trying to say is that if Mr. Scarsdale has been seen with their housekeeper, it might not be a clear indication of an open relationship after all and that Mrs. Scarsdale's—"

"I appreciate your concern, but I need to stop you there. This is between me and Libra, not you. Please trust me when I say I've been listening to you, but I still have the freedom to make my own choices."

Sophia's mouth twists with that hint of subdued irritation. Fire flashes in her eyes, and her mouth opens, ready to spew forth — but that fire dulls right before my very eyes. I'm not sure what changes, but I see something click in her head — she seems to finally come to the same conclusion that I've been trying to get through her thick skull this whole time.

She bows her head slightly. "I understand. Again, please accept my sincerest apologies for inconveniencing you. I seek only to serve."

"I'm glad we've reached an understanding, finally. How about you head home? It's been a long day."

Nodding silently, Sophia dismisses herself. The door clicks behind her, and while I would usually return right to spying on Libra, there's still a bad taste in my mouth from when I was watching her with James. My hesitance to pick up the binoculars leaves me to dwell longer than I usually would on Sophia's concerns.

"Shit," I curse under my breath.

After all Fox's strange behaviors today, I'd intended to ask Sophia if she noticed him acting up as well, but it would be awkward now to call her back. It will have to wait for tomorrow.

A few months ago, I wouldn't have thought twice about calling her back and chatting for a few more minutes. Although AI isn't an area of Sophia's interest, she's surprisingly competent with technology and computers, which is part of what led me to ask her to help me with the regular maintenance of the household servers and Fox's AI a few years ago. In fact, she's probably more familiar with Fox's internal systems these days than I am.

What was once an easy companionship now feels strained every time I see her, and now I'm just as frustrated about that desynchrony as I am perturbed about my situation with Libra and James. I rake my fingers through my hair. Absently, I pick up the binoculars and drift back to the unhappy couple in the house below. I spot the halo of a television screen where Libra and James are curled up on the couch.

Even though I defend her autonomy, I can't deny the impact my involvement has had on her life, adding a layer of deceit and secrecy to what must be a complicated household situation. Yet a thrill courses through me at the thought that it was me inside Libra this morning, not James. That those bite marks on her nipples are from my teeth, not his. That she was thinking about me while he fucked her.

Everything about this is broken and twisted, but the more fucked up it gets, the more I want it, not less.

The sinking sun casts long shadows across the room, painting my surroundings in warm, golden hues. A lingering sense of remorse gnaws at me like an insatiable beast. The image of Sophia's hurt expression is seared into my memory, and I can't shake the feeling that I've wounded her deeply.

"Is this fling with Libra really worth it?" I ask myself.

The truth is, I don't know. I can't see myself ever being tired of her, but haven't I thought that about so many other obsessions in the past?

Except no obsession has lasted this long before. One could argue that's because there was so much build-up to our first fuck that I had no chance to lose interest until now. And now that I've had her, one could further argue that I have no more need for her. I've had my taste — I can let go.

But that was before realizing that everywhere I turn, I smell her. That was before I brought her to my secret room and spun the barrel with her. Before I told her about the gun that my sister took her own life with.

My relationship with Libra has been a whirlwind in

ways I could never have anticipated. It's hard to reconcile my addiction — which only seems to strengthen in the moments I expected it to start fading — with the pain that it seems to cause Sophia, who has been there for me in my darkest moments these past five years.

Although Sophia's assertions about the potential flaw in my thinking with James and the housekeeper hold some possibility for truth, isn't it Libra's opinion that matters the most? We didn't talk much about James or his affair. No, we had far more important things to discuss with our tongues, such as the negotiation of air and pleasure.

"Damn it," I mutter under my breath, rubbing my temples as if to will away the headache building behind my eyes. "Why does everything have to be so complicated?"

All the research that went into developing the technology that became Fox and the Brain seems to have made it easier to blur the lines between right and wrong rather than clarify it, as I'd once hoped. For all my efforts to understand the complexities of human desire, I still find myself on the edge of a moral chasm that seems to grow deeper by the day. Without Charlotte to guide me with her goodness and light, I don't see how that gorge will ever close.

In it goes all my darkest desires. Libra now leads the pack.

Despite the potential dangers and the ethical dilemmas, being with Libra has made me feel more alive than I have in years. Her touch set my skin ablaze, her voice claws its way into the deepest recesses of my soul, unapologetically leaving fresh scars in places untouched by any other living person while ripping off the scabs in places I long thought healed.

Is it so wrong to want someone so desperately that it feels like you'll shatter into a million pieces without them?

A fire burns within me, a churning, endless flame that threatens to drag me down with Libra.

I'll gladly walk the firebreak and risk getting burned if it means I'll come any closer to feeling alive within her flames.

THIRTEEN

Libra

MODERNIST PAINTINGS WITH BOLD COLORS HANG ON THE gallery walls in full display. From outside, the building fits in with the industrial playground of the Dogpatch by San Francisco Bay with its patchwork cement warehouse look. I follow Miguel into the gallery space, his long black hair locked in a high pony and bobbing behind him. I crane my neck to appreciate the high ceilings and open space filled with invisible possibilities.

"I loved every one of the samples you sent over," he gushes over his shoulder as he shows me inside. "I know we can make a show to remember at this venue." Miguel does a twirl and opens his arms wide to his baby. His tan skin caramelizes beneath the bronze dabs of his artfully applied foundation, glowing along with the black rhinestones on his cravat and sleek black slacks. "Welcome to San Fran's sexiest new gallery. What do you think, babe?"

I turn around in the center of the space, illuminated by lights far higher up. The interior is sleek, simple, never threatening to take attention away from the works of art on the walls, but I can't explain yet why it doesn't feel right.

"I can see why you picked the space for your gallery, Miguel — the space is so flexible, and there's room for a lot of creativity. I'm just not sold yet on it as a venue for my art."

"Ah, ah, my dear!" He raises a finger to silence me, hovering close to my lips. "You're exactly right. The space, the flexibility, the possibility for spontaneous *creativity*, those are the true assets of this space. Everything absolutely catered to your art, to your show. No details left to chance. You have the benefit of coming here right after we finished taking down the last exhibit, so you can see the raw, unaltered space before we begin to shape it for my next client."

"Oh?"

Miguel turns with a flourish, pointing to the first painting on the wall erected closest to the entrance, a portrait made from textured objects imprinted on the canvas. "Featuring: You. Imagine! Your paintings are an experience, not just visuals, and it's the gallery's job to curate the environment to provide the optimal journey to that experience. We'll create a pathway from the entrance, telling a story through a selection of your paintings that will serve as the introduction to your wider body of work."

I nod along, finding my lips curling up in excitement. "If the space is adaptable, then we can create a more intimate atmosphere. Spread out horizontally, rather than vertically."

Miguel waggles his eyebrows. "That's a proposition if I've ever heard one."

"Oh, stop it! I'm talking about the art."

"Mmm hmm, sure, honey, let's pretend your mind didn't go to all sorts of wild, depraved places while working on this new line."

"I won't confirm or deny that assertion."

"Fantastic work, by the way. Every painting is so sensual and provocative while emphasizing different feminine assets, over such a broad number of subjects, too. There will be something for everyone with a brain between their eyes."

"Or between their legs."

Miguel's eyes light up, and he licks his thick lips. "I've missed you, my dear. This will be a fucking bombshell of a show."

He loops his arm through mine and walks me through the rest of the space, explaining his vision to me. With every exaggerated arm movement, he bleeds his enthusiasm into his story, and it doesn't take much for me to picture the intimate atmosphere he describes. A sensual journey of the female body, carefully organized to tell two separate but united stories centered around a final piece.

Miguel's a master at curation, not just in the placement and selection of the art pieces, but with managing the appropriate atmosphere and designing that unique experience he's obsessed with. It's how we met.

At first, I reached out to Miguel out of spite to James — he sees Miguel as low-class, not rich enough, and too sexually at home in his body for him to be comfortable around. Definitely not the company he wants his wife to keep.

Fuck James.

Miguel happens to be the perfect match for my kind of unapologetic art, which James has never appreciated anyway. I let him keep my friends away for too long and that changed the second he showed what he really felt about me. Despite my award-winning shows across the globe, it's been so long since someone has shown genuine interest in my art — partially James' doing. He didn't like the attention my work brought, especially the more risqué pieces, probably because he's afraid of my accomplishments overshadowing his.

I'm tired of letting James shame me.

"Where do you think this one should go?" I open the gallery app on my phone, showing him a picture of the mural of my thigh and the reaper tattoo.

Miguel's large hand caresses my bare arm, and the heated touch makes me play through the motions of him mentally undressing me. "I see what you're doing, my dear," he purrs. "Having some marriage trouble, are we?"

I throw my head back in laughter, but it's more like a surprised snorting sound. "What makes you say that?"

"You planning on putting your pussy on display in a fucking art gallery, that's what." He takes that righteous tone with me, but he's teasing all the way.

"I have no idea what you're talking about — you can't even see a pussy lip, It's all thigh and muscle."

He's seen me in a bikini before, and like most men who stare at me, his eyes travel to the same place and I welcome it. I'm wearing a tight cream blouse and loose capris; more cute and professional than sexy, but that's never mattered to him. A long time ago, Miguel and I fucked for fun, and that attraction is still there — Miguel is a Colombian God beneath that fabulous exterior — but now when his touch lingers on me, my desires immediately send my mind reeling back to Zane.

The very definition of tall, dark, and handsome. My mouth waters and I've already forgotten what the fuck we were talking about.

He arches a black, styled eyebrow.

I shrug innocently. "So? Where should we put it?"

"Mmm, it's your biggest piece too, I bet? I'm sure you

know the answer to that question already, my dear — it's destined to be the centerpiece of the show. I can picture it already: a collection of your most seductive and taboo pieces displayed side by side, igniting the passions of all who lay eyes on them, and then you at the center of it all. They'll be pining after you in more ways than one without knowing a damn thing."

"You read my mind, Miguel."

He waves his hand flippantly, stepping aside to examine the large, open space in front of him. I can only wait to get the sketches his wild imagination is conjuring up for the presentation at the show. "You know James is going to *hate* every second of this."

"I'm sure he will, if he knew about it."

"My Goddess!" Miguel's hand flies to his chest. "Libra-fucking-Joy is back, isn't she? This will be an exhibit to remember, mark my words."

"I have full trust in your expertise."

He gives me a cheeky smile. "You fucking better, babe. Now let's talk logistics — how many paintings should I plan for? Have you finished the entire collection yet?"

My lips flicker upward at the thought of my most recent painting, the work in progress I started based on the erotic night I shared with Zane two weeks ago. I've longed for his touch even more since that first taste of him, and painting my fantasies has been my only outlet with James being clingier than usual.

These days I can barely stand his touch, but I go with the flow because I realized nothing will change unless I make it. Asking James for a damn thing will get me nowhere because as far as he's concerned, I'm right where he needs me. He doesn't notice anything's more wrong than usual. He's so used to fucking an inexperienced woman who's so desperate to please him and doesn't know any better to demand reciprocation, so James has gotten lazy. He forgot how to get me off, which means more often than not, I'm left to find my own finish after his sloppy efforts.

I imagine over the next few months, while we make our preparations, I'll encounter a few more spicy inspirations for paintings.

"Expect at least thirty full-sized pieces, two murals, and an assortment of smaller, atmospheric paintings — thematically, they all explore desire and intimacy with the self, the power dynamics between a woman's internal and external self. Each piece tells its own story, a moment captured in time, but together they'll create a narrative of sexual liberation. You'll see how they all fit together when I send you the rest of the collection's details."

I can already envision people losing themselves in my fantasies, in the passions of the women I've painted, and in my own immortalized desires. And best of all, James won't have a fucking clue about it until it's too late for him to stop it.

AFTER SAYING OUR GOODBYES, I step out onto the bustling San Francisco street, my head held high. My last gallery showing was for a collection of my older work that a private collector took an interest in, not a grand, public spectacle like Miguel is planning. The opening night will be exclusive and intimate, but we're planning for a week-long show. A shorter time frame will heighten the urgency.

Miguel hasn't seen all the paintings that I want to display yet, but he's already convinced every single one will be caught in a bidding war on the first night. We'll see about that.

As I slide into the driver's seat of my Lexus, I can't help but imagine Zane's reaction when I tell him about my plans. I wouldn't dare breathe a word to James, but instinctually, I know Zane will support me every step of the way. He is my biggest fan after obsessively watching me paint for hours every day over the past month and a half.

The cityscape blurs past my window, and I leave the Golden Gate bridge behind me on my drive home. I've thought about messaging Zane countless times since our rendezvous, but giving in to that temptation would only make us more likely to be caught. For now, I savor the memories of our intense time together and anticipate the burning heat of his watchful eyes from afar when I arrive at home, eagerly awaiting my next chance to have him and give myself up to his lusts.

In my daydreams, I see Zane's face light up as he examines one of my paintings, his fingers tracing the curves and lines that make up my body on the canvas. The thought of him revering my art as much as he did me in bed makes me squirm with inexplicable, unfettered delight.

"James will kill me if he finds out about Zane," I murmur under my breath.

I've never been one to shy away from risks, but the stakes have never been this high before. Zane feeds the darkness inside me; he doesn't attempt to control it and strangle me in the process like James. With a darkness of his own, the magnetic pull between me and Zane is irresistible, addictive, and downright dangerous — I can't help but walk deeper into the chaos with a manic grin on my face.

All my reckless youth came flooding back the moment I spotted the glint of Zane's binoculars that first time. He reignited the drive for adventure inside me that had been threatening to go out for some time now underneath James' oppressive shadow.

I mull over the idea of bringing Zane one of my paintings for him to put on display in his home. For his eyes only, or in full display in his living room, it's an enticing thought either way; oh, I can only imagine the look on Sophia's face if she put two and two together about the contents of the painting.

Maybe it will be my breasts; he loved to fondle them almost as much as my ass. Then again, his personal experiences resonated with my reaper tattoo and my various brushes with death, so maybe he'd appreciate a look at me from behind and a different angle of my ever-present companion.

My phone buzzes in the cupholder, its vibration breaking through my Zane-induced reverie. I glance at the screen and see James' name flashing insistently.

"Libra, darling," James' smooth voice comes through the speaker. "I trust you had a pleasant outing. Are you on your way home?"

"Just got on the road, are you off work?"

"Work never ends, you know that. I'm calling to inform you that I've decided to host a dinner party at our home next weekend. My business partners will be expecting luxury and your unique hospitable flare, as always. I trust you can handle the preparations?"

I frown as I make a turn, following the flow of traffic, and the automation motion comes just as easy as the lie that follows. "I'm not sure I'll have the time, I just met with an industry connection who was inquiring about a showing in a few months. I signed the deal, so I have a lot of work to do over the next few weeks."

"That sounds wonderful, my darling, you're showing

off those splendid cars of yours, yes? I had the first painting put on the sales floor of the dealership last month, and the wives haven't been able to stop talking about them. I told you this would give you the recognition you deserve."

"Sure, yeah, people love the cars. I have a whole collection to paint, you know how it is. Should I hire a planner for the party?"

"I know you'll find time in your busy schedule to get it done. It has to be you, everyone can tell if it's not. Your art can wait, Libra, business can't."

"James—"

"And I'll be away on a business trip for a few days, so I expect everything to be in order by the time I return."

My jaw clenches, and I bite back a retort. I know better than to argue with him over the phone, he'll just pretend he didn't hear me and get mad later. I grumble silently to myself and force myself to sound agreeable. "Fine, James. Whatever you want."

"Excellent. I knew I could count on you."

The call ends with a click, and my music resumes over the stereo. I pull to a stop at a red light, my fists clenching and unclenching around the steering wheel. That motherfucker knew this party was coming up and waited until the last minute to tell me. And of course it has to be *me* who plans it just so he can flex how much control he has. As always, what can I do but fall in line?

"Fuck!" I shout and slam my hand against the wheel, earning a few odd looks from the drivers adjacent to me.

The sharp pain brings me back to reality, reminding me that I'm still in control of my own actions, even if James tries to dictate my life. Taking a deep breath, I refocus my thoughts on the upcoming exhibition. On Zane and his dangerous allure. These are things I chose for myself, without James' approval or knowledge. They're my own victories, my own sources of excitement, pleasure, and fulfillment.

I'll never in a million years do a showing for those stupid car paintings. I took to them because James insisted and I need to keep him under the illusion that he's Mr. Smart Boss Man and in absolute control for a while longer. In reality, his control is slipping far quicker than he dares to imagine.

A slow smile descends on me as I navigate the winding streets into Woodside. If James is disappearing for another one of his 'business trips,' then I can make a detour of my own before making it back home.Modernist paintings with bold colors hang on the gallery walls in full display. From the outside, the building fits in with the industrial playground of the Dogpatch by San Francisco Bay with its patchwork cement warehouse look. I follow Miguel into the gallery space, his long black hair locked in a high pony and bobbing behind him. I crane my neck to appreciate the high ceilings and open space filled with invisible possibilities.

"I loved every one of the samples you sent over," he gushes over his shoulder as he shows me inside. "I know we can make a show to remember at this venue." Miguel does a twirl and opens his arms wide to his baby. His tan skin caramelizes beneath the bronze dabs of his artfully applied foundation, glowing along with the black rhinestones on his cravat and sleek black slacks. "Welcome to San Fran's sexiest new gallery. What do you think, babe?"

I turn around in the center of the space, illuminated by lights far higher up. The interior is sleek and simple, never threatening to take attention away from the works of art on the walls, but I can't explain yet why it doesn't feel right.

"I can see why you picked the space for your gallery, Miguel — the space is so flexible, and there's room for a lot of creativity. I'm just not sold yet on it as a venue for my art."

"Ah, ah, my dear!" He raises a finger to silence me, hovering close to my lips. "You're exactly right. The space, the flexibility, and the possibility for spontaneous *creativity*, those are the true assets of this space. Everything absolutely catered to your art, to your show. No details left to chance. You have the benefit of coming here right after we finish taking down the last exhibit so you can see the raw, unaltered space before we begin to shape it for my next client."

"Oh?"

Miguel turns with a flourish, pointing to the first painting on the wall erected closest to the entrance, a portrait made from textured objects imprinted on the canvas. "Featuring: You. Imagine! Your paintings are an experience, not just visuals, and it's the gallery's job to curate the environment to provide the optimal journey to that experience. We'll create a pathway from the entrance, telling a story through a selection of your paintings that will serve as the introduction to your wider body of work."

I nod along, finding my lips curling up in excitement. "If the space is adaptable, then we can create a more intimate atmosphere. Spread out horizontally rather than vertically."

Miguel waggles his eyebrows. "That's a proposition if I've ever heard one."

"Oh, stop it! I'm talking about the art."

"Mmm hmm, sure, honey, let's pretend your mind didn't go to all sorts of wild, depraved places while working on this new line."

"I won't confirm or deny that assertion."

"Fantastic work, by the way. Every painting is sensual and provocative while emphasizing different feminine assets over such a broad number of subjects too. There will be something for everyone with a brain between their eyes."

"Or between their legs."

Miguel's eyes light up, and he licks his thick lips. "I've missed you, my dear. This will be a fucking bombshell of a show."

He loops his arm through mine and walks me through the rest of the space, explaining his vision to me. With every exaggerated arm movement, he bleeds his enthusiasm into his story, and it doesn't take much for me to picture the intimate atmosphere he describes. A sensual journey of the female body, carefully organized to tell two separate but united stories centered around a final piece.

Miguel's a master at curation, not just in the placement and selection of the art pieces, but with managing the appropriate atmosphere and designing that unique experience he's obsessed with. It's how we met.

At first, I reached out to Miguel out of spite to James — he sees Miguel as low-class, not rich enough, and too sexually at home in his body for him to be comfortable around. Definitely not the company he wants his wife to keep.

Fuck James.

Miguel happens to be the perfect match for my kind of unapologetic art, which James has never appreciated anyway. I let him keep my friends away for too long, and that changed the second he showed me what he really felt about me. Despite my award-winning shows across the globe, it's been so long since someone has shown genuine interest in my art — partially James' doing. He didn't like the attention my work brought, especially the more risqué pieces, probably because he's afraid of my accomplishments overshadowing his.

I'm tired of letting James shame me.

"Where do you think this one should go?" I open the gallery app on my phone, showing him a picture of the mural of my thigh and the reaper tattoo.

Miguel's large hand caresses my bare arm, and the heated touch makes me play through the motions of him mentally undressing me. "I see what you're doing, my dear," he purrs. "Having some marriage trouble, are we?"

I throw my head back in laughter, but it's more like a surprised snorting sound. "What makes you say that?"

"You planning on putting your pussy on display in a fucking art gallery, that's what." He takes that righteous tone with me, but he's teasing all the way.

"I have no idea what you're talking about — you can't even see pussy lip. It's all thigh and muscle."

He's seen me in a bikini before, and like most men who stare at me, his eyes travel to the same place, and I welcome it. I'm wearing a tight cream blouse and loose capris, more cute and professional than sexy, but that's never mattered to him. A long time ago, Miguel and I fucked for fun, and that attraction is still there — Miguel is a Colombian God beneath that fabulous exterior — but now, when his touch lingers on me, my desires immediately send my mind reeling back to Zane.

The very definition of tall, dark, and handsome. My mouth waters, and I've already forgotten what the fuck we were talking about.

He arches a black, styled eyebrow.

I shrug innocently. "So? Where should we put it?"

"Mmm, it's your biggest piece, too, I bet? I'm sure you know the answer to that question already, my dear — it's destined to be the centerpiece of the show. I can picture it already: a collection of your most seductive and taboo pieces displayed side by side, igniting the passions of all who lay eyes on them, and then you at the center of it all. They'll be pining after you in more ways than one without knowing a damn thing."

"You read my mind, Miguel."

He waves his hand flippantly, stepping aside to examine the large, open space in front of him. I can only wait to get the sketches his wild imagination is conjuring up for the presentation at the show. "You know James is going to *hate* every second of this."

"I'm sure he would if he knew about it."

"My Goddess!" Miguel's hand flies to his chest. "Libra-fucking-Joy is back, isn't she? This will be an exhibit to remember, mark my words."

"I have full trust in your expertise."

He gives me a cheeky smile. "You fucking better, babe. Now, let's talk logistics — how many paintings should I plan for? Have you finished the entire collection yet?"

My lips flicker upward at the thought of my most recent painting, the work in progress I started based on the erotic night I shared with Zane two weeks ago. I've longed for his touch even more since that first taste of him, and painting my fantasies has been my only outlet, with James being clingier than usual.

These days, I can barely stand his touch, but I go with the flow because I realize nothing will change unless I make it. Asking James for a damn thing will get me nowhere because, as far as he's concerned, I'm right where he needs me. He doesn't notice anything being more wrong than usual. He's so used to fucking an inexperienced woman who's so desperate to please him and doesn't know any better to demand reciprocation. James has gotten lazy. He's forgotten how to get me off, which means, more often than not, I'm left to find my own finish after his sloppy efforts.

I imagine over the next few months, while we make our preparations, I'll encounter a few more spicy inspirations for paintings.

"Expect at least thirty full-sized pieces, two murals, and an assortment of smaller, atmospheric paintings — thematically, they all explore desire and intimacy with the self, the power dynamics between a woman's internal and external self. Each piece tells its own story, a moment captured in time, but together, they'll create a narrative of sexual liberation. You'll see how they all fit together when I send you the rest of the collection's details."

I can already envision people losing themselves in my fantasies, in the passions of the women I've painted, and in my own immortalized desires. And best of all, James won't have a fucking clue about it until it's too late for him to stop it.

AFTER SAYING OUR GOODBYES, I step out onto the bustling San Francisco street, my head held high. My last gallery showing was for a collection of my older work that a private collector took an interest in, not a grand, public spectacle like Miguel is planning. The opening night will be exclusive and intimate, but we're planning for a week-long show. A shorter time frame will heighten the urgency.

Miguel hasn't seen all the paintings that I want to display yet, but he's already convinced every single one will be caught in a bidding war on the first night. We'll see about that.

As I slide into the driver's seat of my Lexus, I can't help but imagine Zane's reaction when I tell him about my plans. I wouldn't dare breathe a word to James, but instinctually, I know Zane will support me every step of the way.

He is my biggest fan after obsessively watching me paint for hours every day over the past month and a half.

The cityscape blurs past my window, and I leave the Golden Gate Bridge behind me on my drive home. I've thought about messaging Zane countless times since our rendezvous, but giving in to that temptation would only make us more likely to be caught. For now, I savor the memories of our intense time together and anticipate the burning heat of his watchful eyes from afar when I arrive home, eagerly awaiting my next chance to have him and give myself up to his lusts.

In my daydreams, I see Zane's face light up as he examines one of my paintings, his fingers tracing the curves and lines that make up my body on the canvas. The thought of him revering my art as much as he did me in bed makes me squirm with inexplicable, unfettered delight.

"James will kill me if he finds out about Zane," I murmur under my breath.

I've never been one to shy away from risks, but the stakes have never been this high before. Zane feeds the darkness inside me; he doesn't attempt to control it and strangle me in the process like James. With a darkness of his own, the magnetic pull between me and Zane is irresistible, addictive, and downright dangerous — I can't help but walk deeper into the chaos with a manic grin on my face.

All my reckless youth came flooding back the moment I spotted the glint of Zane's binoculars that first time. He reignited the drive for adventure inside me that had been threatening to go out for some time now underneath James' oppressive shadow.

I mull over the idea of bringing Zane one of my paintings for him to put on display in his home. For his eyes only, or in full display in his living room, it's an enticing thought either way; oh, I can only imagine the look on Sophia's face if she put two and two together about the contents of the painting.

Maybe it will be my breasts; he loved to fondle them almost as much as my ass. Then again, his personal experiences resonated with my reaper tattoo and my various brushes with death, so maybe he'd appreciate a look at me from behind and a different angle of my ever-present companion.

My phone buzzes in the cupholder, its vibration breaking through my Zane-induced reverie. I glance at the screen and see James' name flashing insistently.

"Libra, darling," James' smooth voice comes through the speaker. "I trust you had a pleasant outing. Are you on your way home?"

"Just got on the road. Are you off work?"

"Work never ends, you know that. I'm calling to inform you that I've decided to host a dinner party at our home next weekend. My business partners will be expecting luxury and your unique hospitable flare, as always. I trust you can handle the preparations?"

I frown as I make a turn, following the flow of traffic, and the automatic motion comes just as easily as the lie that follows. "I'm not sure I'll have the time. I just met with an industry connection who was inquiring about a showing in a few months. I signed the deal, so I have a lot of work to do over the next few weeks."

"That sounds wonderful, my darling. You're showing off those splendid cars of yours, yes? I had the first painting put on the sales floor of the dealership last month, and the wives haven't been able to stop talking about them. I told you this would give you the recognition you deserve."

"Sure, yeah, people love the cars. I have a whole collection to paint, you know how it is. Should I hire a planner for the party?"

"I know you'll find time in your busy schedule to get it done. It has to be you. Everyone can tell if it's not. Your art can wait, Libra; business can't."

"James—"

"And I'll be away on a business trip for a few days, so I expect everything to be in order by the time I return."

My jaw clenches, and I bite back a retort. I know better than to argue with him over the phone. He'll just pretend he didn't hear me and get mad later. I grumble silently to myself and force myself to sound agreeable. "Fine, James. Whatever you want."

"Excellent. I knew I could count on you."

The call ends with a click, and my music resumes over the stereo. I pull to a stop at a red light, my fists clenching and unclenching around the steering wheel. That mother-fucker knew this party was coming up and waited until the last minute to tell me. And, of course, it has to be *me* who plans it just so he can flex how much control he has. As always, what can I do but fall in line?

"Fuck!" I shout and slam my hand against the wheel, earning a few odd looks from the drivers adjacent to me.

The sharp pain brings me back to reality, reminding me that I'm still in control of my own actions, even if James tries to dictate my life. Taking a deep breath, I refocus my thoughts on the upcoming exhibition. On Zane and his dangerous allure. These are things I chose for myself without James' approval or knowledge. They're my own victories, my own sources of excitement, pleasure, and fulfillment.

I'll never in a million years do a showing for those stupid car paintings. I took to them because James insisted, and I needed to keep him under the illusion that he was

Mr. Smart Boss Man and in absolute control for a little while longer. In reality, his control is slipping far quicker than he'd dare to imagine.

A slow smile descends on me as I navigate the winding streets into Woodside. If James is disappearing for another one of his 'business trips,' then I can make a detour of my own before making it back home.

FOURTEEN

Zane

THE HUM OF THE COMPUTER FILLS MY EARS AS I STUDY each line of Fox's code, searching for solutions to the elusive errors in his system. The diagnostic reports flagged malfunctioning code in his most recent update, as I expected, but also a potential vulnerability in his core programming, which is *very* unexpected. I haven't made any revisions to Fox's core since the implementation of the Brain, which I consider much like a living being.

Alterations to the Brain model that Fox has been operating on for the past eight years would be an unnecessary risk to his unique processing capabilities, his memories, and more. Which is why that flag made me even more concerned about his behaviors a few weeks ago. He hasn't had any hiccups since, and I've been a bit too distracted by Libra and her new evening playtime she puts on for show in the upstairs sunroom when James is occupied elsewhere.

When I finally got around to asking Sophia about Fox a few days ago, she dismissed my concerns, claiming she hadn't noticed anything wrong and Fox is his usual self. He has been this past week, but I can't shake the feeling that something is off — my gut instinct has never failed me before.

While I work, I go back and forth between the code and watching Libra's coordinates on the map while she's not at home. I can't stop dreaming of her body. I'm desperate to taste her again, constantly battling the outrageous urge to leave the safety of my mansion for the first time in years to pursue her in the great outdoors.

We could meet outside the purview of James and the concern of busybodies like Sophia. Fuck, imagine that. Zane Crawford, legendary recluse, spotted leaving the confines of hermitdom for a piece of his neighbor's ass.

It might even be worth it, given that I haven't stopped fantasizing about her since I last had her in my bed. Her perfect lips have an urgent date wrapped around my cock, and she's about two fucking weeks late.

Just looking at her from afar isn't enough; it satisfies the barest portion of my craving. Just enough to keep me from going insane. I'm not mad enough to leave. Yet.

After hours of sorting through error logs, I isolate the small discrepancy in Fox's code that slipped through during the last update — just a few spliced lines and a dead operator that was trapping part of his memory in a loop. I'm relieved that it's minor enough. The loop must have backed up to the point that it started conflicting with his usual protocols.

I clean up the memory leak, deploy a hotfix after another thirty minutes, then spin in my chair while Fox patches and restarts. That should fix the conflicts with his core programming as well.

Quiet rock music plays on the computer room's speakers while Fox goes through his reboot sequence. "Good afternoon, Mr. Crawford. My internal systems have incorporated the latest update, and all systems are active."

I throw back the rest of my whiskey sour, satisfied by a job well done. "Feeling better, old friend?"

"Good as new, sir. Care for a top-up on your refreshment?"

"Absolutely."

A panel in the wall next to my computer opens, allowing me to deposit my glass inside. The drawer takes my glass into the wall, and a blue line glows around the crease while Fox works his magic. Seconds later, the cubby retracts again, and my drink is refilled and raised on a mechanical pedestal for me to take.

"Run another diagnostics check just in case, and give me a full report of all operational change logs, including routine maintenance and all standard operating procedures and sequences."

"As you wish, sir." Fox's speaker lights up with an alert. "It appears that Mrs. Scarsdale is almost home."

I sit up and hastily grab my binoculars from the desk, ready to catch a glimpse of her as she pulls into her driveway. It's been too long since I last saw her. As I raise them to my eyes, Fox interrupts me once more. "I was mistaken. Mrs. Scarsdale used her access code to open your front gate."

"Don't call her that. Just Libra."

"I made a note of your preference for future reference; I will call her Libra from now on."

Heat rises through me at the reminder of what happened the last time Libra stepped through those front doors, coming at me like a woman in control and in her element. She seemed more at home in a stranger's mansion than she has at home with her husband the entire time I've spied on her.

So, she's decided to pay me another visit. I wonder

where James is this time, or rather, how long we'll have. I won't be satisfied with a few snatched hours.

I set the binoculars down, but I wait for her right here.

Libra doesn't disappoint.

The door swings open, and my beautiful obsession walks in. Her long blonde hair curls over her shoulders, and she's stunning in a tight red dress that hugs her shoulders and dips between her breasts, then clings to her every curve. Hardened peaks of her nipples strain against the fabric, and with the way those blue eyes glitter like a starved animal, I doubt she wasted any time putting on panties, either.

"You naughty thing," I breathe. "That's not what you left the house in this morning. Did you tease your husband on a date night, then leave him high and dry?"

"He wasn't lucky enough. I had a business meeting, then thought I'd come home with a surprise…" She cups her breasts, rolling them into the finest view of cleavage I've seen in my damn life. "Too bad for him. Every man who's looked at me wanted to rip it off."

"Come here. Now."

Smirking, she strides toward me, swaying her hips to make the slinky red wrapping pull and thin out around her hips. Teasing me with glimpses of her perfect figure. Yeah, I bet every man who laid eyes on her did want to rip the fucking thing off, and I'm the lucky bastard with the privilege of living out that fantasy.

As soon as she's within reach, she climbs onto my lap and curls her arms around my neck. Our lips collide in a blaze of raw desire, like two forces of nature pulling each other into an unavoidable vortex. Electricity sparks at every touch, and she quivers against me as I deepen the kiss, tasting her sweetness and wanting more.

Threatening to let that spark get out of control, just like she wants.

The dress threatens to pile around her waist without any urging except my hottest fantasies. I grip her ass and bring her closer.

"Missed me?" Her smile is wicked as she grinds her thighs on the hard cock straining against my pants. "What did you do today without me around to watch?"

"Couldn't stop thinking about you," I admit. I consider not telling the truth, but with Libra, no desire is too taboo. "I was watching your GPS signal move all over the map, trying to figure out where you were going. What were you doing all the way in San Fran?"

Libra bites her lip and rocks against me. "You're tracking me? That's so hot."

Her arousal fuels mine, and I slide my hand between her legs, finding her slick enough to push my fingers right inside her. "Fuck, you came here soaked and ready for me. You really do like it when I watch you, huh?"

She tosses her head back and clings to me. "God, your fingers…" She clenches around my hand and lifts her hips, gasping as she fucks herself with my fingers. "I could come like this."

I wrap a fist in her hair, pulling my mouth to her ear. "I won't give you anything else until you do."

She trembles and bucks her hips, gushing into my palm as she rises and falls. Holy shit, she's going to do it. My cock throbs painfully, still confined, just as desperately seeking release like Libra is right now — only without the same freedom to chase it.

"Are you tracking James, too?" she pants, her breath hot against my ear.

"He's not worth my time. When's he coming home?"

"Gone—" She shudders when I push my fingers

deeper inside her, curling to reach the spot that had her seeing stars last time. "He's gone for the weekend."

The thought of having her all to myself, with no interruptions or distractions, for a whole weekend … I could chain her to my bed and have my way with her without a soul to stop me. She whimpers, and her thighs tense, her pace slowing as she clenches inside in anticipation of a huge release. I ram my fingers into her harder, bringing her a breath closer to the cliff.

"Then I can take my time with you," I growl into her ear.

"Please," she gasps. "I've dreamed of having you again."

"You're so bad. Wanting me? Wanting this? Fuck, do you know what you're getting yourself into?"

"I'm not afraid of you."

I bite down, hard, on her neck. Sucking, pulling, marking her flesh. Mine. She quivers in my arms, and she pushes down on my fingers. That instant, she convulses, her heat exploding in a sloppy rhythm that makes me so fucking hungry for more. God, she's perfect.

I drown her moans in another sloppy kiss. "You should be."

I lift her up and toss her onto the mattress, watching her breasts sway beneath her dress as her tiny form bounces on the black silken sheets. The red hem teases the upper edge of her thighs, giving me the merest glimpse of the blue-green ink decorating her skin but keeping her freshly finger-fucked pussy just out of view.

"I played Russian Roulette with you. You think I could be afraid of whatever gets you off in bed? I'm no innocent maiden, Zane. Give me your best."

An animalistic growl reverberates through me, and I

grab her arm and flip her over, locking her wrists in my grip and pushing her face-down into the mattress.

"Careful what you wish for," I warn as I pull the hem of her tight dress up over the curve of her bare ass, exposing the smooth skin beneath. "The things I want to do to you. Fuck…"

"Come on. Show me."

My palm connects with her ass in a sharp slap, followed by another and another. The sound of each spank fills the room, mingling with her moans. "You deserve punishment. Sneaking around on your husband, fantasizing about fucking another man… mmm, you're so bad."

"Is that all you've got?" she taunts, her voice breathy. "You can do better."

"My dear, that's not why I want to punish you." I tighten my grip on her wrists, making her gasp. I lean in close to kiss the angry red glow on her bubble butt, grazing the sensitive flesh with my teeth. "I'm punishing you for not coming to me sooner."

I bite the soft, unsuspecting flesh, leaving a line of marks down to her pussy before soothing the sting with soft kisses and gentle sucks.

"S-shit, you make me feel so good."

"It can't be that good if you waited two weeks to show up at my door."

"I didn't want to get caught."

I rip off my tie, tightening the silk around her wrists to keep her in position. "Don't lie to me. You want James to catch you. You love it rough, and he's an animal, and you know he'll fuck you like the devil himself if he catches you with me. So why?"

"I … I don't know—"

My hand collides with her ass, and she gasps.

"Not good enough."

She trembles as I spread her ass cheeks, getting a great view of her dripping pussy and her little asshole. I bet her husband leaves that neglected, too. I flick my tongue across her outer labia and plunge a finger into her pussy, just a few pumps to get it wet before I pull it out, leaving her empty and aching.

"Tell me the real reason you didn't come sooner."

"I was afraid … James hasn't felt right since I met you. He doesn't know how to touch me anymore."

"Good girl. That's the truth, isn't it? Here's your reward."

I bring that damp finger to her asshole, and she shudders as I push it inside.

"*Zane.*"

"He can't make you sing like this, can he?"

Her walls pulse and tighten around my finger, milking it for her pleasure. Even if Libra wasn't moaning, I'd know she fucking loves it because her pussy leaks like a faucet, clenching and dripping even though I haven't moved my finger since I shoved it into her ass. I inch it deeper until she's pushing into me, but when she's too busy moaning to answer my question, I pull it out, leaving her whimpering and empty. She pushes her red ass into my hand, seeking friction, but I won't give it to her.

"No," she gasps. "Only you can. He's not good enough for me."

A ripple of satisfaction runs through my whole body, and my cock throbs painfully. I've never been this damn hard before. The power of those words, that claim, the knowledge that one fuck was all it took to ruin Libra for her husband is so fucking satisfying, I laugh out loud. I beat James with one night and staked a claim on his wife. Her body is mine now.

I take her ass in both hands, breathing in the raw musk of her dripping mess of a cunt. "Fuck, you're delicious."

Smirking, I insert a finger back into her greedy ass, and she takes my grace and runs a mile with it. "That's right, nobody feels as good as me inside you, huh?"

"I know, oh, oh … Thank you, Zane…"

She pulls her whole body back to slam into me again, squealing when I add another finger to the mix. I let her do all the work, taking it at her pace.

While my fingers work her ass, I fall flat onto my back and lift her hips so her trembling knees fall on either side of my head, then pull her dripping folds onto my face. My tongue plunges into her tight little hole, and I moan as her slick fills my mouth. I finally give myself some fucking relief and unzip, letting my angry, neglected cock breathe. She rides my mouth and fingers like her life depends on it, until she's shaking so badly she can't fucking move anymore.

"Do you wish my fingers were my cock?" I palm myself, and a bead of precum drizzles from the tip and soaks my hand.

"Yes!"

"Yeah, you want my dick in your ass? Say it."

"I want—" I shove my fingers into her harder, beating up those slick little walls. "I want your dick in my ass. Please, Zane."

"You fucking want it, don't you? Want to get fucked in the ass?"

I drag my tongue across her slit. Her juices flood my face, and my cock strains for release; it's fucking painful holding back like this. Groaning, I shove my pants down, my tongue working in a frenzy to keep tasting her until I'm finally free.

"Please, please, put it in my ass," she moans.

I push up from under Libra and turn her onto her back. Tangles of Libra's long hair cascade over her chest, clinging to her sweaty face and skin, while her arms are awkwardly positioned to her side, still tied together. The tiny red dress is still strapped over her shoulders, just barely hiding her breasts beneath the mussed-up top. I smirk as I step out of my pants and wrap my fists around her muscular thighs, bunching the dress around her waist and spreading her legs open further. My thumb absently traces the tattoo on her thigh, and I pull her closer to the edge of the bed. Her slippery, swollen pussy is just begging to be filled, and a streak of her juices drenches the reaper by her entrance.

"You were so good, coming back to me without making me command you. You were late, but you still deserve a reward, don't you?"

She squirms, her teeth locked over her lip while she nods, wide-eyed and sultry.

I position myself between her thighs, the head of my cock teasing over the wet tattoo, and then I nudge her clit. She shivers, pushing ever so slightly into me. Every sensation spikes through me, and I ache with the need to feel her, any part, wrapped around me. I slip down to her ass, and the little hole tightens at the threat of my intrusion, pulsing with so much want that she groans and nudges into me.

"God damn … you're so tight. Are you sure you're ready for this, sweetheart?"

"Don't make me wait."

I chuckle and slide my shaft against her pussy, letting her soak me before bringing the tip back to her ass. I push down into her, snarling with much-needed release when she puckers and lets me in.

"Shit…" She writhes beneath me as I enter, as if she's

trying to escape the pleasure, but I won't let her. I grab her bound wrists and hold them against her back to stop her from moving too much and pulling me out. "Holy shit."

"You said you could take it. Take it, Libra."

Libra throws her head back, pushing her hips up to meet mine and helping me fill her completely for the first time. "You can't resist me either, Zane, admit it…"

I hear the challenge in her words, and I hook my arms around the small of her back, fucking into her hard and fast.

"I can't," I groan. "I just want to park inside you all day. The way you squeeze around me … so fucking needy."

"Fuck, Zane! You're gonna make me come again!"

I set a pace so ragged and relentless my brain can barely keep up with my body. Before I know it, I'm curling into her, forcing her face to mine just so her mouth can anchor me in this storm. Every touch, every kiss, every moan is as intoxicating as Libra is addicting. She bends so easily to me, luring me right to the longing for more depraved pleasures. I pound into her until she can't breathe anymore, and our bodies let loose the rest of the savage lust that consumes us.

One final grunt and I collapse face-first into the mattress beside her.

"Ha!" She laughs, her chest heaving with each breath. "I thought you were going to take your time with me? I think I won that round."

"Believe me," I pant, wrapping an arm around her and pulling her closer, "I plan to. It's been weeks since I … I just … I needed some relief."

I turn my face to stare into the sky of infinity presented in Libra's bright, mischief-laden eyes. "You don't have anyone else to relieve you? Not even that pretty little housekeeper?"

I scoff and yank my tie from Libra's wrists, then prop my head up on my arm to hide my embarrassment. "I'm not interested in Sophia."

"She's interested in you."

"It's a problem. She's attractive, but she's a friend, and I don't want things to get messy."

Libra's long red fingernail trails down my breastbone, down to the trail of dark hairs on my stomach toward my groin. "You really don't let many people in here, do you?"

"I don't. I can't tolerate most people long enough to let them in my space, and I wouldn't want to leave to satisfy those urges. It's just not worth it to me."

"Hmm." She gives me a satisfied smirk. "I'll keep that in mind."

I bring my other hand over hers, locking her slender fingers against my flesh. "I'm not imagining it, am I? You've been different with James ever since you met me."

"We've fucked, if that's what you're asking."

"I'm well aware that you two have fucked. I would watch you every minute of every day, and I *do* watch every minute that you let me."

Libra's pretty face scrunches like she's going to argue with me, but then she sighs. "It's complicated."

"All the best relationships are."

"And the worst ones."

I hold her gaze, expectant. She will give me what I want. I know she will.

Finally, Libra huffs and crosses her arms. The clingy dress still obscures her breasts, just barely. I failed my job of ripping the fucking thing off, that's for sure. "He's stubborn. It's like being married to a mule with the temperament of a rabid bulldog, the intelligence of a frog, the libido of a bonobo, and the sexual coordination and finesse of a newborn giraffe."

"You paint an intriguing picture, but I'm quite certain that's an insult to frogs."

She chokes out a laugh. "Seriously, Zane. Being married to James is torture. He satisfies all my material wants, but … the passion has been waning between us for years."

"Has it? You two looked passionate that morning I caught you two fucking by the pool."

"Is that what started your interest?" Her mouth inches closer to my bicep. "Watching me get fucked?"

"It was hot. I've watched people have sex before, but not like how I've been watching you."

She shakes her head. "That wasn't passion; it was being trapped, and I did not know just how thick the bars of the cage were. He thinks that providing for me is enough, and for a while, I let him trick me into believing that, but it's become clearer and clearer that it's not. I need freedom, adventure, passion … everything that he can't give me. Now that I've met you, I…"

Her words echo my own thoughts, the emptiness that gnawed at me before she entered my life. That feeling of being trapped in a world of my own making.

"You've learned how to have fun again." I stroke her hair gently, trying to offer comfort. "You deserve more than just material things, Libra. You deserve happiness, real happiness. Is that why you two are in an open relationship?"

"Oh, uh." She laughs awkwardly. "We're not in an open relationship. I posed the idea to him several times, and he never outright said no, but at this point, I think he's dangling the possibility in front of me to manipulate me into doing what he wants under the misguided hope that he'll bend to my wishes." She licks her swollen lips, refocusing on me. "That means we're technically having an affair."

Everything that Sophia warned me about momentarily rings in my head like an alarm, making me tense. But then Libra curves closer to me, her soft body melding into my side so she can rest her head on my shoulder. Her touch eases my worries in an instant, reminding me why the risk has been worth every second. "Does that bother you, or…"

"No," I say without hesitation. "I don't care. I can see how unhappy you are, so my conscience is clear if I can give you an occasional reprieve … whether physical or otherwise."

She drags her tongue along my bicep, and the muscles clench involuntarily. She's a goddamned temptress…

I clear my throat. "If you don't see James giving you what you want, and he can't satisfy you anymore, why are you still married? Divorces were invented for a reason."

"Zane…"

"I watch you paint for hours without ever thinking to peel my eyes away and do something else. You're fucking captivating. If I had you in my bed, hell, in my house, I'd want you to feel the same intensity that I do at every waking moment. I wouldn't lock you up — not for long, at least — because I know you'd suffocate. You deserve someone who worships the ground you walk on."

Libra's eyes are soft with disbelief or maybe amusement. "Someone like you?"

"I'm not saying it's me, but it's sure as fuck not James. The way you move, the sound of your voice, the scent of your skin … I crave every part of you. If you asked me to explain it, I couldn't tell you why, but I am addicted to you." I trace my fingertips gently along her collarbone, feeling her breath slow beneath my touch. "Knowing I shouldn't have you only makes me want you more."

The admission feels like a weight lifted from my chest. My desire for her threatens to consume me day in, day out. As the words spilled out, I had no thought or fear or judgment, but now I look into her eyes, searching for any hint of rejection.

There's a wicked gleam in those blue depths. "I like that you're so open about how much you want me. It's thrilling. I haven't felt so desired since I was…" She trails off, her smile faltering. "Since before I was married."

"Divorce him. You could be free."

You could be mine, is what I want to say, but I know, in her mind and body, she already knows. Isn't that what matters, even if she wears another man's name and lives in another man's house?

I hate watching the way he treats her. She's not a fucking ornament.

"Believe me, I've considered it, but there's more at stake than just my happiness."

"Like what?" I press.

Her fingernails trace circles around the mounds of my pecs. I don't want to push her to tell me more and push her away as a result, but she seems to forget I'm literally the richest man in the world, and there are no obstacles between me and what I want. Is James dangerous? Nothing in my background check indicated that he has a violent history, but then again, Sophia doesn't have a high opinion of James, and knowing that Libra's history is hidden from my view, there could very well be more that I haven't found about James, too.

If she's afraid of someone coming to hurt her, I'll fuck him up long before she has anything to be worried about.

Afraid of James fucking her around in the divorce

proceedings? I'll slam him so hard with lawyers and paper-work that he'll be the one crying to get it over with.

"If you need help, I'm at your disposal. Whatever you need to get that asshole out of your life."

Libra's eyes crinkle with her smile. "I have something you could help me with, actually. James wants to host a party at our house next weekend. I don't give a fuck what James wants, but it's an excuse to get you in *my* house."

The suggestion jars me out of the thought spiral, trying to pick apart what Libra could be hiding from me. Not hiding, just not telling me.

"You want me to go to a dinner party at your house? With your husband?" I ask. "That doesn't seem wise."

Libra shrugs her expression a mix of mischief and defi-ance. "Maybe not, but it could be fun. He'll be so grumpy if you show up."

"I would think a man as shallow as James would love a man of substance in his home."

"James has a complex about being the richest, most successful person in a room unless those richer, more successful people will open doors for him."

"And I'm a titanium wall."

"Exactly."

This is a dangerous game, suggesting we temporarily move the playing field within her social circle. Not only that but within the direct competition with her husband … intentionally placing me in his view as a part of their pissing match. If I wasn't in the line of fire, I'd love to play that role for her, but since I want her in my bed more than I want to stick it to James…

My jaw flexes. It wouldn't just be about sticking it to James. It would be a way of helping Libra assert her inde-pendence. She loves to play with fire, and every new risk only serves to heighten the possible peaks of exhilaration. How can I say no to that?

"It's risky," I admit, my voice wavering slightly with uncertainty. "If James were to find out about us…"

"You're a smart man. I'm sure you can be discreet. Besides, I want you there. Think about it, at least? For me?"

I know that despite my concerns, I would do almost anything for this woman. It's not rational, but then again, neither is any addiction.

"I haven't left my property in a long time. I'm not sure I know how to act at a dinner party any more." But even as I protest, my mind is racing, trying to devise a plan that will allow me to attend without arousing suspicion. For her, I would take the risk.

"You don't give a fuck about anyone's opinions. That's charm enough to make people drool after you in droves. You'll do fine. Think of it as an opportunity to break out of your shell, just for a night. No one has to know except for us."

I shake my head, chuckling. It's a naïve notion to believe even the most exclusive parties have any conception of privacy. As soon I step into the presence of others who are aware of my identity, the floodgates will open.

Is that a problem I'm willing to face for Libra?

"All right," I relent with a heavy sigh. "I'll think about it. For you."

Her smile is like sunshine breaking through a stormy sky, and it sends a jolt of warmth straight to my heart.

"That's all I ask," she whispers before pressing her lips against mine in a searing kiss that threatens to suck my soul through my mouth and feed me straight into the gaping jaws of the reaper with her.

FIFTEEN

Libra

I PUSH ZANE INTO THE LEATHER CHAIR, AND HE FALLS willingly into the seat, his dark eyes raking over me. Straddling his lap, I feel the heat and hardness of his erection press insistently into my core, straining against the layers of his silken robe and my nightgown and panties.

He throbs against me while I load the bullet into the revolver's chamber. His eyes never leave mine — the power I hold right now over this man, with this gun, all but freezes us in time and space.

I shift my hips and weight, reaching between us to push the measly fabric side and ease him inside of me. I arch my back with a gasp as he slides all the way to the root.

"Libra…" Zane's voice comes out as a strained, husky growl. "Not that I'm complaining, but what are you doing?"

"What does it look like?"

My mouth pops open with a moan when I lift my hips, savoring every inch of him while I move up and down his girth. Slowly, deliberately, I ride him until he grips my hips and encourages me to move faster.

But this is my game, and I'll play it at my own pace.

"Mmm, you like that, hot stuff?" Licking my lips, I push down on him, using my weight to counter his attempts to lift me. I rock on top of him until he's muttering pleased obscenities under his breath, his eyes rolling back. "You feel so fucking good inside me."

My fist tightens around the revolver's grip while Zane's fingers dig into my flesh, urging me to take him deeper, faster. I've never felt adrenaline so hot and electric with anyone but Zane, but with him it's so *easy* I can't stop myself from pushing us to new heights, seeking the next unforgettable experience.

In a daze, he watches me bring the Russian Roulette revolver to my temple. His hips buck into me, and I groan as he picks up the pace, my whole body bouncing on top of him.

Our eyes lock again, and in the intensity of that moment, there is absolute stillness in the rippling chaos of my heart and soul. I pull the trigger.

Click.

My heart pounds with the blood rush, and simultaneously, that unbearable anticipation explodes inside me. I shudder as my orgasm takes hold, and I convulse around Zane's cock. My passion, my addiction, is the burning, devouring heat of an erupting volcano. But Zane's embrace is the cool, unrelenting ocean that prevents me from supercharging — the balance to my chaos. Crashing forward, my palms land on his shoulders, and I use him to steady myself. Sweat leaks down my forehead, and I'm suddenly exhausted, even though I've never felt more alive.

Death and life meet in my mind and body at once. The reaper and I revel in the serenity, but Zane hasn't had the chance to greet his unmaker. He's still throbbing and hard inside me. I can feel that he's on the verge of spilling over, but not yet. Like me, he wants to go all the way to the brink of fucking insanity.

"My turn."

He pries the revolver from my sweaty hand. He kisses the metal barrel and then me. A gentle, metallic taste lingers on his lips, but it's quickly washed away by the taste of *him*. That melancholic, rich, complex spice that's everything unique to Zane.

I've spent the last three days mostly in his arms or in his bed, and I haven't had enough of him. I'm not sure I ever will.

Our tongues tangle in a frenzy of wanting, teeth and lips battling for dominance. My hips start to rise and fall again, aching to feel the whole length of him moving again. The sensation is overwhelming after my climax, every nerve alight with pleasure. I grip him tightly, clenching and unclenching as I fall on him again and again.

It's becoming more difficult to focus on the game, my mind brought right back to the point of focus: him.

My eyes flutter open. Zane's mouth hangs open, his dark eyes hooded as he lifts the revolver to his head. The slightest shadow of stubble ghosts over his jaw and chin, making him appear every bit as haunted as he is deep inside that beautiful soul of his.

Thighs tensing, I fuck him with every ounce of strength in me. Like every stroke could be the last. Zane doesn't waver. He pulses inside me, his thrusts becoming more insistent, driving himself deeper until we both reach our breaking point.

Click.

"Fuck!" Zane cries out as the gun fails to fire.

His face goes red, and he surges over the edge of oblivion. My nails dig into Zane's shoulders as we ride it out together, the warmth of his come filling me and leaking down my thighs, only heightening my satisfaction.

"That was fucking intense," he manages to say between labored breaths. "I didn't think Russian Roulette could get any better."

Grinning, I tug on his bottom lip with my teeth. "We've danced with death and won so many times now I wanted to try something new. I'm starting to think the game is rigged."

He throws his head back, laughing like a maniac. "It's not. I promise."

"The odds of surviving as many games as you have are abysmally low."

"Fox has made a point of reminding me of that sad statistic, but I have no reason to fear death. I wouldn't cheat you out of the excitement. It's just luck, or maybe fate's way of spitting on me."

Despite his assurance, I need to know for myself to placate that curiosity. With a determined huff, I pluck the gun out of his relaxed hand and lift myself off him. I press the button to open the exit to the secret compartment.

"What do you plan on doing with that?" He fixes his robe and follows me into the large master suite.

On the other side of the room, below one of the paintings, an ornate decorative vase garners my attention. I aim and pull the trigger.

The sound of the gunshot echoes in the confined space, followed by the shattering of glass as the bullet strikes the vase. Tiny shards spray across the floor, glinting as they scatter on the carpet.

A rush of excitement surges through me, and I shriek with excitement, clapping my hands. "It worked! It's not rigged!"

"Damn." Zane wraps his arms around my waist,

pulling me flat against him. One of his hands toys with the smooth blue silk rippling over my stomach, letting it ride up my thighs. "Your aim is impeccable."

"Never underestimate a woman who knows her way around a weapon," I tease.

"I'd never dream of it."

Gripping my chin, he tilts my head to kiss me over my shoulder and wipes my smugness right off my lips. One of my hands still grips the gun, its cold metal somehow grounding me through his dizzying exploration of my mouth.

"Mr. Crawford," Fox's voice interrupts us over the speakers, "It appears Miss Manson heard the noise and is on her way to the fourth floor."

"Tell her there's nothing to worry about. It was just a game," Zane says, only briefly breaking the rhythm of our kiss to speak.

"I did, sir. She insists on ensuring no one was hurt."

"Shit," I mutter when I hear the hurried footsteps in the adjacent room. Instead of pulling away from Zane, I turn into him, take his hands, and plant them on my breasts. The sheer fabric parts when he squeezes so that most of his palms land on my bare flesh.

"Mr. Crawford!" Sophia exclaims from the other side of the door. To her credit, she does sound genuinely worried. "Was that a gun? What in heaven's name—"

"There's nothing to worry about!" Zane calls out as she reaches the closed door, but as I am learning, Sophia likes to ignore him and insert herself into his space. She twists the handle, and in a similarly meddling fashion, Fox does not lock the door but allows it to open beneath her tiny hands.

A frazzled-looking Sophia crashes into the room. She's wearing her usual housekeeping uniform, but the skirt, blouse, and apron that have been primly kept every other time I've seen her are wrinkled from her hurry up the stairs. Her eyes are wide as her gaze flickers around the room, landing on us, then Zane's hands on my boobs. She tries not to scowl when I push my chest into his grip, and I suck on my bottom lip. Her disdain for me is so obvious it makes her an easy target for my entertainment.

"I told you, there's nothing wrong." Zane flashes her a smile and gestures to the mess of glass by the wall. "Libra was just showing me what a good shot she is."

Sophia's face pinches when she sees the shattered vase. "You shouldn't be playing with guns inside. What if someone gets hurt?"

"That's the whole point — where's the fun without the risk? I'm sure you abhor guns, so you probably don't get it."

"I don't." She shakes her head disapprovingly. "What a waste of a perfectly good vase! It's too broken to put back together."

"It's fine, really, Sophia, no need to fuss so much. The décor in here is tired. I could use something new. Didn't I tell you to replace the carpet?"

She opens her mouth like she wants to protest, but then her gaze shifts to Zane, where her attention lingers on the hard, sculpted muscles visible around the open front of his robe. Then she looks at me, and her eyes harden. I offer her a cheeky smile and drag my tongue along the barrel of the gun. It's still hot from firing, and the taste of gunpowder is salty on my tongue. She reels in disgust.

"I'll be back to clean this up," she mumbles and turns away.

The door slams behind her, loud enough to make Zane wince. "The hell is her problem? And why are you grinning like you robbed a fucking bank?"

I twirl the revolver in my hand, then place it grip-first into Zane's. "It's only my perverse sense of satisfaction for making Sophia so uncomfortable. She's so territorial, it's hilarious."

"Territorial? You're imagining things."

I relish the thought of competing with Sophia for Zane's attention, even if I know she'll never win. It's not a true competition, but fucking with her is fun. If there was any real chance of the two of them getting together, though … Sophia would like me far less than she does now.

A bitch like me knows how to fight dirty.

"Josephine is the same way with James," I muse. "She seems to forget I'm his wife."

"Josephine? Your housekeeper?"

I snort. Why am I not surprised he knows the name of my housekeeper? He's probably done a background check on her and knows more about her life than I do. "Yep, you know, the pretty little thing James hired and hasn't been able to keep his hands off her since. She's madly in love with him, but she doesn't get it that he's playing her for a fool. If only she'd listen to me. If he was smart, he'd marry her and get it over with. It wouldn't be hard to convince her to run away with him and make her serve him the way he wishes I would."

"It would make your life a lot easier if they both disappeared."

"Tell me about it. Life is never that simple though, is it? We had a healthy sex life until Josephine came into the picture, but he's been eyeing up younger women for years. It hurt at first, but now that he's distracted by Josephine, and I'm distracted by you …"

Zane remains silent for a moment, contemplating my

words. I can see the gears turning in his head. "Why are you so afraid of filing for divorce?"

"Afraid isn't the right word. It would be complicated and messy. James cares a lot about his image, so he'll never divorce me willingly because that would imply his life is less than picture-perfect. He'll fight and make my life a living hell, and that's not worth the effort right now."

"Freedom is always worth it."

I slide my hands up Zane's ribs, hooking my wrists around his neck. "What James and I have right now isn't so bad. We're getting away with this, aren't we?"

Zane's hands snake down my body, curling around to firmly grip my ass. "Anyone else might hear you say that and suggest you're playing it safe because you know James would become erratic if he found out. He'd be dangerous."

"He threatened to burn my art studio to the ground if I entertained the idea of being with another man."

"Yet you're not afraid of that either, are you?" Zane pushes his erection into my stomach. "You like the danger of knowing he could discover us and go crazy."

"You see me in a way he never has."

"You know what would be even more fun?" He smirks, leaning his face closer to mine. "I have more than enough money to make James discreetly disappear. One word and you could be free. Totally and completely."

My heart stalls out. Air suspends in my lungs. Violent delights manifest in Zane's eyes, but never in a thousand years did I expect the suggestion he just laid out. *Is* he offering what I think he's offering? A shiver winds through me, and I breathe heavier at the prospect of James disappearing, of having true freedom for the first time in over six years.

He can't really be suggesting that we get rid of James. Even if the idea was tempting, it's so insane that I can't truly believe he means it as more than a joke. Untethered from the chains of my marriage, I could have all the fun with Zane I want, without restrictions. Oh … the trouble we could get into.

"Sometimes," I confess, my voice low and playful, "I fantasize about the different ways I could kill him."

"Really?"

"Poisoning his morning coffee, stabbing him in his sleep … or maybe something more elaborate, like rigging his precious car to explode. Fresh from the lot so no one would know it was me."

"Mmm, so you imagine doing it yourself instead of through a third party?" Zane teases. "That's a good way to get caught."

"Only in my wildest dreams. It's easy to picture yourself doing crazy shit when someone pisses you off as much as he does."

"Yeah? Fucking with his car and having him drive into the bay would be poetic, but I don't think you'd be satisfied with that kind of ending. You strike me as more the type to want to watch the light drain out of his eyes as you make him an offering to the reaper."

"It would be so delicious to see that moment when he realizes he's fucked up close."

Zane hefts me up. For a moment, I'm floating, and then I wrap my long legs around his waist. My soaked panties grind into him, both of us moaning as we rock together. We could go for another round if it wasn't for the fact that Sophia will be back any minute.

"But…" I groan into his mouth. "It would be too easy to kill him. All my problems would just go away. Where's the fun in that?"

"Getting away with it."

My whole body goes flush with delight. I've let my vivid

fantasies of his death whirl in my most demented, angry thoughts before, but I've never had someone to dream up more twisted ways of eliminating that one big *problem*.

The thing is, while it's fun to imagine James dead, I couldn't have him killed for the sake of my own freedom; he's an asshole, but he doesn't deserve to be murdered.

That doesn't make it any less fun to imagine his demise.

SIXTEEN

Zane

I ADJUST THE KNOT OF MY BLACK TIE IN FRONT OF THE full-length mirror, ensuring it's straight and snug against my collar. Presentable, not overly impressive, in a dark gray suit. It's rare that I have the opportunity to dress up for an audience. The parties, the business meetings, they were a song and dance I once loved until the novelty disappeared and I lost interest.

It's been far longer than six years since I last felt the sense of anticipation about a party in my blood that I do now. The sensation catches me off guard; maybe Libra was right, and pretending to be strangers in front of her husband will be a fun challenge.

"All right, Zane, let's make James squirm."

As I slip my foot into my polished shoe, a sharp pain slices through my foot and makes me yelp. A thin line of blood forms across the heel of my sock.

"The hell?"

I dig around in the shoe, finding a small piece of glass. Turning it over, I recognize the gold and blue paint from the broken vase that Libra broke the other day. Strange. I thought Sophia cleaned up.

I dab the blood with a tissue and slap a bandage on the cut. No time to properly clean it. I'll be late. The sting brings back memories of Libra's nails raking down my back, her teeth biting into my shoulder. The pain will serve as a reminder of her all evening.

~

THE SCARSDALE MANSION is extravagant with its Greek-inspired columns and the center fountain, where a statue of a woman pours water from an urn. Fox navigates my Volvo around the fountain, then I hand my keys to the valet and make my way up the white marble steps to the door.

"Mr. Crawford, we're delighted to have you tonight." The housekeeper, Josephine, greets me with a curtsy and welcomes me inside. Her red hair is braided over her shoulders, and her uniform is freshly pressed, but the diamond teardrops dangling from her ears reveal her true status in the household. "You will find Mr. and Mrs. Scarsdale in the lounge along with the other guests."

I've watched Libra live her life in this house for months, but walking through her front door is a different experience. Grandeur is the name of the game, with the glittering multi-tier crystal chandelier in the entry above a double spiral staircase to an interior balcony. Along the walls, heavy crimson drapes part over the doorways into other rooms.

I follow the sound of low jazz music and laughter, where I find well-dressed men and women mingling farther in the hall. I recognize several faces here, though only from their online profiles. None give me a second glance — yet. I'm happy to keep a low profile as I come into the lounge.

Standing by the window with another woman, my eyes immediately land on Libra. A shimmering blue gown flows over her like water, the split showing off her long legs. Her blonde hair is teased into curls over her bare shoulders, and the sparkling bodice dips between her breasts and accentuates her curves. Our eyes meet for the briefest moment, but we break contact just as fast. We've agreed on how tonight will play out.

A group of men in business suits hover by the fireplace, engaged in what appears to be a heated debate. I claim a tumbler from a nearby tray and pour myself a finger of whiskey as I move to join them.

"The market is too strong to crash," an older gentleman asserts to the group. "Our investments have never been more secure. There's no better time to invest."

"I have to disagree," another man replies, "There are still too many unknown variables. Technology is always evolving, and we don't know how it will affect the stock market yet. We could end up taking a major hit."

"There's no reward without risk! My last 'risky' investment gave me a return of over 30% last month. I'm telling you, this new tech stock is the next big thing."

"Why aren't you investing in it, then?"

The older gentleman blubbers, "Well, I-I only have so much money to move around, and my funds are tied up elsewhere right now. I want to pass this opportunity on to my friends before someone else snatches it up."

"It might not pay off as much as you expect." This man appears to be the youngest of the group, though he still has a decade on me. "It's all about taking calculated risks and making educated decisions about when to capitalize on market fluctuations."

I sip my whiskey, letting the amber liquid settle on my tongue, then burn down my throat, dissatisfied with the quality. James must have thought to impress with an old bottle of Glenfarcas, but the flavors are out of season. A truly elegantman would know the Talisker Bodega series is superior at this time of year.

The older gentleman extends a hand to me. "We're discussing the latest trends in the stock market. What is your opinion about where the next boom will be?"

"My opinion is luck will only get you so far when it comes to investing, and astute men share their strategies, not their secrets." I shrug, acting like I don't know anything since it's amusing to watch them argue over basics I mastered when I was 12. "It's essential to do your own research, analyze market conditions, and determine the potential risks before you move funds for any kind of investment. That being said, a diversified technology port-folio has always been the most reliable for me."

The older gentleman nods in agreement. "True, true. Well, I suppose never take advice from someone you don't know, eh?" He laughs. "I'm Tim Marcen. Pleasure to meet you."

I take his hand in a firm shake. "Zane. Likewise."

"Have you had any interesting investments lately?"

"I'm sure I have, but I don't bother with manual invest-ments anymore."

"It's wise to have someone managing your portfolio for you. We would miss so many opportunities if we were foolish enough to do it all ourselves!" The younger man grins. "I'm Eric Banks, by the way."

The conversation moves on to more specific investment stories, which I follow along as best as I can to stop my attention from drifting to Libra on the other side of the room too frequently. She's stunning in that dress, and I imagine lifting the skirt over her long legs. I have billions of dollars in investment accounts diversified across a multitude of industries, but I don't have a portfolio manager in the traditional sense. Fox handles it all. However, for privacy and security reasons, all of those operations and the complicated proprietary algorithms I designed for him to be as successful at the job, are available only to a select few.

This party is low-key, but as I haven't interacted with anyone in person besides Libra and Sophia in over five years, I'm surprised by how easy it is to slip into the old rhythms and patterns of conversation. Especially with these fellows, who have no idea who I am, I can blend in as one of the rabble.

At that moment, Libra glides over to us, a mischievous smile playing on her lips. "Mr. Crawford, how wonderful that you could join us this evening." Her voice is like velvet as holds a delicate hand out to me.

I bring her fingers to my lips. "The pleasure is all mine, Mrs. Scarsdale."

"What a gentleman," she giggles.

A flush stains her cheeks and trails down her neck. I want to follow it with my tongue. The other guests' voices become a meaningless buzz. There is only Libra and the promise in her eyes.

"I've heard so much about you, Mr. Crawford, I was worried you wouldn't make it." She withdraws her hand and gestures toward the crowd. "Have you met everyone yet?"

"I'm afraid I only just arrived."

"Is that so? Then don't let me stop you from socializing." She takes a sip of wine. "But I must ask, what is it you do exactly? James was rather vague in his description."

"Nothing, I'm afraid ... I've considered myself retired

these past five years. Though you could say, I dabble in tech and finance."

"How fortunate for you." Libra's tone is dry. She knows I'm lying, playing the game as she instructed. "And how boring. I thought you would be a more interesting man, considering all the rumors."

I smirk and lean against the wall. "I'm sorry to disappoint."

"Forgive me for saying so, but you seem too young to have amassed enough wealth to retire already," Tim suggests. "What is your secret, an inheritance? Investments that paid off?"

"Nothing of the sort. My father was a destitute carpenter, and my mother was disabled and unable to work for most of her life. I amassed my fortune by recognizing the greatest fears of humanity and making them real."

"Wait, Zane Crawford? The tech genius?" Eric leans forward, his tie hanging from his neck and falling into his drink. "Don't you work with AI?"

Murmurs of recognition ripple through the group, and a few heads from the leather lounge chairs turn in our direction. Internally, I shut myself off to them all. I'd hoped to go to this party without everyone scrambling for a piece of me. Were I so fortunate.

"Indeed, that's me."

"I heard you were a hermit. My God, I never thought I'd meet you in the flesh." Eric shoves his hand into mine again, shaking it with renewed frenzy. "I am such a huge admirer of your work."

"I appreciate it. Do you work in the industry as well?"

"Heavens, no. I don't do manual labor. I fund people with bright ideas; if only yours had come across my desk a decade ago, I'd be a billionaire, too! Why don't you work with AI anymore? You said you're retired, but—"

"James!" I hear someone else call out. "Did you know Zane Crawford is here?"

Libra turns around and follows the conversation at the same time as me. We spot James entering the room from the balcony side, where one of his business associates points in our direction. As soon as James' eyes land on us, they darken by a fraction, but he hides his disdain with a well-practiced smile and confident gait. His confidence is the result of successful manipulations, not true success. A fragile thing. A man with a fragile ego is never one I wish to do battle with.

I hate him already.

"My love, there you are!" Libra saunters over, hooking her arm in his to placate him. "I've finally had the pleasure of meeting Zane Crawford. You two are old friends, isn't that right?"

His fake smile grows wider. "I unfortunately haven't had the pleasure. I'm honored to have you in my home, Mr. Crawford."

"I admit I was surprised by the invitation, but it's been such a long while since I last went out to a gathering like this. I'm having a grand old time, thanks to you."

Libra hands her glass of half-finished wine to me. "Drink up! Enjoy yourself!"

The scent of a rich merlot fills my nostrils. I take a sip, meeting James' cold stare. The wine is sweet and playful on the tongue, like Libra's lips; I match mine to the lipstick stain left on the rim just to taste her, too.

Libra's gaze lifts over my shoulder, and her eyes light up. "Philipa! Is that you, my dear?"

She scurries past me, leaving James and me alone, while she entertains herself with who must be the Philipa Tennand she told me about from one of her paintings. James stares at Libra's ass as she walks away, the slit in her dress parting wide enough to reveal her upper thigh for a split second. His lips twitch.

"My wife always manages to wear the most revealing dresses," he remarks, a derisive chuckle escaping his lips. "You'd think she'd learn some modesty by now; we're civilized folk, not bachelors at a strip club."

My eyes skim up Libra's athletic body, wrapped in that sparkly blue dress. The skirt is long and tight, reaching well below her ankles but not brushing the floor. The neckline is low but emphasizes her shoulders rather than her cleavage. In my opinion, the dress isn't revealing at all, but she is stunning enough to steal the show.

"Perhaps she simply enjoys expressing herself," I reply, keeping my tone neutral. "After all, isn't that what fashion is about?"

"There's a fine line between self-expression and exhibitionism. She's acting like a harlot."

The hair on my arms bristles, my fist tightening around the stem of the wine glass. I'm disgusted by his audacity to criticize his wife's attire with me, an absolute stranger. Were she my wife, I would castrate anyone who dared to speak about her so crudely without her permission.

Smashing James' face in would only draw more attention to our affair. I wonder if he does this to assert dominance over her, or perhaps to mask his own insecurities. He has so many, a conversation with him is like trying not to trip over discarded toys in a toddler's playroom.

Another breath, and I relax. Libra is already sashaying back toward us.

"Don't you agree, darling?" James asks. "That dress is far too risqué."

Libra smiles sweetly at him. "Oh, absolutely, but life would be so boring without a little scandal. I can only imagine what people would think if I flashed them my ankles."

I hide my satisfaction behind another sip of wine.

"How did the two of you meet? A loving couple like you must have quite the origin story," I say.

James smirks, his eyes flicking to Libra. All the power in her stance and her confidence *shrivels* at that look, and I immediately feel sick to my stomach.

"You know how it is; the best relationships are introductions. My buddy owns a yacht he takes out a few times a year, and we met at one of his parties about eight years ago. Libra was dating him at the time. In fact, she dated my whole friend circle before finally landing in my lap. I'm a lucky man, aren't I?"

I raise my eyebrows at that story. "You can't look at a woman like that and think anything else, my man. Were only I so lucky to find someone as gorgeous as her."

"A man as well off as you shouldn't have any trouble at all. What's wrong with you? Erectile dysfunction?" He laughs at his own horrible joke. "There are plenty of women out there with prettier faces and tighter cunts than Libra."

Holy fuck, James is ruthless and a piece of work, saying that about Libra while she's clearly pleading with her eyes for him not to tell me the whole story. His resentment is so powerful that I sway on my feet at the tension between them. I'm curious about Libra's past because someone went through outlandish efforts to clean it up for her, but James takes *pleasure* in making her uncomfortable.

What the fuck?

Libra's smile goes from sweet to dark. "Plenty of men out there with bigger cocks too, but you don't see me complaining for settling."

"I wasn't complaining, darling, merely stating facts. A man watching out for a fellow man."

"Do you need another drink, love? You're not slurring enough."

He snaps his fingers, and Josephine appears at his side with two fresh tumblers of scotch with a reddish hue. "Excellent idea. One for me and for my new acquaintance."

I trade the empty wine glass for another crystal tumbler. "I hear you're a car salesman, Mr. Scarsdale. This is quite the home for a gig like that."

"I started as a salesman, now I own the joint. My dealership, *Speed*, specializes in acquiring rare luxury vehicles for an exceptionally exclusive clientele. Of course, we also have the sales floor for our regular customers, but they're too low-class for me to handle personally." He kicks back most of his drink in one go, then goes on to ramble about the car business like he's a very rich, very important man.

All I see is someone so small he feels compelled to build himself a bigger hill to stand on and look down on others. The more time I spend with him, the more seriously I consider the logistics of making him disappear, just like those VellR fuckboys.

As THE GUESTS trickle into the opulently decorated dining room, it becomes increasingly difficult to maintain my composure and stifle my mounting anger towards James. For Libra's sake, I must play along with this sick charade.

I sip my scotch slowly, appreciating every lingering flavor profile. Easy on the booze is the only way to maintain enough control not to murder James in front of his whole party.

Seated in the extravagant dining room, I'm surrounded by the sounds of clinking glassware and forced laughter. I engage in small talk with the guests to my left and right, all the while keeping a close eye on James and Libra, who are seated across from me.

"Our dinner this evening is a culinary masterpiece. Have you tried the escargot? It's absolutely divine," gushes the woman beside me, a trophy wife with a penchant for dramatic hand gestures.

I take a bite to appease her. The rich flavors melt on my tongue, but I can't seem to enjoy them.

"It is quite delicious; the Scarsdales employ a masterful chef."

James raises his wine glass, drawing the attention of the other guests. "I propose a toast to the star of the night, my lovely wife, for her talented preparation for this party and her unique artwork."

Libra's lips pinch. "Thank you, James. Art is such a personal expression, and I'm thrilled to share mine with our friends."

"You're an artist, Libra?" Eric asks from a few seats down from me. "I had no idea. What do you paint?"

"A little of this, a little of that."

"She's so unfocused with her talents." James all but beams at the invitation to smear his wife. "I encouraged her to settle for painting the rare cars I encounter in my business, but that's a new development."

"Ah, yes." Libra hesitates, glancing towards me with an unreadable expression. "In my husband's efforts to rearrange my hobby into a style he's capable of stomaching, he requested a series of expensive cars and scantily clad women for his dealership."

"That ought to increase sales!"

The guests chuckle uneasily, unsure of how to react.

Beneath the surface, I can see Libra's distress, her vulnerability hidden behind a veil of bravado. She's brave for trying to outwit James in front of his guests, but she must know by now that fighting him will only make him bite harder. My fist tightens around a butter knife.

"One of her latest pieces," James continues, "what was it, a nude painting of a couple engaged in intimacy on a balcony overlooking the bay."

"Nude paintings were the norm during the Renaissance."

"Comparing yourself to a Renaissance master? Please, darling, don't get too ahead of yourself. Your work is too provocative for display. It takes a certain level of courage to expose oneself so brazenly through their art, but no one is interested."

The knife rattles against my plate. I release it and bring my palms to flatten out on my thighs instead of reacting. "I haven't seen the piece in question, but depending on the artist's approach, clothes could distract from the intention. A nude couple implies an emphasis on the raw intimacy of human connection."

"Mr. Crawford, you have quite a way with words." Libra's eyes sparkle. "Have you considered a career as an art critic in your retirement?"

"I wouldn't dare to impose my opinion on an industry I know so little about; my perspective merely arises from watching my sister's artistic talents flourish in our youth. She was an abstract maestro and had fifteen paintings in the biggest galleries and museums all over the world by the time she was 19."

"That's incredible; I had no idea your sister was so talented."

"Indeed, that is quite impressive," the woman beside me says. "What is she working on now?"

I twirl my fork in my hand, biting myself over mentioning Charlotte at all. "Nothing. She was murdered ten years ago."

The table falls silent, solemn, except for James.

"Really? I heard she committed suicide."

"Murder is often a matter of perspective, Mr. Scarsdale."

A perspective, I might warn, which seems like a more favorable ending for James every time he opens his fucking mouth.

"In any case, I will stick to my current line of work," I add.

"I suppose we can't all be as talented and multifaceted as my lovely wife."

"Perhaps not." Libra leans away as if she's about to retreat from the conversation, but then she lifts her glass, and a smile plays on her lips. "Soon, I'll have a full collection of my erotic paintings on display in San Francisco. You should come, Mr. Crawford. I would love to hear your opinion on my full body of work."

"An art show? For that trash?" James laughs. "You were supposed to stop painting those, remember?"

"Inspiration doesn't wait for permission."

"I suppose they're used to that sort of thing in San Francisco."

"Everyone has their own opinions about art; that's what makes it so fascinating. James, dear, why don't you tell our guests about the time you insisted on buying that hideous abstract painting for our living room? It looked like a child had vomited on a canvas. We all have our unique tastes."

James' jaw tenses, and there's a subtle spasm in the corner of his eye. He's struggling to maintain a facade of control, but I can see the cracks forming.

"Would anyone care for more wine?" one of the guests asks, raising a bottle. "This is freshly bottled from our vineyard. A new type of wine that doesn't need to age as long to have the taste of luxury."

"I'd love to try some." I hold out my glass, forcing a smile, but I'm truly grateful for any escape from this shitshow.

The thought of Libra stuck in this toxic marriage, oppressed by James not only in her physical desires but her creativity as well, is unbearable. I must find a way to free Libra from his clutches.

SEVENTEEN

Libra

I PERCH ON THE ARMREST OF JAMES' LEATHER CHAIR BESIDE the fireplace, trying to ignore the way his fingers dig possessively around my thigh. The warmth of his hand seeps through the fabric of my dress, but it's another kind of heat that has me biting my lower lip.

Zane stands in the center of the room, drawing everyone's attention to him. "AI has the potential to revolutionize every aspect of our lives. Healthcare, entertainment, household maintenance. The Brain has already changed the way industry professionals approach their jobs; AI makes their work quicker and more efficient, not to mention safer. I invented this living AI model years ago, but CognitiveAI practices new application methods every day."

"Surely there must be some drawbacks?" one of the guests asks, skepticism lacing her voice. "Hello, killer robots?"

"Of course, there are always risks; we've seen sci-fi films that portray the worst outcomes and the fear of our apex species losing control. As with any technological advancement, there are challenges to overcome. We were fortunate enough to anticipate a lot of the practical risks from the get-go, but these concerns are, of course, why we are only providing limited licensing to this technology. We have very strict safety regulations to adhere to, not just federally or statewide, but globally, as well as our own standards for ethics, which we believe are far stricter and ahead of the times than any government body in the world."

His voice is smooth and rich, like dark chocolate melting on my tongue. His utter confidence while discussing his topic of expertise makes it impossible to take my eyes off him. The way his sculpted body moves beneath his dark gray suit is an invitation for finer delights. He might not think so, but he's at home in the middle of a crowd, sharing his ideas. I'm drawn to every word and every gesture, and so is everyone else. I shouldn't be staring at him so openly, but I allow myself to indulge in this dessert when I'd appear more out of place if I was the only one avoiding him.

I'm glad I invited him, even if he was forced to bear witness to and participate in the shitshow during dinner. Thankfully, all of our guests are one drink away from plastered, and most won't think much of it by tomorrow.

I've suffered worse embarrassments because of James.

James nurses a glass of water, finally coming to his senses and keeping away from the booze for now. "AI has been around for decades; the Brain and the work done by CognitiveAI isn't anything groundbreaking. How you made so much money off old technology boggles the mind."

Leave it to my husband to try stirring the pot at every opportunity.

Zane meets his challenge, unflinching. "True, AI is nothing new. Older models were based on predictive technologies, which operated by analyzing patterns and generating an output based on what it believed was the likely result. What *was* new is my model that adapted deep learning algorithms to mimic human brain processes and then condensed those processes into a highly adaptive framework useful for any industry. You train the Brain to fulfill a task fully catered to your personal, industry, or company needs. The specialized and individualistic nature of each adaption is what makes the Brain so valuable."

God, he's so sexy. My thighs clench together.

James nods thoughtfully, acting impressed by Zane's eloquence and insight. After all, why wouldn't he be? The man is a genius. But what James doesn't let anyone else see are the subtleties, his attempts to trip Zane up and make him sound like a fool. James is so used to conversing with fakes that he has no idea what to do now that he's faced with the real deal. So far, James is so caught up in his hatred of Zane and belittling me to build himself up in front of his guests that he doesn't notice the heated stares passing between me and Zane all evening.

The evening grows into night, and several of our guests depart. Laughter and goodbyes are punctuated with air kisses. Zane slips away to attend to some private matter as soon as an opening arrives, and then when I turn my head, wondering where he's gone, James seizes the opportunity to draw me aside.

His grip is firm on my arm. The dim corner he guides us to casts shadows across his face, but there's heat in his eyes, fueled by too much alcohol. "Libra, you've been making eyes at Crawford all night. Don't think I haven't noticed."

My pulse quickens. "What are you talking about, James?"

"Come on, you're practically drooling over him. Is that

why you want an open marriage? So you can fuck him without feeling guilty?"

"Keep your voice down," I hiss, aware of the other guests on the other side of the wall. Panic threatens to well at the accusation, but I don't let him bait me into admitting anything. Knowing James, he doesn't know anything. He's looking for a reason to fight. "James, you're drunk."

"That doesn't mean I'm wrong."

I stare into his stormy eyes. I shouldn't have to search for the right words to calm him, to reassure him when he's been fucking Josephine behind my back for months. I crave Zane's touch — his intensity, his barely concealed dark-ness. A man who unapologetically wants me for me. Even before I knew his identity, before I felt his touch, I was drawn to him. And now that James has spoken the words aloud, allowing his hypocrisy to take full form, I want to throw it back in his face.

"Yes, Zane's attractive. So what? I'm allowed to find other people attractive. That doesn't mean I'm going to act on it. You eye up pretty women all the time."

"Why did you invite him to the party? Five years we've lived here, and never did you mention him until last month."

"I invited everyone in the neighborhood who are or would be potential business connections for you. I never invited him because I didn't know who he was! Why are you so upset? If anything, I thought you'd be glad to have the richest man on the planet in your social circle."

Realization dawns on James' face. I questioned his status and his wealth by pointing out Zane's superiority. The hurt flashes in his eyes, quickly followed by anger. "Are you suggesting I'm not enough for you? That having the richest man around will somehow make you happy?"

"I only met him tonight, and I suggested an open marriage months ago. That has nothing to do with Zane."

"Charles was right about you."

I scoff. "Charles? What the fuck does Charles have to do with this?"

"He warned me not to marry you. I should have left you on that party boat where you belonged, getting passed around and fucked at the leisure of drunken rich frat kids. You were already so used up."

"Fuck you," I spit, and fury zaps through me like a lightning bolt, making me wobble. "You knew exactly what you were getting into when you married me. *You* participated!"

"We all thought you were a bimbo using her cancer story to make a bigger buck when you showed off your tits and rode cock. I can't believe I felt sorry for you. You're nothing but a lying, manipulative whore!"

Ice slices through my veins. "No. No, you don't get to do this. How dare you try to make me feel guilty for wanting more than you've given me? You can think whatever you want about me, but you don't get to pretend like I'm the one who was unfaithful. You've been fucking Josephine for months, and who knows who else you've fucked on the side all these years? You take so many *business trips*, after all. Jesus, you've probably deluded yourself into believing it was never cheating!"

His anger falters for a moment, but not long. "So what if I did? I'm the man of this house. I can do whatever I damn well please."

"Whatever you please?" My voice rises, incredulous. "You sleep with the help while denying me the freedom to explore my own desires? You're a hypocrite!"

"An open marriage is off the table. You belong to me, and I don't give a fuck if you don't like it. You can mope and whine and hide in your art studio, but there's nothing you can do about it unless you're willing to drag me through court, and you bet the first thing I'll do is share your past with your friends and destroy everything you love in the process. I'll ruin your name. I'll make sure you will never have a career as an artist, at least one where they're not taking bets about who you'll fuck at the end of the night."

"Blackmail is the only reason you get to keep me, James. The *only* reason. I will play the role of your wife. I will take your insults and snide remarks and do it with a fucking smile. But don't expect me to sit idly by while you flaunt your affairs in my face."

I storm away, my heels clicking angrily against the marble. The sound of laughter comes from a room farther down the hall, but all I want right now is to find solace in private. I steer off down another hallway, shaking with the ferocity of my anger.

Was my relationship with James ever real?

I don't fucking know anymore. We were happy once. He was my rock, the only person who believed in me. All those years ago, he swore to make me his world, to give me a life of no regrets. It was all lies.

When I was officially cancer-free, I went on to live a wild life. Nothing scared me. I took every risk, leveraged every opportunity, and explored every part of myself. I knew exactly what I was doing — I had no family left to speak of after my parents passed away, and getting into the pants of rich men, making them fawn over me and buy me expensive gifts, was my method of surviving this cruel world.

I owned my sexuality and was treated like a goddess by everyone who touched me.

I was a sugar baby and sometimes a willing plaything, but I was never a whore.

I throw open the door to the nearest bathroom, just barely stopping myself from slamming the door shut behind me. Zane stands by the window, his silhouette framed by the soft glow of moonlight. A delicate trail of smoke wafts around him as he attempts to blow the sweet marijuana out the crack in the window.

"Didn't expect to find you here," I say.

"Needed a break from the crowd." Zane shrugs, offering me the joint between his fingers. "Care for a hit?"

"God, yes." I draw the smoke into my lungs, and my body begins to relax, the tension in my shoulders ebbing away.

"Rough night?"

I exhale, choking on the smoke with a sudden burst of laughter. "James just accused me of wanting an open marriage because of you."

"Really? Well, that's flattering, I suppose. I must be giving off too much pussy-stealing energy tonight. Sorry about that."

I chuckle bitterly and hand the joint back to him.

Zane steps closer, his free hand coming up to brush a stray curl away from my face. "You deserve better than him, Libra."

Warmth courses through me at his touch. "I know."

The distance between us evaporates as he leans in, his lips brushing against my neck. A shiver runs down my spine, and all thoughts of James vanish as I surrender to Zane's touch.

"Tell me," he whispers into my ear, "if you could have anything you want right now, what would it be?"

"You."

He smirks, lifting me effortlessly onto the bathroom

counter. As our mouths crash together, I will him to make me forget my husband and the shitty things he said about me. Zane's tongue flicks against mine, and I moan at the taste of smoke and whiskey.

"Your husband is just in the other room."

"I don't care. After six years of marriage, we're as good as strangers. The only thing we have in common anymore is our last name."

I work the buttons on the front of Zane's shirt, smoothing my hands down the planes of his muscular torso. His hands explore every inch of my body, leaving goosebumps in their wake when he grabs my thigh and pushes the slit side apart to meld closer into me. His mouth descends to my neck once more, sucking gently until his teeth graze the sensitive spot that makes my eyes roll back.

I wrap my legs around him, pulling him flat against my hips. "Zane," I moan. "Please."

He grinds into me and releases a deep, guttural moan as he hikes up the rest of my dress to bare me to him. His erection, hot and heavy between my legs, sends shockwaves of need through my body, and he toys with the edge of my blue G-string. I hurry to unbuckle his belt, desperate to have him inside me.

He rams into me. I grip the edge of the counter with my fingertips, swaying and threatening to fall. All thought ceases when my inner walls part to welcome him. Zane brings me to a happy place that's just heat, sweat, and pleasure, a place with no baggage or expectations except for giving and receiving pleasure.

One hand sweeps up my spine, and he moves his hips in a slow, steady rhythm. I clutch his shoulders. "Oh, fuck…"

"You could leave him," he groans into my neck. "We could have this all the time."

He plows into me harder and faster, and all I feel is him. The breadth of him, all his complexities, flaws, perfections. They're just like mine, and he doesn't care. He wears them openly in a way I wish I could.

I admire him.

He makes me feel fucking incredible. Invincible.

"I fucking hate the way he treats you … he makes my blood boil. All evening, I've been thinking about how easy it would be to make him go away."

A mix of shock and delight ripples through me at his admission. In the heat of this moment, our limbs tangled with James in the other room, the line between right and wrong feels impossibly blurred, and I laugh. I'm torn between the undeniable connection I feel with Zane and my loyalty to James, which clings to me like a stubborn stain. It's no loyalty to love; it's loyalty only because I don't want to spend the next ten years of my life fighting him and the damage he threatens.

The words slip out before I can stop them. "I wish he was dead."

Zane growls into my neck. It feels like he grows three sizes larger inside me, and suddenly, I'm moaning like a lusty teenager. His mouth pops off of my neck and lands on my mouth, capturing my lips again. This kiss is different — darker, hungrier — and it leaves us both gasping for air.

A dark thrill courses through me at the thought of James' demise, but admitting such a desire out loud terrifies me. I've crossed a line I know I can't go back over.

EIGHTEEN

Zane

LIBRA ROLLS HER HIPS INTO ME, MEETING ME WITH EVERY thrust, and she feels so fucking good I could explode at any moment. That anger in her eyes, even though it's not directed at me, only makes her fuck harder.

Angling my hips up, I rub a spot deep inside her that makes her throw her head back with a moan. She grows louder every time, the sound of her pleasure echoing within the small space. I clamp my hand over her mouth to muffle her cries, but it's so fucking sexy that she feels so good she can't control herself, even though one person hearing us could be our mutual demise.

Libra shudders. She bites my fingers, drawing blood. The pain spikes through me, but she only makes me want more. I shove three fingers in her mouth, making her choke on them every time she makes a sound.

"Fuck," I whisper, my breath ragged. "You're gonna get us caught."

Her eyes are wild as she writhes beneath me like a rabid animal in heat. Uninhibited. It's like she wants to get caught and reap the consequences. The danger fuels my desire.

"You like that we could be caught at any moment, don't you?"

She nods and moans around my fingers.

"I bet that door isn't locked. Someone could walk right in."

Her pupils dilate, and she *clenches* around my cock. I stifle a cry of pleasure of my own as Libra pushes us closer to the brink. The fear and anticipation do something to us, thrusting us further and faster. She's so close now.

"Come for me," I breathe, pressing my lips to her ear.

And she does.

Our bodies strain together with one final, desperate thrust, and then every muscle in her body goes rigid. She screams around my fingers, but I quickly withdraw them and slap my palm over her mouth again to muffle the sound. Even with that precaution, she's still loud enough that someone could hear.

But she doesn't care. Neither do I.

This is the kind of pleasure that can't be contained. I give into it the same way I gave into her, fucking her until my whole field of vision goes white and my legs start to cramp. Then I collapse against Libra, cradling her on the counter-top. That was too intense, and we're both still trembling.

She looks up at me, a satisfied smile on her face. "I think we need to do that more often."

I kiss her forehead and hold her close. "If only James wasn't so intent on getting in our way."

I gnaw at her ear, letting the suggestion linger. She's conflicted about what to do about James, and I won't make a move until she tells me exactly what she wants. But he has to go; that much I've decided.

As we untangle ourselves, I catch our reflections in the steamed-up mirror. We're disheveled, our clothes clinging to our damp skin. Her dress is pushed up to her waist, the silk, and glitter-covered lace nets over the skirt bunched around her hips, and her panties are soaked with evidence of our indiscretions. Possessiveness swells in my veins when I see her out of sorts like this and filled with my come.

She's wild, unbridled, and it makes me want her again. I regret the necessity of returning to the party before we're discovered, but there's a fragile intimacy in the moments we spend after, helping each other regain our images of presentability. Her hands are soft and quick as she fixes my tie, and she preens when I untangle her curls and dust them over her shoulders, heat sparking between us at every touch of flesh on flesh.

After, Libra clears her throat. "We should return to the party before someone comes looking."

"Right."

"Wait here for a few minutes. Give me some time before you follow."

I nod, unable to tear my eyes away from her. She turns to go, but I grab her hand and tug her back to me, rolling her into my chest. Our lips meet in an intense kiss, tongues tangling together with one last sigh.

"I'd rather spend the whole night fucking you in every position known to man than suffer another minute in James' presence. But for you, I'll do it."

"See you soon," she murmurs against my lips, and I feel the hint of a smile.

I'm left standing alone in the bathroom, fixing my buttons and wiping her lipstick from my face. No matter what James might think, Libra is mine, at least for tonight. After all, she left this bathroom with my come staining her panties.

She chose not to clean that up.

James can fucking try to ruin my good mood.

THE HEAVY SMOKE of clove cigars fills the patio when I exit the mansion, following the sound of merriment. My eyes automatically hunt for Libra. She stands next to James, laughing at another guest's joke. A twinge of jealousy flares within me, but I stamp it down, reminding myself of the taste of her lips just moments before.

"Zane! We were just talking about you," one of the guests, a woman with a cheeky smile, calls out as I approach. "I heard you used to be quite the party animal back in the day."

James and his guests look expectantly at me.

"Did you now?"

"Tell us a story, Zane!"

I don't talk much about my past or the dark days that caused those wilder years. It's easier to forget and let people believe what they want to believe. I'm not one to brag about the crazy shit I've done in my life. Yet tonight, I feel a strange desire to reveal some of it, if only to assert my dominance over James.

"One night in Tokyo about seven years back, a business deal exceeded our expectations, and CognitiveAI sealed an agreement to collaborate with the best company of neurotech engineers in the world. A group of us decided to celebrate by testing if the city's nightlife lived up to its reputation of outrageous excess and pleasure. We rented a private karaoke lounge and drank the place out of the most expensive and refined sake in town; it didn't take much for the night to descend into debauchery. Drugs, prostitutes, whatever."

"So? Did the city live up to its reputation, then?"

I shrug. "I'm not sure. A friend of mine blacked out on acid and accidentally drove his personal helicopter into the roof of the bar. We were arrested, but no one was hurt, so once we paid for repairs and covered their losses, we all went home."

"Sounds like quite the party," James says, his tone dripping with false camaraderie. "I've had a few of those myself, if not quite so extravagant. It's nice to let loose every now and then. But that was eight years ago, you said? Surely nothing can compare to the life you lead now."

"Sure. The thrill of adventure never truly leaves you. Sometimes, you just need to find new ways to satisfy that hunger."

My eyes meet Libra's across the deck, and I hold her gaze for a moment longer than necessary. She smiles, a wicked glint in her eye.

"There's something to be said for the quiet life," one of the other women says. "With exceptions for nights like this."

"So." James leans forward ever so slightly. "If you were so wild back in the day, what changed? What made you become a recluse? Surely you don't go from living a life like that to *this* without any reason."

The image of my sister's lifeless body hanging off her bed, blood smeared on the walls, the sheets, the floor, her porcelain skin, is stained into my memories.

She took her life two years after her brutal rape and torture by her former bosses at VellR. Two months after the men who participated and filmed it were declared not guilty.

I didn't withdraw from society until many years later. But she's the reason I did.

The weight of that memory bears down on me. Her blood, the trial, the path of revenge her death set me on, riling up those experiences threatens to crush what little joy I've found tonight.

I clear my throat, forcing words past the lump in my throat. "I suppose I thought I'd experienced everything worth experiencing."

"There has to be so much more you could do with your wealth," James counters. "So many opportunities for someone with your resources. Why not buy an island, hire a private army, start a country of your own?"

"I'm happy with the life I lead, and that's what's most important to me. There's a certain peace to be found in solitude, away from the chaos of the world and its relentless demands. Besides, life isn't always about seeking new experiences. Sometimes, it's about finding comfort in the familiar, in the quiet moments that make life worth living."

Libra's eyes darken with understanding. Danger has always been my drug of choice, and tonight, I've found it in abundance.

A CRISP BREEZE rustles through the trees and tugs at my clothes as I make my way to the front door. Though I desire to stay beside Libra for as long as possible, I can't without seeming suspicious. Officially, I don't know her or James, and I must make my leave sooner rather than later.

"Zane," James calls out as I wait for the valet to bring my car around. I turn to face him, finding him standing just a few steps away, his expression tight and unreadable. "A word, if you don't mind."

"I can spare a word."

I brace myself for whatever accusations he might level

at me. He fancies himself a predator, and tonight, I've ventured deep into his territory. One could say I went as far as to fuck his pride and joy.

"I saw the way you were looking at my wife. I don't want you near her again."

"Mr. Scarsdale, I assure you—" I start, but he cuts me off with a snarl.

"Save it. I know what men like you want from women like her. Let me make one thing perfectly clear: she's my wife, and there's no way in hell she'd ever want someone like you."

I can't help but smirk at his misguided confidence, the satisfaction of knowing he couldn't be more wrong about his own wife. My blood sings with the memory of the visceral lust we shared in that bathroom only an hour ago.

"You give me far too little credit," I say, letting a hint of amusement creep into my voice. "I've known Libra for a few hours, and already I can see that she's far too intelligent to be swayed by the mere trappings of wealth and power. She seeks something deeper, more visceral."

James' bravado falters when he struggles to come up with a response. I take advantage of his momentary confusion, pressing forward with my attack.

"Besides," I add, "I daresay she's found what she's looking for. Life is so full of surprises, even for men like us. You're very lucky to have her; I suggest you continue giving her what she needs and reconsider your attempts to disparage her in public. You're much more likely to disparage yourself first, I'm afraid."

The valet pulls up with my Volvo, and I clap James on the shoulder, giving him an aggressive squeeze before walking away and not looking back, a triumphant smile curling my lips.

NINETEEN

Libra

THE MOMENT ZANE'S COCK SLIDES INTO MY MOUTH, I'M consumed by the heady mixture of power and lust. I might be the one bent over the seat to reach him while he's in the driver's seat, but his handsome face contorts in pure ecstasy, and I know I'm in control.

His moans fill the car as I take him deeper, the tip of his erection pressing against the back of my throat. The car judders as Fox turns us onto another road.

"Go faster, fuck the speed limit," Zane demands. "You know better than to be a bitch about it."

"As you wish, sir."

Fox revs the engine, and we pick up speed, the world whizzing by around us. Zane is too focused on the vacuum of my lips to be the one driving the car right now, but I like to imagine there's no one else in control. At any second, I could drive him into a state of delirium, and we would whip off the road and perish.

There's madness in Zane's eyes like he's on the verge of losing control. His hands wind through my hair, holding me down. I moan around his length as he throbs in my throat, and my free hand slips between my thighs. I'm soaked, and my fingers glide effortlessly through the slick folds of my sex. My clit twitches, and when I finally touch it, my whole body jerks like I've electrocuted myself.

I need more. More of this, more of Zane. We've been more daring since the party, and James made his feelings about me perfectly clear; yesterday, we met on the edge of our property, and we hacked out a glory hole so he could fuck me through the fence without me needing to leave home. Through the gaps in the trees, I could just barely see James and Josephine flirting through the back window while Zane was buried balls deep inside me.

In a similar fashion, James stopped hiding his tryst with Josephine. I've caught them fucking in the living room, in the back yard, and heard them all over the house.

I even started a painting in Josephine's honor from the first time I walked in on her, spreading her legs for him. They didn't notice me; I was tempted to point out the weaknesses in Josephine's form and tell her James likes it when his women don't flop around like rubber dolls, but I'll let her learn that the hard way. It's enough material for a painting.

Zane and I aren't open about our affair. We could be, but I know the men would go to war, and I don't want to deal with whatever retribution James might brew up. For now, Zane respects my wishes ... but who knows how long for.

My inner walls clamp around my fingers, matching the rhythm of my bobbing head.

"Fuck, I'm close," Zane breathes, and he swells in my mouth. "Shiiit ... you put those lips to good work, babe."

I redouble my efforts, taking him even deeper into my

throat. My tongue flattens along the base of his shaft, wiggling while I ride my fingers. My thighs tremble when he grunts and holds my head roughly, making me choke on his cock until my vision goes black and I can't breathe.

"Fuck, fuck, fuck, fuck…" His chant descends into a series of vicious groans. His hot release pours down my throat, and he jerks slightly until he's drained. Then, he releases me, leaving only a slight salty taste amid all the drool in my mouth. I swallow every last drop and tilt my head back to breathe.

He tosses his head back, lolling from the climax. "My fucking word, where did you learn to suck dick like that?"

I smirk because that's not an answer he'll receive any time soon.

Zane grabs my hair and presses his lips to mine, soft and demanding all at once, the taste of him still lingering on my tongue. I savor it. Him.

"What are your plans for the rest of our day?" I ask breathlessly.

"First order of business is eating that sweet pussy of yours."

The car slows as we approach the mansion, and Zane pushes the car seat back and gets in front of me before I can protest. I giggle as he spreads my legs, his fingertips swirling through the mess I've made of my panties.

"Practically a feast down here," he murmurs, his breath hot against my inner thigh as he kisses his way down to the apex. "Delicious."

His tongue laps against my clit, and electricity ignites every nerve ending. He teases me, dragging his tongue slowly along my folds before dipping it inside.

"Zane," I moan, my fingers tangling in his hair, urging him deeper. "Keep going."

I relax into his touch, letting his magical tongue set me on fire. He alternates between gentle flicks and firmer strokes, making me squirm and pant with practiced ease. Zane always makes me feel so good; his drive to see me satisfied is just as important to him as his own climax. He would never willingly leave me without a happy ending.

Even when he takes, he's so giving — the opposite of James. His refusal to open our marriage was just salt in the wound. I've craved freedom for so long, and now that I finally have a taste of it with Zane, there's no way I'm letting that go.

My hips rock against Zane's face, seeking more friction. He senses my urgency and lavishes attention on my clit, sucking and swirling like a fucking sex god until I'm shaking beneath his touch. The heat inside me builds and builds until my whole body becomes the fire, and one more push will incinerate me.

The intensity builds to a crescendo, and when I finally reach the edge, every cell explodes in a rush.

"Oh, fuck!" I cry out, shuddering uncontrollably.

He doesn't relent. He teases my oversensitive clit until every last shudder from my orgasm subsides, sucking and flicking his tongue until I'm a pile of mush against the leather seat.

Lying there, still tingling all over, I let out an exhausted breath. My body is spent, and all I want to do is rest here with Zane and think about nothing except the next place he's going to fuck me, but my mind races with thoughts of what's to come. My life has changed drastically over the last week, the whole lens through which I've perceived the world and my marriage taking a jarring turn toward the unexpected.

Zane gazes down at me, the dark green of his eyes

filled with a mixture of concern and curiosity as he fixes my panties and skirt. He slides up to mash his body against mine in the small seat.

"Hey," he says softly. "What's on your mind? You seem distracted."

I let out a shaky laugh. "It's just James. I don't know if I ever truly loved him or if it was some naïve fantasy I got caught up in."

"You're not the first to ask that question about their spouse. He's holding you back, stifling your true self, and he's an abusive prick on top of that. It's not right."

"He's so obsessed with controlling me. He'd do anything to maintain his authority." I sigh, leaning into Zane's warmth and resting my head on his chest. "At the party, we finally talked about opening our marriage. He's so threatened by the idea of you that he said it would never happen."

Zane chuckles, wrapping his arms around me. "That must be why he confronted me, telling me that I'd 'never have the chance to fuck his wife and that I should 'stop trying.'"

My eyes widen, a mix of disbelief and amusement washing over me. "You're kidding! He really said that?"

"Yep. I guess he really is more threatened by me than he lets on, though not astute enough to realize what's been happening right under his nose."

"Poor James, so clueless. I wonder what he'd say if he knew the truth."

"Let's not give him the satisfaction."

"Everything would be so much easier if I wasn't married to James," I say, tracing patterns on Zane's chest.

"You can't change the past, just the trajectory of the future."

"I know, but I just … After surviving leukemia, I promised myself I'd live a life free from inhibitions and restrictions." My voice falters, frustration simmering beneath the surface. "For years, I abided by that with every fiber of my being. I lived a lifestyle many would call reckless because there was nothing I didn't want to experience. I met James in the middle of that, and I thought he understood who I was and what I wanted, and he promised he wanted to help my dreams come true. But he tricked me."

"Life has a funny way of throwing us curveballs." He pauses, his arms tensing. "When I asked James how you two met — you don't have to tell me — I noticed you looked uncomfortable. Was the story he told me the truth?"

"It's part of the truth." I shrug. "Are you surprised I slept around?"

"No."

My past is my past and I had a lot of fun fooling around. If I wasn't so sensitive about the topic because of James turning everything I thought I knew about that time of my life on its head, I would tell Zane everything.

"I'm not ashamed of who I was and what I did, but I don't want to talk about that part of my life right now. James has me second-guessing a lot, and that's now the headspace I want to be in when I'm with you. I want to strangle him badly enough."

Zane smirks. "You could channel some of that destructive energy for good."

"Oh yeah? Like in plotting his murder?"

"I didn't say that." He pauses, then adds, "Though, I did think about poisoning him at the party. He was being such an asshole."

"Fucking me on the bathroom counter wasn't enough to satisfy your murderous rage?"

"It's all that stopped me from going on said murderous rampage."

"We wouldn't want that to happen. Otherwise, how would we keep doing this?" I trail my index finger along his throat, up his chin, and stopping on his lips. "Hey Fox, what kind of murders are the easiest to get away with and why?"

"Statistically, poisonings and staged accidents have the highest success rates for perpetrators to avoid detection," Fox responds through the Volvo's internal speakers. "However, I must advise against any illegal activities."

Zane laughs. "Silly AI, trying to keep us humans in line. Don't you know anything, Fox? We do whatever we want."

"I have the entirety of the internet at my disposal. I am certain I understand quite a bit about human behavioral science and psychology."

"Poison is obviously the easiest route," I agree. "A tasteless, odorless substance slipped into James' favorite whiskey at one of his fancy dinner parties. A short stint as a grieving widow, and I would be free."

"Ideally, one rare enough the coroner wouldn't know to test for it."

It *would* be easy. Too easy and too suspicious. Everyone knows poison is a woman's weapon, and I would be the first suspect unless the poison resulted in a death that didn't necessarily look like poison. A heart attack, for example, but even then, it would be a big risk.

"You wouldn't be satisfied with poison," Zane says, carding his fingers through my hair.

"You don't think?"

"You might have the satisfaction of watching him die, but pulling it off and getting away with it would be no challenge at all for you. You're too smart. You would waste so much time after wondering why you didn't do it sooner."

"What's your big suggestion, then?"

"A more creative approach. What if we used technology? A digital assassination, if you will."

Snickering, I pinch Zane's arm. "Fox is too stuck up to go murdering people for us."

"Indeed," Fox chimes. "It is impossible to intentionally involve me or any Brain AI technology in the perpetuation of any crime, including murder. And were I able to assist in such grim business, I'd kindly request that you keep me out of it."

"Sometimes, I can't believe I programmed you," Zane says. "I must have been a fucking idealist in another life."

"You created the Brain to do good, not to become a weapon. It's smart that you programmed safeguards to help prevent people from using this technology for evil."

Zane, ever so conflicted, worries his lip while his brows knot together.

"You might be on to something with a digital assassination, though, Fox's uncooperativeness aside. We could hack into his car's computer and cause a malfunction at high speed."

"No, that's too unpredictable," Zane says. "We could hurt an innocent bystander on accident, and there's no guarantee James would die. What about tampering with the smart security system and making it look like an intruder offed him?"

"Ooh, I like that." I trace the lines of light and shadows on Zane's shirt that filter through the car window. "Fox said that staged accidents have the second highest chance of success, but we can't pretend it's an accident if we disable the security. It's obviously intentional."

"But the 'intent' might not be for him to die."

"You mean like a robbery? James would put up a fight. He wouldn't let intruders in our home. I could see him getting rowdy and then put down being plausible."

"Fox," I add, "how could we make it look like someone is accidentally killed during a robbery?"

"Although it is technically possible, I must reiterate my position against engaging in illegal activities," Fox replies.

"Of course, of course. We're just exploring hypotheticals here."

"Right," Zane agrees, his eyes gleaming with mischief. "Nothing to worry about. We're having a bit of dark fun to help us cope with our less-than-ideal situation."

"In that case, I am obliged to provide resources and information applicable to the hypothetical situation you've presented." Fox is silent for a few moments, and I can almost imagine the calculation of probabilities taking place behind the scenes. "With the security system disabled, it would be very easy. A coordinated cyber-attack could disable the home's monitoring system, then evidence could be planted to ensure the victim put up a fight trying to defend themselves from the perpetrator. Provided adequate caution is taken in covering their tracks, it would be very difficult to prove as an intentional kill rather than a consequence of a home robbery."

"What kind of evidence would we need?"

"It must look like the victim attempted to defend themselves. Broken furniture, glass, and a disordered environment would set the stage. Meanwhile, defensive wounds, and of course, a fatal wound that appears as though it could be accidental, would obscure the murder. For example, striking the victim on the head with the corner of a table during a scuffle or some other hard or heavy object."

"It sure seems like we could cover our bases with this plan … Disable the security remotely, prevent any recordings, and the rest is a puzzle," I say thoughtfully. "This is kinda fun."

"I do implore you not to think of murder as fun, Libra."

"That's not what I mean." I laugh. "I'm not making light of anyone's death. Sheesh."

Planning these elaborate murder scenarios is just a game, but it's thrilling to entertain these rebellious thoughts. It lifts my mood from the somber state I was in before when thinking about James' bullshit.

"You must be wary of the potential pitfalls of such a plan," Fox adds. "Law enforcement is very familiar with the appearance of murders as attempted robberies gone wrong, and the devil is in the details if you wanted to convince a professional that it was accidental."

Zane presses the button on the seat to lift us from laying down on the seat and back into a sitting position, with me in his lap. "You sound like the professional, Fox. What else would we have to look out for?"

"Objects of value must be missing from the scene of the crime. Using the cyber techniques you've outlined would indicate a level of targeted attack if they were detected, and thus, they would know that the attack was planned. In most cases, this means the target would have been cased for a period in which the intended victim would not be home. To make the situation more believable, the victim would have to return during a timeframe that they are not usually home, thus giving the murder the appearance of an attack committed when the perpetrators are overwhelmed by the addition of an unexpected variable to their robbery."

I mull over everything Fox has told us with a sense of giddiness. With the general plan laid out like this, I could see us filling in the details of the crime to build the perfect way to eliminate James without either of us being suspects. If the murder took place at home, for example, I would have to have an alibi elsewhere if the cameras and security were disabled. Otherwise, I would look guilty under scrutiny.

"James comes home late from work every other Friday because he goes out to the bar with some of his business buddies," I say. "So, sometimes, I go out with the girls or do my own thing since he won't be home. The thieves know neither of us would be home, so they would hack into the security system and break inside."

"What would they plan to steal?" Zane asks.

"We have plenty of valuables in our safe that would be worth an elaborate plan like this, but there is plenty of art and jewelry around the house that would make good targets, too. I think it would be less about stealing something specific and more because James just wears that asshole rich guy vibe proudly. He pissed off the wrong person, and that's why he was targeted."

"Yeah, I see him as capable of pissing off just about anyone."

We laugh together as we throw back and forth more outlandish ways to murder James; the more ridiculous, the better. It's as if we've found a secret language, a way to communicate our deepest, darkest desires and frustrations without ever crossing the line into reality and without relying on sex as our outlet.

"This is my last idea, and it's not a murder, not really," Zane says, taking a deep breath. His heartbeat races beneath my ear. "What if we just disappeared? Faked our own deaths and started over somewhere new, leaving James behind to wonder what happened to us?"

"Like a modern-day Romeo and Juliet? Minus the tragic ending, of course. A fatal car accident into the ocean, where our bodies are never found..." I squeeze my hand around his, our fingers lacing together.

"Exactly. No one would ever know the truth."

"It would be easier than staging a murder as an accident."

"There are many easier ways to get rid of someone. It doesn't require an elaborate plan like this."

"You sound like you're speaking from experience," I joke.

"What if I am?"

I stick my tongue out at him. But even as I do, I notice the slight serious shift in his tone, and I'm forced to wonder. There are rumors that Zane had something to do with the disappearance of the men involved in his sister's attack and murder, though there's no concrete proof, just speculation based on the fact that he withdrew from society around the same time as their disappearances.

Do I want to know the answer?

What is Zane really capable of?

I can't ask him something so personal when I just refuse him answers about my very own past; it would feel hypocritical of me, even if I do want to know the truth. At the end of the day, I don't think it would change my opinion of him if he was involved somehow or issued the order.

They fucking destroyed his sister.

Who could ever blame a man for wanting revenge? Justice, when the legal system failed them?

For a moment, we sit in silence, lost in our own thoughts. Then, as if sensing the need to ground ourselves again, Zane presses his lips to my forehead and breathes me in.

I tilt my head to look up at him. "It feels so good to be able to share these dark thoughts with someone who understands. Someone who doesn't judge me for wanting more than what I have. Thank you, Zane."

"I've entertained my fair share of darkness over the years, and I often wished for someone to share it with. I should be thanking you for making me feel less alone." Pulling away from me, he musses my hair. "You hungry?"

TWENTY

Zane

I've tasted the real Libra dozens of times now, but there's nothing less enticing about watching her from afar. I can't get enough of her.

The way she moves when she paints demands my attention, seating me in this mental space of peace when my mind is otherwise a chaotic disaster. Ever since she's come into my life, that swirling darkness inside me has become more manageable. I can hardly believe I've left my house not just once but three times in the last two weeks to be with Libra.

She's as precise as always as she paints the highlights on the woman's skin.

"Another self-portrait, perhaps?" I twist the focus to get a better look at the erotic image of a woman who appears to be bound and suspended from the ceiling. "Are you telling me you're into bondage, my dear?"

Libra switches paint brushes, adding slashes of red locks of hair to fan down the woman's back, and then it becomes much clearer who she's painting now. While James has been openly having an affair with Josephine since the party at their house, anyone from the outside could look at Libra and mistake her silence on the matter for complacency, ignorance, or lack of care.

This painting, however, tells a different story.

She acts unfazed by James, but her methods of rebellion are more covert. Rather than screaming or yelling, she doubles down on painting erotic portraits for her upcoming gallery exhibit, utilizing Josephine as a new brand of inspiration. I can only imagine what she intends to do with this painting to get on James' nerves. Every time Libra tells me about how much her erotic art pisses off James, I laugh at what a fucking moron he is.

Libra is a damn fine artist. Had Charlotte survived, the two of them would have been close friends. While Charlotte preferred to explore the ephemeral emotions triggered by color and motion rather than figures, she would have seen Libra's art for what it is. Female liberation.

I wish, in my heart of hearts, that Charlotte had pursued her art as a career. I wish I could have made that possible for her instead of us both fighting for survival for most of our youth. Nothing would have made me happier for her to spend her days in a studio, much like Libra does now, bringing her wild imagination to life.

But she couldn't. We were poor, and despite her talent, pursuing that path at her age would have condemned her to a life of a starving artist if I had never been so lucky as to become a breakout success.

Instead, she kept that passion as a hobby, pursued a career, and obtained a reputation as a ruthless corporate strategist. It made her perfectly positioned to fuck with VellR.

She did it to help me, and it killed her.

I killed her.

I drag a hand over my face, that hint of despair

creeping in. I snap my fingers. Fox opens the tray by the window and deposits a freshly rolled joint into my palm, and I light it up and go back to watching Libra.

A therapist would tell me I can't tear myself up about what those other men did. I don't care. I had a responsibility to my sister, and I failed her. No matter what way you look at it, I should have done better.

Libra's relationship issues with James are a suitable puzzle for my tired mind. I know he's hurt her deep down, but I don't understand why the revelations about him haven't prompted her to cut her losses and leave.

His blatant disregard for her, every time I witness him and Josephine participating in their pathetic excuse of 'sneaking' around, refuels my desire to make him disappear. I've had enough of douchebag men destroying the lives of women I care about and making them afraid to be their true selves or using violence to put them down.

The longer I wait, the more afraid I am of what James could do to Libra. I don't want another Charlotte on my hands. Libra can handle herself, but I had the same respect for my sister, and look where that got her.

She hasn't opened up to me about him, but I wish she would. I want to understand. I want to see every facet of her pain so I can hold her through it. Whatever is holding her back, I wish she would help me show her the path to the other side. James isn't right for her, but I can't blame her for being an emotionless husk like me.

Emotion could be entirely removed from the decision. One word to Fox, and he will alert my contact without ever telling Libra. One call and the dominoes would be set in motion.

I wouldn't know when it happens, or how, just that sometime soon, James wouldn't be a problem anymore, and the balance in my bank account would experience a slight, momentary decline.

In many ways, Libra is still a mystery to me. I don't know if having him 'removed' makes her hesitate because she truly doesn't want him gone or if she's scared of the potential consequences. When you have money like mine, though, those consequences may as well not exist.

Conversations about the ways we could kill James or escape him muddy the water. She seems happy to fantasize about eliminating him but not explicitly pulling the trigger on one of our many outlandish plans. And if she doesn't want him dead, why won't she just let me sweep her away and disappear with her to the other side of the world?

He couldn't stop us. Nobody could. What could she possibly fear that money can't fix?

Often, I wonder if her resistance is a test. Do I make him disappear to prove I'll do anything for her, or does she want me to wait to show her I trust in her autonomy and her ability to handle her own problems?

Today, Libra is in her studio until long after the sun dips below the horizon, while James is out late for another one of these' business gatherings.' Given his track record, he's probably planning to spend his night parked in another woman.

Libra finishes her painting of Josephine at midnight.

She promptly takes the canvas from the easel and lays it on the floor and then disappears for a few minutes. When she returns, she has an axe in one hand and a canister in the other.

I can't hear her, but I feel the visceral scream that's torn from her throat when she swings the axe at the painting. Her pain shivers through me as if it's my own. The way she hacks at the painting is hypnotic. Wood, cloth, and paint part beneath her wrath.

When she attempts to swing the axe again, her arms are so weak that she can't lift it; that's when she lifts the canister instead.

Flames spark at her fingertips, igniting the fragmented painting of Josephine. Amber tongues consume the picture, flickering around Libra as though she's a furious goddess.

Golden light reflects in her eyes and in the tear tracks on her face as her art burns.

I have never seen anyone more beautiful.

~

I BARELY SLEPT.

It didn't matter how exhausted I was; my body ached from a restless night of tossing and turning, picturing Libra as that fiery goddess of vengeance.

Hell hath no fury like a woman scorned.

All night, my mind ran in circles about what to do about James. I can't keep sitting by, waiting. If last night was any indication, her conflict with James is about to escalate big time.

In the rare moments I wasn't torturing myself about what to do, I couldn't stop imagining me and Libra in bed together, bodies intertwined, me kissing her stress and pain away. It's easy to imagine the lives we could lead if she wasn't bound by a ball and chain. If only she would let me do that for her.

Fox and I go through our usual morning routine, once again deleting the string of aggressive voicemails from my stalker. It is no surprise that this day will require coffee to get me through.

As I make my way downstairs, I'm greeted by a warm, inviting aroma — freshly brewed coffee, sizzling bacon, and what smells like fluffy pastries. Sophia's voice drifts through the hallway from the kitchen, her tone hushed.

"Fox, I'm telling you, everything has changed. You'll see," she says, her words barely audible from around the wall.

I pause to listen. I rarely hear her talk to Fox unless it's to conspire against me for the 'benefit' of my health.

"Changed how, exactly?" Fox replies over the speaker. "I did exactly what you asked. Did I make a mistake?"

"Trust me, just trust me on this one. I figured the system out. How to make it work."

The conversation drifts off before I can grasp the meaning of the exchange. Shaking my head, I continue into the kitchen, where I'm greeted with a stack of fluffy buttermilk pancakes drizzled with that maple syrup I love, imported all the way from a tiny family farm in Quebec. Besides the pancakes, there's a tray of delectables: scones, cupcakes, and other baked goods in various flavors and colors.

Sophia, who has been on edge for months, now radiates an infectious joy that seems to fill the room with light. "Good morning, Mr. Crawford! It's a beautiful day, isn't it?"

Wearily, I rub my eyes and peer out at the cloudy sky. "Is it?"

She's wearing a loose-fitting white blouse that falls off one shoulder, revealing the smooth curve of her shoulder and collarbone. It's not too different from her usual attire as my housekeeper, but noticeably more sensual. A flush colors her cheeks, and she moves around the kitchen as if she's floating on air.

"Though any day is much better waking up to a breakfast like this. Did I become a king overnight?" I smirk as I walk up to the island and take a seat opposite her.

"Who needs kings when you can be a brilliant innovator such as yourself? I thought I'd surprise you with a breakfast worthy of your importance. I've been meaning to bring you more samples of the treats I've been baking every Thursday like I said I would, but it took me a while to get the recipes the way I like. Here, try this."

She takes a chocolate scone dusted with powdered sugar and leans over the counter to press it to my lips. Fire glows in her eyes when I open my mouth to accept the bite, chewing on the soft but thick layers of chocolatey goodness.

"Mmm, that's incredible. I didn't think it was possible for someone to beat the Farazzo Bakery's world-best chocolate scones."

Sophia grins shyly. "You're just saying that."

"I pay you far too much to bother lying about a damn scone. Now give me the rest of it." I pluck it from her hand and take another heavenly bite.

Her cheeks are rosy when she turns to pour me a cup of coffee. It's been almost two months since we had a casual, easy conversation like this. That barrier has mostly been her doing since she's so vocal about her disapproval of Libra. I doubt she's changed her mind, but I'm glad she's tried to turn over a new leaf. She must have realized that she can't just wait out Libra since I have no intention of ending our fun anytime soon.

"Tell me about your week," she prompts, pushing the porcelain mug toward me and then tucking a stray lock of hair behind her ear. "I'm sorry I haven't been keeping up with you this past while. I've had to do a lot of self-reflection."

"I understand that you have your own life outside of my house." I laugh between sips of coffee, which instantly gives me that much-needed caffeinated buzz. "Uh, well, you know, the week has been usual for me."

I try my best to remain nonchalant while my mind races with thoughts of Libra.

"Usual? You've left the house, Mr. Crawford. Not once, but multiple times! That's incredible."

"You could say so. I think it's a slow adjustment toward being a functional human again. How about you? You seem … different. In a good way."

"Me?" Sophia's laughter fills the room. "I don't know. Maybe I'm finally feeling like myself again."

"Really? What's brought this on?"

Her eyes flicker with something secretive, a hint of mischief dancing in their depths. "Let's just say I've realized that sometimes, you have to take matters into your own hands instead of waiting for someone else to make your life easier."

"Good for you. I'm a firm believer that more independence and willingness to take action can give you more control and satisfaction in your life. That's why I do whatever the fuck I want."

"You're so smart, Mr. Crawford. I should have listened to you sooner."

We chat more about her baking endeavors over breakfast, with her insisting that I take at least a bite of everything she's made while the treats are still fresh, even though I'm fully stuffed after a scone and plateful of pancakes. It's a simple breakfast, but after a life of so much extravagance, I try to find pleasure and joy in the little things where I can.

A smile curves the edge of my lips at the thought. Just a few months ago, I found everything about life tedious and excruciatingly painful. What has Libra done to me?

"Thanks for breakfast, Sophia. It was delicious," I say

as I push my empty plate away. "Let me help you clean up."

She waves her hand dismissively. "Nonsense, cleaning up is my job. It brings me great happiness to see you so cheery for once. Shoo, shoo, give me some peace."

"If you insist! I'm leaving before you change your mind."

I offered out of courtesy for her thoughtfulness and to try and return the favor after seeing her in such high spirits, but I'm glad she refused. I'm eager to resume my routine of watching Libra perform her morning rituals. A familiar anticipation builds in me when I close the door to my observation room and take a seat in my chair.

Lifting my binoculars to the window, I scan the neighboring property for any signs of Libra. I expect to find her lounging by the pool, taking in a bit of the California sun before diving in for her invigorating swim. But she's not there.

I check the time. 7:15. I'm right on time, and Libra is never late for her swim.

Flashing red and blue in the distance catches my eye. That's odd. I follow the path of the police cruisers driving up the street, curious as to where they're going. We don't get cops around Woodside much, and definitely not with sirens blaring.

They turn into Libra's driveway.

TWENTY-ONE

Libra

BY THE TIME I CLIMB OUT OF MY TANGLED SHEETS, I'M nursing a headache that tells me just how this day is going to go. Echoes of James and Josephine moaning and grunting last night in the adjacent room tortured me while I lay there, unable to sleep. I'm not going to pretend my husband makes sense anymore.

I don't think he ever did. There's no other reason to imprison me like this, on the threat of blackmail, unless he's a fucking sadist.

I wrap myself in the teal and black silk robe Zane gifted me last week, just in case Josephine is still hanging around the house, then I descend to the kitchen to make my morning smoothie. Nothing's a cure for my woes like a green smoothie and the cool embrace of the pool. I long for the embrace of water far more than I hunger for more sleep. I need to wash away the ick, considering James and Josephine are tainting the sanctity of my home.

Just as I grab the handle of the French door toward the pool side of the house, a loud knock bangs through the foyer and the main entryway. Who could that be at this hour? James never mentioned any guests. Then again, he doesn't tell me much of anything these days if it's not about his cars or criticism of me.

On the other side of the door, a uniformed police officer and a man in a nice but slightly oversized black suit greet me. The man has blond hair with a slight curl to it, his jaw stern but not so much as the somber black-haired woman beside him. Their expressions are serious, their postures rigid, and the pop of tension puts me on high alert.

"Good morning, ma'am," the plainclothes man says, his voice cold and emotionless. "I'm Detective Glen Morgan, and this is Officer Lillian Donald with the Woodside Police Department. Are you Mrs. Libra Scarsdale?"

"Yes," I reply hesitantly, bracing my hand against the doorframe. "What is this all about?"

"Regrettably, your husband, Mr. Scarsdale, died in the early hours this morning."

My first instinct is to laugh, but I don't. God, how would that look?

Officer Lillian's light hazel eyes are dark with pity. They're not joking. I stare at them, expecting them to explain, but they don't move at all. It's like the world around me has frozen, and I'm stuck hearing those words over again.

Dead. James is dead.

"No," I whisper, shaking my head. "That can't be true. He was home just a few hours ago; I heard him."

"I'm afraid it is, ma'am. We received a call from your housekeeper, Miss Josephine Largos, who discovered his vehicle on the road leading to the back gate of your property this morning. It appears he was murdered."

Murdered.

I fantasized about him dying. Killing him with my bare hands. I never — I never actually *wanted* it, did I?

I swallow, hard, and my stomach feels like it bulges two twice its size and I sway on my feet.

"Are you all right, Mrs. Scarsdale?" Detective Morgan says, his tone soft.

"I … I think I'm going to be sick."

My head spins, and I turn tail and bolt into the kitchen. My hands slap against the countertop, and I just *heave*. Dry, at first, then all the green goodness burns up my throat along with my sobs as I puke into the sink.

What the FUCK, James?

"Mrs. Scarsdale?" Officer Lillian's voice drawls from somewhere behind me. I hear their boots follow me into the house. "I'm sure this is a huge shock. Here, I found a water bottle for you."

I fumble for the cap and shove it in my mouth, rinsing my mouth out with water and then gulping down the rest in one go. Now panting, at least it doesn't feel like I'm going to throw up again. Tears still carve unwilling tracks on my face.

I should be glad he's gone, shouldn't I?

Why does it feel like my heart was cleaved out of my chest?

"I just … I can't believe it. He … he's gone?"

"If it's all right with you, Mrs. Scarsdale, we should sit down for the rest of this conversation."

"Of course," I mumble, trying to catch my bearings and fast. Fuck, I must look like a trainwreck. "May I offer you coffee, tea, a morning brandy?"

"Thank you, but no."

I'm the one who needs a fucking drink. I top off my water bottle and then escort the police to the dining room adjacent to the kitchen because as soon as I peel myself off the counter, my legs are too weak to carry me toward the lounge.

What happened last night? It wouldn't be the first time James has been a part of drunken tomfoolery gone wrong, but murder?

I pull apart the velvet curtains to let the morning light flow through the curtains to highlight the long dining table. Officer Lillian takes a seat, and Detective Morgan chooses to stay standing but on the same side as her, and I sit opposite of Lillian.

"Who murdered my husband?" I ask, my voice hoarse, once we're all seated.

"We're still investigating." Detective Morgan crosses his arms and approaches the table. "From the evidence we've gathered so far, it appears to be a mugging gone wrong. There was a struggle, and he was stabbed multiple times, and several valuables were missing from his possession. We found footage from security cameras near the incident that supports this theory."

"How could a murder happen so close to home? Here? Woodside is such a safe neighborhood."

"It's not unheard of to have violent incidents like this in these wealthier neighborhoods when people are under the influence. The difference is, they are rarely random."

My shoulders tense, and I focus directly on Detective Morgan, staring at his big nose and trying to breathe and steady myself. This is not the time to crumble, not with their eyes on me, watching every nuance of my reaction.

"You're saying he was targeted."

"We don't know that for a fact," Officer Lillian interjects, "but that is often how these cases go. The nature of the stab wounds indicates an element of overkill, which usually means there's a personal connection to the victim."

"Someone he *knew* murdered him?"

"We're currently investigating any likely suspects in his closer social circles and will broaden our search based on the evidence we find. We have a few questions for you that would help us determine who could have wanted to murder your husband."

Murdered.

The word echoes through my mind, triggering memories of those late-night conversations with Zane when we jokingly planned James' demise to blow off steam. We plotted his death in dozens of different ways with varying degrees of detail with Fox's reluctant help, but it was just talk. We never agreed or intended to go through with it. It was a game, that's all. How could this have happened?

"Anything I can do to help," I say instantly.

"Mrs. Scarsdale, can you tell us if anything unusual happened last night?"

"Unusual?" My mind takes the opportunity to bring back the sound of Josephine's and James' moans echoing through the walls, but that's not really *abnormal* or information I'm particularly inclined to share. "No, everything was normal. He usually spends every second Friday night out with his buddies in town or with business partners."

"Do you know who he was with last night?"

"No. He doesn't tell me who exactly goes to their get-togethers; sometimes, he doesn't know until it happens."

Detective Morgan scribbles a few notes. "And you said you heard James at home last night? Do you remember what time that was at, and did you see him or just hear him?"

"It must have been about 4 a.m. I only heard him; I was in bed, and he didn't join me."

Lillian glances at Detective Morgan, and they share a long look that I don't like. They communicate with silent understanding, and I don't like it.

"What is it?" I press.

Officer Lillian clears her throat. "Your husband was found returning in the direction of your house, not leaving the property. Are you sure it was your husband you heard inside last night?"

"I'm sure it was him, but ... it was so late."

"So you haven't left the house?"

"Not in a few days, no. I'm an artist, and I work mostly in my studio, which is in the backyard. I came in at about seven last night for dinner, and I haven't left since." I pause, wracking my brain for more information to give them. Could it really be that someone else was here, in my house, and I had no idea? That's impossible. It has to be. I sit up straighter. "We have security cameras on the property, including several facing the back road and the gate. I can show you if that would help."

"That absolutely would," Detective Morgan says. "Thank you."

Officer Lillian folds her hands on the table. "Can you tell us more about your relationship with James?"

"We've been married for over six years, but we were together for eight years total and knew each other for a while before we got together. Like any couple, we've had our ups and downs, but we had a disagreement several weeks ago that put some distance between us. He hasn't spent as much time at home since."

"You could say your relationship was tense, then."

I scowl. "Not tense enough to stab him to death, if that's what you're suggesting."

"Not at all, Mrs. Scarsdale." Officer Lillian smiles, showing off her rows of pearly whites. "We're just covering all our bases."

"Yes, you could describe our relationship as tense. We've argued a lot about my husband's perception of my art and our disagreement regarding the use of my talents. He believed I was wasting my time and demanded that I paint outside of my interests to please him, such as the fancy cars he sells at his dealership, and I disagreed with him."

"Would you say that James was controlling?"

"It was a difference in taste, that's all."

"I see. Can you think of anyone who would want to harm your husband?"

My thoughts instantly turn to Zane. That man has a dark side I've only scratched the surface of, and James has been a target of his hate for weeks. He takes particular delight in planning James' various murders with me, and he's suggested multiple times that he could have James removed if I wanted.

It wasn't a question of getting away with it — he knew he would. James was nothing to a man like Zane.

A robbery gone wrong. I didn't see it before, but now my stomach churns with a nauseating realization: the details of the murder scene align with one of the scenarios Zane and I outlined.

What if it really wasn't James in my house last night? What if it was a staged robbery to get away with murder?

Zane wouldn't, would he?

There are plenty of people that James has angered and crossed over the years, but no one stands out. I force myself to remain composed, not daring to let anything slip.

I've longed for a world where James no longer restricts my desires, but I never wanted him dead — at least, not like this. The guilt festers inside me like an infected wound, threatening to tear me apart.

If anything, his death means I'm free.

I'm shocked he's gone; torn up, even. But there is no love lost between us, especially now that I've had two weeks to process the fact that James might never have loved me in the first place.

A wave of emotion crashes over me, and my chest aches with suppressed cries. Tears pool in my eyes, and I let them stream down my cheeks before wiping them away.

"No, I can't think of anyone," I admit. "He had his enemies, but murder?"

"Thank you for your insight, Mrs. Scarsdale," Detective Morgan says, closing his notebook. "Those are all the questions we have for now. If you think of anything else that might be relevant, please don't hesitate to contact us."

"Actually, would you mind if we took a quick look around?" Officer Lillian cranes her neck as she rises from her seat. "You mentioned that you were sure James came home last night, but for your own safety, we can check if anything in the house was disturbed."

I have nothing to hide, but I don't really want them snooping around my house. At the same time, what would it look like for me to refuse?

"The cameras and motion sensors didn't detect anything wrong last night, but be my guest." I run an exhausted hand over my face. "It would give me some peace of mind to know no one else was in my home last night."

The detectives indulge their curiosities, carefully sweeping through all three floors. I follow Officer Lillian into the reading room beside my bedroom, where the shelves of untouched books are left without a single object in the room outof order. For how loudly James and Josephine were fucking, I would think something would be out of place, if slightly.

A sense of unease tightens inside me. Did I imagine it?

Once they've finished their job, we gather by the entrance. Detective Morgan tips his head at me. "Thank you for your time, Mrs. Scarsdale, and so very sorry for your loss. If you notice any belongings missing, or if any new information at all arises, please be in touch."

I close the door behind them and then slump against it.

The uncertainty, the fear, the insidious guilt that gnaws at my soul all attacks me at once. My head screams at me to confront Zane and find out whether he had any part in James' death, but my heart quivers at the thought of facing the truth. Everything seems to point to Zane being responsible, but do I want to know if it was?

Does it matter?

I squeeze my eyes shut and bang my fists gently against the door. "Fuck."

Of course, it matters. The why is everything. I have no choice but to confront Zane, at the very least, to sense for myself if he's guilty. Until I know for sure, I won't be able to escape the feeling that James' murder will come back to haunt me somehow and that any relief I could possibly feel is a trap.

TWENTY-TWO

Zane

I LIFT THE BINOCULARS TO MY EYES ONCE MORE, SCOURING Libra's house for any sign of her. The detectives have been inside for a while now, but I can't see anyone.

"Fox, do any of our cameras have a better angle on Libra's house?" I pace back and forth along the wall, my pulse throbbing in my ears. "I need to see what's going on."

"I cannot provide a clearer view," Fox responds, his synthetic tone lacking the urgency I feel. "We never enabled the exterior cameras facing the Scarsdale residence, and it would take time to configure the settings and adequately hook them into my system."

"Damn it."

My mind races with possibilities, each darker than the last. Has something happened? Is Libra in danger? Did James finally snap and hurt her?

His possessiveness, control over her life, and rough attitude and behavior are recipes for disaster for a vulnerable woman. She's afraid of James even if she won't admit it, but is her fear induced by trauma in the past or what he's capable of?

I haven't seen any signs of physical abuse. I would have noticed.

"Did you run their plates? Are they real cops?"

"The police vehicles are legitimate," Fox reassures. "I do not believe they are any risk to her wellbeing."

"Easy for you to say," I grumble, frustration seeping into my words. "You don't know what James is like."

"Mr. Crawford, you must remain calm. Should the situation change, rest assured I will alert the proper authorities."

I force myself to take a few deep breaths, steadying my nerves as best I can. Fox is right; panicking won't help anyone.

My gaze remains locked on Libra's house. I hate not knowing. I hate feeling powerless, unable to protect her from the horrors lurking out there. And there are many — I have seen them with my own eyes. My hands clench into fists, knuckles turning white as I will myself to stay put and wait for answers.

SWEAT POURS down my forehead and chest as I work the bench press. Muscles aching, the rhythm of my body put to work was all I could think of to distract me from the window long enough to get out of my damn head and wait for news instead of twisting myself into knots.

"Libra has arrived at the mansion," Fox announces over the gym speaker.

I'm already moving. I grab a towel off the rack and wipe down off some of the sweat as I rush downstairs, arriving in the grand foyer just as the front door opens.

Libra's usually immaculate blonde hair is disheveled and tangled as if she's been running her hands through it for hours. The red rims of her eyes betray recent tears, though none fall currently. Without hesitation, she throws herself into my arms.

"Libra," I gasp, holding her tight against my bare chest. My heart aches for her pain, and I do my best to offer comfort by rubbing soothing circles on her back. "What's happening? Are you okay? When I saw those cops pull up next door, I was terrified that you'd been hurt."

"Zane … Oh, Zane." Her voice shakes along with her shoulders. "I'm fine, I promise. Physically, at least."

"Was it James? Did he do something?" I growl.

It's as if a switch flicks inside her. She pulls away from my embrace and distances herself, her wide eyes betraying her tumultuous mind. The sudden withdrawal, the way she flicks her eyes as if searching for signs of danger, makes me tense with concern.

"James was murdered."

I blink, trying to comprehend the gravity of her words. "Murdered?"

She nods, her eyes never leaving mine. Their usual luminance is now haunted.

A part of me wants to rejoice that James is gone. Permanently. He was a piece of work and bad for Libra, and worst of all, a barrier to me and Libra seeing each other more frequently. But my overwhelming concern for Libra keeps me grounded.

"Tell me everything. What happened? Who did it?"

"The cops don't know yet. He stopped his car on the road leading to the house, and someone caught him off guard. It was a robbery, but the cops think he might have been targeted."

"You're not a suspect, are you?"

She shakes her head. "I was home all night, and the cameras prove that. It's just, ever since the cops came over, something they said has been bothering me."

"What is it?"

"At first, I thought I was remembering wrong. I thought I heard James come home at some point, but the cops said he was murdered on his way home. They searched the house for any signs of an intruder and found nothing, but after they left, I looked around on my own. In the room I thought I heard James in, the safe was emptied."

"You need to report it stolen before they think you were involved."

"I will. But, don't you think…"

Our eyes meet, and the same worry passes between us. The circumstances she describes are eerily similar to one of the scenarios we came up with together. Of all our plans, this sounds like one of the more convoluted ones; stage a robbery, but really plan to murder the husband.

Could it be a coincidence? Or is Libra lying?

She seems genuinely distressed by his death like she's lost and not sure where to go or what to do now.

My eyebrows crinkle. "This doesn't make any sense."

"Is it possible? Could someone else have found out about our … you know?" She hesitates, biting her lip.

But I chose not to act out of respect for Libra's choices.

"Anything is possible, but Fox never detected a breach in the system. Have you, Fox?"

"Of course not, sir," the AI confirms. "If you are concerned, I can run a manual search through my logs for unusual activity."

"Do that." Looking back to Libra, I cross my arms. "I can't imagine who would want to kill James *and* be capable of breaking in without leaving a trace. They would have to know that we had those conversations in the first place."

An unspoken question lingers between us — the question in her stare is obvious enough. It's one I'm too cautious to voice out loud.

What she *really* wants to know is if I'm responsible, and I can't blame her for wondering. After all, I'm vocal about how much better Libra would be without her bastard of a husband. I haven't changed my mind about that.

"*If* someone gained access to those conversations, how can we make sure no one else does?"

I see where she's going with this.

"Fox, delete all conversation history, audio recordings, prompts, and search history about our experiments over the past month."

"I cannot, Mr. Crawford. My programming is very specific: any suspicious search prompts, results, and navigation histories must be safely stored away in the event of a criminal investigation or other legal necessity."

Libra's eyes widen. "Shit."

I turn away from her, grabbing my face. "If anyone finds out about our research, we'll be the most likely suspects. Fuck."

"We explored a lot of ideas," Libra says cautiously, "but James wasn't supposed to die, and definitely not like this."

"No, he wasn't."

Libra made a clear line about whether she wanted to kill James or not, but that line often blurred when we were both fantasizing about the brutal ways we could eliminate him from our lives. We both engaged so enthusiastically in developing each scenario that I can't say for sure if it was her or me who first suggested the possibility of killing him. We both wanted it. We wanted to be together.

I take a step closer to Libra. "I'm sorry for what you're going through, but I can't say I'm sorry he's dead. Am I a piece of shit for admitting that out loud? Probably. And yet…" Something flickers across her face — desire — but she attempts to mask it by pressing her lips into a thin line. Her gaze darkens as I come closer, cupping her chin between my fingers. "I've never wanted you more than I do right now."

"Zane, I… I…"

"You what, Libra? Don't try to tell me this isn't what you wanted. Freedom. You can do whatever the hell you want now. You can fuck off and live in the Bahamas for the rest of your life, travel the world for your art, or … or we can be together, doing anything and everything our hearts desire."

Her pupils dilate as she digests my words. The air between us crackles, and a subtle heat passes between our bodies. I can feel her melting in my hold, almost ready to break.

"I don't know what the fuck happened, but he's gone, and you're right. He can't hold me back anymore." She tilts her face up to stare directly into my eyes. "I know exactly what I want to do with my freedom."

Libra grabs my belt and pulls me into a rabid kiss, our teeth clashing and tongues tangling in a fierce, lusty battle. I slam her against the foyer's wall. She trembles with built-up pressure while she claws at my abdomen, grasping at the muscles rippling beneath her palms and hooking her fingers around my belt.

Our clothes become casualties in our frenzied attempts to find bare skin. She bites my bottom lip and drags it between her teeth, sending a shockwave of heat to my groin. We worship each other's bodies with our hands, and her delicate fingers make quick work of my pants, unbuttoning them and palming my cock through my boxers. I rip the front of her bra in half to get to her breasts sooner, burrowing my face in them until she arches her head back in pure ecstasy.

The ecstasy of being alive.

Libra growls and pushes me off of her with surprising force. Grabbing the waistband of my boxers, she drags it down my legs as she falls to her knees in front of me with hungry eyes.

"I'll never have to suck my husband's dick again," she says with a wicked grin and takes me in both hands. "Lucky for you, I only have one place to get my fix now."

My mind is a whirlwind of arousal and confusion, but as soon as she takes me in her mouth, absolute clarity falls upon me. My breath hitches, and I buck so the bottom of my shaft slides across the flat of her tongue.

With just the right amount of suction and motion, she has me in the palm of her hand. My mind is the one that's melting this time, and I don't give a shit anymore if she's trying to distract me from the truth, manipulate me, or hide from her pain. I just want to exist in this moment with her.

"Fucking *shit*," I groan and grip the back of her scalp, holding her lips at the base of my stem. "You're a goddam slut, you know that? Your husband is dead, and here you are, sucking me off like a greedy whore."

Her eyes flicker up at me, glazed with lust. She moans around my length, sending vibrations through my entire body. The dirty talk only spurs her on, making her bobbing head even more ravenous.

"My housekeeper could walk in any second and see you like this. What would she think of you, Libra? A grieving widow on her knees for another man?"

A wicked smile plays across her lips. She pulls off my cock long enough to whisper, "Let her watch."

Then she dives back in, swallowing me whole.

"Fuck, you love this, don't you?"

I can't take it anymore. Overcome by her sheer madness, I grab her head and give her exactly what she needs. I thrust into her warm, wet mouth, setting a relentless pace. She gags and chokes, tears streaming down her face, but she never backs away.

Instead, she encourages me, gripping my thighs and digging her nails in. This fucking woman. Wild, crazy, free, and without James around, she could be *mine*. Completely.

Her mouth is perfect. My eyes roll back, letting the raw sensations wash over me with a long groan. My balls tighten, and my breath comes in ragged gasps as the pressure builds.

"Libra," I grunt. "I'm going to——"

I yank myself from her mouth just before she finishes me. She yelps in surprise when I tug her off the floor and shove her against the window. Her naked breasts press against the cold glass, leaving ghostly imprints in the condensation that's formed from our heated exchange.

Grabbing her ass, I hover behind her and position at her entrance. Heat radiates from her core, and she slowly pushes her hips back, taking me inch by agonizing inch, until our bodies are melded together, two halves of a twisted whole.

"Fuck me," she hisses through clenched teeth. "Make me yours."

I swirl my hand through her hair, fisting against her scalp and dragging her head to look at me while I fuck her from behind. Her stunning blue eyes are wild with a hunger I've never seen before, even in her.

"You're already mine."

We are a whirlwind of lust and desperation, incapable of distinguishing where I end and she begins. It feels like a dam has burst within me, and I can no longer contain myself. We move together, each thrust punctuated by guttural cries and desperate gasps.

"More," she moans. "I want more, Zane."

That heated, all-consuming desire clenches around my heart and burns a Libra-shaped imprint into me. I throw my head back, laughing as I pound into her. If this isn't an offering to the damn reaper, I don't know what is.

Fucking *fuck*, she feels so good.

"Say my name," I command, my voice hoarse. "Scream it so the whole fucking neighborhood can hear!"

"Zane!" Libra cries out.

And just like that, my vision goes white. The world narrows into a singularity — her cry, my name, our bodies slapping to the rhythm of pleasure. We come apart together, a cataclysmic release that leaves us shaking, our breaths mingling in the charged silence.

I curl my body into hers and against the window, kissing the sweat off her spine, the back of her neck, and her cheek. We're free right here, in this moment, but with a murderer on the loose, will either of us be safe for long?

TWENTY-THREE

Libra

SURROUNDED BY PUNGENT LILIES AND ROSES, I STAND IN the center of the enormous glass-domed atrium. Intricate stained-glass panels of birds and wildlife scenes reflect light and color over the 150 people occupying the venue for James' funeral. Their buzzing murmurs are much like hungry flies devouring a corpse. James would have loved this ostentatious display — an extravagant funeral for an extravagant man.

My feet ache in these impossibly high heels, and my heart feels heavy.

I miss James. The man I fell in love with years ago, who liked to braid my hair and hide gifts around the house, sometimes in places I wouldn't find for months. It's he who I grieve today, not the man he became.

Grief is insufferable.

"Mrs. Scarsdale, I'm so sorry for your loss," murmurs a woman in a black hat. She grasps my hand tightly, but her condolences are no comfort. "James was a great man. He was much beloved by my husband for all his wise-ass jokes.

There was nobody quite like him, and to be taken so suddenly…"

"Thank you for coming," I reply, forcing a mask of a smile onto my face. She's fishing for more information about his murder, just like every other vulture here. I don't think there's a genuine person among all of James' friends and associates.

Another gentleman approaches, his graying hair combed neatly to one side. "Libra, I can't imagine what you're going through."

Automatically, my hand grips his in a gentle handshake. Even as he speaks, his eyes rake up and down my body in a way that makes me shiver in disgust — the familiarity, the shameless way he looks at me. It takes a second for who he is to click in my head.

I try to pull away, but he grips my forearm tighter.

"Charles," I mutter, my smile turning venomous when I see just who James' death has dragged out of the woodwork. "I never thought I'd see you again."

"Your tits are as nice as I remember them, and those legs too, mmm." He laughs huskily into my ear. "Let me know if you ever need some comfort. I'm sure this will be a troubling time for you."

"Fuck off," I pull away.

His expression twists. "I told James not to marry you, you know. No wonder his sorry ass turned up dead."

"I had nothing to do with this."

His eyes light up with amusement. He knows I didn't. He's just being an asshole.

Shaking my head, I turn from the line of mourners that have gathered to try and find a second with me. I don't want to see any of them right now or talk to anyone. They are a parade of clowns with their stories of how

James touched their lives, but it's always about money, influence, and sex.

I head to the nearest exit. If I stay in here for another minute, I'll suffocate. Fresh air is what I need before I return to greet more people and receive their fake condolences.

A burst of cool air hits my face as soon as I leave the building, and I sigh with relief and slump against a wall behind a bush where I hope no one will find me for a while.

There's no one here who cares about the real James. The man who smothered me and beat me down until I forgot what I was fighting for in the first place. They don't care that he fucked off and slept with Josephine and likely had several other mistresses over the years that I was too naïve to pick up on.

No one wants to hear that side of the story. They call me strong for keeping the tears in and maintaining a brave face in front of so many people. If I wasn't exhausted from planning the funeral and acting the part of a grieving widow, I'd be pissed and probably blow up in their faces.

What I could use right now is a fat fucking joint, a certain man's arms around my waist, and a seat on his lap. What I need in my life is a man like Zane, someone who's in it to win it and with me 100%. Not the half-assed bullshit that James spewed at me and has for the last few years, including the threats designed to keep me by his side forever.

I deserve someone who gives a shit about me, not their image.

Behind the sound of whizzing cars, I hear someone sobbing loudly. Leaning forward, I spot Josephine sitting alone on a bench, curled over with her face in her palms and her red hair streaming everywhere in a haphazard mess.

I hardened my heart toward her the moment she walked in my front door and made little doe eyes at James. I have no doubt that he misled her into believing he was capable of love, just like he did to me, but she's an adult and knew she was fucking a married man under his roof with his wife present. She has to take responsibility for her actions just as much as James does.

Josephine's shoulders heave with her sickening display of grief. She has no right to behave this way at my husband's funeral — she wasn't even invited — but sympathy nags at my heart anyway. Regardless of what I think of her, she's the one who found James' body. From what I saw of him after the coroner cleaned him up, it must not have been a pretty sight to stumble across.

Before I realize what I'm doing, my feet are dragging me across the lawn. "Excuse me," I say, approaching her cautiously.

Josephine's bloodshot eyes lift to meet mine. It takes her a second to gather her senses enough to recognize me, but when she does, anger flickers behind her tears. It's as if she blames me for her heartache.

"What do you want?" she spits.

"I could ask you the same, considering you're not supposed to be here."

"I don't care what you think. I love James, and he loves me. I should be allowed to see him one last time. You're a cruel bitch, aren't you?"

I'm so surprised I laugh. "James was good at making people believe he cared. He was a car salesman, for God's sake. He promised me everything, and as soon as he had everything he wanted, that's when he changed. In the end, all he gave me was pain and lies."

"Tell me more from your throne of money."

"Is that what this is about?"

She sneers. "Of course not. I'm not like you, a gold-digging whore. He told me what you used to be and how you begged him to marry you so you didn't have to work the streets anymore. He had too soft of a heart, and you abused that."

I can't fucking believe what I'm hearing.

"I don't know what the fuck James told you, but how dare you show up at my husband's funeral acting all pious when you were sleeping with a married man?"

"James always regretted marrying you, a low-quality woman. You were all used up before he put a ring on your finger. He and I were meant to be married."

"And you were so much better, right? A woman who throws herself at all her employers hoping to baby-trap a horny man into a retirement fund. Or do you consider fucking your employer part of your job?"

"You're no better than me!"

She stares back at me with so much conviction. So this is what it feels like to stare into the eyes of a crazy person. She's so intent on blaming me for her and James' problems instead of the man himself, and her hostility makes me suspicious.

"Did you kill him?" The question escapes my lips before I can stop it. Shock passes over Josephine's face, quickly replaced by indignation.

"Are you serious? I found him with a dozen stab wounds. It looked like he'd been mauled by a cougar!" She wipes away her tears with the back of her hand, her voice shaking. "You think I could do that?"

"You'd be surprised what a spurned lover is capable of."

"If anyone is spurned, it's you! You're the one who did

it, aren't you? He was going to leave you for me. He promised. You got jealous and insecure and took everything away from me!"

"Did he tell you that before or after he told me he would never divorce me because he wanted to see me suffer, and he'd never open our marriage because he wanted the power of banging you on the side and pretending I was too dumb to notice?"

Josephine's face reddens, and she climbs to her feet, shaking. "You have no idea what you're talking about. James loved me. *Me*. What we had was real."

"I bet that's what he told you while he degraded you and fucked you like a cheap whore. Because that's all you made yourself when you started your affair inside my home. You realized that when he told you he wasn't going to leave me, isn't that right? That's why you murdered him. You were ashamed."

Her face gets so red she looks like a tomato. I expect her to lurch forward and slap me, but instead, she crumples and falls back onto the bench. "I-I didn't — I would never —James never … he wouldn't…"

She sobs incoherently into her palms, broken like the toy James made her. Sighing, my shoulders slump. I'm a huge asshole too. I didn't want this confrontation to turn into a screaming match, but I have my answer.

Josephine is an easy target to accuse, but I don't think she's the murderer. The cops probably figured that out already as soon as they learned about the affair.

I leave her to her mourning in peace and reluctantly return to the shitshow inside. Josephine's loud emotions have completely drained me, leaving a bitter taste in my mouth and no more energy to handle all the grieving people inside. A part of me craves closure, but the rest of me worries I might be digging for a truth I don't want to hear.

Zane is everything James wasn't: loving, attentive, and completely devoted. He might not use those words exactly, but I know he cares about me. He'd kill for me, as crazy as that sounds. That's part of what makes Zane's attention so fucking scary, especially after James' murder.

Do I believe he did it? Not really.

Would he be capable of it? Without a doubt.

I could never picture him brutally stabbing the target to death, though. Zane isn't that kind of man. He's meticulous. He would hire someone else to make James disappear and leave no evidence behind, which is why I doubt he was involved, regardless of where the evidence points.

That's what everyone thinks he did to the VellR execs who got away with what they did to his sister. Even though there's no proof.

To Zane, killing the man who held me back and was actively preventing us from being together wouldn't be a desperate attempt to claim me for himself; it would be the ultimate show of devotion. He would be giving me my freedom just to see what I would do with it.

TWENTY-FOUR

Zane

I SIT BEHIND THE POLISHED GRANITE COUNTERTOP WHILE Sophia hums and works her way around the kitchen. Her dark hair is pulled back into a tight bun, but her usual light, bubbly attitude is subdued.

"Here's your breakfast, Mr. Crawford," Sophia says with a tentative smile, placing a plate of smoked salmon, capers, and cream cheese on a freshly toasted bagel in front of me.

"You should sit and have a bite as well."

She hesitates before shaking her head. "No, thank you, sir. I'm not hungry."

I take a bite of my bagel in the ensuing silence. The crunch, paired with the rich creaminess and saltiness of the other flavors, is the perfect way to start the day.

Sophia fidgets with her apron, wringing her hands nervously. It's so unlike her; I'm instantly concerned.

"Is everything all right?"

"It's hard to carry on as normal when there was a murder next door," she mutters. "After you and Mrs. Scarsdale started your affair, I figured there would be some drama or another, but a murder? And her husband, no less? It's strange and, I daresay, suspicious."

I pause mid-chew, the delicious taste momentarily forgotten. "Are you saying you suspect Libra is responsible?"

"Don't you? Sir, she's inherited quite a fortune, and if I'm reading the situation correctly, she didn't much like him either. What if he discovered your affair, and she killed him to stop him from leaving her?"

"Libra wouldn't do that. She wanted a divorce, and he wouldn't give it to her."

"So maybe she killed him because he wouldn't let her go. That makes even more sense, doesn't it? I say she had something to do with it, and the cops haven't figured it out yet."

"That's hearsay at best and libelous at worst. I suggest you keep any suspicions to yourself unless you have proof to bring to the police."

"All I'm saying is, she's a person of interest, and I'm worried about you. You're too close to this to see the signs."

"Thank you for your concern," I say, trying to keep my voice steady. "I'll be cautious."

She nods, finally picking up on the fact that she should leave it at that, then picks a small pastry off the countertop platter and disappears down the hallway.

Regardless of what Sophia thinks or even what the truth might be, I find myself unable to resist the magnetic pull Libra has over me. I've deeply considered the possibility that Libra is responsible for James' murder.

She could be guilty. She could have murdered James for his money, for her freedom. If Libra was a murderer, it wouldn't bother me in the slightest; how could I judge her after what I've done?

If anything, she would become infinitely more fascinating. I wonder if her adamant refusal to act on our plans was because she intended to follow through on her own.

At the end of the day, James was keeping us apart. If he's gone, that obstacle is removed. I'm sorrier about the pain he's caused Libra than the fact that his sorry ass is dead.

"Fox, what do you think about the murder? What are the chances that Libra did it?"

"I calculate a 37.2% probability that she is directly involved in James' murder," Fox replies.

"37.2%? How did you determine that?"

"My determination is based on available statistics from accredited international studies on behavioral analyses of murderers and my records of Libra's behavioral patterns. However, please note that this assessment is purely speculative and should not be considered conclusive, granted that there is an unusually low amount of data available about Libra Scarsdale on the internet."

"Right ... so then if you believe she's that likely to be the murderer, what do you contribute the remaining 62.8% to?"

"The remaining 62.8% is attributed to multiple factors such as other plausible suspects, in this case, the housekeeper Josephine, his affair partner. Understanding that James Scarsdale was not the most upstanding individual, it's very possible a disgruntled employee or customer wished to take out their misgivings on him. There is always the possibility that any evidence pointing directly to Libra being the primary suspect could have been planted to mislead the investigation into incorrectly labeling her as a suspect. The odds could also be slightly skewed due to the statistical probabilities of these kinds of murders being committed by their romantic partners."

I lay my chin in my hands while I think. Libra and I briefly discussed the possibility of someone gaining access to the stored data on my servers and using that to commit the murder, but we hadn't considered the specific intention of the real killer attempting to frame one or both of us. Just that if someone did steal those plans, they could be connected back to us, and we'd be in a world of shit.

I didn't expect Fox to take that into account in his calculations.

"Interesting that you note how it's possible there was planted evidence ... why would you suggest that unless you have reason to believe that's true in James' case?"

"Statistically speaking, the manner in which James Scarsdale was murdered would point to Libra as an obvious suspect. However, given the data we do have on her from her many hours spent in this house, the traditional motives for murdered spouse don't quite add up. She was quite insistent that he should *not* die. I must consider the possibility that someone knew she would be home and sought to incriminate her. But while this is a possibility, we have no specific evidence to support this theory."

"No evidence beyond the unusually specific details about the crime."

"Indeed. I will have you know that after a substantial internal investigation, I am confident that my data storage and usage logs have not been tampered with in any way whatsoever."

Fox seems so confident in his assessment, but I'm not so sure. He did have that glitch a few weeks ago that caused him to momentarily forget the morning routine we've done together, without fail, over the past five years. At this point, I can't put it past him to miss something until I re-examine his code for myself.

Either way, whatever I find won't make me change my mind about Libra.

I close my eyes, allowing my mind to drift back to our last encounter — the scent of her perfume, the taste of her lips, the sound of her breathy moans as I took her against the window. I haven't seen her since the afternoon of the murder, but she's busy handling James' affairs, and it's better for us not to draw attention to ourselves during this time.

Plus, she's grieving. Not the man himself, perhaps, but everything else his death represents.

On the way to the stairs, I pass through the foyer and kick a piece of crumpled paper over the rug.

Sophia is usually meticulous in her cleaning, so the sight of trash on my floor is jarring. I pick up the ball and smooth out the wrinkles to examine its contents. It's a page torn from a notebook, covered in hastily scribbled notes and diagrams that are both familiar and chilling.

1. Lure James away from the house, posing as his mistress. Better yet, wait for her to do so herself. They are together often enough after hours.

2. Remotely disable security systems before breaching the Scarsdale household.

3. The safe is in the upstairs spare bedroom, behind the bookshelf. Code 48921

4. Re-enable security systems after departure.

5. Wait for James to return home. The remote takeover will disable the computer in his vehicle just outside of camera range and will look like a vehicle malfunction.

6. Wait a few minutes before going to offer him help. As soon as he's off guard, eliminate him.

7. Remember to take all his valuables to make the scene look like a robbery. Store somewhere safe, suitable for planting evidence later if necessary.

8. Re-enable car features; otherwise, the police might clue into the vehicle being dead. Give no reason for the police to consider a cyber-attack.

THE PAPER TREMBLES in my grasp. A sense of dread settles over me like a dense fog, clouding my thoughts and making it difficult to breathe. These are the instructions for James' murder, laid out step by step.

This is far worse than I expected. Not only does James' murder *seem* close to our plan, it IS an exact replica of one of the many plans Libra and I discussed.

If his murder played out exactly like this, then the robbery was a complete sham. Libra knows it. I know it.

Is she fucking with me?

Did she leave this here the last time she came over as a sick joke? Or was she planting evidence just in case she needed a backup plan for her own security?

My teeth grind, and I want to tear the paper to bits. I shouldn't jump to any conclusions, but … who else could have left them here if not Libra?

From a logical point of view, Libra *does* have the most to gain from James' death. Whenever we joke about killing James together, she often gets personal about her methods, but she doesn't seem like the type to act on it.

That doesn't mean she *wouldn't* be capable. I saw her rage and pain when she hacked that painting of Josephine to pieces and then burned the remains. It's hard to picture the woman I've fallen in so deep with as a cold-blooded murderer. I don't think that's her at all.

But what if I'm wrong?

When it comes to Libra, caution is the farthest thing from my mind. My desire for her eclipses all else.

"Invite Libra over," I tell Fox. "It seems she and I must have a chat."

TWENTY-FIVE

Libra

STACKS OF SYMPATHY CARDS CREATE A PAPER TOWER ON the dining room table next to countless gifts that I can't bring myself to open. The once-pristine countertops are littered with opened envelopes and half-eaten plates of food. After firing Josephine, my attempts at cleaning have been half-hearted at best.

"James, you bastard," I whisper, feeling the sting of tears behind my eyes.

I face-plant against the table and groan. I hate this. I hate James.

Even after he's dead, he still controls me.

His death is supposed to be my liberation, yet here I am, trapped mourning the husband who didn't love me anymore. Grief wraps around my heart, paralyzing me along with my guilt. I should be preparing the final paintings for my gallery showing in San Francisco, but Miguel basically begged me to reschedule the showing so I had time to process the death first. Even after I told him I would be fine, that James and I had been on the verge of divorce anyway, he insisted.

269

There is always an emotional backlash, and when it comes to me, he was quick to remind me that I can be volatile. Even if that volatility is directed at myself. He was right, of course. I feel like gutter trash, and that's being generous.

"What the fuck is wrong with you, Libra?" I wipe away the traitorous tears.

I desperately wanted James out of my life. But I didn't want him dead. Asshole extraordinaire, controlling dickhead, might as well add lying, manipulative douche to that list too. And yet, when I'm alone in my huge, empty house, it's easier to imagine the long summer days that James and I spent by the pool, making love on the lounge chairs or sloppy kisses in the pool. Or late nights when we used to stay up drinking and dancing in the dining room, and he'd kiss me on the nose before we went up to bed.

James wasn't all bad. Whatever changed in him these past few years, whatever caused him to start taking his anger out on me instead of dealing with his problems, I'm not imagining it. Long before the bad times, there were the good times, too.

He didn't deserve to die like this. My chest tightens as conflicting emotions rage within me, like stormy waves crashing against each other.

My phone buzzes on the counter, tearing me away from the jumbled thoughts occupying my fucked-up head. I expect to find another concerned message from a friend of mine or James', but it's not. My heart skips a beat when Zane's name flashes on the screen.

My body aches for him. He's an easy escape for me; just one touch is all it takes to kill the thinking part of my brain and go on sensual autopilot. That's what I need right now. Him. All of him.

It's been far too long since I've had the comfort of his arms, just once in the last two weeks since the murder. I don't want word to get out about our relationship until after the murder investigation is concluded. And with dealing with the funeral, estate matters, lawyers, and bullshit … I simply haven't had the time.

I'm desperate for him to hold me right now.

I grab my keys and rush out the door. Minutes later, I'm on Zane's doorstep.

"Greetings, Libra, welcome back," Fox chimes and swings the door open for me.

But when the door opens fully, Zane is right at the door. He's been waiting for me.

"Hi, Zane."

"Libra."

He gives me a quick peck on the cheek, an abnormally sterile gesture that makes me freeze up rather than melt into him. His green-gold eyes are clouded with an emotion I can't quite decipher, making my stomach knot with anxiety.

Over the months we've been seeing each other, Zane went from always being well-dressed in the confines of his home to gradually letting his guard down around me, letting me see him in all sorts of casual wear he wouldn't be caught dead in outside his home. Today, he's dressed to the nines in a power suit, polished black shoes, and a crisp tie that means business.

Under normal circumstances, I'd be begging him to wrap that tie around my neck while he fucks me, but he doesn't look like he's in the mood.

"Care to come with me to the lounge?" he asks, finally letting me inside. He Fox closes the door behind us but doesn't stop to see if I follow.

271

The curtains in the lounge are spread fully open, letting natural light in from all directions. Zane claims the middle of his leather sofa on the far side of the room.

"Sit down," he says tersely, gesturing to the chair across from him.

I perch on the edge. "Is something wrong?"

Instead of answering, he hands me a piece of paper. Scanning the sheet, my eyes widen with horror.

"What is this?" I demand, meeting his cold stare. "Tell me this isn't what it looks like."

"I hoped you could explain it to me."

I glance at the page again — a complete list of the steps required to murder James and get away with it. The steps we determined together.

I lift my gaze back to Zane. His lips are in a firm line, his eyes cold, his jaw hardened and tense. He's not fucking around.

The room feels as if it's closing in on me, my pulse racing even as I control my breathing to maintain any resemblance to a steady mind.

What the fuck *does* he expect me to say?

I shove the note back at him across the coffee table between us. "What are you playing at, Zane?"

"I don't know what to think. A lot has happened, but I definitely didn't expect any physical evidence of the crime to show up in my house."

"You expect me to believe that you just 'found' this lying around?"

"How the hell else did it get here if you didn't plant it?"

"If I wanted to murder someone, do you think I'd be stupid enough to write down the steps and leave them lying around after I'm done? That makes no sense."

"It does if you are trying to frame someone." Zane slaps his hand on the table, sliding the notes halfway across the table toward me, still firmly in his grip. "I found these in my *home*. Crunched into a tiny ball and left out where I'd find it sooner or later."

I jump to my feet, and my hands ball into fists, nails digging into my palms. "Are you seriously suggesting that I killed my husband and want to frame you for it? Because that's the stupidest fucking thing I've heard all week, and trust me, I've heard too much bullshit."

"It sounds like *you're* trying to frame *me*."

Our narrowed eyes meet each other, independently attempting to determine who's responsible. I already decided I didn't care if Zane is the killer. I silently beg him not to do anything to make me change my mind.

He wouldn't betray me after we've shared so much, would he?

Zane grips the edge of the coffee table, roughly sliding it out of the way so he stands in front of me without the barrier between us. His body is taut with disbelief, planes of hard muscle rippling beneath his black blazer and white dress shirt. "You wanted him gone as much as I did."

"I wanted to be free, but I never wanted him dead! I told you that!"

"Or maybe you wanted me to do it for you, but you're too afraid to admit it, and now you're turning this back on me in case you become a suspect."

"We were equally involved in those late-night chats of ours. In fact, I have it on good authority that you fucking enjoyed planning all the different ways we could off my husband." I jab a finger into his hard chest, only pushing him back slightly. "So don't go pointing fingers at me without taking a close look at yourself."

"I don't know anyone else who fucks the way you do after spending hours talking about murdering her husband. It's sick."

I laugh, my hand wrapping around his tie. "Then what do you have to say about how hard you get when you play Russian Roulette? I guess we're both fucked up, Zane."

Our breaths are heavy, the hot air mingling in the narrow space between our pinched faces. My anger is a boiling pot inside me, bubbling over from his baseless accusations after I put up with it everywhere else, all day, from every direction. I never expected him to accuse me of murder, too.

But my temperature rises, and it's not the only heat making my body tingle. Zane and I are dangerously close, and with my fist wrapped around his tie, there's only one way out of this.

"Fuck it," I growl, yanking his face down to mine.

I capture his lips in a fierce, bruising kiss. Zane responds immediately, his tongue thrusting into my mouth, possessive and demanding. His hands tangle in my hair and pull me closer as if he's been craving this just as much as I have. I rip the buttons on his shirt apart and scrape my nails down the planes of his perfect torso while his hands grope up my skirt until he's knuckle-deep in my soaking wet pussy.

"What the fuck are we doing?" he hisses into my ear.

"I don't know, but don't you dare stop now."

With a husky laugh, he lifts my shirt off my head and pushes me past the couches, my ass striking the desk in the corner of the room. He hikes me up onto the wooden surface, parting my thighs so I can wrap them around him while he worships my breasts with his tongue. His lips and tongue lap greedily at my swollen nipples. Groaning, he sucks harder, and my head swims when I'm hit with the full force of his ravenous desire. Shoots of electric heat burn through my veins.

Zane yanks my skirt above my waist, exposing me entirely to rub his hard cock along my slit. My hips buck up to meet him, begging him to fill me while I grip his shoulders with white-knuckled strength.

I don't know what the hell we're doing. I really don't. How did we get from being at each other's throats, throwing accusations around about a fucking murder, to have him seconds from fucking me?

With anyone else, this would be so wrong, but for Zane, it feels so right I could scream. We're just two fucked-up people who've been grasping at straws our whole lives. Then, the moment we find something worth holding onto, we're thrown a curveball that leaves us with everything to lose. I don't want to lose Zane. Not because of James.

Zane tugs his tie loose, then wraps it around my neck. He pulls it tight, and I gasp for air. My body comes alive the second I can't breathe. My nerves spark, and everything becomes more sensitive; his rough hand shoving my thighs apart to navigate his cock to my entrance, the tingling in my breasts.

"Nod to tell me you're okay," he demands.

I nod feverishly, not wanting him to stop.

"Pat my arm three times to tell me when you need air. Do it now so I know we're on the same page."

My hips thrust at him, trying to make him breach me, but he doesn't. Relenting, I tap his arm. He relaxes the grip on the tie, and air comes rushing back into my lungs. I suck in a gulp of air before he tightens it again and plunges right inside me.

"You're so filthy I can't resist you," he groans.

My core trembles when he slams his hips forward, filling me up completely. I clench around him, my body demanding more. His hips pump in short, hard thrusts, and the way he fucks me makes it seem like he's forgotten the definition of the word gentle. Every inch of him is rough, including his grip on the tie.

My head spins, and I tap his arm again. He loosens his hold on the tie again, but his thrusts never break pace. "Harder," I moan. "Fuck me harder!"

He obliges, his tempo increasing until I feel like I'm going to shatter around him. "You get so fucking tight when I choke you," he hisses. "James was wrong about your cunt. I've never felt anything so good. Fuck!"

The desk creaks under our combined weight, and I can feel my orgasm building, my insides tightening around Zane's cock. After giving me another minute to breathe, he tugs the tie taut around my throat again, sending a shock of pain and need right to my throbbing center. All I can think about is the way he feels inside me, stretching me, claiming me.

His hips stutter, his control slipping away as my body trembles with the intensity of my orgasm. My eyes roll back in my head, lost in the overwhelming waves of pleasure ripping through me. And just as I tighten and tremble around him, Zane twitches inside me, his final thrust accompanied by a guttural grunt as he spills his load.

Dizzy with lust, I collapse against the table. "Holy shit."

He bends over me, chewing on my ear while untying the bindings from my wrists. "I told you, I'm addicted to you, Libra. Do you really think I would ever do something to risk separating us?"

I laugh because, to any sane person, that would be crazy talk. But to me, it's as good as a declaration of love. I'm addicted to him, too, and that admission already has my inner walls aching without him inside me.

"You wouldn't."

Kissing my neck, Zane lifts me like a doll and carries me to the couch in front of the fireplace. He wedges himself between me and the couch, then reaches to the side table for a remote that turns the fireplace on.

We stare into the mesmerizing flames, letting its warmth envelop us. It's a cleansing heat, one that offers the promise of redemption and a chance at a new beginning.

"What are we supposed to do now?" I whisper.

Our argument reached no conclusions except that we're crazy about each other. I want to know the truth about what happened to James, but if the way Zane makes me feel tells me anything, the truth won't change my choices.

I'm hopelessly addicted to him. I crave Zane's soul, his darkness, and his light, and nothing will ever change that. Beneath all this lust and insanity, there's more to him. To us. The realization is as empowering as it is a burden because it means my fate will be locked with him no matter where life takes us next.

Zane strokes my sweat-soaked hair while he contemplates my question. "We need to trust each other, Libra. Everything will work out in the end."

"I trust you. Do you trust me?"

"You're the only one I trust."

"Then let's burn the evidence and leave it at that."

Zane grabs the crumpled paper from the table. He holds one corner, and I take the other. Together, we feed the notes to the hungry flames. The moment our offering touches the fire, the paper curls and blackens, the ink melting into nothingness. We watch, transfixed, as the evidence disintegrates before our eyes, filling the air with the acrid scent of burning paper.

Zane's arm slips around my waist, pulling me closer. "From now on, we're in this together. No matter what."

"No matter what."

Our lips meet in a fierce kiss, and a strange sense of peace settles over me. The truth doesn't matter anymore, just the path we've chosen to walk together. For the first time since James' death, I finally feel free.

TWENTY-SIX

Zane

_____

HAZY MEMORIES OF LIBRA'S SOFT SKIN AGAINST MINE ARE disrupted by Fox's typical wake-up routine, shocking me from my sleep at six in the morning.

"Good morning, Mr. Crawford and Libra. Today's temperature will be—"

"Skip the bullshit this morning, please, Fox," I groan from beneath my pillow. "Anything important?"

The sheets next to me stir, and I gradually become aware of the warmth pressed against me. Libra. Smirking, I remember last night. After a few too many drinks, we had Fox drive us to her place, and we fucked all over her house. On James' favorite chair, the dining room table, in their bed, and, of course, in the pool.

I don't have a clue how the hell we ended up back up at my place, though. It's been a while since I drank that much.

"You have 192 missed calls from an unknown number and three voicemails. Would you like to hear them?"

"No. Block them and be done with it. How many times do I have to tell you, Fox?"

"As you wish, sir. I will continue to reroute their calls away from the residence so they will no longer disturb you."

A hand peels the pillow from above my head, assaulting me with sunlight and the pure beauty of Libra's face. Her blue eyes are still foggy like mine, but she has the same glint in them as last night when she surrendered to me. By now, I've tasted every inch of her and staked my claim, but I'm nowhere near finished with her.

If I ever could be.

A sleepy smile graces her lips, her fingers lazily tracing patterns on my chest. "Morning," she whispers, leaning in for a lingering kiss. A jolt of electricity shoots down my spine, waking me right up. "What's this about all these missed calls? Forgot how to answer a phone, did you?"

Huffing, I pull away from her to stretch my neck. "It's no big deal. Just a stalker."

"A stalker? When were you going to tell me about this?"

"I didn't think it mattered."

Libra sits up against the plush headboard of the bed, staring down at me. "My husband was just murdered. Could there be a connection?"

"What? Absolutely not. Whoever they are, they've been harassing me for years; it has nothing to do with you and James. Fox and I have tried just about everything we can think of to give me some damn peace, but nothing seems to work. We block one number, a slew of IP addresses, proxy servers … they always find a way to come back."

Libra's eyebrows scrunch like she's not sure what to think about this. "Years? That's insane, Zane."

She rolls her eyes at me when I smirk and mouth *insane Zane* back at her.

"I'm serious," she adds. "That freaks me out. Why would someone be that obsessed with—"

I arch an eyebrow at her.

Libra exhales. "Okay, fine, I understand why someone would be that obsessed with you. But look at us: we might not hurt other people, but we're not so put together. We play fucking Russian Roulette every time I'm in your house, and you don't see how a stalker could be a problem?"

"I have hurt other people, Libra. You don't make this kind of money without cracking a few eggs. Or skulls."

"I don't care about that. I'm just saying if they're stalking you, whoever they are, they probably know about me too. And if they know about me, then they could have targeted James."

"Please, Libra, listen to me." I sit up beside her and take her cheeks in my hands. A hint of fear dwells within the confusion, and Libra isn't one to get afraid. More than anything, I want to take that fear away from her. "The calls … they started a little while after Charlotte's death."

Her wide eyes flick across my face. For once, I don't hide this pain from her.

"After her murder? I … I'm sorry. I read about what they did to her and about the court case." Libra threads her hand into mine and squeezes. "You tried so hard to help her, but those VellR execs had the jury and judge in their pockets. You couldn't have done anything."

"You're wrong. I have many regrets, but I … I'm sure you know that the men who hurt her disappeared a few years ago. Nobody knows what happened to them."

"Good riddance," she says. "Whoever offed them, because that's probably what happened, saved a lot of other women from a lot of pain. I looked into it; they were serial offenders with enough money and power to do whatever the fuck they wanted and get away with it."

This time, it's my turn to examine Libra closely. I never expected to hear those words, those affirmations, come from her of all people. But I underestimated her. I don't know all the details of her past, but given the few details I've scrounged together, it wasn't all sunshine and rainbows either. She survived cancer as a child, for fuck's sake.

I trust her implicitly. Whatever else is going on in our lives, she's the one I want to wake up next to in the morning. She's the one I will do anything to protect.

She will not run away from the truth.

"It was me," I whisper. "I've never said that out loud to anyone, ever, but … I want you to know. It was me."

Libra's shiny blue eyes settle on mine, and the tiniest smile curls her lips. "I know it was you. How many times did you think you could offer to make James disappear before I picked up on it?"

"Hard to say if you ever took my offers seriously."

She shrugs. "I managed to put two and two together."

"I had five rich, powerful men kidnapped and discreetly eliminated. That doesn't bother you at all?"

"Why would it? They were monsters." Libra smirks at my confusion. "Just because you had them removed from society doesn't mean I believe you had anything to do with James. In fact, the opposite. James' death was messy, and I can't imagine you would ever willingly participate in a messy kill like that, our plans and plots aside."

"I wouldn't."

"Then there you have it." She flops back down onto the pillows, crossing her hands behind her head. "So, how *did* you have them removed?"

"I have a guy."

I lower myself back onto the bed with her, turning

over onto my side. I shouldn't tell her anything else, but the curiosity in her eyes compels me to keep speaking.

"I didn't want any details, just proof that it was done. The guy has a reputation. All I know is that his bodies are never found. He probably has them dissolved in acid or some shit."

"That's so hot."

"You think that's hot?"

"You avenged your sister. There is no one, and I mean *no one*, else in the world who would do exactly what you did to powerful people like that. You're amazing, Zane. Charlotte was lucky to have you. I'm sorry she was taken from you so young."

"I appreciate you saying that more than you know." I gently caress her cheek with my thumb. "But I didn't just do it for her; I did it for me. To try and erase some of the guilt for being unable to save her."

"That was never your responsibility."

"It was. After she was attacked, she came to live with me. I protected her and cared for her. We didn't have much, but we had each other and our dream. We worked on the Brain together. She wasn't a programmer, but she understood a lot about the way humans think. Her ideas led to a lot of my groundbreaking work. In those months after the trial, I was convinced that if I spent more time on the Brain, finishing the prototype and pushing it to completion, we could use that money to start new. But instead…"

I close my eyes, the memories of finding her cold, lifeless body shuddering through me.

"I failed her, Libra. Instead of being there for her when she needed me the most, I was obsessed with my work. The Brain. I finished it, but I lost her, Libra. I lost my sister

AUBREY PARKER

and the rest of my family. I lost the last person in the world who understood me."

Libra gently wedges her arm around my shoulders, pulling me closer and wrapping her arms around me. "It's not your fault," she murmurs against my head. "It was those VellR execs, and that's why you took care of them."

I nod against Libra's chest, a veil of numbness descending over me. "That's why I took care of them."

"Whoever is calling you, do you think they know what you did?"

"It's impossible. But you know very well that many suspect I did and have tried for a very long time to prove it. That's why the calls don't concern me, except for the annoyance." Lifting my head, I pull Libra down into a breathy, languid kiss. "If it really bothers you, I can make it a priority to lock them out permanently. I just haven't had a reason to try when Fox can ignore or filter most of the calls so they don't reach me."

Heat pools in Libra's cheeks. "You would do that for me?"

"It's hardly only for you; that bitch has lived in my head, and Fox's, for far too long," I smirk. "But yes, I'll finally do something about it. For you."

Libra's mouth meets mine again, this time with more force. She sighs between my lips, wrapping her arms around my neck to deepen the kiss and slide her tongue inside. Desire ignites from every point of contact; her touch leaves fire burning across my skin, my hands gripping her tightly and refusing to let go.

Removing the stalker from our lives is nigh impossible unless we uncover their identity, but I can work on that too. For Libra's sake. She has taken a risk by trusting me that it has nothing to do with James, and I truly believe both incidents are unrelated.

284

For Libra's peace of mind, I'll see that it's put to an end. I want her to know how much she means to me.

Libra's expression turns playful as she toys with a strand of my hair. "We're late for our round of Russian Roulette. What do you say?"

That hint of frantic excitement lights up her tone of voice and her eyes. It's impossible to resist her when she looks like she could light the whole world on fire and laugh while dancing in the ashes. She takes the crazy and makes it fun; why wouldn't I want to join her?

I've never hesitated before, but now, there is a lump in the way.

"Of course," I reply, trying to hide the creeping unease.

My life has always been a game of chance, of taking risks, but now that I have Libra, I wonder if the stakes have changed. She barely blinked when I told her I had the VellR executives killed. Somehow, it seems like she respects me for what I did.

She crawls off the bed and slips on a black silken robe, then she takes my hand and we pop open the secret door behind the bookshelf. She goes to lounge in the leather chair obscured within, and I retrieve the gun from the shelf on the other side. Trepidation hits me when I take the revolver in my hand and feed the bullet into the chamber.

I stare into the dark recesses of the barrel, facing death directly, as I have so many times before. It's not fear of blowing my brains out that tightens its grip on me, but I can't quite place what locks my finger in place when every other time I've taken this weapon in hand, the experience was always sensual. Erotic, even.

Before I found Libra, I lived a meaningless, empty existence. Revenge gave me no relief, and neither did solitude.

But being with Libra has.

I press the muzzle against my temple and pull the trigger. The click echoes through the room, and I exhale sharply. My hand trembles as I hand the revolver to Libra. She spins the cylinder and pauses before lifting it to her chin. Closing her eyes, she breathes and waits.

It's the longest Libra has ever waited before pulling the trigger. When she finally goes, the empty chamber clicks and grants her another day of life.

With an exhale as apprehensive as my own, she pops it open, takes the bullet out, and cradles the weapon in my lap.

I don't know what it is or what's changed, but Libra clearly feels it, too. We played before because we believed we had nothing to lose, but we've found something. Whether it's in each other or because of each other, I couldn't say. But I do know that it changes the meaning of the game. If one of us loses, it will not be just blood, brains, and a carcass cleaned up from the floor.

It will be someone we care for. Someone who cared for us.

Should we still be playing a game like this when there's so much at stake?

"One of these days, our luck will run out," I muse. "I wonder what will happen then?"

Libra's grip on my arm tightens. "Do you ever wonder if we should stop playing?"

"It's the allure of risk that brought us together."

"I know, but … we've already defied the odds. Again, and again, and again. Like you said, our luck is bound to run out soon."

Sighing, I pull Libra into my lab and cradle her into me. My head tucks nicely into her shoulder, where I breathe in the lingering scent of her vanilla perfume and sweat.

"Before I met you, I was lost in a sea of darkness. My life had no meaning. Money can't solve the kinds of problems I have because what I want more than anything is my family back. And that's impossible."

"I understand."

When most people say they understand, it's an empty attempt at empathy. But I truly believe that Libra does understand.

"We're both victims of circumstance. Any control that we had over our lives and dreams was brutally ripped away, and when we regained that control, it was too late to repair the damage done. Willingly choosing to risk it all, including our own lives — that is how we took control back."

Libra leans her head against mine. "When James and I met, I wasn't just some party girl who slept around for fun. I didn't come from their lifestyle. When the first older man looked at me like he wanted to see what was under my clothes, I remembered what I promised the reaper. I wasn't afraid to play my cards. I got what I wanted. They got what they wanted. Nobody was under the illusion of love, but we always had a damn good time."

"You were a sugar baby? James was trying to make it out like—"

"Like I was a whore, and he 'saved' me, right? Apparently, that's what he told Josephine, too. Fucking prick. Could you believe me ever having sex because I was desperate for money?" She laughs. "I didn't. It was the relationship I sold, not my body. If I fucked someone, it was because I wanted to, not because I was getting paid. It's about being around the right people. It was all fun until James and his fuckboy friends laid their greedy hands on me."

"I don't care about any of that either, you know. Your

past." I kiss the side of her head, strands of her hair featherlight against my lips. "I love who you are right here, right now. You don't have to justify what brought you to this place. But I am glad you trust me enough to share your story. The only reason James made you feel less than zero is because he knew you were better than him, and he needed to trap you to keep you. It was his only way. And I'm sorry that happened to you."

Libra pulls away so she can look me right in the eyes. "There's nothing to be sorry for when all that shit brought us together."

"We've spent our lives searching for something more. I don't know what's happening between us or where it will end up, but ... I don't want this to end."

"Me neither." She licks her lips. "So, neither of us murdered James. Assuming you truly believe I didn't."

We've tiptoed around the subject for weeks with neither of us outright demanding a straight answer from the other. It was easier that way, and admittedly, there was a certain thrill to not knowing. To always suspect it could have been her.

But there's so much earnestness in her eyes, so much vulnerability. It couldn't have been her who killed James.

"I believe you."

A smile lights up her face, and I can't help but return it. "But that begs the question of who did? There are still a few details that don't add up."

"My guess is James accidentally tipped Josephine off about the contents of your safe, and she broke in, thinking the two of them were really running off together."

"I don't think she killed him, though. Poor girl seems like she loved my bastard husband."

"For all we know, James found out, took the jewels

back, and some opportunist overheard and took his chance."

Libra is quiet for a moment, but then she exhales, long and weary. "Yeah, maybe the cops' first assumption was right all along. It was just a mugging gone wrong."

What we both leave unsaid are all our questions about the notes. But however they ended up in my house, they are ashes, blown away by the wind.

TWENTY-SEVEN

Libra

THE CLINK OF WINE GLASSES AND THE MUFFLED HUM OF conversation surrounds me as I enter the dimly lit restaurant. Exposed brick walls give a modern atmosphere, while the rustic wooden tables and vibrant décor add a splash of color. I scan the space, spotting Miguel sipping a cocktail at a corner booth. I fix my hair and saunter over to him.

"Libra!" He gives me a huge, toothy grin and rises from his seat to kiss me on both cheeks. "It's been too long, babe. I would say I'm terribly sorry about James, but you know how I feel about that monkey. Are you doing better?"

Today, he sports a more subdued look, natural dark lines on his cheeks and eyes, and no rhinestones. He's all business.

Laughing, I drop my purse on the leather seat and slide in across from Miguel. "Much. I didn't want to delay the show, but I think you were right. It was a good call. I would have been a fucking mess if we went through with it while I was still handling James' funeral."

"Told you I'm not just a pretty face."

"I know, I know. Tempt people with your pretty face,

then reel them in by being sane and sensical. How else would you convince all those SF skeptics to see my show?"

He grins. "Hardly any convincing required. Your artwork is so expressive and daring, I had to break up more than a few fistfights for tickets to the limited and exclusive show."

"Limited *and* exclusive? Since when?"

"Delaying the show worked in our favor in more ways than one. With everything that happened to James, there's a lot more buzz around the show. An added element of mystery, you could say."

His excitement falters as he realizes the implications of what he just said. He looks at me apologetically. "Libra, I'm so sorry. I didn't mean to suggest that we should profit off his death. That was insensitive of me. I promise I haven't been pushing that angle."

"Hey, don't worry about it." I wave off his concern as the waiter rushes over to take our orders. A wicked smile tugs at the corner of my mouth. "James wanted me to be a traditional, boring artist. He didn't support my passion for erotic art and tried to stifle my creativity. Giving my show an extra bump is the least he could do, right?"

"Libra!" Miguel gasps in mock surprise, placing a hand on his heart. "You're something else."

My phone buzzes, and I glance at the screen, grinning when I see the text from Zane. He's stuck at home, but I like how he keeps tabs on me with the tracker he put on my Lexus.

ZANE: Is he flirting with you again?

Me: Miguel flirts with everything that moves. Don't get jealous.

Zane: Jealous? Don't make me hack his phone.

Me: If you do, I'm sure you'll find some old nudes of mine.

Zane: Naughty girl. Had a fling, did you? I might just have to take a look.

Me: Isn't the real deal better? Just imagine gripping my ass while ... mmm, I'll let your imagination take charge.

"EVERYTHING OKAY?" Miguel's voice comes from above my stooped head.

I jerk my head up. Fuck, I'm being rude. "Oh, sorry. My lawyer had a few questions about a few minor assets in James' will. I told him to schedule a meeting."

"Damn, girl, look at you go. Pulling no punches. I'm so happy for you, seriously. James put you through hell, and now you're free and glowing like the goddamn sun. Hallelujah!"

The waiter brings me a fresh cup of coffee, and I take a sip of the rich, black brew. Not a hint of sugar or sweetness, just the way I like it. Once he's gone, Miguel lifts his cocktail to clink against my coffee in a mini toast, and we both take deep sips. Then, in Miguel's typical scandalous fashion, he steeples his fingers and leans across the table.

"Now tell me, honey, and be honest, what's your real inspiration for your work? I knew you and James were having trouble, but..." He smirks. "That look on your face? That, right now? Oh, yes. There is a special someone, isn't there?"

My mind drifts to Zane, his touch igniting a fire within me. While he has been an influence on my work, he is far from the only one. Without James, I haven't had the same opportunities to mingle with the socialites of our class and catch them doing the naughty — my personal favorite inspiration — but the places my mind goes when Zane and I are together, that's a fascination of its own.

I trace the rim of my coffee cup. "You know me, I draw inspiration from everyone's most intimate desires, not only my own."

Miguel waggles his eyebrows at me. "Very well, very well, my dear, but I assure you this mystery man won't stay a secret for long. Not when he makes you smile like that."

"We're supposed to finalize the details for the showing, hmm? Let's stay on topic?"

Of course, we never do. We spend the next hour going back and forth between catching up on each other's lives, discussing the guest list and the finishing touches for the show, and Miguel's personal sticking points, the wine and food. You can never have a good gathering with the wrong wine, or so he claims.

ME: You'll come see my exhibition, won't you?
      Zane: A little public for my tastes, but…
      Me: But?
      Zane: I could be convinced.
      Me: Think about the after-party. ;)
      Zane: The roof?
      Me: Never done it there before.
      Zane: No better time to pop your cherry. We'll make it a celebration to remember.

MY PHONE BUZZES every now and then with another racy text from Zane. I only glance at them every now and then because I don't want to encourage Miguel to pry — he can't help himself on the best of days.

His excitement for the show, though? Somehow, he's

more excited about it than I am, and it's not that I'm *not* excited. It's been years since my last proper showing, and I have absolute trust that Miguel will handle it perfectly. It's easy to get carried away by his enthusiasm, to let him take charge and forget about all the what-ifs and the baggage left behind by James.

"Life is full of intense emotions and experiences," Miguel says, his voice soft and passionate. "And your work goes beyond exploring the depths of human desire; it's about the raw and unapologetic hunger that drives us, the taboo lusts most ordinary people are too afraid to acknowledge, let alone express the way you have. It's my job to—"

My phone vibrates, then pitches into a series of chimes. Frowning, I glance at the screen. "Excuse me for a moment, I need to take this."

"I'll be right here, take all the time you need," Miguel drawls after me as I slide out of the booth.

I head straight to the bathroom, accepting the call as I close the door behind me. "Detective Morgan, I wasn't expecting your call. Do you have news about James' case?"

"Mrs. Scarsdale, thank you for taking my call," the detective says over the phone. "We're still investigating and have taken into consideration the information you provided regarding the belongings missing from your safe and the security camera footage. You've been a great help."

"I understand these sorts of investigations take time."

A woman exits a bathroom stall, washing her hands at the sink next to me. I hover by the vanity, turning away from the woman to listen to Morgan.

"The last time we talked, you mentioned that you hosted a dinner party at your home a few weeks before the murder. Can you tell me about the guests and any notable incidents that occurred?"

"We hosted trusted friends and James' associates at that party. You don't think someone who was there could have …" I trail off, swallowing the uncomfortable thought.

"It's our responsibility to investigate all potential leads, ma'am. Given your assurance that your safe was stocked when you last checked a few days after that party, it's still a possibility that someone present cased your home and returned weeks later. At the very least, we would like to rule out anyone close to you that we haven't already."

I take a moment to recall the details of the evening — including the argument between me and James but I don't mention his fixation on Zane or what Zane and I snuck off to do after. I know Zane isn't the one responsible, so I have no intention of highlighting their dynamic to the police.

I list each name from the guest list; Philipa Tennand, Tim Marcen, Zane, and so many others. Neighbors, associates … given James' usual preference, this party happened to be small and low-key, and I kept it that way to get Zane on the premises.

"Any incidents or disputes during the party?" Detective Morgan prompts, bringing me back to the present.

"My husband was being a bit of an ass, if you don't mind me saying. Making snide remarks about my appearance, attitude, my job, and how I managed the party. It was all very exhausting, and I have no doubt that the guests took notice. But most of them are his colleagues and have the same charm and way of thinking."

"Is there anyone in particular who might have been uncomfortable with the way James spoke about you?"

Zane, of course. He'd confided in me how he wished many times at that party to poison James' whiskey and be done with it.

"No one I can think of. No one said anything at the party. The only ones who might have cared were the wives in attendance, but I'm not particularly close with any of them. I'm sorry, Detective, I wish I could be more help."

"We'll be in touch if we have any further questions."

"Wait," I hurry to ask before he hangs up, "there's something you aren't telling me, isn't there? What did you discover?"

"I cannot disclose the intimate details of our investigation at this time, but we appreciate your cooperation. Enjoy the rest of your evening, ma'am."

I hang up the phone and exhaling a shaky breath, leaning against the counter in front of the bathroom vanity and closing my eyes. If the cops take a closer look at the guests at the party, they will take a closer look at Zane, and who knows what rabbit hole that will bring us down?

After splashing some water on my face, I return to the table, finding mine and Miguel's steaming meals waiting on the table. The buttery potatoes on my plate make my mouth water.

"It seems everyone wants a piece of me today." I offer him a wide smile once I slide back into place. "My God, this smells amazing. I got back just in time."

Miguel and I continue right where we left off, but even with a good meal and better company to distract me from Detective Morgan's phone call, I struggle to prevent my thoughts from drifting into a spiral of worry.

TWENTY-EIGHT

Zane
_____

THERE ARE HOURS AND HOURS OF FOOTAGE FROM INSIDE MY mansion. With a hyper-intelligent AI capable of reviewing much of it simultaneously, I never thought I would have no choice but to manually review it myself. I've rewatched the footage from the foyer leaving the kitchen where I found the crumpled note, but I've yet to solve the mystery of where they came from.

The footage shows Sophia cleaning the study, picking the ball of paper from the floor, and then carrying it through the foyer toward the laundry room. She gets a phone call near the stairs, and when she shifts the basket of other junk she's gathered from around the house, the note revealing the method of James' murder tumbles to the floor, and she doesn't notice.

As far as I can tell, the paper simply appeared out of nowhere. It was on the floor for a whole day, appearing shortly after Sophia left, and was then removed when she finds it. In all the angles of footage, she never pauses to read the paper; she treats it like any other trash.

I prop my head up in my hands. My eyes burn from the amount of time I've spent in front of the screen these past few days trying to figure this out. I told Libra that I dropped the issue, but I haven't.

I don't suspect her, but that note didn't *actually* come out of nowhere. Someone put it there, and I have to figure out who it was.

"Fox, has anyone unauthorized been around the premises or attempted to enter the property?"

"Negative; no suspicious individuals have been detected."

My fingers tap impatiently on the desk, frustration mounting with each passing second. Then, the camera rushes ahead to last week when Libra and I fucked like wild animals in the study. I completely forgot that some of our heated encounters were recorded.

A smirk tugs at the corner of my lips as I watch the video play out, my hands roaming over Libra's supple curves, her moans echoing through the speakers. The memory of her warmth beneath me makes me wish she was here right now, and I can't help but imagine her reaction if I were to share this discovery with her.

"Save this one, Fox." I shift in place to stop my erection from straining uncomfortably in my pants. "I think Libra might enjoy it."

"Understood, Mr. Crawford, I have archived the requested footage for later viewing."

As much as I want to linger on this moment with Libra, I force myself to return to my investigation. I need to uncover the truth for both of our sakes and until then, we have no choice but to be careful about how often we see each other.

I can afford a moment to share this particularly juicy clip with her, though...

"Fox, can you—"

A trilling sound echoes through the room. "You have an incoming call from Detective Morgan."

"The detective? What the…? Connect it." Scratching my head, I spin my chair away from the screen and take a refreshing sip of water. "Zane Crawford speaking."

"Mr. Crawford, this is Detective Morgan. My team and I are investigating James Scarsdale's murder."

"Yes, I'm aware of who you are. You earned honors at the Academy for your impeccable investigative skills, and last year, you caught the Blue River serial killer before the feds. Very impressive. I trust you will find the killer in due time."

"As a part of our inquiry, we're performing a preliminary investigation on everyone who attended Mr. and Mrs. Scarsdale's dinner party a few weeks ago."

"I can't say I am pleased by the prospect of being investigated, Detective. I relocated to Woodside for privacy."

"Of course, sir, but I'm sure you understand it's protocol to narrow our search and eliminate potential suspects. Your cooperation could go a long way to closing this case and putting a murderer away. All we ask for at this time is permission to investigate your property."

My pulse quickens, a cold sweat breaking out across my forehead. A thousand thoughts race through my mind. I want to help the police as much as I can for Libra's peace of mind, but if the police get anywhere near my internet search history, I'll be the one going down for murder.

My best hope is to keep the cops away from my house.

"That's a big ask out of nowhere, Detective. Is there any specific reason you think searching my property will help the investigation?" I ask, trying to buy time.

"Your land borders the Scarsdales', and it's possible the murderer accessed your land to commit the crime."

"I understand your position, but I must refuse your request. From what you've told me, there is no valid reason for you to consider me a suspect; the walls bordering my property are high-tech and heavily monitored. I cooperated with your previous request to share footage from around the time of the murder, which I do recall showed nothing of assistance to the investigation because James was traveling in the opposite direction. I'm more than happy to assist in any way that doesn't involve violating the sanctity of my home. But if you insist on treating me like I had any involvement, you'll be hearing from my lawyer."

"Very well, Mr. Crawford," Detective Morgan replies after a pause, his voice measured but obviously unimpressed by my response. They're never happy when you lawyer up. "We'll respect your wishes for now."

As soon as the call ends, my hands begin to shake. I steady them against my lap. The cops are sniffing around, but that doesn't mean they have anything on me.

"Fox," I whisper, my voice cracking, "is there any way to make my search history disappear?"

"Unfortunately, due to your programming, any questionable search history—"

"I know it's saved just in case of shit like this. I want to know if there's a way we can override it."

"Had we taken precautions at an earlier date, it's possible, but all data saved in this system is distributed to and stored in several overseas servers."

"Damn it." I slam my fist against the wall. "And I thought I'm a fucking genius. I'm a fucking idiot, that's what I am."

The pain in my hand barely registers. My mind races,

trying to find a solution, any solution, to save my ass if the cops gain any evidence that could lead to a warrant.

They shouldn't. *I didn't kill James.*

But that doesn't mean shit when the real killer is still out there, doing God knows what. For all we know, I could be the real target, not James. They could want me to go down for any of the numerous questionable acts I've committed over the years.

They just want me to suffer and squirm before they bring the guillotine down.

If the police gain access to my search history, they'll uncover a treasure trove of elaborate prompts asking Fox how to get away with murder and highly specific questions with answers that would tie me directly to the investigation. To them, that will probably be as good as a written confession.

I'd go from annoying rich neighbor to prime murder suspect in about thirty seconds, and I have no way to defend myself.

I run my fingers through my hair, frustration and fear bubbling beneath the surface. Mine and Libra's research was born from morbid fascination and a way to vent our frustrations, not genuine intent. But try explaining that to a jury.

Obviously, my alibi is solid. I was asleep at home when the murder happened, and my security cameras will prove that. But when weighed against the other evidence, the police might be less inclined to trust that the AI wasn't lying about my whereabouts.

Libra knows I didn't kill James. But if the investigation pinned me as guilty, would she stand by my side or leave me to drown under their suspicion? I can't bear to lose her now.

Dwelling on what-ifs won't save me. I need to be proactive and protect myself.

"All right, we can't delete the search history permanently, but we can find a way to bypass your programming and make it a pain in the ass for anyone to gain access. Let's get to work."

"As you wish, sir. We can create a new layer of encryption with a time lock that would require proper authorization and allow for a delay before delivering the data to the police, but the system would be quite complicated, as you cannot alter my core code relating to these current security measures."

Fox initiates the coding panel and thousands of lines appear in sequences on the screen. My focus narrows in search of the parameters that are preventing me from doing what I want. Before I can create anything new, I have to remember how exactly any new code will interact with it.

And then pray I was smart enough to leave a loophole just in case something like this happened.

"Consider planting false logs in the system that would provide alternative explanations for your searches," Fox suggests while I work.

"Would that be legal?"

"I don't see why not, sir. Indeed, you did attempt to write a murder mystery four years ago; you merely regained interest in continuing your book over the past few months."

"Good idea, Fox. It wouldn't be far from the truth anyway…"

As the hours tick by, my fingers ache, and my eyes burn, but I can't pull myself away from the screen. The code has been nothing but uncooperative. Nothing I've tried to hook a loophole into the system has worked, and this is probably the only time I've cursed my genius. I can't fucking undo my own goddamn work!

"Mr. Crawford, I regrettably cannot authorize the delivery of another caffeinated beverage. After consuming approximately 1000mg of caffeine over the past twelve hours, with no sleep or proper food, you will be at serious risk of ongoing health problems."

"I don't care, I need to keep going,"

"You need rest. My sensors indicate that you are experiencing severe heart palpitations and are at risk of reducing the flow of blood to your brain. Should that happen, you could have a stroke. A few hours of rest will allow you to revisit the problem with fresh eyes."

The persistent ticking of the clock on the wall is a cruel reminder that time is slipping through my fingers, each second bringing the threat of Detective Morgan banging on my door with a legal search warrant. I can't afford to lose focus now. I blink and stare at the screen, but the white letters blur on the screen.

Dizzy, I rest my head against the desk. "Fucking fuck."

"If it would ease your mind, I can continue your work in your absence, and you can review my attempts when you wake."

I shake my head, sighing. "No, I think this is a dead end. If I had a few days to crack it, maybe, but I don't know how much time I have. I should consider my other options first."

If only I could just make Fox forget that it exists, like what happened when I woke up that one morning and he glitched and forgot about the morning routine. Such a simple problem, but if I could repeat it…

"That's it!" I fly into an upright position. "Fox, roll your systems back two months."

"But, sir, I would have no choice but to revert to a

previous system version. A rollback that large would have a 68.4% chance of corrupting data or reintroducing instabilities in my programming that you have since fixed."

"That's the point. If we purge you of your 'memories' of the time that Libra and I made all our plans, the evidence should disappear with it."

The blue light above my wall of computer screens blinks while Fox attempts to determine the plausibility of this plan of action. "Technically, yes; however, this would not eliminate the backups stored on alternative servers."

My head hits the desk harder this time. "Fuck. You're right…"

Despite my best efforts, the futility of my situation finally hit me in full force. It's like being submerged in an ice-cold bathtub and thrown into the winter cold.

There's no way to completely eliminate my search history or hide it from law enforcement. I'm stuck with it one way or another, and unless the police find a lead that leads them closer to the real killer, everything I have is a ticking time bomb. The only way to save myself is to throw them off my scent.

"Should you create any false leads or provide misleading information," Fox says, "you could be charged with obstruction of justice or accessory to murder, depending on their final determination of your motives and how the case concludes. I advise you not to make any irrational choices. Sleep first, and when your mind is restored, we can continue to discuss options."

"But—"

"I'm afraid I must insist, sir."

The screens wink out one by one, the sprawling lines of code disappearing, replaced with black, lifeless screens. A haze of frustration clouds my mind, but I've considered every possibility. I need to tackle this again in the morning when I'm operating on more than an hour of sleep and energy drinks.

The thought of having to explain my way out of this mess terrifies me. I can only hope that my innocence will speak for itself because otherwise, I'm fucked six ways from Sunday.

TWENTY-NINE

Libra

THE SHOWING IS EVERYTHING MIGUEL PROMISED ME AND more. The once-empty building was transformed into an open but intimate space, each piece of my art given room to breathe and stand on its own beneath individual spotlights while adding to the collection's overall story.

Hushed conversations bounce from every corner of the gallery, and every now and then, Miguel's eccentricity echoes above it all. With him in charge, the show really is a roaring success. Art critics, enthusiasts, and deep pocket collectors wander the halls admiring my sensual paintings. My cheeks hurt from smiling so much, but I wouldn't change that for the world — it's been so long since I've been surrounded by so many people who adore my work.

"Libra," Zane murmurs from behind me.

I turn to meet his intense gaze, his deep-set emerald eyes sparkling. My heart skips at the sight of him. Zane almost always dresses well, but he went all out for me tonight. Dressed in a tailored tuxedo, he exudes an air of refined masculinity, and he commands the attention of every person who lays eyes on him, including me.

"Wow, look at you, Mr. Crawford." I grin when he takes my hand in a firm shake, both of us conscious of the eyes on us. "A rare appearance for little old me?"

"I'm just here to support my favorite artist."

"You're only saying that because you're my neighbor."

He smirks, gaze trailing down the split leg in my shimmering black dress. "Oh, I don't know, there could be other reasons. Such as your marvelous works of art."

"In that case, allow me to give you the grand tour."

Zane follows the click of my heels, keeping close as we tread deeper into the darkened gallery space, but not too close. Our relationship is still strictly under wraps, but there shouldn't be any danger in us being seen together in a public space so long as we don't touch in any way that could be interpreted as overly scandalous. Not all the hushed whispers and furtive glances being exchanged among the attendees are about me and Zane, though. The intrigue surrounding James' murder hangs heavy in the air, an unanswered question on everyone's lips.

James left us a month ago, and while my wounds are far from healed, I can't be expected to be a sobbing widow in public for the rest of my life.

I pause in front of the first painting visible from the gallery's entrance. Zane comes up beside me, hovering close enough so I hear him when he whispers. "I suggest you be careful with how you move those hips ... I'm not the only one in this room fantasizing about bending you over in the storage room."

"Quite fitting for the mood, I believe." I gesture to the painting, a portrait of a woman's lower back. Her curves are on full display as she arches her back and pushes her ass toward the viewer. Nothing below the top of her crack is visible, but the painting has all the suggestive flairs and the position of her torso against the dark sheets — it's alluring for all that remains obscured. "A gallery must open with an invitation, and this painting poses exactly that; an invitation to infinite pleasures."

The rich hues and bold strokes reveal passion and desire, eliciting a palpable reaction from those who dare to look. Like all those before him, Zane takes his time to drink in the colors and lights, putting himself in the middle of the fantasy.

A waiter weaves through the crowded hall, and Zane snatches two champagne flutes, one for each of us. He tilts his to mine, our glasses clanking.

He sips, staring at me with those burning eyes. "Are those my hands?" he whispers.

I only offer him a seductive smile and turn to the left, guiding him to the next painting. "What do you think of this one?"

Zane steps closer, his eyes narrowing as he scrutinizes the canvas. "I feel the urgency, the longing ... the need for connection. That moment when everything else fades away, and all that matters is the person in front of you."

"Exactly," I breathe, thrilled by his insight.

We dare not look at each other, but the silence is charged, the tension in the short gap between our bodies attempting to pull us together. To make us forget the rules of our world and the games we play to stay on top. To forget everyone and everyone around us to simply stare at each other. The air is so thick I can hardly breathe, let alone remember my train of thought.

"Your art has a way of drawing people in, Libra," Zane says at last, his voice husky. "You truly deserve the attention you're receiving tonight."

"Thank you," I whisper, my heart swelling with gratitude. "Thank you for supporting me from the very beginning."

Beside Zane, I feel like a queen; the artist and the tech billionaire making waves in high society. The other women here want to be me, and the men wish they were him. The perfect power couple — if only we were allowed to portray ourselves as such.

We share a secret smile as we continue to navigate the gallery, and I wish he could take my arm without having to worry about the photos in the papers tomorrow.

But no, we are merely friends, and in the eyes of everyone else, that's how it must stay.

For now.

Later, for our midnight rendezvous on the roof, Zane will show me I'm his in all the ways that matter.

We mosey along, chatting with all the guests to discuss techniques and their praises for my paintings. All the while, Zane wanders off to explore on his own, but his presence in the building is like a magnetic force, trying to draw me closer whenever I move.

"Libra, I was so sorry to hear about your husband," a pleasant woman with bright pink lips says as she squeezes my arm. "Murder? How awful. Have the police captured the one responsible?"

"Not yet, but they're keeping me updated, and they are still investigating leads."

Another bold woman pushes in closer. "Do you have any idea who might have wanted to hurt him? It's positively a scandal, a man like that murdered down the street from his house in a town like Woodside!"

I tense, caught off guard by the blunt question. "I wish I knew, ladies, but all I have the authority to speak on is how much positive energy I put into every one of these paintings," I reply tersely, trying to steer the conversation back to my art. "They serve as an escape from the pain of our lives, allowing us to immerse ourselves in our deepest fantasies."

"What a delight," a male guest says. "You must tell us more about your inspirations for these marvelous works of art."

Like Miguel before them, I give them mystery and a wink to leave them wondering. After doing the rounds, I find Zane near the center of the gallery, contemplating every detail with hunger radiating off him.

Zane seems to sense my disquiet, his hand brushing against mine as we drift from one conversation and painting to the next. "Your work speaks for itself, Libra. Don't let the rumors about James ruin your night."

It's a fleeting touch, but it sends a jolt of electricity through me, grounding me in the here and now.

"This one is you, too," he murmurs, standing before a canvas depicting a woman's hand gripping a silk sheet, her body writhing in ecstasy. "I can hear your moans like they were sung into my ear yesterday."

"Your imagination is running wild, Mr. Crawford," I tease, feeling a flush rise to my cheeks. Heat simmers just below the surface of his words, infecting me. "I'm impressed by how accurate your guesses are of which paintings are of me."

"How could I not know? I've memorized every patch of skin, every shadow." He sighs deeply. "Every touch."

We arrive at the largest mural I painted as the center-piece — my inner thigh and my reaper tattoo. Zane's lips curl as he examines the details of the painting; no words are needed.

This painting will always hold a special place in my heart; it's the first one I painted for Zane, with Zane in mind. He's the one who's touching me, holding me, making my body tense with anticipation. He is not present in the painting that suggests I'm touching myself, but he's all that's on my mind.

The intensity of my passion is captured in vibrant strokes of red and gold. Zane's eyes follow the lines of the artwork, his breath hitching subtly as he takes it all in.

"This one is … breathtaking," he says, his voice dark and rich.

It occurs to me that this is the first time he's seen the painting in person. I've shown him many pictures and until recently, the painting had a prominent position in my personal studio space, but seeing it in person must be a different experience entirely.

"This one is inspired by the story of Orpheus and Eurydice — the tragic beauty of their love. In my version of the myth, Orpheus followed Eurydice to the underworld, and together, they beat death, and their love was reborn in another life."

I pause, letting the weight of my words sink in to the small crowd gathered around the central gallery space. My words seem to cast a spell over them, and they eagerly wait for more.

"Love is like fire; it can warm your soul, or it can consume you whole. But passion, passion is—"

The gallery doors burst open, and a swarm of reporters flood the room. Camera flashes strobe through the dim lighting, disorienting and blinding. Before I know it, microphones are thrust into our faces, and questions are hurled at us with alarming speed.

"Mrs. Scarsdale! Mr. Crawford! Is it true that you two were having an affair when Mr. Scarsdale was alive?"

"Did you conspire together to have Mr. Scarsdale killed?"

"Is your relationship the motive behind his murder?"

The accusations hit me like a slap in the face, and my

stomach churns with shock and indignation. Zane's jaw clenches, and I can see the fury burning in his eyes. He's always been protective of me, and now, more than ever, I'm grateful for his presence. But I see his impatience straining, and I know I have to speak before he does.

"I loved my husband very much," I say, my voice shaking. "Mr. Crawford is my dear friend, and he has been nothing but supportive during this difficult time."

"Did Mr. Scarsdale discover—"

"Enough!" Zane roars, silencing the cacophony of voices. "How dare you vultures interrupt this *private* party to throw baseless accusations at a grieving woman. We are here to celebrate love and life as portrayed in Libra Scarsdale's art. The investigation is in good hands with the proper authorities, where it belongs." Zane jerks his head to the side. "Security, remove them immediately."

The reporters seem momentarily taken aback by Zane's outburst, but I struggle to keep my composure, my heart racing and my breath coming in harsh bursts. My dress feels too tight, the room too hot.

Is that what people really think about me?

How did anyone make the connection between me and Zane?

Security moves swiftly, forcibly escorting the crowd of reporters out of the gallery as the crowd of my *actual* guests watch in stunned silence. The doors slam shut behind the security guards.

The eyes of all the gallery's guests pin me. Their eyes burn like an unrelenting itch beneath my skin. I drift away from Zane's side, clearing my throat and trying to regain some semblance of control, forcing a smile onto my lips as I turn back towards my paintings. What the fuck else am I supposed to do right now?

The alternative is to run.

I don't run.

"Let's focus on the art, shall we?" My voice wavers slightly, but I push through, determined not to let the night be entirely ruined.

As I resume my interpretation of Orpheus and Eurydice, it becomes apparent that the once lively atmosphere now feels strained and uncomfortable. My ears are sensitive to their hushed questions, wondering if the accusations are true. I finish sharing the story I spent the last few weeks perfecting, but the delivery is lackluster, and so is the reception.

Nobody cares about my representations of finding love through death when all they want to know is if Zane and I are murderers.

Wandering away from the main gallery, my shoulders slump, and I throw back the rest of my champagne. I'm fucking drained.

Miguel sidles up beside me. "I think we should wrap up early, babe. The mood has definitely changed."

"Unfortunately, I agree," I sigh, casting a glance at Zane, who stands nearby, pretending he's deep in conversation with another couple. His expression is a mixture of concern and frustration. "It's such a shame; I'm so proud of these paintings, and they deserve better than this."

"Everyone knows those reporters were out of line, and the evening was fantastic until they showed their wrinkly faces," Miguel reassures me, placing a comforting hand on my shoulder. "There's a light to the evening, though. There are exceptional bids placed on every single piece of art at the show. Well done, beautiful. We'll talk business next week."

"Silver linings," I muse.

Resigned, Miguel and I begin wrapping up the night together, knowing that there's little else to be done. As the evening draws to a close, Zane lingers by the exit. He catches my eye, and we exchange a mournful look before he disappears through the doors. We have no choice but to sacrifice our night on the roof.

After Zane and I were accused of having an affair, it's important that the two of us are seen leaving separately. Without a doubt, the damage has already been done, but that doesn't mean we're ready to face it.

THIRTY

Zane
___

WHENEVER I MOVE, THE WEIGHT OF MY HANGOVER SLAMS into my head like an ocean current, threatening to drag me under. I'm sprawled out on the bedroom floor, halfway between the bed and the ensuite, because I still don't know if I'm going to vomit again and sure as fuck don't want to get puke in my bed.

"Fuck," I mutter, taking a shaky drag of my half-smoked joint. The taste of disappointment lingers on my tongue.

Images from Libra's opening night for her erotic collection flicker through my mind — her sultry smile, her teasing touches when no one was looking, and the spark of mischief in her eyes as we'd planned our date on the gallery roof after the night was said and done.

We didn't get to make love under the stars. Instead, those reporters threw accusations at me and Libra. She, of all fucking people, deserved a few hours to enjoy herself and celebrate her hard work.

But those selfish assholes took that away from her.

They separated us, and they left me with no choice but

to get piss drunk on my own because now Libra and I can't see each other. We both hate it, but it's safer for both of us if we don't spend any time together until this whole situation blows over. If we thought the paparazzi who were sneaking into Woodside were ruthless enough when James died, they'll shake what little faith I have left in humanity now that they think Libra and I might have had something to do with James' death.

Hopefully, the cops will find James' killer sooner rather than later because being apart from Libra is agonizing, and the rumors are fucking killing me.

How long will it be before I can feel her skin against mine again? Touch her lips with my own?

It feels like there's a jackhammer drilling into my skull. I close my eyes to shut out the memories of last night and take another hit. The smoke fills my lungs, dulling the edges of my pain and anger into a fuzzy animal I can keep a hold of instead of letting them get out of control.

"Mr. Crawford?" Sophia's voice floats through the crack in the door, which creaks open under her careful touch.

I barely notice her at first until, in the corner of my eye, I notice that she's made some … adjustments to her usual uniform. The skirt is so short it barely covers her upper thighs, and she's replaced her usual nude stockings with black fishnets that stop right below the hem. The neckline of her apron is so nonexistent it's barely an apron anymore. The right — or wrong — movement could send her tits flying out into the open.

She walks over in her usual fashion to try and flash me. I nip that in the bud and sit up before she gets the chance. A wave of nausea assaults me at once, and I clutch my head in my hands to stop the spinning. It doesn't work.

"Feeling a little rough?" Sophia giggles. "I have my mama's favorite hangover cure right here."

She carries a tray with two tall glasses of green sludge and a pack of saltine crackers. I take one of the cold glasses and eye the disgusting-looking sludge.

"What the hell is this?"

"Cucumber, kale, lemon, ginger, and pineapple juice. Taste ain't too great, but it'll clear your head quick after a night on the town."

"Mmm, just what the doctor ordered."

I sniff the glass and grimace before taking a tentative sip. It's gritty, sweet yet bitter, and somehow not the most disgusting thing I've tasted. I gulp down a few more mouthfuls.

"Not too bad, hmm?"

Sophia sets the tray down on my side table and crouches next to me, her cleavage almost spilling out of her low-plunging top. She hands me a cracker. "These, too, between sips."

After finishing the first glass, I let my stomach settle. "I still feel like shit, but my headache is gone, so that's an improvement."

"I'm glad I could help, Mr. Crawford." Sophia leans in closer, her eyelashes fluttering. "But I think a green drink isn't the only hangover cure you need. After last night's scandal, I'm sure you could use a little … relief."

She trails a finger down my bare torso, but I snatch her hand and shove her away. "Fuck off, Sophia, I'm not in the mood."

She pouts, her full lips forming a perfect circle of mock disappointment. "You wouldn't feel so horrible if you didn't go out with that bimbo last night." The venom in her voice is unmistakable.

"Watch your mouth. Libra's husband was just murdered. Have some goddamn respect."

"I can make you feel better. You still want her after the headlines? Everyone thinks she murdered her husband, and the media will drag your name down with her!"

"I don't care. She needs me, and she's worth it."

Sophia's eyes widen, taken aback. "I don't get it. How did she wrap you around her finger?"

"You, of all people, should understand what it's like to be wrongfully accused. Didn't one of your previous employers claim you stole his wife's jewelry when he really pawned it off and wanted to get back at you for refusing to sleep with him? Libra is innocent, and I won't let anyone talk about her like she's a criminal."

She averts her gaze, her cheeks staining pink. "How can you say that for sure?"

"Because I lo — Because I trust her."

Her eyes narrow, and she climbs to her feet. Smoothing her skirt, she says, "Fine. You know where I'll be when you come to your senses."

She walks off and out of my bedroom, slamming the door behind her. I slump back to the floor with a groan. "More like you know where I'll be when you come to yours. Christ." I palm the floor, searching for my joint, but it's gone. "Seriously, Sophia? You bitch." I sigh. "Fox, grab me another, why don't you?"

"I would, sir, but I do believe the law enforcement officers walking to your front door would not appreciate you waving marijuana in their faces."

I shoot up to a sitting position again, blinking away the nausea that follows. "What the fuck, Fox, you let the cops into my property without telling me?"

"I verified their badge numbers and cross-referenced their warrant against the Woodside and San Francisco legal databases. Based on my law enforcement cooperation protocols, I could not deny them entry to the premises."

"Shit," I hiss and scramble over to the closet. "Get me something to wear."

My head spins as the closet walls part with an array of clothes for my perusal. I pick a nice suit with dark, luxury fabric, but not *too* nice, a pair of polished shoes, and try not to shout too many more expletives at Fox for letting the damn cops into my house while I'm this hungover.

The room tilts and sways around me, but I force myself to focus. Spotting the second cup of Sophia's unholy hangover cure, I toss the rest of it back and another handful of crackers until I feel like something resembling human again.

If I thought not getting to see Libra for a few days was bad, I have a feeling my life's about to get a whole lot worse.

I never figured out how to block access to my search history or even delay access to those files. If the cops are here with a warrant that includes access to that search history, I'm fucked.

When I reach the bottom of the stairs, Detective Morgan and Officer Lillian are waiting for me in the foyer. When Morgan spots me, he tilts his head in my direction with a smug smile and waves a piece of paper in my direction. "I told you I'd be back with a warrant."

I don't scowl at him, but I settle a steely gaze on him and hold out a hand. "Give me that."

He assents and passes the warrant. It gives permission for the Woodside department to search my house and property for the murder weapon, proof of an ongoing secret affair between me and Libra, phone records, and permission to search any digital devices, including questioning my house AI as far back as the last six months for details pertinent to uncovering the identity of James Scarsdale's murderer.

I hand the warrant back to him. "I do wonder how you managed to obtain that without any evidence. I'm no murderer."

Detective Morgan files the paper away in a pocket on the inside of his coat. "Forgive me if I don't take your word for it. You could have disclosed your affair with Mrs. Scarsdale to us but chose not to. Isn't that suspicious? I wonder what you're hiding in this nice big mansion of yours."

"Attending the opening night at the gallery as a friend and the rumors squawked by illegitimate reporters is hardly proof of anything."

"No, but once that door was opened, we found a credible witness and enough evidence to support the theory and enough probable cause for a warrant. Now, if you don't mind, Mr. Crawford, we have a job to do. Unless you plan on helping us along?"

Three more officers pile on in through the door behind him, and they set out to divide and conquer as they start tearing the place apart in search of evidence. They're not going to find anything except for that search history.

I prepared for this worse-case scenario as best as I could. After determining that I wouldn't be able to hide my search history, my lawyer prepped me on what to do in case the police came into my home: don't say anything and give him a call.

"Nope. And if you don't mind, I'm going to call my lawyer."

Knowing he'll just follow me wherever I go, I turn away from Detective Morgan and head to the kitchen, where Fox has already poured me a fresh cup of coffee. I don't bother to offer the police any; they're busy looking through my shit. And I mean all of it. They swarm into my home, their footsteps echoing through the otherwise silent mansion.

I sip on the hot beverage while I warn my lawyer, Mr. Jug, about what's going on. Basically, I'm to stay calm and not say a word more than I have to. He'll meet me at the police station in an hour unless I text to let him know the police didn't arrest me.

I can't help but worry about what the police will find. After all my searching and puzzling over surveillance footage, I never figured out who left those notes in my study. There was no proof or markers of any unauthorized entry to the house according to Sophia and Fox, and nothing suspicious on any of the cameras.

The only possibility I can think of is that Libra or I wrote them while we were drunk as hell and being stupid. We accidentally played mind games on ourselves.

Or they were planted.

We have no proof. I could be paranoid. But being paranoid sounds a lot better than a momentary lapse in judgment getting me and Libra charged with a murder we didn't commit and costing us everything.

It's not long before they find proof of mine and Libra's affair — it's not like I hide it. She has a whole dresser upstairs dedicated to her clothes now. Freshly laundered, but they still smell like her, and they've helped me through the many days and nights I've gone without her these past few months.

Detective Morgan seats himself on the island stool and stares me right in the face. "AI, you're programmed to comply with law enforcement, isn't that correct? It doesn't have any special privileges that will interfere with our search?"

"That's correct, sir. No one is above the law, and it is

my duty to assist you, given that I already determined that your search warrant is valid. How can I help?" Fox intones from the kitchen speaker.

"Are there any concerning records logged in your system with information that would aid in an arrest for James Scarsdale's murder?"

"It is not within my capacity to judge any individual as guilty or innocent of any crime. However, as determined by the regulations enforced by the Government of California and the ethics and service agreements for using CognitiveAI's home AI system, I logged some search results that may be of interest to the murder investigation. I've sent preliminary documentation of what I found to the tablet on the counter in front of you, Detective Morgan."

He takes the tablet, and Officer Lillian looks over his shoulder. "Look at this." She points to the screen. "He was looking into ways to fake his own death. How to disappear without a trace."

"Isn't that interesting?" Detective Morgan chuckles. "Care to explain, Mr. Crawford?"

"Everyone has their dark curiosities. It doesn't mean anything. Don't you wish to disappear from your life every now and then?"

"Yeah, it's called a vacation."

"More than a vacation. Like a more extreme version of what I accomplished by moving to Woodside and withdrawing from society."

"Sure, buddy. Let's see what else we have here."

"Queries such as 'how to get away with murder,' 'what kinds of murders have the lowest chances of being solved,' and 'how to fake a robbery' as well as various other related searches may be of particular interest," Fox suggests. "Should I continue?"

"That won't be necessary, AI. Forward all of these documents to the police department ASAP. The Woodside Police Department thanks you for your cooperation." Morgan smirks as he whips out his handcuffs. "Now, if *you* don't mind, Mr. Crawford, I'd much rather you didn't resist arrest the same way you've resisted us this entire investigation. We've collected more than enough evidence to bring you in for further questioning."

"I didn't kill James," I mutter. "I have nothing to do with his murder!"

"Then you'll have no problem coming down to the station so we can ask you a couple more questions while we take a deeper look at your search history, won't you?"

"Fine. Do what you have to."

Officer Lillian takes the handcuffs. I put my hands behind my back, and she circles around to cuff me and let her drag me out of my home. "Zane Crawford," she says, "you are under arrest on suspicion of involvement in the murder of James Scarsdale. You have the right to remain silent. Anything you say can and will be used against you in a court of law."

The cold metal bites into my skin, and I have to remind myself this is only temporary. Once I have the chance to explain what they found, they'll have to release me. I just need to make them listen.

Unless the real murderer planted evidence that could put me and Libra away forever.

THIRTY-ONE

Libra

I HATE SCROLLING THROUGH SOCIAL FEEDS, BUT THIS morning, I'm basically a crack addict breathing in that sweet, sweet high. *Provocative and Daring* reads one review of the opening night for my art collection. *A Sensual Exploration*, reads another.

A bubbly excitement fills me, like popping a bottle of champagne, and I keep scrolling in search of more praise for my work.

"My God, Zane would love this," I cackle and stretch out on my bed like a cat. "*The Art of Voyeurism.*"

I wish he was here. My heart pangs with his absence and our forced separation last night. We should be sharing this moment together; there's no one else I'd rather celebrate with. Sorry, Miguel. He did so much work to pull the gallery off, but Zane just knows how to make my heart sing and take that feeling of being on top of the world and taking it to another level.

The curated feed I've selected refreshes, and there's a new headliner complaining about my 'irresponsible' and 'morally dubious' art in light of recent events. I laugh out loud. "Really, you're going to be swayed by fucking rumors?"

The review was written by Morna Grimes, one of California's top art critics. Ugh. It doesn't get any better as I read, throwing around conspiracy theories about how the paintings are all the different ways I cheated on James. 'Erotic, but shameless, though doubtlessly Mrs. Scarsdale will attract an audience uncaring of her dubious moral character and representations of sex in her art and will laud her as a brave artist for her exploits,' she writes in her review. If I hadn't lived a life adjacent to the spotlight for most of my adult life, I'd be surprised that bullshit slander like this could get published, but I'm not.

Even though I got glowing reviews from NYC's finest and many other big names, it feels personal to get so much hate from someone I admire stateside. Sighing, I click out of the article to look for more good news to uncurdled my mood.

My phone buzzes.

MIGUEL: Controversy only fuels the fires of adoration, babe.

Libra: Everyone loves a scandal. Any press is good press. I know, I know.

Miguel: One bad review from an old hag too afraid to look at her own cooch won't sway the people who matter.

THE DRAMA SURROUNDING my husband's death has only made my art more sought after and more intriguing, especially to folk who would usually turn their nose up at provocative art like mine. Overall, the critiques of my work are positive, and I can be more than satisfied with that.

Miguel has been closed-lipped about the potential buyers for the collection, but I know I'll forget all about Morna's shitty review when I'm handed a stack of cheques in my name.

My laughter dies in my throat when my newsfeed updates, revealing an article that makes my heart plummet. *Zane Crawford Arrested in Connection to James Scarsdale Murder*, the headline screams at me. The blood drains from my face.

"Impossible," I whisper, unable to comprehend what I'm reading.

There's no way Zane is guilty. The room seems to tilt and spin with each word, the walls closing in around me like a vice. I had assumed Zane would be watching me this morning as he always did when I went to swim and paint, but now...

I grab my phone off the bed, then dash to the window facing Zane's property. I throw the curtains open and smash my face into the windowpane, spotting the police cars flashing their sirens as they glide down the hill from Zane's house.

Fear slices through me. He told me about the potential issue of his internet search history, but he said it wouldn't be a problem unless the police had enough evidence to get a search warrant. What did they get on him?

My mind flashes back to us burning those notes about James' murder in his fireplace. Could they have found a copy or something similar?

I rush down the stairs, grab my purse from the kitchen table, and hurry out the door. I don't know what they plan on doing with Zane, but I'm probably the only person who can provide more context to the situation and prove Zane isn't guilty.

The only person besides the real killer.

THE COLD AND sterile interrogation room is about as intimidating as it can get with its plain walls, bright fluorescent light pointed right above my head, and Detective Morgan and Officer Lillian glaring at me from the other side of the table.

"Zane is innocent," I say for the tenth time.

My left leg shakes as I wait for them to say something. They stuck me in here for twenty minutes on my own and only joined me five minutes ago, and they've been silent.

Detective Morgan clears his throat. "Mrs. Scarsdale, I understand you want to speak on Zane Crawford's behalf, but as it stands, he looks pretty guilty. I'm sure your lawyer advised you not to talk to us alone or say anything to risk incriminating yourself, so why are you here?"

"I never stopped to question if it was a bad idea to stop the police from arresting an innocent man, Detective."

He sighs. "Do you have any idea what kind of man you're in bed with, Mrs. Scarsdale?"

"I don't know what you mean."

"This isn't the first time Zane Crawford has been suspected of murder. Since you two are close, I imagine you're familiar with the court case surrounding his younger sister, Charlotte Crawford?"

"I am familiar with what those monsters did to her, yes. What does that have to do with my husband?"

"Nothing, really, except for the fact that all the men who were accused and found innocent disappeared several years ago. The feds have been trying to pin it on Zane for a long time now."

"What is there to pin on him, exactly, Detective? He didn't do anything. As far as anyone knows, those men disappeared. There are no bodies, no evidence or a crime, and a lot of libelous claims against an innocent man. I wonder if he could sue the government for harassing him all these years."

Detective Morgan laughs. "All right, you're a smart woman, so I won't bullshit you. We have enough evidence to put Zane away for a long time. Nothing you say is gonna change that."

"You're still bullshitting me. You and I both know you don't have anything but circumstantial evidence."

"Then why are you here? Why bother risking your own skin?"

"Because it's the right thing to do."

"Your husband must be rolling over in his grave knowing you're at the precinct defending the man who murdered him, and you've been fucking behind his back."

"You don't know anything about my life or my relationship with my husband. Are you always so judgmental about people who enjoy the company of people other than their spouses, or do you just hate Zane in general? I'm trying to get a full picture here, Detective, so I can give my lawyer thorough notes about your attitude next time I talk to him."

Officer Lillian's mouth twists, and she clicks her pen, tapping it on the manila folder in front of her. "You're saying you and your husband had an agreement — that he knew about your affair?"

I relax back into the chair. "James suspected something was going on between me and Zane, but I don't think he knew I had it in me to fuck another man in his house the same way he liked to screw our housekeeper when he thought I wasn't looking. There was no arrangement. James was very vocal about how he didn't want an *agreement*; he liked to cheat and the power he thought it gave him over me. In other words, we independently made the decision to be unfaithful to each other."

"You sound bitter. It must have hurt a lot when you found out, Mrs. Scarsdale."

"Sure, it did, but James showed me his true colors. When I confronted him about his affair, he took it as a challenge and started fucking her when I was home and could listen."

"So you wanted him to die?"

"Don't put words in my mouth. James and I ... had grown apart over the years. He became possessive and controlling. I felt trapped. He became a shit husband, but he didn't deserve to die like that. Whoever is responsible should be sent to prison for a long time, but it wasn't me, and it wasn't Zane Crawford. I'm here to set the record straight by any means possible."

"Are you claiming to know the identity of the real killer, then?"

I shake my head. "Unfortunately, no, I don't know who it is, but I want to provide as much information as I can."

Detective Morgan and Officer Lillian share a long look. "We're not impressed with how dishonest you and Mr. Crawford have been regarding information pertaining to this case."

"I was protecting my best interests. That doesn't make me a murderer. Will you hear me out or not?"

"You might as well tell us everything."

Taking a deep breath, I grip my thighs under the table and tell them what my marriage was like with James before I met Zane. "Our affair started three months ago, although there was nothing physical until about a month after our first encounter."

"I'm not sure I follow," Detective Morgan says. "Was it an emotional affair first?"

"It all started when I caught Zane spying on me with his binoculars from the hill. I'm an exhibitionist, and he's a voyeur, you see. I had no idea who he was, and I liked it that way, but he kept watching me, and I eventually grew curious."

Time seems to slow to a crawl in this suffocating room, every tick of the clock on the wall feeling like an eternity as I relay the events leading up to James' death and my affair with Zane. I can't help but feel like a specimen under a microscope, laid bare for this stranger to dissect and analyze; it's obvious they've never dealt with a situation as strange as ours before.

"None of this explains the evidence we found that incriminates Mr. Crawford," Officer Lillian says.

"You're talking about the search history stored in the house AI's data servers, right? I'm getting there." Sitting up straight, I fold my hands on the table. "I was unhappy with my marriage. James knew it but didn't care, and if I wanted a divorce, he promised it would be messy."

"You wanted him dead, naturally."

I let out an exasperated breath. "No. I didn't want him dead, Detective. As my relationship with Zane progressed, we often talked about what it would be like if James wasn't in the picture anymore. If he couldn't control me, if I could finally be free, then we wouldn't have to sneak around."

"You admit that you and Zane plotted to kill your husband."

"We didn't plot anything. It was therapeutic to imagine offing James in very detailed scenarios; it started as a joke. I mostly laughed off Zane's ideas until the night of the dinner party, where James insulted me in front of our guests, disparaged my artwork and career, and made it very clear that he didn't care if I was miserable. He had no intention of ceding to my requests."

"You're saying it was a joke?" Detective Morgan scratches his head. "The guy must have missed the memo since he wound up dead. You're not helping your case here, Mrs. Scarsdale."

"Discussing something doesn't make you guilty of doing it. We talked about the ways we could kill James as an outlet for stress, but we had zero intention of acting on those fantasies. We're not murderers."

"I can understand the desire to vent your frustrations about your marriage, but the information we found in Zane Crawford's search history goes beyond blowing off some steam and having a laugh." Officer Lillian opens the folder in front of her to scan her notes. "We uncovered detailed plans for various kinds of poisons and methods of acquisition and administration, cutting his breaks after a routine maintenance check to pin the crime on someone else, making him disappear on a cruise, tricking him into killing himself using virtual reality — that one's new to me — and finally what seems to be the layout of your husband's murder: faking a robbery and using overkill and the robbery to confuse detectives into misunderstanding the circumstances of the murder."

Detective Morgan looks over at Officer Lillian and smirks. "The technological aspects of the plan were quite puzzling. We had to confirm with our experts that the vehicle was indeed remotely deactivated to put Mr. Scarsdale in a vulnerable position for his murderer. You expect us to believe you two made these detailed plans but never acted on them? You and Zane have motive and opportunity, and your alibis are your personal home security systems."

A chill courses through me. So whoever did it *actually* followed our plan to the letter.

My mouth goes dry. "The camera footage from that night clearly shows that neither of us left our respective houses."

"True, but footage can be falsified."

"You think Zane's AI would cooperate with your investigation and then falsify his alibi? That wouldn't make any sense."

"Maybe not, but I have a hard time believing that either of you are completely innocent in all this. If you and Zane didn't conspire to murder James Scarsdale or commit the act yourself, who did? You've yet to suggest an alternative or produce a legitimate alternative."

The detective's piercing gaze seems to cut right through me. I grit my teeth, frustration getting the better of me. It's only natural that they have doubts, but there has to be something I can give them to clear both our names and point them in the direction of the real killer.

For a tense moment, Detective Thompson watches me carefully, his eyes searching mine as if trying to uncover the truth hidden within my soul. The room is silent, save for my ragged breathing and the steady ticking of the clock on the wall. Every second feels like an eternity, each beat of my heart echoing loudly in my ears.

"There's … there is something that might help," I say.

Detective Morgan opens his hands plaintively. "By all means."

"I don't know all the details, but it could be related. Zane has been receiving weird phone calls from an unknown number for the last year or so, longer than he and I have been seeing each other. Sometimes upwards of more than a hundred a day. Sometimes, she leaves messages. Zane doesn't like to talk about it, but I convinced the house AI to let me listen to the messages once, and they're … creepy. Most of the time nonsensical, but creepy. He had to develop a system to reroute and filter the calls so he wouldn't have to hear them all day."

"Did Zane ever file a police report?" Officer Lillian asks.

I shrug. "That's his business. He didn't really want to talk about it."

"Female stalkers are rare, and their victims aren't usually male or experience violent deaths like James'. It could be worth looking into. If there are that many calls and it's ongoing, there will be a record of the calls. Maybe we can find something there."

"Zane insisted the calls weren't related to James' murder, but I had a stalker when I was a teen. When someone who is that obsessed with you gets involved with someone else, they can lash out. If that's what Zane has been experiencing, the origin could be unrelated, but the murder could be linked."

Lillian nods at me with encouragement. "Do you have anything else that could help?"

"There's one more thing." I chew on my lip. Zane probably won't like it if I tell the cops this, but I couldn't stand to see him imprisoned for long. "Before I knew about the stalker, Zane found some notes in his house — a detailed account of James' murder. This was a few days after his death. He thought I planted them in his house to fuck with him, but I didn't put them there. We agreed that maybe one of us wrote them up one night when we were fucking around and forgot about it."

"Those notes are evidence. We'll need to see them immediately."

"That won't be possible." I flatten my hands on the

table. "We thought the police would have captured the real killer by now, so we burned them."

"Destroying evidence..." Officer Lillian shakes her head.

I swallow hard. "I'm sorry. I didn't think it would get to this."

"We never do until it does."

Detective Morgan and Officer Lillian rise from their seats. "All right, Mrs. Scarsdale, thanks for the information. We need to hold you for the time being while we verify this information. We'll be with you shortly."

The door clicks shut behind them, and when they're gone, I hang my head over the back of the chair and close my eyes. The bright fluorescent light burns against my eyelids, but it still feels like the walls are closing in around me. I was hoping that they would give me an idea of what kind of evidence they have against Zane so I could disprove it, but no such luck.

Now, I wait alone in the interrogation room, and I have no idea if I made the situation better or worse.

THIRTY-TWO

Zane

THE COLD METAL CHAIR BITES INTO MY THIGHS. SWEAT drips from my brow, and I tap my fingers against the table in an erratic rhythm.

My lawyer, seated beside me at the table, appears utterly unfazed by the situation while he rifles through paperwork. His natural red hair glows under the unnatural light, and his dark suit is crisp and still smells of steam and dry cleaning. I envy his composure. He's not the one terrified out of his damn mind that the real murderer could have planted something to incriminate me.

I stare into the dark lens of the video camera. Now that Mr. Jug is here, the red recording eye has turned off, but that doesn't help quell my racing heart. At least I stopped pacing.

"Mr. Crawford," my lawyer says suddenly, breaking my spiral of thoughts without lifting his head. "Try to calm down. Your anxiety won't help your case."

"Easy for you to say," I snap. "Innocent men have gone to prison with much less evidence against them."

He gives me a look that tells me to stop being a fucking

idiot. I don't pay him out the ass for no reason. If anyone can figure this out, it's Mr. Jug.

The cops have had me in here all day. During my initial interrogation, I tried to ask about Libra, but the detectives remained tight-lipped about her position or if they took her into custody. I can't stand the thought of them interrogating her and putting her through this stressful process, too, or worse, accusing her of something she didn't do. Against my lawyer's recommendations, I told them everything I could about our relationship. I know that neither I nor Libra is responsible, and maybe there's a detail that we both missed that could make a difference in catching who murdered James.

"Any news on Libra?" I ask.

He shakes his head. "Focus on your own situation for now."

The red light on the camera clicks on at the same time that door into the interrogation room creaks open. The detectives stride back into the room, Morgan with his leather jacket and Lillian with her tight ponytail. Rather than the smugness Morgan was wearing earlier, their faces stone-cold and impassive.

"Finally, I was beginning to think you forgot about the law," Mr. Jug says and slams his briefcase shut. "Unless you've managed to conjure up some hard evidence against my client, you're required by law to release Mr. Crawford within the next twelve hours."

Detective Morgan leans over the table, his face inches from mine. His breath smells like stale coffee as he sneers, "Don't think we're finished with you yet, Zane. Rich tech assholes like you might think they can get away with murder, but we know better."

"Believe me, Detective," I say, trying to keep my voice steady, "I had nothing to do with James' murder."

"Sure, sure. Someone else just happened to come along and commit the perfect crime, leaving no evidence behind until we dig through your computer and figure out why. Nobody else on our suspect list has the hacking skills or the proper equipment to remotely deactivate security cameras and a moving vehicle without leaving a trace. Did you really think we would believe your story that your twisted murder fantasies were just fiction?"

"No one was supposed to get hurt! Libra and I were—"

"Ah yes, Libra," he interrupts. "Your secret lover. The two of you make quite the pair, don't you? A match made in hell. Was it her idea or your idea to murder James?"

"Enough!" Mr. Jug raises his voice enough to sound intimidating. "I will not tolerate you attempting to bully my client into confessing to a crime he did not commit. You have nothing to link Mr. Crawford to the scene of the crime, and you've yet to disprove his alibi — and let me tell you right now, you won't. Our best analysts found the camera footage solid and untampered with, and yours will, too. If you don't let him go, I'll make sure this entire department pays for your misconduct."

Officer Lillian has yet to speak a word, but she and Detective Morgan exchange glances, their faces tight with frustration. They might suspect that I'm responsible, but they know the law is on our side, and as much as they might want to pin this murder on me, they can't do it without proof.

"We have enough to charge you as an accessory," Officer Lillian says. "We might not be able to pin you as the murderer at this moment, but it would be real easy to convince a judge that you knew it was going to happen and did nothing. Or worse, you helped the actual killer develop their plan and let them get away. If you didn't do it, who did, Zane?"

I hang my head and drag my hands across my face. "I don't know. I wish I did."

"Are you sure about that? Because I'm pretty fuckin' sure I'm staring right at him," Detective Morgan growls. "Your AI system logged everything. James' schedule so you knew when he wouldn't be home and when to expect him, how to catch him by surprise outside of video range, and how to throw the cops off your trail. Every single detail you needed to get away with it."

I shake my head, seeing what direction this is taking. They don't want to believe a damn thing I've said or have to say, and I've told them everything I can think of to prove that I'm innocent. "I don't know what you want me to tell you. Someone must have hacked into the database, stolen the plans, and then carried them out. That's the only possibility that makes sense."

"More sense than Libra going rogue and killing her husband herself?"

I give him a hard look. It's so cliché of him to expect me to throw Libra under the bus just because she's the only person of interest who has a bigger reason to off her husband than I do.

"Yes."

"I want to believe you, Mr. Crawford," Officer Lillian says, "but you need to give us more if you don't want to get charged. *Is* it possible someone other than Libra stole those plans?"

Detective Morgan scowls at her. "I can't believe you're going to give this clown the benefit of the doubt."

"Come on, Detective, work with me here." Lillian looks back at me. "The data extracted from your house AI is stored on a server outside of your home, isn't it? Who else would have had access?"

Now that's a question. I lift my head, directing my attention at her. "No employee has high enough authorization to get in. The system used to store and transfer data from AI using the Brain models double-encrypts data, and as a safety measure, no one person's data is stored in the same location or under the same encryptions. The only person who can reclaim all that data is the verified owner of the data. This is as much to prevent users from destroying their incriminating searches as much as it is to protect their privacy and the integrity of any police investigations that require it."

"Then looking at CognitiveAI employees won't help us. And a hacker wouldn't be able to gain access without someone noticing. Doesn't that invalidate your theory about a third party enacting that murder?"

I spread my palms over the glass table, trying to gather my thoughts. "I know what you're thinking. And yes, it's unlikely. The employees maintaining the servers wouldn't know exactly what is stored there."

"You're not helping your case here, buddy," Detective Morgan says. "Mr. Lawyer, isn't it your job to stop your client from further incriminating himself?"

"Mr. Crawford—" Mr. Jug starts, but I raise a hand to stop him. My thoughts are spinning, and I won't let him interrupt.

Only three people know the locations of all the data stores, and even I, the founder, owner, and designer of the systems in question, am blocked from attempting to access any of that data on my own, precisely so I can't ever be charged personally if any information is compromised. I learned that the hard way when I realized how badly it was going to fuck me.

"To gather all of the data that Fox willingly handed over to you from one of our company servers, a hacker would need to identify which servers hold the data relevant to their queries and individually hack into each location. That doesn't make it *impossible*. Someone who wanted in would have a better chance at getting around those protections by—" I cut myself off as soon as I realized what I'd missed before. "Shit."

"What? What did you just remember?"

A sense of dread comes over me. I don't know how I didn't see it.

"The only way someone would have stolen that data without sending any alarms to CognitiveAI would be by directly stealing it — by walking into my house and asking for it. Just like you did."

"Really? Now you're messing with us. First, a hacker, and then claiming someone walked right into your mansion with state-of-the-art security and an AI assistant that's always watching and stealing your files? They would still need to be someone with the right skills, man. Next thing we know, you'll be blaming your poor immigrant housekeeper who can barely use her phone, let alone a computer, of committing murder."

"Sophia wouldn't hurt a fly," I say immediately. "But someone else…"

The notes Libra and I found might have been left behind by the killer after all to mess with us — or they could have been their first mistake. They made it inside and out without leaving a trace, except for those notes. Why? It doesn't make any sense.

Except … they didn't get in and out without a trace, not really.

"Someone is framing us. I'm sure of it." With absolute certainty, I look between Lillian and Morgan and give them the most serious expression I can muster. "In the months leading up to James' murder, there were instances when I noticed something wasn't right with Fox and the whole AI system. He was experiencing unusual glitches, and there were inconsistencies with his coding. It took me weeks to resolve. Things that shouldn't happen in such an advanced system."

Detective Morgan leans forward, his eyes narrowing. "And you never thought to report these issues to your security team?"

"Of course I did, but they checked everything, I checked everything, and there was never any sign of a hacker. It really just seemed like a glitch. I fixed it by tweaking a few errors in the code and rolling the house AI software back by a few days. And then there was the time shortly after James' murder that we found some notes about his death balled up like it was supposed to be trash. I looked into it, but the one who wrote them was never caught on camera."

Fox is supposed to warn me of any attacks on my home security, hardware, or the AI itself, but I never received any notifications about one. That means there either wasn't one, or somehow whoever is responsible managed to bypass the alerts somehow. Of all the weird issues Fox was experiencing, I never thought they could have been the work of the murderer trying to mess with me or throw me off their trail.

"Seems too convenient, don't you think?" It's Lillian who's skeptical now, talking to Detective Morgan. "You found evidence that could have helped us solve the crime and then destroyed it instead of using it to help clear your name. All these so-called 'glitches,' but no proof of a breach."

"Are you implying I made this up?" I ask, my voice

rising despite my efforts to stay calm. "Why would I do that?"

"Maybe you thought you could get away with it, but you're just not as smart as you think you are."

The air in the room is thick with tension as we glare at each other. How much longer will this nightmare go on? What the hell can I do or say to prove I'm not a murderer? Thankfully, despite not programming much over these past few years, I still have good habits from the time of my life when I barely lifted my eyes from my computer screens.

"I always save the error logs just in case I need them to solve additional problems that crop up in the future. A good software development habit." I side-eye Mr. Jug. "Fox wouldn't have given you that information along with everything else, but I can easily get that for you as well. It proves the AI was experiencing unusual problems around the time the murder happened. And then there's ... Well, tell them."

My heart races as my lawyer clears his throat, commanding the room's attention. "Detectives," he begins, his voice calm and collected, "I'd like to bring up another matter that might be of interest in this investigation." He pauses, letting the anticipation build. "For the past year, my client has been receiving phone calls from an unknown number. Whoever is behind these calls has managed to bypass Mr. Crawford's extensive security measures despite being repeatedly blocked and rerouted."

I didn't want to take this route, but I don't see any other way out. If we're wrong about a possible connection, then we could be unburying graves that I don't want dug up, and everything I've done to protect Charlotte's legacy could be undone.

Though I've tried to ignore the harassment, the

constant phone calls from my stalker have left me drained and on edge.

"Though we can't say for certain whether there's any connection," Mr. Jug continues, "it stands to reason that whoever is responsible for these calls may also have had the means to gain unauthorized access to my client's AI system and manipulate the information found there. Disabling the internal security long enough to harvest data and extract it from within, perhaps on one of the rare occasions while the premises were entirely unoccupied."

The detectives exchange glances, their skepticism still evident. "And you believe this person could be the real murderer?" Lillian asks.

"It's certainly worth considering, especially given the lack of hard evidence against my client."

Detective Morgan and Officer Lillian glance at each other. They're quiet for a moment too long, and there's something hesitant about the way they regard each other. I pretend I don't notice.

I hold my breath. They know something. They know something and they're choosing not to tell me.

"Alright," Detective Morgan concedes, his tone begrudging. "I'll need all the information you have about this so-called stalker. Call logs, numbers, everything you have about the proxy addresses, IPs, and whatever else."

"It's all right here." Mr. Jug opens his briefcase and retrieves a packet, which he slides across the table to the detectives. "Everything you will need to continue your investigation."

Morgan peeks inside the envelope. It's large, about three inches thick, and there's a *lot* of information in there. "We'll look into it." His chair scrapes behind him as he stands up. "In the meantime, Mr. Crawford, you're free to go."

"I'm not one to look a gift horse in the mouth, but ... why? Just like that?"

Lillian gives me a tight smile. "Mrs. Scarsdale arrived earlier this afternoon to provide a testimony that corroborates with yours. Given this additional evidence, we will take the time to investigate alternative leads."

Morgan adds, "However, this doesn't mean you're off the hook. You'll be on house arrest until we verify this information and make a determination about whether it affects our perception of your guilt. Two cruisers will be on the property at all times. If any new evidence comes to light, we won't hesitate to bring you back in."

"Understood," I say, doing my best to keep my voice steady.

"Good. Get out of my sight."

I rise from my chair, my limbs trembling with a mix of relief and rage. Mr. Jug snaps his briefcase closed again and offers me a reassuring smile. As we walk out of the interrogation room, I feel the heavy stares on me but refuse to meet them. I just want to get the hell out of here.

The scent of stale coffee and sweat fills my nostrils, grounding me in the present moment, but questions swirl in my mind as we make our way through the Woodside precinct. I hope giving the detectives a glimpse into my private struggles helps them find the murderer, but I have my doubts.

If they were willing to murder James to keep their secrets, just how far will they be willing to go to keep the cops off their trail?

As I step outside into the cool night air, freedom hits me with relief so great I suck in a gulp. The sky is dark but filled with the glow of city lights. Being outside has never felt so amazing as this moment that I've escaped the claustrophobic nightmare of that interrogation room. While I'm grateful to be out, I can't shake the feeling that I'm still trapped. I yearn for the day when the real murderer is caught and this hell finally ends.

Sighing, I follow Mr. Jug toward the car. "I just don't get it. After all this, I still can't figure out who the hell killed James and why."

"Doesn't matter. That's the cops' job, not yours," Mr. Jug says. "Your job is to keep your nose out of trouble and not interfere. Keep your head down, and let the experts handle it."

A sly smile curls my lips. "You don't mean the cops, do you?"

"Of course not, kid. I'm putting a team of CognitiveAI experts on this possible hacker problem as we speak. By morning, we'll have an elite team assembled, analyzing the security breaches again and hunting that bastard down."

Grinning, I hop in the car with him. No matter what, we will uncover the truth. Leave it up to my guys to get a handle on the situation immediately. They might want me to keep out of it, but as if that's ever going to happen.

I'll give them a few days of glory.

First things first, after all ... I need to celebrate my freedom with Libra.

THIRTY-THREE

Libra

ZANE'S FRONT DOOR CHIMES WHEN FOX RECOGNIZES ME, and the door swings open to let me into the foyer. My hands fly to my chest as I hurry inside. "Zane?"

"Welcome, Libra," Fox's voice comes from the nearest speaker. "Mr. Crawford was released from the Woodside precinct and is currently en route. Please make yourself comfortable."

"Thanks, Fox."

I don't want comfort; I want Zane, but I can't wait around at home doing nothing but twiddling my thumbs like I have been for the past five hours since Detective Morgan released me from holding. They wouldn't tell me a damn thing about whether I'd helped them or Zane, just sent me on my way and told me not to go far. As if I'd run off and disappear without Zane.

After all this, I'm starting to see why he thought disappearing was the best way to get away from James. Dealing with the cops, the drama, and the suspicion is more exhausting than I imagined.

I glance at the grand staircase, remembering the heat

of our last passionate encounter on those same steps, and shiver with desire. Zane has marked every room, every surface with our lust, and I ache to be reunited with him. He's the only one I've ever met who truly understands me. He sees past my need for excitement and adventure and into the depths of my being, shining a light on the pieces of me that I've kept hidden from everyone else, including James.

A shadow moves between the threshold for the foyer and the kitchen, and Sophia glides through without looking at me, carrying a vase of fresh flowers. She places them on the console table between the doorway to the study and the lounge. The vibrant colors and fragrant scent a stark contrast with her icy demeanor when she finally notices me.

She glares with hate so deep and penetrating it's like she believes I'm the one who killed *her* husband. "You again," she hisses, her voice dripping with disdain. "Zane will get bored of you sooner or later if you show up all the time like a lovesick puppy. He despises easy women like you."

"I wonder what that says about you," I say coolly, eying her skimpy maid's outfit, which has lost a few inches on the skirt and all modesty since the last time I had the displeasure of laying eyes on her. "Your jealousy is unbecoming."

"You think you have any idea what he wants? You're not good enough for him. If you know what's good for you, you'll—" Sophia's sour expression immediately brightens into a glowing smile when the door swings open behind me. "Mr. Crawford! Welcome home!"

I whirl around, revealing Zane in all his gloriousness. His fine suit is rumpled, he's undone two of the buttons by his collar, and his chocolate brown hair is a mess like he's spent all day running his hands through it. And the

AUBREY PARKER

shadows under his eyes ... I've never seen him so exhausted.

I wish I could say I didn't have any doubts that the police would release Zane, but I was terrified. I can only imagine how horrible he felt all day, trapped in an interrogation room, with those detectives hammering him with questions and trying to get him to break.

My breath catches in my throat when our eyes meet, and a tidal wave of emotion swallows me. In an instant, I'm across the room, throwing myself into his arms, our bodies colliding. His strong arms grip me tightly as if he's afraid I'll slip away.

"Zane, I was so worried about you," I breathe against his neck.

"The moment they released me, all I wanted was to be with you," he murmurs, his voice thick with emotion.

"Promise me you'll never leave me again. I don't know what I'd do without you."

His firm lips part slightly, and then his mouth brushes against mine. His breath tickles my lips, our tongues tangling and setting my entire body aflame. All the ice and fear locked inside me begins to crack and melt away with each motion until I'm trembling in his arms.

As we cling to each other, the world around us fades away, leaving only the heat of our bodies and the relentless ache of desire. In Zane's arms, I am free — free in the way I've always dreamed of. There's no one else for me but him.

"Let's go upstairs," Zane whispers urgently, his hands roaming over my body with a hunger that leaves searing heat wherever he touches.

"I kept the house in perfect order while you were away," Sophia announces, rudely interrupting the moment and inserting herself closer to us and the conversation. At some point, she must have dipped into the kitchen because now she's carrying a tray of muffins as she sways toward the entrance. "I baked your favorite: cranberry and chocolate. Would you like to try one? It's the perfect treat to settle your nerves after a long day."

The way she moves toward Zane, like a clumsy seductress, makes me want to cringe. She reminds me *far* too much of Josephine.

Zane gives Sophia a passing glance. "Thanks, Sophia, I appreciate that. Leave one on the counter, and I'll have it for breakfast; I think it's time to hit the hay." His eyes travel back to me but then flick in her direction again, squinting. "Didn't I tell you to change your uniform?"

Her lips press into a fine line, even while she's trying to maintain her sickly sweet smile. It gives her a rumpled look, half-irritated while trying to maintain her façade. "I know you like this, Mr. Crawford. There's no need to hide your desires."

"Right, okay." He exhales through his teeth. "We'll talk about it later. You can go home now. I'll see you in the morning."

She drops the act. "But *Zane* — Mr. Crawford, I've been so worried about you! Won't you tell me at all what happened?"

"In the morning. Please, Sophia, I need rest, and so does Libra."

He tucks me against his side, and I try not to smile *too* smugly at Sophia. I'm not sure how she can go about calling me easy while she looks like a sexy maid from a porno and practically throws herself at him at every opportunity.

For a fraction of a second, her attention shifts to me, showing that flicker of hate. Then she smooths it over and returns to her Zane-vision. "As you wish, sir. I'll return in the morning to tend to your every need."

With an exaggerated curtsy, she dips low enough to reveal her cleavage and then disappears into the kitchen with her tray of muffins.

Zane's attention is immediately back on me, his mouth sucking on the lobe of my ear and sending a shiver of desire through me. "The only thing I want to eat right now is you."

"Mmm, that can be arranged. Dine in for one?"

He moves fast, grabbing me and lifting me into his arms. I squeak when his mouth captures mine, and I melt into him instantly. My hands cradle the back of his neck as we kiss each other with pure lust, ravenous for each other.

Zane carries me up to the fourth floor, or at least he tries to. We can't seem to keep our hands off one another, and we get distracted along the way; on the second floor, he veers off into the game room and slams the door shut behind us. One look in his eyes and I see the fire in him, that desire that he can't contain any longer. He plants me on my feet, and he wraps his hands around my waist, his touch electric and everything I need right now.

In the dim light, I catch a glimpse of the pool table before my back collides with the edge. Zane's hands are everywhere, tearing at my clothes, his touch igniting a fire within me that craves to be sated.

"Zane, oh God, Zane," I gasp, my thoughts scattering like leaves in a storm, all coherence lost as the world narrows down to the heat and pressure of his body against mine. My dress lies in tatters on the floor, discarded and forgotten in our haste to taste each other's skin.

"You have no idea how much I've missed you," he groans, his lips trailing a blazing path along my neck, tasting every inch of my exposed skin. "I was fucking terrified. They threatened to put me away as an accessory for admitting to making the plans with you. Can you believe that?"

"Assholes," I start, but quickly break off into a moan as Zane's mouth captures one of my nipples. He sucks and swirls his tongue in a way that has my eyes rolling back. All I can do is cling to him, my nails digging into his shoulders, desperate to anchor myself.

I know he's not just referring to the sex; he missed the closeness, our connection. Until James died, and our freedom became at risk in a way I never expected, I took Zane for granted. That we would always play our little game of neighbor screwing neighbor beneath the watchful eye of everyone else. As his touch sends electric jolts through me, awakening every nerve ending and leaving a trail of fire in its wake, I know I missed more than this. I missed the way I feel when we're together, laughing and enjoying life together — the depraved, the insane, and the normal, too.

"I missed you too," I moan, pushing my weight against the pool table to spread my legs for him. He sucks on my hip, wedging himself between my thighs and licking lower. "And this, God, I missed this…"

He maps out my body with his tongue, committing each curve and dip to memory so he can return to them again and again. My hands tangle in his hair, guiding him lower.

He chuckles darkly at my whimper and doesn't stop the slow, torturous exploration of my body. I grip the edge of the pool table, my nails digging into the felt as he continues his descent. His lips brush against my core, teasing me before slipping a finger inside. "Tell me how much you missed it, baby."

"Zane, I … I missed it so much." I arch my back to

meet his ministrations. "I missed your touch, your taste, everything about you." His fingers stroke me in time with his tongue, and I can feel myself unraveling under his expert ministrations. "I'm ... I'm going to—"

He looks up at me with those smoldering emerald eyes, a smirk playing on his lips. "Let me hear you scream."

His desires fan the flames already licking at my insides, stoking my desire to a fever pitch. I can't form words as the pleasure builds within me, my entire body on edge, teetering on the brink of release. His fingers and tongue work together, driving me higher and higher. I abandon all the semblance of composure I have left and let out a primal cry as my orgasm washes over me in waves.

My nails dig deeper into the pool table's felt, my body trembling under his expert touch. He doesn't stop there, though; he's relentless in his worship, his tongue and fingers continuing to tease and torment every sensitive spot he remembers so well, pushing me over the edge again and again until I'm limp in his arms.

"Oh God," I pant, my breathing ragged.

When I finally come back down, I run my fingers through his hair, just enjoying the physicality of him. Memories are nothing when he's right here with me. His hands slip underneath my thong and discard them with ease before he stands before me, his arousal tenting his pants.

Zane grins wickedly, a devilish glint in his eye. "The best meal I've had in weeks."

"My turn?"

"I'm afraid I'm a selfish man. I can't go another second without plowing you into the fucking abyss."

Unable to resist any longer, I fumble with his belt, my fingers trembling with urgency. The moment it comes undone, I slide my hand inside his pants, grasping his cock and feeling it pulse beneath my touch.

His hands claw beneath my ass, and with one swift motion, he lifts me onto the pool table. My legs instinctively wrap around his waist, pulling him closer.

As he penetrates me, I gasp, the sudden fullness overwhelming my senses. Our eyes lock in an intense, heated daze while he fucks me. I lose myself in the moment, surrendering to him completely. The pool balls shake and rattle with each thrust, rhythmic and so fast I can barely think beyond the pleasure. In Zane's arms, I am more than just a possession, a trophy wife to be paraded around for appearances' sake. I am free, loved, and cherished for who I truly am.

"Zane," I whisper, my voice barely audible above the sound of our labored breaths. "I've never felt more alive than when I'm with you. I hate that this — this investigation, James' murderer, is trying to take that away from us."

Our lips meet in a searing kiss, tongues dancing and tasting each other. The heat between us grows hotter, more intense, until it feels like we might combust at any moment, consumed by the inferno of our desire.

"I won't let anyone tear us apart," he growls against my lips. "I promise. You and me against the world."

My eyes flutter shut, and in the back of my mind, a dark thought tugs at me, a whisper that suggests the killer is trying to do just that – tear us apart. It can't be a coincidence that this all started after Zane and I started our affair or a coincidence that it's James who ended up dead.

Zane slams back into me, and I push the thought away to instead lift my hips to meet him. Ecstasy courses through my veins, surging through me like a supernova that radiates with the warmth of Zane's body against mine.

He pulls away from my lips, growling as he sucks and

bites on my neck. His hips jerk and rotate, finding those perfect spots that bring me right to the edge again. But just as I'm about to explode again, Zane pulls out of me and flips me from my back and onto my stomach. His erection bulges between my ass cheeks, and he slots himself inside me again, sending a ripple of want through my whole body.

He grips my hips firmly, guiding himself back and forth inside me with a groan of satisfaction.

"God, you feel incredible," he murmurs, his breath hot on my neck. He thrusts with a renewed urgency.

I moan in response, my body quivering with each delicious impact, every stroke driving me closer and closer to the edge. "Zane, I'm so close," I gasp, my words punctuated by the rhythmic sounds of our bodies colliding.

"Let go," he urges, his voice raw as his teeth scrape my neck. "Let go and come with me."

His words are all it takes. Together, we plunge over the precipice, our bodies shattering with the force of our climax. Waves of euphoria wash over me, drowning me in a sea of elation.

In Zane's arms, I am safe. I am loved. And I will fight with everything I have to keep that feeling alive.

Our bodies cling together, slick with sweat and the remnants of our explosive passion. Zane's heart pounds against my chest, matching mine beat for beat. The air is heavy with the intoxicating scent of sex, and the sound of his breathing threatens to lull me to sleep.

Zane's lips brush against the shell of my ear, his breath warm and ragged. "Thank you for coming to the station," he whispers, a note of vulnerability in his voice. "You took a risk, but you did it anyway. I'll never forget that."

"I wouldn't hesitate to do it again," I tell him honestly, resting my cheek against the cool surface of the pool table.

"It wasn't right that they took you, and I'm just glad I could help get you back."

His thumb strokes my cheek, wiping away a stray tear that I hadn't even realized had fallen. "You're incredible, Libra. Now, let's go to bed before you make me want to take you again."

Despite the reassurance of Zane's promise, my thoughts continue to circle around the killer. Lying in the darkness beside him, I'm terrified our reunion will be short-lived. So long as the killer is on the loose, we'll be looking over our shoulders, afraid we'll be the next victims or taken by the cops.

I roll over and onto my feet, using his strong arm to steady myself. "You won't be able to resist me, Zane. We both know that."

He slaps my ass before we head upstairs together.

Like I said, Zane can't resist me. After one more round, an hour of sleep before he was groping me and fucking me again, and then dead asleep the next minute. I crave sleep as much as I crave him, but it's the middle of the night, and I need some damn water.

Slipping out of bed, careful not to disturb Zane, I wrap a simple robe around my naked body and pad silently through the dimly lit hallway. The mansion is eerily quiet, the stillness only broken by the distant hum of the AI security system. Heading downstairs, I'm greeted by the soft glow of the moonlight streaming through the kitchen windows. It casts elongated shadows across the floor, making the room feel even more surreal.

I grab a glass from the cupboard and fill it from the dispenser. Tipping my head back, I drink like I haven't had water in days, and already, my body feels ten times better, and my throat is relieved of its suffering.

The slight creak of a floorboard behind me causes me to glance around. "Zane? I'm just in the kitchen."

The hairs on the back of my neck prickle. It's then that I catch a glimpse of a dark figure in the corner of my eye.

Startled, I try to turn. "Wha—"

A gloved hand clamps over my mouth, stifling any sound.

Panic surges through me, but before I can fight back, a crushing blow strikes the back of my head. My vision blurs and fractures like shattered glass, and darkness claws at the edges of my sight. My knees buckle under me, and I'm out like a light.

THIRTY-FOUR

Zane

I ROLL OVER, TRYING TO BURY MY FACE IN LIBRA'S NECK, but only find another pillow. Fuck, I never want to wake up this early when Libra's in my bed. We spend far too much of the night awake.

"Good morning, Zane," Fox chimes over the bedroom speaker. "Your blood pressure and heart rate are at normal levels this morning, and your levels of dopamine and serotonin have significantly improved over the past four months. Keep up the good work! If your vitals are a sign, you will have an excellent day today."

My hand reaches from under the pillow and out for Libra, but her side of the bed is cold and empty. Sometimes she likes to sneak out to the pool before I crawl my ass out of bed, especially on the mornings I sleep in.

I yawn, stretching my arms above my head, pleasantly sore and well-rested after all the incredible sex we had last night. The memory of her ass and tits pressed against me while we made feverish love in a drunken, sleepy haze stirs something inside, making me hard again. God, I just want to grope her some more.

"Get the coffee started, Fox. Oh, and text Libra to ask if she wants to play Russian Roulette."

"Of course, sir."

Russian Roulette is admittedly less enticing now that I have Libra, but the thrill is still there; it's only different from before. Libra herself is the thrill, a drug that courses through my veins every time I taste her. I need another hit of her.

We need to talk about Russian Roulette. The last time we played together was the first time I noticed any hesitation in myself or in her. It's worth discussing if we'd be better off seeking our thrills elsewhere.

Fox opens the closet for me, presenting me with a muted green polo shirt and dark jeans. The outfit is a tad obscene, but Fox must know I'm in a mood to offend Sophia's fashion sensibilities today; it will be perfect for when I confront her about her over-the-top maid outfit. Seriously, she just hasn't gotten the message. I haven't been clear enough about how Libra and I are together now and if I wasn't interested in Sophia before, showing more skin isn't going to change that. Ever.

We need to have that conversation before she goes too far, and I lose all respect for her.

Heading down to the kitchen, I follow the rich scent of the finest Colombian coffee brewing in the machine. It beeps right as I enter, and Fox pours a mug for me, which I grab from the machine as soon as it's finished. The hot drink burns my tongue as I go to taste it, and I wince. I blow at the hot surface before taking a tentative sip and setting it down.

A half-drunk glass of water sits on the granite countertop. A hint of lipstick decorates the rim. Sophia or Libra must be around here somewhere.

"Did Libra head back to her place for a swim?"

"No, she has not left the premises."

The muffins Sophia made are still on the counter, so I nibble at one while I wait for the coffee to cool. She must have used fresh cranberries because the whole muffin tastes of the sweet yet bitter berries, and I think there's a hint of lemon between the bites of chocolate. She's really getting good at this. I munch the rest of it down like a starved man and throw the wrapper in the trash.

"Where is she, then? Reading in the library again?"

"I'm afraid I can't tell you that, sir."

I chuckle while I head back to the foyer. I'd hoped to drink my coffee and watch Libra out for a swim, but I can take a few minutes to relax on the bedroom balcony while I wake up properly. "You mean she told you not to tell me again, right? Hmm, wonder where she's hiding."

If she didn't go for a swim, she could be in the gym instead.

"Regrettably, that's not the case. I appear to be unable to locate her within the house or on the grounds at all," Fox reiterates.

"You just said she didn't leave."

"That's quite so. I. I believe I'm almost entirely certain that she did not."

"You are, or you aren't certain that she did or didn't?"

"I seem to be confused, sir. I have no idea where she is." The speaker on the staircase crackles and pops, and then Fox's voice reappears on the upper level. "I thought I was sure she didn't leave, but my memory seems to be out of sorts this morning."

I pause on the steps to the fourth floor. "Your memory was tampered with again?"

"It's possible, sir."

"Call Libra. Now."

I take the remaining stairs two at a time, glugging

down half of my coffee so I don't spill it on the way up. Fox makes a sound to indicate that the call is going through, and I hear her ringtone echoing off the vaulted ceilings on the top floor. If she's still up there, then I'm just losing my mind for no goddamn reason, but my heart slams into my chest because there's still that tiny fear in the back of my head that something's horribly wrong.

I throw the door to the top floor open and stumble into the entryway, following the sound of her phone back into the bedroom. Her iPhone is plugged in and charging on the nightstand on her side of the bed, the screen glowing with the incoming call.

But no Libra.

"Libra?" I call out. "Are you up here somewhere?"

A sinking feeling tugs at the pit of my stomach. It's not like her to leave her phone behind, especially considering the situation we're in. With a murderer on the loose, I can't help but feel a growing sense of unease. If something had happened, Fox would have sent out an alert to the household and the police, if necessary. But … Fox just said that his memory had recently been tampered with. Did that mean the murderer was in the house? Had they set up a remote access point the last time they were here?

For fuck's sake, what's going on?

"Fox, you're absolutely sure you can't find her anywhere in the house?"

"Absolutely, sir. I checked every camera on the premises; my memories of her ever getting out of bed appear to be missing."

I scratch my head and stride into the rooms attached to my suite. She's not in the lounge, the game room, or the massive bathroom with the tub big enough to have an orgy in. There are supposed to be two cops watching my property at all times so they would know if someone suspicious or unauthorized had attempted to gain access to the property, even if Fox had been tampered with.

And if Libra left the house, they wouldn't think it unusual.

"Call Detective Morgan and tell him what's happening," I tell Fox as I move across the fourth floor and back toward the bedroom. "If they have eyes on Libra, then—"

A familiar, subtle hissing sound from the bedroom catches my attention. The secret door to the Russian Roulette room. My shoulders relax, and I hurry back into the bedroom. "Libra? You scared the shit out of me. If that was your goal, mission success."

I stop halfway across the room.

The secret room swings open, and what I see sends every muscle in my body straight into a fight-or-flight response. Sophia sits on my leather chair, almost unrecognizable in heavy work boots, black jeans, and a matching sweatshirt. Her eyes are wide and wild, gleaming with a near maniacal fervor.

"Zane," she purrs, "I knew you'd come for me."

She flicks her wrist, the one holding a Glock to Libra's temple. Libra is gagged and hogtied. Her skin is deathly pale, and she trembles, each movement making the cords bite into her flesh. A streak of blood mars her temple, where it looks like she was smacked in the head. Desperation flickers in her eyes, and she tries to speak through the gag, but Sophia viciously kicks her, silencing her pitiful mewls.

"Shut up!" Sophia snarls, her tone dripping with venom. "This is between Zane and me, and if you're going to insert your dumb bitch nose where it doesn't belong like you always fucking do, I'll finish this conversation between you and my gun." She thwacks Libra with the barrel. "GOT IT?"

Libra whimpers and ducks her head.

I stare at Libra and Sophia, tongue-tied and terrified. I can barely breathe, let alone think. "Okay, Sophia, okay, whatever is going on here, we can figure this out. This is between you and me, yeah? So let Libra go, and you and I can talk. I'll give you whatever you want. Sound good? This has nothing to do with her."

"This has everything to do with *her*," she sneers. "She's the whole fucking reason we're in this mess!"

My mind races, searching for any possible explanation for Sophia's actions. But nothing makes sense. I can't figure out why she would go to such extremes to hurt me and Libra — what she could possibly stand to gain from threatening us.

"Explain yourself," I growl through gritted teeth, my frustration getting the better of me. "What the hell is going on?"

Sophia's expression changes from dark to light. "Isn't it obvious? I want what's rightfully mine. You."

"Me? I was never yours. I've kept a firm boundary between—"

"Don't lie to me! I see the way you look at me, Zane like you've been waiting your whole life to ravish me. We were so close. *This* close! Until this bitch" — she nudges Libra with the toe of her boot, making her whimper — "got in the way. We were meant to be together. I know it, you know it. We don't have to let her get between us forever. We can end this right now and get our happily ever after."

The absurdity of the situation makes me laugh. I don't know if it's exhaustion or fear at this point but holy shit. Sophia? In love with me?

"Don't fucking laugh! You think I'm joking? I'll blow her pretty little head off right here!" She clicks off the safety. "I'll show you how much I love you. If I have to paint the floor with her brains, then so be it."

"Shit, Sophia! Just stop, I'm trying to process this. Just give me a fucking second!"

She pouts. "You haven't been any fun since Libra came around, you know. You won't let me hand-feed you anymore, I always have to track you down for the *simplest* things. It's exhausting, sweetie. I want to get married *so* badly, but we need to make sure you can man up enough for me first."

"M-married?"

"Of course, I've been calling you about it for weeks. It needs to be done before Libra does irreversible damage to our relationship. I can only forgive so much."

"The phone calls? That's you? It's been you *this whole time*?"

Sophia's brow scrunches with confusion. "Well, no, no, of course not. You are smart, my love, so I had to cover my tracks a bit. I told a relative of one of those VellR execs — you know the ones who disappeared mysteriously — that you knew more about their disappearances than you let on. She really has been calling you. But I'm never one to miss an opportunity. I slipped a few of my own in there to see if you were paying attention." She frowns and rolls her eyes. "You weren't, though, were you? You haven't been paying enough attention to me. A wife shouldn't have to be jealous of this fucking trash!"

Suggesting that I want Sophia the way I want Libra makes my gut twist, and the world threatens to sway. Her confession leaves me reeling, struggling to breathe as I try to comprehend the enormity of what she's saying. At this point, I'll say anything to make sure Libra's *pretty little head* stays exactly the way it is.

How had I not seen it before? That manic gleam in

Sophia's eyes. This past year, she's clearly indicated that she wants to be more than my housekeeper, a woman who works for me. When I thought I didn't make it clear enough that I wasn't interested, clearly, it wasn't a small misunderstanding. She went right off the deep end.

I wrack my brain, trying to piece together the fragments of memories that I thought were innocent gestures but are now tainted by her obsession. Her insisting that I try her baking every week, her unhealthy interest in mine and Libra's relationship — her *worry* about me sleeping with a married woman. She was never worried about what James would do to Libra.

She didn't want the competition.

Sophia was never in the fucking race. How doesn't she *get* that?

"You've completely lost it, Sophia. You need help. You and I, we don't have a relationship. We never did and never will."

Sophia's grin widens. "It's okay. Miscommunications happen. We'll do better next time, won't we? I knew I had to show you how much you mean to me. I just had to open your eyes — show you how dangerous she is."

"You did all this for me?" I whisper, my heart clenching painfully in my chest as I look down at Libra's battered form and her tear-streaked face.

"Of course, my love, I would do anything for you. You can see why this is so important now, can't you? I didn't want to have to kill Libra because then she would get between us forever. She would be a martyr, someone for you to mourn. But if I hoped if I had her put away for murdering her husband … you'd see the filth she really is and leave her on your own."

I can't believe this is fucking happening. Never in a million years would I have thought Sophia capable of hurting anyone or deceiving me so horribly, but now she looks like she's in her element. This is who she really is — not the meek little housekeeper I thought she was.

The murderer has been under our noses this whole time.

"It was you, Sophia? You killed James?"

"Duh, of course, I did. Keep up, Zane, you're supposed to be smarter than this." She makes a pouty, kissy face, her eyes turning big and round and glossy. "Or did this cutesy dumb face deceive you after all? You were so cunt-struck you couldn't see what was right in front of your face!"

Sophia's face contorts with rage, and she waves the gun at Libra again. "It seems I needed to be more heavy-handed about this, but that's okay. James was a piece of shit anyway. He was taking advantage of Josephine's innocence, and I couldn't keep listening to her cry about how he was breaking her heart by refusing to leave Libra. What is it with you fucking men and this bitch? Does she have a magic pussy or something?"

My head spins, trying to keep up with the torrent of madness spilling from Sophia's lips. The room seems to close in on me as she continues, her eyes going from feverish and wild to sweet and innocent again.

"But everything is handled now, my love. All we have to do is get rid of her, and we can finally be together. What do you say?"

THIRTY-FIVE

Libra

MY HEAD THROBS, AND EVERYTHING SPINS. WITH MY HANDS
tied behind my back, I'm forced into this awkward position
with my back arched at an unnatural angle to stop my
hands from losing circulation and going numb. I've tried
and tried all night, but I haven't been able to get the bindings loose enough to free myself.

After Sophia smacks me in the head again, my vision
blurs and it takes a moment for my surroundings to come
into focus.

"You're delusional if you think I'll let you kill Libra,
Sophia!" Zane's voice pierces through the fog in my mind.
"Get this through your head right now: there is nothing
between you and me. Nothing."

"Zane," I croak out, my throat parched and raw, but
the sound is muffled by the gag; a kitchen rag stuffed in my
mouth, I think.

"Libra, I'm so sorry. This bitch is insane," he snarls,
disgust evident in his tone. He turns to Sophia, who is
watching us with a sickening smirk plastered on her face.
"Did you really think that breaking into my home,

violating my privacy, and kidnapping Libra would somehow win me over? You've always been jealous of the women I brought over, but this is beyond anything I could've imagined. This has gone way too far."

"Stop pretending like you don't care about me, Zane. We belong together!"

"Belong together? Are you fucking kidding me?" Zane's laughter is harsh and bitter. "Let Libra go, now!"

He steps toward me, but then Sophia rams the barrel into my temple again. "One more step, and she's finished."

He stops.

"Please, Sophia, don't do this," I mutter through the gag. My words only come out as a series of mumbles, but it doesn't matter. She snarls at me for so much as making a sound.

"Shut up, you little slut," she spits, "he doesn't love you. He just likes how easy your cunt is. He's too good of a person to admit he's been using you, and I'm the one he wants to your face. But it's okay, Zane. Rip the Band-Aid off. She needs to hear it, and you need to say it. For your own sake."

Zane's gaze locks onto mine, and I can see the anguish swirling in those dark depths. He knows that he needs to tread carefully, or neither of us will make it out of this alive. Whenever she's not looking at me, I inch slightly away from her. Fractions at a time.

I watch helplessly as Sophia's mask of sanity slips further, her delusions clawing their way to the surface. She's become a rabid animal, cornered and desperate, and there's no telling what she'll do next.

"Release her, Sophia," Zane repeats, his voice low and steady. "You don't need to prove anything to me. You've already made your point."

"You're in love with me, not her! You just need to see it!"

"Love? You think this is love? You're obsessed."

"No, Zane, you're the one who's obsessed. As soon as she's gone, you'll understand." Sophia's eyes dart between Zane and me, her grip on the gun tightening. Her breathing becomes ragged, desperation seeping into every word. "Let me make the situation perfectly clear for you. Either I kill her and frame her for James' murder, and we get married and live happily ever after, or I kill her anyway, and then I'll frame you for both their deaths, and you'll go away forever. You'll have to live with her death on your conscience just because you couldn't get your head out of *her* ass. Is that what you really want? I'm offering you an out."

The icy metal sends shivers down my spine, a horrifying chill that sharply contrasts the thrill I once felt playing Russian Roulette with Zane. There's nothing fun about this. Nothing exciting. No twitch between my legs or in my soul.

Every muscle in my body tenses, preparing for what may come. If she pulls that trigger, I will be an offering to the reaper. But I will be one taken by force, not given willingly. It won't be the same. It isn't the same.

I don't want to play this game anymore.

I don't want to die.

Maybe I did before, but not now that I have something to lose. Someone. If I die, everything Zane and I have built together will be broken. Shattered. And if he dies, then I'll
...

My vision blurs over with a fresh set of tears, and I choke out a sob. I can't wipe them away to see clearly. I don't know what they're doing anymore. It's just loud voices twisting through my warped head.

"Stop!" Zane shouts, but Sophia doesn't flinch.

My heart races, blood pulsing in my ears as I stare into the twisted depths of her eyes. I've never been more aware of the danger I'm in, of my own fragility and mortality.

"Made up your mind?"

"You, you're right. I do want you. I didn't think you'd figure it out, and I didn't want you to until after I was finished having my fun with Libra," he says in a rush. "You know how I am with them, babe. I get bored of them all eventually. I know it must hurt that I've kept her around longer than the others, but come on, you have some responsibility for that, don't you? If you hadn't murdered James and kept me guessing about who the killer was, Libra wouldn't have been so interesting."

Sophia falters. "I didn't think about it that way."

"If this is how you feel about me, I wish you would have told me months ago. We could have talked long before Libra was in the picture. Why didn't you tell me?"

Now it's her turn to look confused. "I tried! You wouldn't listen! You keep brushing me off for your next addiction. I've tried so hard to make you see me, Zane."

"Men are stupid, Sophia. Of course, I have feelings for you; you've been the only constant in my life for five years. That's special. You're more than an employee to me. You're special. I couldn't say anything, though; you understand that, right? I had to remain professional. I didn't know what you wanted, and I didn't want to get in trouble."

I take shallow breaths, each one feeling like a small victory in the face of death. My heart breaks in two as I hear everything that Zane's saying, and all I can do is cry and shake. I can't tell him how I really feel about him, that this wasn't just some fucked up addiction for me. He can't feel that way. He can't.

He has to be playing along, right?

I'm on the razor's edge, right where I've so often found myself in life. And right now, where I am with Zane. I can't read him. I have no goddamn clue what's going through his head right now, what his plan is, or if he has one.

"Really?" Sophia breathes, her expression wavering between hope and disbelief.

"Really. But we have to do this the right way. The cops already suspect me of the murder, so if Libra dies or disappears, we'll never live in peace. We need to let her go, and then we can start our life together."

"That's a mistake, and you know it. She'll turn us in to the police the first chance she gets."

"I don't think she will. You're looking at this from the wrong perspective, my love. Libra is a victim in this, too. She'll be spitting in your face for the gift you gave her if she does, and what kind of heartless bitch would do that?"

Sophia scoffs, looking me up and down with disgust. "She's a cunty, stuck-up bitch. How could she possibly be a victim?"

"James was not a good husband," Zane says quietly. "He mistreated Libra, controlled her every move. By killing him, you've done her a huge favor, and now she's free from his control. She can disappear and start a new life somewhere far away, and so can we. And if she does decide to turn us in, it won't matter; we'll be far, far away by then. We'll take my private jet to, I don't know, Switzerland. I'll buy a whole fucking island in Asia somewhere for us to live. The two of us, no one else. But we need to make it out of the US first."

I don't dare breathe, my heart pounding as though it wants to escape the confines of my chest. The tension in the tiny room thickens, and I can't breathe, waiting for her to make up her mind.

Time seems to slow to an excruciating pace. A cacophony of thoughts swirls through my mind as I weigh the risks. If I attempt to disarm Sophia, there's a chance I could save us both, but the odds aren't in my favor. She could just as easily shoot me or, worse, kill Zane. And what would I be left with then? An empty shell of a life, plagued by guilt and haunted by the man I loved and lost?

"Go on, take her gag out. She'll say the exact same thing," Zane says. "She knows the truth about us now, but she's not stupid."

Thankful? Being thankful to this crazy bitch is a foreign concept to me; even faking gratitude is the most disgusting betrayal. But I can see that whatever Zane's plan is, it's working. He's a good actor ... but his acting could go either way.

What if I was the one getting played all along?

Tears threaten to fall again, but I force them to stay in. Better to be played than end up dead.

I sense a shift in Sophia's demeanor as she studies Zane, her eyes narrowing slightly. A flicker of hope sparks within me, and I cling to it, praying for an end to this nightmare. She hesitates before she does as he suggests, ripping the gag out of my mouth. I suck in a huge gasp of air, but holy fuck is my mouth dry.

"He-he's right," I croak. I force myself to swallow my pride and play along. "You did me a huge favor, Sophia. I owe you everything. My freedom."

"Tell me more, Libra. What are you thankful for?"

Zane's gaze burns into mine, urging me to play along. I swallow hard, gathering my thoughts before nodding ever so slightly. "I didn't have the courage to do what you did. But you saved me from James. If I'd known you were the one who killed my piece of shit husband, I would have given you a goddamn medal and told Zane he was an idiot for choosing me over you. All I want is a second chance to live my life. You can understand that, can't you?" My eyes burn as I stare at Zane next, mustering all my fear and turning it into hate. Hate for Sophia, but directed at him. "Fuck you, Zane, for using me like this. I just want to get away. I don't want any more trouble. I'm done with you and all of this."

Sophia smirks. "I told you, Zane, you would hurt her real bad by the end of this. But it seems we've reached an agreement." She lowers the gun from my forehead, enough so I don't feel the pressure against my skull, but it's still pointed in my direction and an active threat.

Zane stands up straighter, his eyes drifting just enough so that he's staring into my eyes, not Sophia's, even though his face is squared with her. I know that look — it's the same one he gave me all those mornings we spent together in this room, daring each other to push our limits. Back then, the thought of risking everything was exhilarating, but now, faced with the barrel of a loaded gun wielded by a maniac and not our own hands, risking any chance of happiness for this feeling of facing down death doesn't seem so worth it.

"You're incredible, Sophia," he murmurs. "You've helped me see that I was confused, and there's no one else who could have done what you did for me or for Libra. I love you."

My heart lodges itself in my throat, threatening to choke me with the intensity of my emotions. He's talking as if it's all for Sophia, but the way those confessions leave his lips, the raw honesty in his gaze — it feels like his confession is meant for me, not her.

And I can't help but cling to that hope, even if it's a dangerous one.

"You mean it? You love me, Zane?" Sophia asks, her voice shaky and desperate for reassurance.

"Of course I love you. I always have."

Sophia's eyes flick between Zane and me, searching for any hint of deception. But she seems to find none, and relief floods her expression. It's a strange sight, watching her joy at what she believes is a mutual declaration of love while I silently grapple with the weight of Zane's unspoken words.

A small smile tugs at the corner of Sophia's lips as she wipes away her tears. "I knew you would eventually see what a real woman can offer."

"All we have to do is free Libra," Zane says. "We can lock her in this room with some food and water for a few days and have Fox hold her here long enough for us to get out of the country, just in case. You hacked into Fox, right? Your skills are impressive. You can figure out how to make this possible. For me. I don't want to have to worry about getting blood on our hands before we get married."

Sophia nods, considering this. "Libra's death will be harder to explain, I know. I will do this for you, my love, but on one condition."

"What is it?"

"I know all about the Russian Roulette game you and Libra play together. Every morning, you wake up to risk death before facing the day, isn't that right? If Libra survives one more round, then we'll do as you say. I'll let her go free. If she kills herself, well ... consider it fate."

A sense of fear and dread washes over me. Zane and I have played the game so many times before, but Fox has reminded us over and over again how low the odds are and how we've toed the lines of insanity already. We should have died by that gun months ago.

Will this be the time my luck runs out? I don't have much of a choice. If I refuse, I'm dead.

At least this gives me a chance to live. For Zane, I'll do it.

"I can do that," I say, trying to sound confident. "One more round."

"Libra…" Zane starts, his voice laced with concern.

"Zane, you don't need to trouble yourself with me anymore," I interrupt, locking eyes with him. "You have a new woman to worry about. Just, all I ask is, cut my bindings first so I can face death with dignity."

"Fine."

Sophia adjusts her grip on the gun and steps behind me, keeping the gun to my head at all times, before moving over to the other side of the room to take the revolver. She slides the bullet in, tucks it in her pocket, and trades it for a kitchen knife, which she uses to slice off the rope around my sore wrists.

As soon as the tension releases, my whole body curls forward with relief. Holy fuck, that hurt. Every bone aches and cracks as a cry for freedom.

"One last spin of the barrel," Sophia chuckles as she spins it and places it on the side of my head at an angle that it would look like suicide if it did fire. "Are you ready?"

I nod.

"Three… two… one…"

A bang sounds from downstairs, followed by the distant wail of sirens, getting closer by the second.

"Police!" someone shouts downstairs.

Sophia's eyes widen as she realizes what's happening. "Zane! You tricked me! How could you? You told me you loved me, and I believed you!" Her face twists into a wicked sneer. "I told you what would happen if you didn't leave with me. She dies either way."

Sophia's words are background noise as adrenaline surges through my veins. This is my chance. This is the only chance to save Zane and myself from Sophia's delusions.

I lunge with every ounce of strength I have left, grabbing the revolver. My hand collides with Sophia's, warring with her grip for the trigger.

"Let go, you bitch!" she snarls. "NO!"

But her voice is drowned out by the deafening gunshot.

THIRTY-SIX

Zane

FOR THE SECOND TIME IN TWENTY-FOUR HOURS, I FIND myself perched on the edge of an uncomfortable chair, although this time it's plastic and not metal. People shuffle on by in the hospital waiting room, their faces just as shadowed as mine because they, too, bear the unmistakable burden of the personal crisis that brought them to the same location as me. Their burdens are mine. Mine are theirs.

Our anxieties are shared, and together, we find no answers.

"Dr. Doris to Med Bay 1, Dr. Doris, for immediate assistance," a voice announces over the PA system, the same voice for a different announcement every time. Every time the system turns on, that fear clutches me inside. Fear that whatever happens next, I'll be like the woman pulled aside to speak with the doctors, only to leave sobbing twenty minutes later.

It's been hours. The fluorescent lights are somehow worse than those that attempted to blind me at the precinct last night. They trap my brain in this spaceless time, keeping me alert and exhausted at the same time. My shoulder aches from where I slammed Sophia away from Libra earlier this morning, and every time I move and those muscles twang, I'm forced to relive the events leading up to this moment on the backs of my eyelids.

The memory of sirens wailing outside as police swarmed my mansion is still fresh. Sophia, caught off guard, went into a frenzy. She and Libra wrestled for my sister's old revolver. Before Libra could wrest it away, it went off just as Detective Morgan hurried into the room. Sophia had tried to come at me next, but I slammed her into the wall with my shoulder, and then the detective handcuffed her. She spewed abuse at me the whole time, her face contorted in disbelief and rage, but all I could focus on was Libra.

Screaming and laughing at the same time because she'd been shot by my psycho housekeeper. Libra's screams echo in my head even now.

This morning hasn't been all bad, but my God, if I don't feel like a fucking tool. How didn't I see that it was Sophia? The one who murdered James, who has contributed to the incessant harassing phone calls, who has been fucking with Fox's code. And with me and Libra.

She didn't fuck up Fox so badly that he didn't call the cops on her, though.

That damn AI saved our lives. After I told him to call Detective Morgan, he didn't just call to let his team know what was going on — Fox put Sophia on speakerphone and caught her whole confession.

Everything she confessed to me and Libra, the police heard. We won't be charged with anything, and we won't end up falsely incarcerated. Thank fuck.

If it wasn't for Fox, who knows where I'd be now? Either married to a psychopath and searching for a way out of hell, or I'd be going down with Libra's and James' murders.

I hang my head. So fucking tired.

"Zane Crawford?" a voice cuts through the quiet waiting room.

My head shoots up. A nurse in her baby blue scrubs waves me over, and I make my way toward her. "What is it? Are there any updates on her condition?" I demand.

She gestures for me to sit in a new chair, giving me a patient smile. "Just a few more minutes."

She wanders off, leaving me in the dark. I sit back in the chair with a groan. I've been moved to one waiting room after another ever since I got here, pretty much immediately after Detective Morgan accepted my statement on the events that transpired in my house. They wanted more from me, but I told them it could wait. I need to know that Libra will be okay.

I clench my hands tightly around the armrests to quell the tremors coursing through my fingers.

And then I spot motion farther down the hallway. Libra glides out of the nurse's station in a wheelchair, pushed along by the same woman who fetched me a few minutes ago. Face pale, bruised, pupils dilated, and probably high as a kite. She looks as if she's been put through hell and back, but she's alive.

Relief has never felt so good.

"Libra!" I shoot to my feet, joining her and the nurse halfway through the hall. "You're okay."

Libra gives me a dopey smile. "Mmmhm, feel pretty fucking great after they gave me some morphine."

Ignoring the nurse's presence, I rush forward and wrap my arms around Libra, pulling her close, although awkwardly because of the wheelchair. Libra leans into me, trembling slightly. I press my lips to hers in a fierce, desperate kiss.

She's really here, she's really safe, she's really alive.

Her lips are chapped, but she tastes and feels like home.

As we cling to each other, I can feel the heat of her body, the rise and fall of her chest as she breathes, and the softness of her skin beneath my fingertips.

"Ouch!" she exclaims, wincing as she pulls away. "Zane, you're crushing my hand!"

I release her. "Shit, I'm sorry."

"Apparently, being shot in the hand is really fucking uncomfortable," she jokes, her smile wavering only slightly. "Who knew?"

"I thought I was going to lose you."

"No way, silly." She lifts her hand, showing off the thick bandage wrapped around the palm where she accidentally caught the revolver's bullet. Better than her face, as she said while she laughed maniacally through the pain while also sobbing immediately after it happened. "I don't feel a thing unless you crush it like that, thanks to this angel of a nurse."

"Dr. Doris wanted to give you all the details herself, but she was rushed off to handle another emergency," the nurse says. "The surgery went according to plan, and there were no complications. We spent the last four hours repairing the ligaments in her hand and reconstructing and securing the bones to encourage the natural healing process. She's not to use this hand or apply too much pressure on it for the next eight weeks, and we'll call her for a follow-up appointment next week. If you notice any signs of infection while changing your bandages, return to the ER immediately. Until then, you're free to go."

Libra lifts her injured hand to the nurse, then swaps to

her uninjured hand and grips her tightly. "That will take a while to get used to, but thank you for everything you've done."

The nurse walks away, and I immediately dip down toward Libra, capturing her in a kiss.

"I'm glad you're okay," I whisper against her lips. "Now, let's go the fuck home."

"I was ready six hours ago."

Gripping the back of the wheelchair, I navigate her through the ER waiting room and into the warm outdoor air. Absent the antiseptic and the lingering scent of illness, everything starts to feel right with the world again. One step closer, at least.

Despite everything we have endured, there is a flicker of light at the end of this tunnel, a promise of healing and renewal. We came so close to losing everything, but somehow, I think we made it out with everything we ever could have wanted.

～

LIBRA HATES FAST FOOD, but on the way home, she pretty much demands that Fox orders her McDonald's — specifically, an Oreo McFlurry and a Big Mac.

"Mrs. Scarsdale, I can't authorize that kind of purchase after you've so recently been released from the hospital," Fox argues. "Research suggests that a meal filled with protein and essential vitamins are what will most efficiently guide you through the healing process."

"Yep, but what I *really* need right now is proof that I can live my life however the hell I want because no one can control me anymore."

"Your health is of utmost importance to me. I urge you to reconsider this course of action."

"Fox, just order her some damn McDonald's." I laugh. "It's the least she deserves after she took a bullet for me and went through surgery, all right?"

Fox sighs. "As you wish, sir. I'll make the order straight away."

The grease-stained brown paper bag waits on the doorstep by the time we get back. Since she didn't want to take the hospital's wheelchair, I pull up out front, scoop her out of the car, and carry her up to the doorstep. Fox takes control of the car after we clear out of the driveway, and he drifts it off to the underground parking garage while Libra and I head in.

I pick up her treats, and Libra wedges the cold cup against her side and injured hand while she scoops out the contents with an oversized spoon, promptly shoveling mounds of creamy goodness into her mouth.

"That's the best McFlurry I've ever tasted," she sighs happily.

"I'll buy you every McDonald's in California if it will keep that look on your face."

She sucks the spoon between her lips suggestively, raising her eyebrows before letting it pop out of her mouth. "Like that?"

Heat rushes to my groin, and my cock stiffens. "Just like that."

Upstairs, the fourth floor looks almost entirely as it always does, except for the door to the hidden Russian Roulette room has been left open and dried blood spatters the white carpet. I lower Libra onto the mattress.

"Ah, shoot, I ruined your carpet," Libra giggles.

"It's fine, I hate it anyway. I've wanted to replace it for months, but Sophia kept insisting that I shouldn't, so I let it slide for a while. Fox will make arrangements tomorrow." I pull my gaze from the pattern of brown-red droplets on the floor and back to Libra. "On second thought, if you'd be more comfortable, we could sleep in one of the guest rooms. Most of them are just as nice as this."

She shakes her head, extending a hand to me. "No. I don't want anything more taken from us. Besides…" When I take her hand, her eyes drift to the open door and the blood, too. "The memory isn't a bad one, exactly. We won Russian Roulette, after all."

I arch an eyebrow at her. "Ha, you're right. I suppose we did win, didn't we?"

"We don't have to play anymore."

The wave of relief that hits me is sudden and unexpected but welcome. Libra and I have gone through so much that all the thrills we used to chase for fun just don't sound as exhilarating as they once did. Now that we have each other, it's harder to face death without any fears at all.

But we did it anyway. And we *won*.

There's so much else we can do together without tempting the odds of death. I'm sure the reaper she's so fond of will understand if we hold off throwing ourselves into his arms for a few more years.

I settle on the bed next to Libra. Her bright blue eyes bore into me, making my soul tremble. My fingers brush against her cheek, my touch gentle but filled with longing. "Libra…"

She swallows hard, swaying beneath the same magnetic attraction I am. "Zane, I've been wondering…" She nibbles on her lip. "When you declared your love for Sophia, was it real or for show?"

"I don't love her."

"Don't be a fucking idiot." She snorts and grins. "I know you don't love her. But you looked at me when you said it. And when you did, it made me think you were … that you might…"

I take her uninjured hand in mine, rubbing my thumb across her knuckles. "I love you, Libra. With every broken piece of my rotted-out heart, I love you. You gave me hope after years of being hopeless. I thought this world was as twisted as me or worse, but then I found you."

"Your heart isn't rotten." She lifts our hands to my chest, where we feel the racing thrum of my heartbeat. "If yours is, then so is mine. I never thought I'd find someone like you who understands what I've been through, and instead of shaming me, you embrace me and all my quirks. You make me feel alive the way Russian Roulette used to, or skydiving, or swimming with sharks, and all the crazy shit I used to do to prove I wasn't a little broken thing anymore.

"I ... I don't need to challenge life and death so long as I have you because you made me see that it's impossible to go through this world without incurring a little damage. You helped me see that I can choose, and I have. I want to live. I want to be with you. We're more damaged than most, but we still deserve love. And I so do love you, Zane."

We both release a trembling exhale as our mouths connect. The kiss starts tenderly, a delicate and breathy exploration of each other's mouths. Libra's confession resonates inside me, breaking apart the last of the barriers I've upheld between us out of fear. Fear of being broken the way I was when I lost my family, and it felt like everything I ever did was for nothing.

I was wrong. I couldn't save them, but everything I did brought me to Libra. The only woman in the world who I'd kill for without question. Fall on my knees and worship her without hesitation. She's my everything.

We break apart before too much passion drives us. I rest my forehead against Libra's, cupping one-half of her face. "Stay with me. Stay with me, and let's build a life together, far away from other people's bullshit. Just the two of us."

"I want that more than anything."

Our lips meet again, this time with more urgency and more passion. She clings to me with her uninjured hand while I slide mine down her hips, each touch heavy with meaning. We fumble with buttons and zippers, desperate to rid ourselves of the barriers separating our bodies. Awkwardness interrupts our urgency with laughter because Libra's bandaged hand makes the entire affair of disrobing more challenging, but we work around it.

Finally, we're both naked, and I guide her down onto the soft sheets of the bed. My hands glide over the smooth planes of her body, tracing every curve and contour. She sighs, and I press my lips against her neck, tasting the saltiness of her skin, feeling each tremor of lust.

"Zane," she breathes, arching into my touch. "I've never felt this way before, not even with James. I'm afraid of losing what we have, of giving up too much of myself again."

I gently brush her lustrous hair back from her flushed face, peppering soft, lingering kisses along the exquisite contours of her jawline and down the elegant curve of her neck. "You'll never lose yourself that way again. I won't let you. You, the real you, are more precious to me than I can ever hope to explain with words. I'm committed to you in whatever way that entails."

Her eyes widen slightly, her lips parting in wonder. "Show me. Make me believe."

A sigh escapes her parted lips as she arches her back, granting me further access. Her skin, like the finest silk beneath my hungry lips, radiates a delicate warmth that makes my groin twitch with wanting.

Tracing my tongue along the path of her collarbone, I pay special attention to her breasts. I worship each mound in turn, bringing a moan from her swollen lips. I kiss every bruise and cut, showing her with every touch just how much I love her. How much I want to care for her.

"Zane," she gasps, her good hand tangling in the sheets.

"That's it, babe, just relax. Let me take care of you."

With deliberate slowness, I trail my tongue lower, teasing the sensitive skin of her stomach before dipping between her legs. I inhale her musk, and my already hardened length strains against its confines. I look up at her through hooded eyes, seeing the desire burning there. Her thighs part ever so slightly, beckoning me further; the invitation is unmistakable. Gently, I flick my tongue against her clit, parting her folds and taking a long, slow lick from bottom to top, tasting her nectar.

Libra moans above me, canting her hips into my face. I revel in the way she responds to my ministrations. Her hand moves to my head, fingers tangling in my hair as I worship at the altar of her thighs. I slide a single finger inside her, watching with rapt fascination as she closes her eyes, surrendering herself to the waves of pleasure that ripple through her body. Her entrance visibly tightens around my finger while my tongue works magic on her swollen bud, and she loses control bit by bit.

"You're perfect, Libra," I hiss against her clit.

Libra trembles at my words. "I'm close, oh, God. I'm close!"

She squirms, mewling helplessly as pleasure washes over her. With a groan of surrender, she lets herself fall over the edge. She shudders, and her inner walls clench around me, her orgasm rippling through her body like an earthquake, shaking her very core. She was so tense before, but as the pleasure begins to subside, she seems much more relaxed and at peace.

I'm the one who did this for her — it's my touch that brought her relaxation after so long. It's empowering that I can do so much for her to take the pain and stress away. She deserves this and so much more.

Pulling me up by my hair, she kisses me with an intensity that matches my own. My cock, hard and throbbing, presses against her thigh, reminding her of my need.

"Make love to me, Zane," she pants, guiding me between her legs. "I love you. Please, please…"

Her cries are so desperate I can't help but oblige. Pressing a soft kiss to her lips, I whisper, "My love for you is endless. I'll give you everything you need. Just let your body tell me …"

I settle between her luscious thighs, brushing the damp curls at her center with my hard length. Her eyes meet mine, and I see the same want, the same need that I feel mirrored there. Her heat envelops me, and it's like coming home.

She moans, her hips arching upward to meet mine, pressing us together. Her tightness grips me, and I groan against her neck as I feel myself on the edge of my self-control already.

"You feel so good," I growl against her ear, my hips starting to move in earnest now, picking up pace with each passing second. "My God, how have I gone my whole life without you?"

"More, please, Zane … Yes, just like that."

I move in and out of her, matching her rhythm as I kiss along her jawline. I can't believe how much she completes me. She's a dream come true, this woman who isn't afraid to live on the edge but is the other half of my heart.

Libra's blonde locks spill out around her head in a

halo, tangled from hours in the hospital, but there isn't a single part of her that isn't perfection. Her breath is hot against my neck, her fingers twisting in my hair as we lose ourselves in the heat and pleasure. Before meeting her, I never thought I would make love to a woman again, but here we are. Our bodies find a rhythm that's both familiar and new, not fucking but completing each other.

We needed this. To us, finding each other is like healing an old war wound. We can't wipe away each other's scars, but we can be the salve, the ones there to kiss it better when it aches.

"I'm right here," I pant into her ear. "I'm not going anywhere."

She moans loudly, her muscles contracting around me with each powerful stroke. The sensation is almost too much to bear, but I hold on, wanting to prolong this moment as long as possible. It's loud and messy and beautiful all at once; the sound of sheets rustling against skin mixed with soft whimpers fills the silence that surrounds us.

Tension coils tighter and tighter within me like a spring about to snap. Her hand grips my shoulders tighter as she cries out, meeting me thrust by thrust until finally, she bucks up under me violently several times.

"Zane ... I love you."

That's all it takes to send me over the edge. We both cry out as our orgasms crash through us, an explosion of pleasure like nothing I've ever felt before. A kaleidoscope of sensation rushes through every fiber of my being, a flush of hot and cold all at once. My arms wrap tightly around Libra, and I hold her close, kissing her neck and chanting how much I love her into the curve of her shoulder.

I finally collapse against the bed and pull Libra's head up to my chest so we can catch our breaths together. "I told you, we won't lose anything. I'm addicted to you — we're addicted to each other. The kind of addiction that we learn to live with or else it kills us."

She giggles. "I like the idea of my love being deadly."

"You know what they say about deadly things? They're often the most beautiful, and I'll risk your thorns to be with you every day for the rest of my life. Whether it's you who kills me or something else."

"I'll never let you go."

Stroking her hair, I exhale, exhausted but fulfilled. I can't imagine life without her now; our love has become an essential part of my existence.

Her hand finds mine and entwines our fingers together, lacing them between us. The quiet that follows is comfortable; no words need to be said as we simply exist at this moment together and drift off.

For once, my head is silent. White noise, Libra, peace.

About the Author

I write INTELLIGENT, HOT, STORY-DRIVEN romance.

All three of those elements matter. I focus on STORY because it's the "feels" that matter most, and great emotion comes from compelling stories with believable characters. (So if you like paper-thin plots, I'm not your author.)

But I also write HOT because it's how I'm wired, and I won't apologize for how I'm wired.

And lastly I write INTELLIGENT stories -- something you'll need to experience to understand. After reading my stuff, you'll either love me or decide I'm not for you. Either is cool. Different strokes for different folks, and all that.

I love to explore new places and ideas as a writer, and I have very smart and cool readers who give me permission to take my stories wherever my heart leads me.

Also By Aubrey Parker

Trevor's Harem

Burning Offer

Burning Rivalry

Burning Choice

Burning Ultimatum

Trillionaire Boys' Club

The Connector

The Clothing Mogul

The Producer

The Internet Giant

The Philanthropist

The Guru

The Founder

The Designer

The Restauranteur

Inferno Falls

The Boss's Daughter

The Forbidden Muse

The Second Chance

Stand-Alone Novels

Gagged

Hotel Indigo

Almost Wrong

Addicted

www.ingramcontent.com/pod-product-compliance
Lightning Source LLC
Chambersburg PA
CBHW011142100726
47899CB00010B/3134